WILD HORSE ISLAND

Don Oylear

Published by Don Oylear

D1736717

Cover design by: Don Oylear
Library of Congress Control Number: 2024915675
Printed in the United States of America

To Ann Mary, Thank you for your endless love and support.

CHAPTER 1

February 17
Tuesday 6:55am Eastern Standard Time

Could he do it? Yuri moves now. Moving slowly, forcing his body through a thick syrupy fluid. Water. But not water. His feet barely touch the bottom. He has only thirty seconds of real time to accomplish the deed. Is it possible? Time is not real. This is relative time. It is as if he is in a dream. The CP Pak is like a Disney ride. Twelve seats and twelve rows with aisles in the middle and down the sides. For loading, faded blue recessed light on the ceiling and walls gave the passengers all the light they needed. It is nearly dark now during the Transport and Yuri can smell the soft scent of an expensive perfume.

He has practiced the act at least one hundred times, but now it all seems to be taking too long to do anything. He has only two steps to take, yet each step demands all his concentration and strength. He must keep moving through the shimmering thick fluid. Everything is dead still all around him. Silence, yet he is not alone.

Finally, Yuri reaches his goal in the row directly ahead of him. He slips his hand slowly into his pocket and pulls out the cellulose twine, as strong as a piano wire and only slightly larger. With all his concentration and strength, he wraps the twine around the neck of Xing Tsua Ten and pulls hard with all his might. He estimates that he needs to count to thirty in this "time relative" environment. Xing Tsua Ten struggles. This is a relief to Yuri. He enjoys feeling the life flow out of his victims. There have been many over the years.

Exactly at his own count of thirty, he releases the grip and begins his struggle back two steps to his own seat in the CP Pak. Was the deed done? Only time will tell if Yuri Rosov, "*The Thorny Rose*", assassin for the Russian mob, has made his first CP Pak transport kill. As Yuri takes his seat among the other 143 passengers, he blacks out momentarily. The hatch door to the CP Pak transport opens in Seattle. Now, to get away!

Yuri Rosov walks briskly out of the CP Pak concourse. He moves quickly, but not so much as to draw attention to himself. He stops for a bottle of water and quickly places a call to be picked up at the Sea-Tac CP Pak baggage terminal. She is to meet him outside baggage claim.

As he walks, he opens the water and slips the cellulose twine inside. Within thirty steps, the string dissolves and he begins drinking. After a few long chugs, it's gone. Yuri discards the empty bottle. Now, even if he is detained, the murder weapon will never be found.

Yuri clears the exterior doors on the baggage claim level, spots his driver, Petra Zane, climbs into her rented Mercedes E Electric 360 and they are driving away.

Phase One, the easy part, is completed. Now Phase Two, the more complex part of the plan, will commence. Yuri's team needs to make sure whoever investigates the murder can't track the murder back to Yuri, or God forbid, back to the contractor who has hired him for this "*Job*".

CHAPTER 2

February 17
Tuesday 4:44am Pacific Standard Time

"REID! GOL DAMMIT REID! WAKE UP! REID!"

"Whaa. What the hell? Carlos is that you?" Reid Daniels responded.

"REID, WAKE UP! I NEED YOU OUT HERE!"

Slowly, the FBI Northwest Regional Director for Cyber Crimes, Reid Daniels, awakens and figures out that it is the FBI Regional Field Commander, Carlos Sanchez, on the agency issued ICP (Instant Communication Phone).

"Yeh, okay, I'm awake, Carlos," Reid finally offered in the voice you only have when you are waking from a deep sleep. "What the hell is going on?"

"I am out at Sea-Tac, Reid; it's a murder!"

"Ookay, soo why are you calling me? Did somebody murder their Samsung phone?"

"No, Reid. I'm at the CP Pak Terminal. A CP Pak Transport arrived a little before 4:00am from D.C. and a Chinese diplomat has been murdered. Nobody saw it. Nobody saw or heard anything. It's as if he was strangled during the CP Pak file transfer," Sanchez said.

"That's impossible! The elapsed time of a file transfer is only a few seconds," Daniels said quietly, as if he were speaking only to himself. His mind raced at the prospect.

"Hey, but again, Carlos, why are you calling me? I've never been involved with a murder investigation in my entire career."

"We need a team with tech knowledge onsite fast, Reid.

We know how he was killed. It was strangulation. Even more improbable, it appears to have happened during that file transfer time. Get out here as fast as you can, Reid. I think you and your team are our best bet to get on this one quickly. Director Russell agrees. Oh, and Reid. BRING YOUR GUN!" Sanchez said, then, he hung up.

"*Bring my gun?*" Daniels thought. "*What am I getting myself into?*" He laid for a few moments in the king size bed of his Mercer Island townhouse thinking about the conversation he had just had, then he quietly moved out of the bed.

As Daniels prepared to head to Seattle Tacoma International Airport, his mind wandered alternately from how a strangulation murder could take place in the brief interval of a CP Pak file transfer, to the daunting challenge of conducting a murder investigation in the field.

In the back of his mind, Charlie was asking questions; "*what was Regional Commander Sanchez thinking and why was he, Reid Daniels, being asked by Sanchez to head a murder investigation in the field, what was special about this Chinese diplomat, who else was travelling in that CP Pak, what were the international implications, when was the last time Reid had fired his weapon?*"

That last question stuck in Reid's mind. It had been maybe two years since he had fired his 40-caliber semiautomatic Glock 27. Jason Shields, a classmate at Quantico, oversaw the training range and had oversight of the more than 50 Primary Firearms Instructors.

Shields and Daniels had become close during their training at Quantico, and Shields remembered that Reid, as a cyber sleuth, had been more than proficient with the standard issue Glock and rarely, if ever, needed to use his weapon. As a special treat for his friend, when Reid's marksmanship training cycle would roll around, Shields would introduce him to new weapons like the S&W M&P 15 Semi, the KAC SR-15, the FN SCAR 16S carbine and the Colt LE6940 MRP.

It was all great fun, but it meant that Reid had not fired

his own Glock in two years. That creates doubt in the mind of an FBI computer nerd.

"Don't forget to bring your gun," Reid mocked the Sanchez command out loud. "Jesus, what are we getting into here?" Reid asked himself and, by extension, asked his wife Charlie.

Daniels hurried around the neat and comfortably appointed townhouse collecting items Charlie thought he might need. *"Who knows when you'll get back home. You'll need field boots* (more like hiking shoes), *agency issue field pants, shirt, pullover windbreaker and an FBI jacket."* Charlie then reminded him, *"Throw in a change of civilian clothes and put extra underwear into your duffle as well."*

Reid showered quickly, leaving two days of stubble on his face, and headed out the door. As he drove his Audi A6Z to Sea-Tac airport a little over the speed limit, Reid called Cyber Crimes team member, computer systems geek Robin Medallon. Medallon was 25 years old and brilliant. He was also a healthy, young, heterosexual male, who, like most nerds do, struck out with the ladies nearly 100% of the time.

"Robin, you there?" Reid asked into his ICP. "ROBIN! I know it's early."

"Whodda? Who is that?" said a tired female voice.

"Shhh. Shhh, it's my boss," Robin whispered.

"You mean the auld fart you were tellin me about las nigh?" she said smiling.

"SHHH, yeh. Reid I'm here."

"Auld fart! I'm only 42 fucking years old! Look, Robin, we need to talk in private."

Robin moved into the kitchen of his Queen Anne Hill apartment. It was small but had a terrific view of the Space Needle and the Seattle skyline to the south. If you leaned way out on the deck, you could get a peek at part of Elliot Bay. *"Apartment with a View"*, the ad had said.

"Sooo, you got lucky Robin my boy? What, is she dumb or ugly?"

"Reid, it's like you wouldn't believe! Two of them from Czechoslovakia, absolutely gorgeous, with one making eyes at me from across the bar last night!"

"Multiple choice, huh? Did you Czech box one or Czech box two?"

"Ohhh, I get it. Very funny. Well, actually box two, (pause) a few times."

"Yeah, I bet. At least that way, you're not talking *"nerd speak"* and driving her away. Okay, Robin, here's what I've got for you. We're on a murder investigation."

"WHAT!" Robin exclaimed.

"A Chinese diplomat was killed during, and we do believe during, a CP Pak Transport from D.C. to Seattle about 4:00am this morning, Pacific Time."

"Is that even possible? But wait! What the hell are we doing investigating this?" Robin asked.

"Regional Commander Sanchez wants our team on the case due to the high-tech nature of the crime and the fact that we can get on it right away. I need you to get the team to the office ASAP and have Bert start breaking down for us who else, besides our dead guy, was transporting in that CP Pak early this morning," Reid said.

"I can get on that right from here. I have full capability from my notebook," Robin replied.

"No, I want the full wrap security that you can get at the office. We just don't know what we are getting into here," Reid said. "Also, please call Chris and have him meet me out at Sea-Tac CP Pak Terminal. Tell him to pack some clothes in case we need to travel to DC or wherever."

"Okay, but I'm going to have to say goodbye to Analka."

"Is that a nickname you've given her?"

"No, her name is Analka," Robin said.

"Well say goodbye and get to the office ASAP, studka."

Reid punched his ICP closed. His mind raced back to his deceased wife, Charlie, and the daunting job at hand. He welcomed the change of pace, then he felt his side to make sure his Glock was still holstered there.

CHAPTER 3

Pre-Dawn February 17
Ketchikan, Alaska

Kendall Hughes had a sleepless night in Ketchikan and was up early. Something was bothering her. "Goddamn I hate this feeling," Kendall said to no one.

Something big was coming; and it was not good. Her late mother had told her that she had her grandmother's gift; the uncanny ability to sense a major change coming. Her mother joked that the little girl had ESPN. A joke Kendall never quite understood as a child.

As she grew older, Kendall came to learn that the change she could feel coming might bring good or bad; she never could tell which, she only sensed that major changes were on the way. Her G-ma said, "It isn't a matter of whether changes are coming, cuz when you feel it, they always are. The most important thing, dear, is how you respond to the changes."

Something troubled Kendall last night. She didn't look forward to what it might be.

"When changes come, sometimes they knock you down hard, dear, but you have to get back up and figure out how to be the best you can be in spite of how hard life smacks you," G-ma had said.

Kendall couldn't help but think about some of those hard smacks. She had not always been Kendall Hughes. She started life as Shelby Ellison, most recently Doctor Shelby Ellison.

As a 16-year-old, it was almost more than she could endure when both of her parents contracted the Corona Virus in the 2020 Pandemic and died. The same feelings that had hit her last night had been there before that event. In her late thirties, the feelings were there again before the U.S. government started the process to declare Eminent Domain and take ownership of the major scientific breakthrough, she had led her team to discover.

In the early morning hours in Ketchikan, as she thought about those previous feelings and what they had meant, Kendall toughened her resolve to follow her G-ma's advice and be the best person she could be despite what might be on her horizon.

In the first third of the 21st Century, Dr. Shelby Ellison and a group of scientists worked, with private funding, on the New World Columbus Project. Their research opened a new dimension of transport and travel.

Funded by billionaire Angel Investors, thought to include the Gates Foundation, the Warren Buffett Foundation, Jeff Bezos, and Elon Musk and headed by a brilliant young physicist, Dr. Shelby Ellison, the Columbus Project broke the code of transporting "objects" over the Internet as simply as one could send an email.

As a little girl, Dr. Ellison didn't understand why a document could come to her father from far, far away in seconds, while it took her father days, sometimes a week or more, to travel somewhere for business.

"Why can't daddy just jump on the internet like a piece of paper and not be gone from me for so long?"

Then, after the 2020 Pandemic that took her parents, a teenage Shelby saw the need for people to be able to travel long distances quickly and in a medically safer environment than an airplane.

The research group she headed started with the theory that inanimate objects could be broken down and then bundled in a manner like Zip Files going into a Drop Box. Technology was expanded from Magnetic Resonance Imaging to the breakdown of nano-molecular cells into completely organized patterns that could be arranged into byte-sized files. These files could be bundled and sent over the Internet. At the other end, they could be rearranged just as quickly and easily as if they were an emailed document.

Within five years, the well-funded New World Columbus Project had perfected the science. FedEx, seeing the writing on the wall, entered into a trillion-dollar deal with CP Pak, the marketed name of the new technology. Angel Investors were paid off, bills were being paid in full, and Shelby Ellison, along with many of her fellow scientists, looked to become some of the wealthiest humans on the face of the earth. They all knew the real achievement was yet to come, so they poured the profits back into the program and continued their research.

During the original research on objects, it became clear that the CP Pak Process could be expanded further to the breakdown of complex objects such as living organisms. The Project started with small experiments.

Within another three years of breakneck research and development, two scientists from the group, nick-named the Wright Brothers, were sent from Seattle to Portland via the Internet. The concept of *"beam me up Scotty"*, first introduced by Gene Roddenberry in the 1960s Star Trek television series, was now a reality.

Her drive and ambition as a scientist, a researcher and an inventor was to create an overwhelming and long lasting benefit to mankind. Driven by that, Dr. Ellison and her team had created a faster and dramatically more environmentally friendly way to transport everything.

People and objects could be sent via the Internet to anywhere in the world where CP Pak Encoders and Decoders could be housed. Airlines, railroads, oceanic freight movers were in near panic for the fate of their businesses.

Rarely had a technological advancement threatened to turn the world economy on its ear in the manner that CP Pak technology could. Major companies in potentially affected industries were going all out in lobbying efforts in the House, the Senate, and the Whitehouse.

As the noise level climbed in the government with political donations driving the narrative, CP Pak technology became a concern of *"national security." "The technology"* had to be controlled by the government for the good of the people. In the interest of National Security and under the guidance of the FCC, which had responsibility over some aspects of the Internet, CP Pak technology was taken over and administered by the U.S. Government

Dr. Ellison, by then nearly 40 and having devoted the past 15 years of her life to CP Pak research, was disgusted by the government action. In her heart, she knew that the US Government wanted to keep the most useful aspects of CP Pak technology for the military. She hated the people in the government who was doing this to her, most of them men. Her greatest fear had always been that greedy shallow-minded men would try to use the CP Pak invention to enrich themselves.

Dr. Ellison determined that she would not let the government steal her work. Travelling all over the U.S., she fought the government with all of her being. Through spurious legal maneuvers in the interest of *"the people,"* Ellison's financial claims to CP Pak were stolen. She was fighting to get them back and was gaining traction in public opinion before she fell gravely ill. Months later she was found to have been poisoned.

As she became too weak to fight and as a means of quieting her anger and her voice against the government, Dr. Ellison was offered a quasi-Witness Protection Program under the name Kendall Ann Hughes. The government encouraged her to take this offer by including a lifetime monthly stipend with COLA adjustments every year. The caveat was that she needed to get as far away as possible from CP Pak and her past life.

Ellison grudgingly accepted the offer so that she could

recover and live to fight another day. Under this duress, Dr. Shelby Ellison became Kendall Hughes.

Eventually, the military took what they wanted and afterward CP Pak technology was parceled out, through government use fees. Major corporations who would suffer the most as the technology came into public use were given the inside track on the use-fee bidding. Instead of survival of the fittest, old laggard companies were propped up by government interference while taxpayers footed the bill for their inefficiencies and lack of creativity.

Shelby Ellison knew, *"The government would never do this to an invention created by a man,"* which made her even more bitter.

With few exceptions, established airlines and railroads gained control and were slowly evolving into the CP Pak age. They had been handed this gift on a platter after sizeable and well-placed political donations. Microsoft, Google, Amazon, and newer more nimble entities had all begun lawsuits because they were crowded out of the use-fee process.

Major airports became staging areas for CP Pak travel. The airlines charged a premium for personal travel even though the technology saved the travel giants hundreds of billions of dollars every year. Each CP Pak could carry a load of 144 people in its 12 by 12 configuration. The travel capabilities were available to and from all major cities across the globe. Smaller rural airports, which could not afford the technology, connected through major airports and continued to use air travel.

In her new persona, Kendall Hughes owned a tourist shop in Ketchikan, Alaska. With a deep-seated mistrust of men and the government, she refocused her enthusiasm and made a new life for herself. She became a good citizen of Ketchikan doing things she had not allowed time for previously; she found friends including some men she grew to trust, and she enjoyed outdoor activities in order to fill her new life, but she never forgave, and she never forgot.

Her transition from Dr. Shelby Ellison to shop owner Kendall Hughes was not easy, but she had made a success of it. CP Pak technology had eventually helped mankind the way she envisioned it. Yet, she continued to feel that there was a void in her life that she did not know how to fill. She was a scientist, a researcher, and a problem solver. This new life didn't use those skills. That was the void.

The foreboding feeling that had come over her in the wee morning hours last was an unwanted irritation, yet at the same time, Kendall was intrigued by the possibility of major changes coming to her life.

Staring out of her hillside townhouse window at the tiny distant lights of Ketchikan in the predawn morning, Kendall said aloud, "Let's just see what this brings G-ma, and we will pray that it will be a good thing."

At that same time in Seattle, Reid was driving to the CP Pak Terminal of Sea-Tac International airport. He was taking in the early morning beauty of the distant bluish white light that haloed behind Mount Rainier. The halo was turning to a deep orange, with flashes of green and streaks of gray across the partly cloudy sky, like a spectacular sunset, only this was the opposite. The light was foreshadowing a winter sunrise. In winter, the position of the sun, low against the southern horizon, created picturesque hues of color on these semi clear bitter cold mornings. Reid loved the views around Seattle. His wife Charlie had loved them as well.

Growing up in San Rafael, north of San Francisco, Reid and Charlie had always heard that it continuously rained in Seattle but having lived here for the better part of 10 years before Charlie lost her battle to breast cancer, they grew to love the vast beauty of the snow-capped mountain peaks and the incredible seascapes of water offset by the evergreen shorelines. Seattle was to Reid and Charlie, one of America's most beautiful cities. God, he missed her, even to this day. Charlie left a huge void, and he could not get over her being gone.

Reid and Charlie had led idyllic childhoods. Each played sports while attending St. Mark's School from K through 8th grade and Marin Catholic High School where Reid excelled at baseball, basketball and lacrosse and Charlie excelled in golf and softball.

Their relationship began after she asked him to the *Frozen* Winter Prom. Charlie was a sophomore and Reid was a Senior. They were nearly inseparable from that day forward. Reid graduated from high school and in the fall, he headed to Seattle where he had a scholarship to play baseball for the University of Washington Huskies. The two love birds were miserable for the entire school year, only able to see one another every few months. The calls bordered on pornographic.

Reid came home for the summer and the teenage lovers became sexually active. By late summer, they were a young couple in trouble. They knew without hesitation that they wanted to get married. Reid was 19 and Charlie was 17. Three months after they were married, Reid's parents were killed by a drunk driver on Christmas Eve. Even though it didn't show to the outside world, Reid was devastated. Reid Daniels was 19 years old with a 17-year-old wife and a baby on the way. It was not quite the future that Reid or Charlie had planned on.

Reid had no other family in Southern California and Charlie's family had problems of their own, so the young couple decided to move to Seattle where Reid had worked for a restoration company part time during the previous school year. Reid had to forgo college and his baseball scholarship and work full time to support his young family while Charlie completed her high school diploma with honors. Charlie, dressed in her cap and gown with a gold honors braid, held their two-year-old son Michael in her high school graduation ceremony pictures.

With a bit of good luck, forced savings, a small amount of life insurance from his deceased parents and Charlie working full time, Reid was able to return to the University after three years away from college. He eventually completed his master's degree in computer science. It was never easy, but if you asked Reid and Charlie, it was never a struggle either because they had each other. They just put their heads down and worked hard to get their lives back on track to be what they had always wanted.

In one anniversary card to Charlie in those early years, Reid wrote tongue in cheek,

"If I had known that being married to you would be so fun and so easy, I would have married you earlier!"

Foregoing college, Charlie devoted herself to supporting Reid and the family while he earned his degrees. She was his rock, the foundation that got him through the loss of his parents, through the hard times in those early years and through college.

Joining the FBI shortly after graduation took Reid, Charlie, and Michael away from Seattle for six years. Reid advanced quickly in the FBI with that same head down, hard-working attitude that got him through college. It all paid off and he was assigned to head up the Cyber Crimes FBI Office for the Northwest and they were headed back to Seattle. After two years back and feeling they had re-established themselves, they were just beginning to attempt to add to their little family. That is when Charlie's four-year battle with cancer began.

Charlie had been gone for two years now and Reid was still not seeing anyone and did not want to move on to a new relationship. He told himself that it was not that he was still grieving, he just couldn't fathom finding a woman who could replace Charlie. They did everything together. They played golf together, binge watched television series together (a lot of Rom Coms) and played on FBI coed softball teams together. They were best friends, lovers and man and wife.

Their son, Michael, was also devastated when he lost his mother. Charlie had fought for so long that Michael had fooled himself into believing that his mom was going to beat the disease. After her death, father and son were able to console one another as Michael lived at home while he attended the University of Washington. He had a goal of becoming a cancer researcher. Michael was now 21 years old and living on his own with a girlfriend while completing a bachelor's degree and preparing for graduate school in Biochemistry at the University of Washington.

After he lost Charlie, Reid buried himself in his work. Special Agent in Charge, Reid Daniels was not a sad-sack moping individual. On the contrary, he was upbeat, jovial, fun to work with and fun to be around. He was simply a guy who was not ready to give up the day to day, hour to hour memory of his deceased wife.

Reid's four-person team worked on financial fraud and child porn investigative cases. Russian and other international hacking was handled at Quantico. Nearly 100 percent of the time, Reid's team never actually came in contact with criminals, with the exception of Chris Keller.

The final take downs and arrests of criminals were made by field agents, which sometimes included one-time Navy Seal, Chris Keller. This occurred after Reid's team had identified and geographically located the perpetrators. The Team had one of the best records in the entire agency of tracking and shutting down perpetrators of Cyber Crimes.

It was extremely rare for Reid to be called-on to head a field investigation and zero would describe the number of murder investigations he had been involved in during 14 years with the FBI. He committed in his mind that his small team would wrap this up quickly, so they would not lose time on the cases they were currently working. Like everything else he had ever done, Reid lived by the premise, as NASA's Robert Frost is known to have said, "The only way out is through."

As he drove to the airport, Reid was asking Charlie what

advice she might have for him as he started this perplexing murder investigation. When Reid had these conversations with Charlie, she was sitting right there next to him. She always had on a powder blue, hooded sweatshirt top with matching sweat bottoms, white tennis shoes and her shoulder length blonde hair tucked under a pink Nike swoosh small-billed baseball cap.

Charlie was telling Reid that he was the composite of all the talents that he possessed and not simply a computer geek. Charlie reminded Reid that he had high levels of intelligence, empathy, intuition, a drive to win, and most of all a capacity for love.

"Just be yourself and you will do a fantastic job whatever the challenge," was Charlie's advice.

CHAPTER 4

February 17
Early Morning Pacific Standard Time

Yuri placed a quick call to another of his six-person team. "Analka, are in place?" Yuri aked.

"Ya Yuri. Snug as a bug in a rug. You guessed right. Da high-tech FBI team from
Seattle is on the case," Analka whispered. "Da boss just called."

"Will you be able to hack lover boy's computer?"

"Oh ya. I just need a little time to verk on it."

"You will be our eyes and ears Annie. Do whatever you feel comfortable doing to stay in the good graces of lover boy, so you can have access to his computer."

"Will do boss."

As he hung up his phone, Yuri felt a little smug about his hunch. The FBI Northwest Cyber Crimes group would be chasing him, and that gave him a little time to relax. He assumed they lacked field experience and that their inexperience could play in Yuri's favor.

Analka Hrapla was "cute as a button" her mother always told her. Robin Medallon was correct describing her as beautiful. Analka kept herself in shape and turned more than a few heads wherever she went.

Analka would have no problem having complete access to Robin and his computers. Her good looks and winning personality belied the fact that this 24-year-old girl had been a first-rate computer hacker since the age of 11. Analka Hrapla had a genius IQ and knowledge of science, computers and the Internet that was well beyond that of Robin Medallon.

It was Hrapla who had broken the *mineral* code which had allowed Yuri to have *full* animation, while in the CP Pak transport, when he killed the diplomat Xing Tsua Ten. Brains and beauty are a most deadly combination and Analka's possession of both gave Yuri extreme confidence.

Although Analka had committed the crimes of a Russian hacker, she was not an assassin and Yuri kept her shielded from the real work of his team.

The fact that the first phase had gone so well, would no doubt greatly please his employer. It bothered him that he had made the first kill of this *"job"* and he still did not know who his employer was or what the end game might be. It was impersonal and Yuri liked it better when his killings were personal to him.

What Yuri did not know was, ten months earlier, four diplomats, each nearly at the bottom of their country's diplomatic Corp, had been vetted and chosen for a secret meeting in Paris. They had all signed a serious pledge of silence and non-disclosure regarding what they were about to hear.

The four were trade diplomats. Each one of them was from an authoritarian led country. These four traded in agricultural products with the United States. It seems that authoritarian countries have one thing in common regarding feeding their people. Unelected leaders spend huge portions of their country's wealth on arms to protect their own position of power. Making sure that their people did not go hungry was a secondary concern. In each country, food goods had to be purchased somewhere else and the United States is the food market for the world. They each traded with the United States for large quantities of agricultural products.

Present at the meeting was Xing Tsua Ten from China, a long-time international diplomat, who had no real rewards to show for his years of good works for China.

From Iran came Shahnaz Latifpour, an Iranian diplomat. Petroleum for food from the United States had been a good deal for the Iranians for a long, long time. Though he held an important position, Latifpour *knew* he was capable of so much more.

Next in the group was Park Soo-Hoon, a North Korean diplomat. He had the most difficult job of all. He was charged with making agricultural trade agreements with America, even though the two countries have not had open trade relations for nearly 80 years. North Koreans had an even greater need for agricultural products from America than the Chinese or the Iranians. Park held an important yet unrewarding position. He was intrigued by America and in particular New York. He could see himself living there someday.

Finally, in attendance was Russian trade diplomat Kostya Ivanov, who felt he had been overlooked for more important diplomatic assignments for far too long. Ivanov was first to learn about the opportunity being laid before them that night in Paris, and he was completely sold on it.

All four diplomats were in Paris performing backwater grunt work for their diplomatic delegations during the annual nuclear non-proliferation meetings.

Joining the unhappy group for a private dinner at the prestigious Spring restaurant was Luba Krupin, the beautiful 28-year-old assistant to Kostya Ivanov. Krupin had dark hair, hazel eyes and a nice figure. Her presence in the room commanded attention from the invited diplomats, all of whom were in their late 50s.

The Spring restaurant was chosen by Krupin because of the classy setting in the converted 17th century home in Les Halles in the heart of Paris.

Luba Krupin attended schools for gifted children as a teenager, then with a scholarship, studied finance at Harvard, where she graduated Cum Laude with an MBA. After graduation she worked as a trader for Morgan Stanley in New York for 2 years before joining the Russian Diplomatic Corp. Her primary goal in life was to use her intelligence and her education to become fabulously wealthy. No small dreams for Luba Krupin.

Luba's greatest fear was that she will remain a relatively poor Russian with no wealth, no power and no connections. Her greatest weakness was her impatience. Her plan, which she named The Marco Polo Alliance, was to use these old diplomats to jump start her own wealth by utilizing their money in fast-track trading and stock manipulation. She doesn't dislike the *old* men, but she doesn't have much respect for them either.

The meeting started with each diplomat wearing earbuds tucked neatly away and connected to a Microsoft Elucidation Translation Machine. Krupin began the meeting by introducing the diplomats to The Marco Polo Alliance concept. They were all international traders, hence the choice, by Krupin, to call the group Marco Polo Alliance in honor of the thirteenth century Venetian merchant trader. What Luba was presenting to them was a high return investment opportunity. She explained how The Marco Polo Alliance was an investment group on steroids.

The plan, she explained, revolved around the ability to hack into the Securities and Exchange Commission, which allowed the hackers to gain information about stock reports ten milliseconds before the information could go public. Artificial intelligence would then make the call to buy, sell, go short, go long, or ignore the information about a particular stock. It all happens in mere milliseconds before other market traders can see and react to the information.

Trades themselves would be made using high frequency trading networks, which are also known as fast-track trades, nano seconds ahead of the market. Krupin had hacked into the SEC system and has run 100 out-of-market tests, to make sure the system worked to make money. "It is a fool proof locked and loaded system to make large sums of money for the investors."

Over 50 bogus accounts would be set up to make the

trades when the plan went live. All stock moves in these accounts would not be winners. Some would be intentional losers but would not lose large amounts of money.

The parties behind these trades were these diplomats present in the room from China, Russia, North Korea and Iran. They would not act on behalf of their governments. They would work wholly in their own self-interest to become personally wealthy. Krupin would receive commission and, over time, spin off money to run her own accounts.

In the end, Luba would make the most money of all of them. Of course, she does not share this fact with the old men, because she needs their money to get started. They should be ever grateful to her for what she is doing for them. Worst case, after a year of operation, Krupin will make some excuse about the process becoming too dangerous and The Marco Polo Alliance will disband. At that point, she will run the scheme solely for herself.

It Is the oldest Idea since stocks were first traded. Gain "insider" information about stocks and securities and make trades before this information becomes public knowledge.

Krupin explained that each of the four diplomats needed to put up $50,000. She would begin trading in a handful of accounts, eventually building to over 50 accounts for each diplomat. They would each become billionaires, she promised.

Her tight low cut little black sweater and grey skirt accentuated her body which mesmerized the older men. The Iranian, Shahnaz Latifpour, who paid close attention to such things in women, in his own creepy way guessed a C cup.

By the time the desserts and after dinner wines were being served, Luba Krupin's presentation had captured the minds of the middle-aged diplomats not only for the wealth that it promised to each of them, but also because of her intoxicating beauty. They would become outrageously rich, remain protected behind a wall of false identities and in no way compromise their loyalty to their own governments.

They saw The Marco Polo Alliance as sheer genius. And,

it was!

CHAPTER 5

February 17
Tuesday 6:05am Pacific Standard Time

When Reid arrived at the SEA-TAC CP Pak Terminal, he recognized some familiar faces from TSA, Airport Security and the King County Sheriff's department along with his boss Carlos Sanchez. Reid played in a softball league with most of these men and women.

"Nice you could make it Sleeping Beauty," chided Mike O'Brien, a heavy-set King County Sheriff's deputy.

"You beat me 'cause you had a shorter drive from Top Pot Donuts, Mike. How are the bacon-maple cake donuts this morning?" Reid shot back.

"Damn good, just like always Reid."

"You better cut back to just one per day or you'll never make it to first base with those weak ass hits of yours. You already look like you're pullin an anvil when you run down the first base line," Reid joked.

"Reid, we've got a forensics team covering this CP Pak carrier and they're coming up with nothing other than normal prints passengers would leave. It looks, for all the world, like this strangulation murder took place during the CP Pak transfer. Can that even happen?" Regional Commander Sanchez asked.

Janet Ballard, head of Airport Security, joined in, "The victim's name is Xing Tsua Ten. We were able to catch a few of the passengers here at the airport because they had connecting regional flights. To a person, they say they didn't notice a thing. They thought the guy was slow waking up, you know how that happens. We're checking video on the other passengers to see if any of them acted strangely; threw anything away, that sort of thing, after they departed the transport. We've seen nothing so far, but my folks will call me as soon as they have something."

"Right now, it appears to be strangulation. The victim has ligature marks around his neck. Not a wire, something softer than wire, but strong enough to do the job," said Veronica 'Ronni' Johnson of FBI Crime Scene Investigation, as she stepped out of the CP Pak pod. "We can't rule out a chemical injection until we get him to the lab. That would certainly make for a more traditional crime investigation, but right now it looks like strangulation was a part of it."

Reid started organizing next steps. "Okay, let's get him to Bellevue to get a definitive on the cause of death. Janet, see if any of the people you were able to detain have anything that could be used to strangle someone, let's collect the trash to see if someone threw the weapon away and let's use this passenger list and your video to place everyone who was in that CP Pak and what they did when they departed the transport and left the airport. My group will get on top of who the victim is beyond his name, who would want him dead and how in the world this crime could take place in a CP Pak transport. Mike, you hang out at Top Pot Donuts, in case we need you to bring a dozen or in case we need help with an arrest, if we get lucky right away," Reid said with a smile.

Mike O'Brien just shook his head and smiled back at Reid.

As the group was breaking up to focus on their tasks, Carlos Sanchez caught Reid's attention. "Reid, we have to work on this as quickly as possible. Right before you got here, I got an earful from Director Russell. This case is already sensitive given the victim is from China and the mystery surrounding the death," Sanchez said. "Please get your team engaged as quickly as possible. I am always available to help out when you need me, but for now I'll step out of your way."

Reid went to Airport Security to have a secure place where he could call Robin Medallon. When he was stepping away from the crime scene tape, he met Chris Keller, an agent from his team. Chris was more of a field guy than anyone else on Reid's team.

When the team had tracked down hackers or porn perps, many times, Chris would lead local law enforcement on the take down, whether that was on domestic or foreign soil. Chris was an ex- Navy Seal Team Six combatant, a Native American from the Nez Perce tribe of eastern Oregon and northern Idaho as well as being six three and 225 pounds. Chris was the guy to have on your side in any kind of conflict. Not only that, Chris, loved and sometimes matched Reid's sense of humor.

"Let's talk," Reid said. "We have a dead Chinese diplomat. It looks like a strangulation that took place on a CP Pak Transport. We don't know how that happened or even if it can happen. Because of the high-tech nature of the crime, our team has the investigation".

"Not only high tech, but highbrow," Chris mused. "Like the old Paul Simon song, there must be 50 ways to kill someone. The only reason to do this in a CP Pak is to show off. In addition, this is the work of a team. One guy does not pull off something like this."

"I think it was *50 Ways to Leave your Lover*, the Paul Simon song, but you're right," Reid said. "Why did this guy get killed this way? Could this be a warning? Could we expect a next move by this killer? Here's what I need from you Chris. I believe we need to talk to the person who invented the CP Pak and that means we are likely to be travelling by the end of today. We will travel separately with you under false identity provided by Robin. I want you to hang back, sort of like the Air Marshal Service, but be there when I need your help."

"I'll be like a helicopter mom."

"I'll try to imagine you in mom jeans and nice MILF boobs", Reid quipped, "and you might want to cover all of that up with body armor, cause I'm packin my Glock."

"Jesus Reid, being hit by friendly fire has always been one of my greatest fears."

"Whether you believe it or not, I used to be considered an expert marksman," Reid said with a retriever-like tilt of his head.

"Well, the 'used to be' part sure makes me feel better," Chris offered with a wry smile. "How about we agree that you only shoot at me, if I am shooting at you."

"That sounds fair. Hey, give me a minute while I call Robin."

Reid stepped into an empty office. "Robin, what do we know so far about the victim."

"Looks like the victim is a long-term diplomat working mostly in agricultural trade," Robin said. "He appears to have climbed as far as he was ever going to go in the Chinese foreign service. He has connections in the government, so even though he was not the brightest penny in the jar, his job appears to have been secure and a threat to no one. The Chinese embassy says that he was headed to Seattle for talks about wheat and beef purchases with farmers associations from around the Northwest."

"I would doubt that this is connected to that," Reid said.

"I agree. Hold on Bert has something for you, handing her the phone."

Roberta "Bert" Hamilton is a 23-year-old computer hacker extraordinaire who worked for Reid's FBI team. Bert is FBI. She pulls together other hackers who are on the payroll of the FBI to reverse hack the criminals who are perpetrating crimes on the Internet. Beginning as a child of 8 she hacked every establishment organization she could think of. Bert hacked retailers, banks, hospitals, etc. to demonstrate the flaws in their Internet Security.

She wanted to show how easy it was to pull records on the Internet. All her hacks dead ended with dummy servers in Russia or Iran. Those countries always caught heat from the U.S. State Department, though they vehemently denied the accusations of their involvement in the hacks. No one could pin these hacks to a young black girl from Seattle's Wallingford neighborhood.

Bert attended Carnegie Mellon in Pittsburgh on academic scholarship and graduated magna cum laude at the age of 17 with a master's in computer science. As the only woman, the only female minority, the only bi-sexual and the most tattooed member of the team, Bert added brains and spice to Reid's group.

"Reid, before I start, I have to tell you that I attended the most unbelievable music event in Portland last weekend. It was the most algid music weekend I have ever experienced. Can't we move our offices to Portland?" Bert bubbled, as music blared in the background.

"What is algid? Is that a type of music?"Reid asked.

"No, it means *cool,* like you used to say something was cool or awesome or rad back in the olden days of being a teenager," Bert said.

"Yeah, I seem to remember the olden days and they weren't that long ago," Reid steadily raised the volume of his response to make his point without shouting. "Okay, what do you have for me? I hope I will think it is really algid."

"Okay, I have been hacking us. I know how you hate that, but it is the only way to keep a secret of what we are looking at."

"You know how I love it when you do that."

Bert was eager to get to what she had discovered. "Yes, I found Dr. Shelby Ellison, the person who led the discovery of CP Technology, is living in Ketchikan, Alaska under the name Kendall Hughes. She holds the key to it all!"

"Shelby, or rather, Kendal owns a little tourist coffee, gift and bookshop up there called The Dog and the Butterfly, ya know like the Heart song your grandparents might have listened to? I know how you love that old Country music, but you must have heard about Heart back in the day."

"Yeah, I know Heart. Charlie said I was a Magic Man."

"There ya go old white dude. Well, Kendall Hughes

is under a program like witness protection under the U.S. Marshal Service, so her real identity stays hidden."

"It was the deal she made with the government, so she wouldn't lead protests against the 'military only' use of the CP Pak technology. She agreed to go into hiding, if they agreed to keep the technology 'military only' for 3 years or less. That was 5 years ago. Kendall is now 45 years old."

"What are the chances she can help us with whether this crime could have happened in a CP Pak during the transport phase?" Reid asked.

"Like I said, she holds the key. Shelby is one of my tech heroes Reid. She is brilliant and like, a real person. From everything I have read about her, Shelby err Kendall is really algid," Bert gushed. "Notice how I worked your new word of the day in there? It's like Sesame Street for old white guys."

"Great job Bert! Let me talk to Robin again."

"Robin, looks like you need to book Chris Keller and me to Ketchikan asap."

"Already on it boss. You can use your own ID but everything behind your name will be an alias. No one can track you. You will show as clearance with TSA to carry your weapon."

"Nice work Robin. I need you to do the same for Chris. He will be travelling with me, but we need to be separate. His identity will be sealed. Chris will have my back."

"Got it," Robin replied. "You will both be on an Alaska Airlines flight at 4:00pm and will arrive at 5:40pm. It is a two-hour flight, but it's a time zone thing. You get to go across Tongass Narrows in the dark."

"Tongass Narrows," Reid mused. "Oh yeah, that is where the "Bridge to Nowhere" was supposed to be built in the early 2000s."

"Yup," Robin replied. "The mountains surrounding Ketchikan are so steep, there is not much flat ground, so the airport is on one side of the Narrows and Ketchikan is on the other side. It's about a 15-minute ferry ride. The ferry leaves the airport on the top of the hour and the half hour and the Ketchikan side to the airport on the mid quarter hours."

"Thank you for the travel bureau information. No one can accuse you of not being thorough."

"True that. And here is the last piece of information for you. Your investigative target, Kendall Hughes, has a little shop called The Dog and the Butterfly, you know like the Heart song from way back in the day?"

"Yeh, Yeh I know." *"Why don't they think I know who Heart is?"*

"Dog and the Butterfly is located on Creek Street. You're going to love it. It's easy to find," Robin continued.

"Thanks Robin. You seem like you are in a hurry," Reid said.

"I promised Analka I would be home for a shower a and a bite to eat around noon."

"Good golly man, you're like an Irish honeymooner," Reid said.

"What does that mean?"

"You and Analka are going to keep going until Peter goes to Dublin," Reid joked and paused for effect. "If you find out anything else that I should know Robin, give me a ping."

Reid caught up with Chris Keller, gave him the plan and then headed to his car to pick up the clothes he had packed. On the way, he went over his team with Charlie. Robin Medallon, computer systems geek, Bert Hamilton, able to hack anything, anywhere whether it was connected to a wire or not and Chris Keller former Navy Seal and team muscle. Even though they had never done anything like this murder investigation before, he liked their chances of quickly solving this first one.

CHAPTER 6

February 17
Tuesday 8:56pm Saint Petersburg, Russia
11 hours ahead of Seattle's time

It had been 9 months since The Marco Polo Alliance had been formed. Kostya Ivanov and Luba Krupin had just received the news that Xing Tsua Ten had been found dead after a CP Pak transport to Seattle, Washington in the United States. Neither knew what to think about this strange death. Luba rushed to Kostya's office in downtown Saint Petersburg.

In nine months of operation, The Marco Polo Alliance had been an unqualified success. Luba's shared reporting to the Alliance stated they had reaped over one million dollars for each member of the team. There was a plan, already in the works, for the Alliance to get together in Paris in three days. It was felt that they could easily meet in public and use the name The Marco Polo Alliance for these meetings under the guise of working on a mutual agreement for agricultural goods from the United States. Kostya could not believe the bad luck with this news about their Chinese Alliance partner.

Had Xing Tsua Ten shared the secret of the Alliance with someone? Could their plan be falling apart just as they were beginning to make real money? Luba Krupin asked Kostya if their lives might be in danger. She began crying just talking about that frightening prospect.

"There, there Luba". Kostya put his arms around her in a fatherly comforting manner.

Luba melted into his warmth expressing her vulnerability at that moment. Kostya had always felt like a father figure to her, but as Luba's shapely body pressed against him, Kostya began to feel less than fatherly. What a dream come true it would be to share his growing wealth with a young woman such as Luba Krupin.

Luba had pursued a job directly with Kostya, telling him that a friend had recommended that she go into Foreign Service. Kostya was more than happy to find a spot for this beautiful and brilliant young woman. Within a few weeks, Luba was on Kostya's team.

As his mind drifted, Kostya was startled by the ringing of his phone. The digital voice instructed, "Please turn on secure Microsoft Elucidation translation." Kostya made the adjustment to his phone. "Hello, this is Kostya".

"Kostya my friend, have you heard the news of Xing. What do you think is happening?" questioned Shahnaz Latifpour, the Iranian member of the Alliance. "Do you think the foolish old Chinaman has told someone about The Marco Polo Alliance and, in so doing, compromised us all?"

Shahnaz Latifpour and his family were distant relatives of the Pahlavi Royal Family of Iran. He was named after a great aunt. Latifpour and his family were not royalty but had been allowed to make their way in Iran after the Shah was overthrown in the late nineteen seventies. The Latifpour family had been international traders for over 200 years. The Ayatollahs had needed their expertise in trade, so staying in Iran after the revolution had made the family quite wealthy. Shahnaz had worked for the government for a time funneling money to gifted students in various countries to help fund research they might be conducting. In this way, the Iranians could stay on top of technical research which they could not have done for themselves.

Because of his family's station in Iranian life, Shahnaz was always overly confident and even annoyingly arrogant.

"I don't know Shahnaz my friend," Ivanov responded. "Luba is quite distressed and thinks that our lives might be in danger as well."

"That does not seem to be rational to me at this time," Latifpour advised. Shahnaz, like all Iranian diplomats, had served in the Intelligence arm of the Iranian Guard and felt like he was best qualified to analyze this situation.

"Remain calm," Shahnaz said, "We can be on the alert and employ bodyguards. Let's contact the others and continue to plan to meet in Paris in three days, as originally scheduled. It is likely not to be appropriate to be discussing this without all parties present."

Kostya reflected on this statement and realized that Shahnaz was not being swayed to the side of panic by the tears Luba Krupin. "As always, Shahnaz, you give sound advice. We will continue to plan to see you in Paris in three days."

When Shahnaz got off the call, he immediately made a secure voice translation call to Park Soo-Hoon, the North Korean partner in the Alliance. Better to keep everyone in line and on the same page.

"Park, my friend, you have no doubt heard the sad news?" Latifpour asked.

"I have heard the news and I believe we must all be in danger," Park said.

"Why do you think that? Do you know something?"

"I believe it to be too much of a coincidence. Just when we are beginning to show some real profits, one among us is murdered mysteriously. Do you trust the Russian?"

"I just got off the phone with Kostya. He was quite shaken, and I could hear Luba crying in the background. She is very shaken. Poor young thing," Latifpour said.

"Look Shahnaz, I am headed to Seattle now and plan a quick trip to Mexico City to lay the groundwork for some, ah, why am I telling you this, oh well, we must trust each other. Laying the groundwork for some produce trade from Mexico to North Korea. I plan to go from Mexico City to our meeting in Paris. Are we still meeting in Paris?" Park asked.

"My experience and my gut tell me that the FBI is on this, and that security will be tight right now, especially on CP Pak transports. So, even if this has something to do with The Marco Polo Alliance, we are safe right now," Latifpour professed.

"I think you should carry out your plan to travel to Mexico, then, let's see what we think in one more day. Right now, the meeting is on for Paris. I don't know about you, but I could use even a small pay out of the investment funds," Latifpour said.

"What you say makes sense Shahnaz. Good to have your expertise and insight. Goodbye for now. Be safe," Park closed.

"You, as well, my friend. Be safe," Latifpour concluded the call. He was confident he had quelled all the concerns of his fellow investors.

CHAPTER 7

February 17
Tuesday 10:37am Pacific Standard Time Seattle

After a drive-through breakfast with Petra Zane, Yuri had spoken with Analka Hrapla who had hacked Airport Parking to find that FBI Special Agent, Reid Daniels, had parked his car. It was on the 5th Floor of the main terminal at Sea-Tac International. Petra and Yuri returned to the airport and drove to the 5th floor. As passengers came and went, Petra positioned her car to a space about 20 yards from Reid's car in a place where they could watch Reid if he came out.

Petra and Yuri had worked together internationally for more than ten years, wherever Yuri's contractor bosses decided someone needed to die. Petra had previously worked as a model and supplied Yuri with makeup and disguise elements, so that he could escape detection to the casual observer and on facial recognition cameras. She provided higher, plumper cheeks, thicker eyebrows, nose additions and a variety of baseball caps which Yuri can pull down close on his head to shield his face.

Yuri had no idea what movements Agent Reid Daniels would make, but until he had hard facts from Analka about what Daniels was up to, he wanted to keep an eye on him. It was estimated by his employer that they needed to create five to ten days of investigation delays before the entire plan could fall into place. The Thorny Rose could then retire for several years or forever on the proceeds of this "*Job*". Yuri and his team could disappear into the night, go their separate ways and, with relatively modest living, Yuri would be taken care of for the rest of his life.

Causing delays in an investigation was not something that Yuri had ever done before. Normally, he painstakingly stalked his prey with a final goal of murder. Now, he was stalking his prey with the goal of impeding an investigation. This would take some finesse and Yuri would give it his best, but if Reid Daniels got too close to uncovering Yuri and his Russian assassination team, then Daniels or any other members of Daniels's FBI team would forfeit their lives. Yuri's creed had always been, "I will kill for you, but I will not die for you."

The Thorny Rose had been hired, anonymously, because of his reputation for killing. Yuri had developed a reputation as the assassin even though he was well educated and as a young man he had set his sights on business. Yuri's parents had scrimped and saved to send him to the United States to stay with his father's brother, Mikhail in Philadelphia, while Yuri was still in high school. Russia was changing and knowledge of capitalism would serve a young man well.

Yuri became a good student and was able to get scholarship help to attend the University of Pennsylvania. After an undergraduate degree, he went on to the prestigious Wharton School of Business. During that seven-year period of high school through college, Yuri poured everything into his education. He did not socialize, he did not play sports, and he did not have girlfriends, even though there were plenty of opportunities. Yuri appreciated how much his parents and his uncle were sacrificing just for him. His education was everything to him. He meant to make his parents and his uncle proud and to be able to pay them back.

As a recent MBA graduate from a highly regarded American college, Yuri was picked up immediately by Epic Energy, the largest oil and natural gas Company in Russia. Epic Energy was formed when the Soviet Union was privatizing its industries. Like many other private companies formed in

Russia during that era of "newfound capitalism", Epic Energy evolved through the shady purchase of oil and gas fields, refineries, and assets from the government by a consortium headed by Leonid Polachev, who was no friend to Vladimir Putin.

Polachev had been a government minister of industry and his group got a sweetheart deal for what was to become Epic Energy. Many western business writers said that it was such an Epic deal that it certainly must have been how the company got its name.

Epic hired smart, well-educated Russians, like Yuri Rosov, who helped develop a modern energy company. All of those in the original consortium became billionaires and people like Yuri were on their way to becoming rich as well. Yuri was able to share his wealth with his parents and his uncle right up until it all fell apart.

Vladimir Putin, whom history has shown to be greedy and controlling, wanted control of everything and that included Epic Energy. He pushed for court trials to show that the government did not receive the true value for the original assets of Epic Energy. This was easily proven. But then, rather than have this extremely successful company pay the true value to the government, Putin took back the company under government control and placed some of his cronies in charge. Not only that, so as not to be challenged by these now powerful men from Epic, all of those in the consortium were placed in jail with their assets seized by the government.

People like Yuri did not go to jail, but his assets and those assets gifted to his parents and his uncle were also clawed back by the Russian government.

Yuri was outraged. All that he had worked for had been taken from him. His parents were now old and could not recover from this major financial loss. They were nearly starving in government housing and his father caught deadly pneumonia standing in line for food. Yuri's mother took her own life shortly thereafter, which pushed Yuri to a new level of anger and despair.

Yuri had determined that he needed to strike back at a government that had dealt so much grief to his family. He knew he could not act impetuously. He had to be smart. He put all that he had learned about analyzing business problems and developing solutions into figuring out how to kill as many of these Putin government loyalists, as he could, without getting caught. His plans had to be deadly and untraceable.

Yuri first set his rage on those who had the most influence on bringing down Epic Energy and the life he had built for himself and his family. Through a great deal of research, Yuri narrowed his death list to 8 individuals, all connected to the Ministry of Economic Development; the Minister of Economic Development, the Economy Minister, the Minister of Property, the Vice Minister of Property, the Minister of State Resources, the Natural Resources Minister, and a pair who had both been researchers for Putin and were now Directors in the Natural Resources Division.

All these people had reason to falsify, and in Yuri's opinion, HAD falsified documents, in order to bring down Epic Energy. As Yuri saw it, they all had to pay for what they had done to his family.

The way Yuri killed each of these *"scum"*, became a pattern of death that would repeat itself in Yuri's repertoire as a killer for hire.

He especially remembered his first killing, because it needed to be close and personal to release the pent-up rage that Yuri had grown inside him.

Vassily Zaikov, the Minister of Property, was a political appointee on his way up. He was a little older than Yuri and had always lived a life of privilege. Yuri was certain that Zaikov had begun the push to investigate the formation of Epic Energy, so it was only fitting that Yuri mete out his punishment to Zaikov first.

Zaikov lived a princely life in a spacious 8,500 square foot home on the shores of Meschora Lake near Moscow. The home was built in the design and finish which was popular in the mountain regions of the Western United States; lots of earth tone colors, windows, spacious second floor decks facing the water, and timbers exposed on the ceiling inside. The exterior had brown rockwork with highlights of a deep golden yellow which covered a few feet up the walls from the ground. This same deep golden yellow stone was used to beautifully landscape around the house.

The home had a semi-covered 1800 square foot patio facing Meschora Lake, complete with a rockwork barbecue, a fire pit and a hot tub. The home had a ten-foot-high rock wall fence, which ran 50 yards in front of the house, then down past the home to the shoreline of the lake. A secure gated entrance allowed automobile entry from the driveway connecting the compound to the main road. The compound and house sat on approximately 10 acres of wooded property which Zaikov owned. Zaikov lived there with his young wife and three young children.

Most days, Zaikov would work from his home and did not have to make the 90-minute commute to his offices in Moscow. His everyday actions demonstrated that he knew there were those out there who might want to harm him. In addition to the compound walls, his home was heavily secured with cameras and a 24-hour surveillance security team of 4, with at least 2 security members always on duty. When the Minister of Property did commute from his home, he always had a driver and a bodyguard with him, and they had a dozen different routes which were taken randomly to and from his office.

With care to be a well-hidden stalker, Yuri studied Zaikov's habits. He knew he needed help and a certain expertise. With money he had managed to save, Yuri hired Georgy and Luka Pajari, two brothers who had both been ousted from the Russian military, one for a major supply theft and the other for attacking and nearly killing his commanding officer. Yuri was surprised how easily one could find unsavory characters in Russia who were willing to do anything for money.

With the help of hackers he hired, Yuri was able to gain access to the surveillance cameras and had spent months looking for a way into and out of the Zaikov compound while remaining undetected. Finally, in late June, Yuri saw his opportunity.

As the weather had warmed, Zaikov began swimming back and forth each morning from his dock to the dock of a neighbor about 100 yards away. Zaikov would swim over and back three times. At one point in between each lap, as he turned from his own dock to head back to start his next lap, Zaikov was out of camera view for a matter of seconds. Additionally, sometimes it was a little longer time out of sight if he paused to tread water for a half minute at the end of his second lap. When Yuri saw this happening, his heart raced. It was the opening he had been looking for.

On the 300 feet of lake front within the Zaikov compound was a brief bit of shoreline, which had brush growing down to the water. The Zaikov dogs, frequently, were called back from that area when they went berserk barking at raccoons or some other natural invader.

On Alibaba, an Amazon competitor on the European continent, Yuri located a small underwater rebreather device and ordered four of them along with a wet suit, mask, and fins. True to their promise, in three days, Alibaba delivered to a nearby mail drop apartment which Yuri had taken under an assumed name.

The excitement to release the rage began to build. Yuri determined that on the first moonless night after a Zaikov commute to the office, he would put his plan in place to make his first kill.

He selected a secluded area, 300 yards down the shoreline from the Zaikov property, from which to make his approach. The reflection of the early morning sun off the water helped obscure this area from the view of the Zaikov compound. Yuri would enter the water from this site and work his way to the brushy area on the Zaikov's property. Georgy and Luka would be waiting at this starting point for Yuri's extraction after the deed was done. If necessary, they would storm the compound to rescue Yuri.

At 1:00am, Yuri entered the 55-degree water at the secluded spot down the shoreline. "How could Zaikov swim in this water? How can I swim in this water?" Yuri thought. He checked to make sure he had all four breathing devices tucked into the pockets of his wet suit. Each device had two little tube like tanks on either side of a mouthpiece and measured about 8 inches in length. Depending on the rate of breathing, a diver could get ten to fifteen minutes out of each device in less than 20 feet of water.

It was a tight fit, but Yuri got them all tucked away in his suit, and he slipped into the water, pausing to recheck the knife which Luka had given him to strap to this leg. "Never go anywhere without a knife," Luka had said.

"TOO COLD" was his first thought! He had to collect himself and refocus his anger and rage against Vassily Zaikov. The refocusing helped. He swam slowly on a route to a point about 100 yards out from the shoreline, then headed for the brushy area on the Zaikov property. It was a moonless night. Moonless and dark! Overcast! Panic set in! Yuri had been so eager to get his first kill; he had not checked the weather! Could it be cloudy and raining in the morning? Could Zaikov abort his swim for that day? Why had he not checked the forecast? Would his first attempt at revenge be a failure? He had to put all of this out of his mind.

About halfway, Yuri stopped to practice breathing with one of the devices. He twisted the valve, placed the device in his mouth and began breathing. The breathing was fine, no bubbles, as advertised, but Yuri could not stay under the water. He had no weight belt. He would swim down using the breather, but then, quickly pop back to the surface as soon as he stopped swimming down.

He decided that he needed to grab some rocks along the shoreline and zip them into his wet suit, so he could remain under water. After doing this and after several minutes under water, Yuri decided he had practiced enough. He tucked the breather away and continued his slow swim to the brushy area feeling a little warmer since the exertion to stay under water had warmed him.

After nearly two hours of slow swimming and practice time, Yuri reached the brushy shore. It was a tangled mess and there appeared to be no way to crawl quietly ashore and remain out of sight. Yuri again had to refocus on what he was here to do. Slowly and quietly, he began moving rocks and dirt with the knife Luka had given to him. The activity had awakened the Zaikov dogs and after 10 minutes of barking, one of the security guards came down to the water to check things out.

Half in the water, Yuri willed himself to remain perfectly still until the guard was satisfied that it was a false alarm. He gathered the dogs and headed back toward the house, no doubt keeping an eye on the area with the security cameras.

After another 45 minutes, Yuri was able to slide completely up under the brush. An hour after that, the first light of day was creeping over the lake, the clouds had cleared, and the sun would be rising soon. Excitement began again to build in Yuri's heart. *"I will kill this scum and my life and my parent's death will be avenged."*

Yuri waited until Vassily Zaikov came down for his swim. When Zaikov started out on his first 100-yard swim to the neighboring dock, Yuri would slip into the water. He would make his way under water to where the Zaikov dock touched the shoreline, the blind spot. He would wait there until Zaikov would make his first turn out of view of the cameras to start his second trip to the neighbor's dock. At that point, Yuri would again go underwater and wait for Zaikov to get to his short rest period between the 2nd and final lap of his morning swim. That was the time and the place.

Just as Yuri was readying himself to get into the water, the dogs were back. This time they were going berserk. Two security guards came running. Yuri was quite certain he could not be seen. Time was slipping away. The first morning light was streaming through the foliage. Yuri's dark wet suit matched well with the dark dirt from the ground. *"Sheer luck,"* Yuri thought. *"In the future he could not rely on that."*

The light dappled across the ground and across Yuri. The guards were certain they could see something in the brush. One pulled a gun and fired shots at a point near Yuri. Panic surged through Yuri's heart. He wanted to get out of there as quickly as possible.

"Had to focus! Had to think!"

One of the guards had run to the dock and was shouting to Zaikov who had stopped swimming. Luckily, the talk was of an animal which they were trying to scare out of the brush.

Another pair of shots into the brush! By blind luck, Yuri had not been hit. Quickly, Yuri positioned himself to move some rocks with his feet. This made splashing sounds in the water. Success! Even though the dogs were still barking, the guards were pulling back and taking the dogs with them, all the time shouting reassurances to Zaikov, who began swimming again.

Yuri had to move quickly now. Again, he stuffed rocks into his wet-suit and pulled a breather from his pocket. He quietly put on fins and his mask and pushed into the water. His only chance now was to go out in the water to the point near where Zaikov would make his turn and commence his short rest stop at the end of the dock. Yuri would take Zaikov at that point.

The rocks in the wet suit were working. Yuri was swimming along the bottom, and he hoped he was heading in the right direction to hit the end of the dock. He used the slope of the bottom as his guide and could tell by the pressure in his ears that he was getting deeper.

AIR! *He was running out of air! How long had it been, who cares, focus!* He grabbed another tube and stuffed the empty into his pocket. Abruptly, he noticed the swimmer above him and to the left. He turned his focus to Zaikov and followed at a distance deeper in the water. Zaikov stopped! He was at the blind spot at the end of the dock!

With all his strength Yuri swam to Zaikov's knees. He struck with the speed of a cobra. He grabbed Zaikov by the knees from behind and pulled him under water. Zaikov was flailing at Yuri with is arms. His legs were trying to kick Yuri away. Yuri held tight. Yuri could feel the rage giving him abnormal strength. Zaikov panicked.

Yuri held him under water for about 20 seconds. Somehow, Yuri had maintained his breathing device even though his diving mask had been knocked askew and was hanging around his neck.

"You will not get away from me, you scum!" Yuri thought as he quickly released his two-handed grip on Zaikov's lower legs. With one hand, he grabbed the top of Zaikov's hair from behind. With his other hand he grabbed a low point on a piling of the dock. This repositioned Zaikov to hang upside down in the water with his feet now pointing up but not out of the water.

Zaikov scratched at Yuri's hand and forearm, but the wet suit gave protection. Yuri was able to hold Zaikov down. Slowly, Zaikov was losing strength. His life was slipping away. Yuri Rosov pulled Vassily Zaikov's face to where he could see it up close. *"You got what you deserved, bureaucratic scum bag!"* Yuri thought. Zaikov stopped moving and in a few more seconds Yuri allowed the dead body to float to the surface.

Yuri turned and went deeper away from the dock, and he began following the contour of the lake bottom to his takeout point, all the while feeling a sense of relief and accomplishment that elated him. The getaway was a complete success.

In the following days, Yuri reflected on all that had gone

wrong and all that could have gone wrong in his first revenge killing. He vowed to become even more diligent and to become laser focused on the details.

The authorities eventually ruled the Zaikov death was a homicide, yet they could not find one clue to follow. Very quickly the investigation ground to a halt.

To raise the necessary funds to continue the killing of those on his list, Yuri and his team put together a hacking scheme that reaped hundreds of thousands of dollars from individual European banking accounts. This is where Yuri first utilized the talents of the young hacker Analka Hrapla, whom he called Annie.

Next, Yuri Rosov turned his thirst for revenge to the other seven individuals whom he deemed responsible for the cruel pain that had ruled his life over the past two years.

One by one, all of those whom Yuri Rosov had selected for assassination were eliminated, two in a car crash when the brakes failed, one in a hunting accident, one in a natural gas leak and home explosion, one in a staged suicide, and one in an abduction-rape-murder carried out by the Pajari brothers. In each case, Yuri needed to be close enough to watch, or to see video of the deed to gain the satisfaction he needed to assuage his lust for revenge.

Yuri Rosov soon gained a reputation with the Russian underworld. These types had high profile targets and deep pockets of money. Thus began the legend of the assassin "The Thorny Rose". Yuri's team had grown to 6 operatives and killers; Analka Hrapla, the genius scientist and hacker, Petra Zane, a beauty who could be called upon as a driver, a makeup artist or for certain under covers activities, Faddy Zolnerowich also known as Fatty Sandwich, a documents forger and travel logistics expert, Vadik Kozlov, an expert bomb maker and finally the cold-blooded killers Georgy and Luca Pajari. The team Yuri had assembled had performed countless underworld assassinations and this same group was the lethal team now after Reid Daniels and his team of computer geeks.

CHAPTER 8

February 17
Tuesday 10:37am Pacific Standard Time Seattle

"Any news Annie?" Yuri asked.

"Ehlo. Robin is on his way back to me and I have bout twenty minutes to hack his verk computer and see what he has been up to. Call you right beck?" Analka said in one breath.

While he waited for Analka's call back, Yuri got out of Petra's black Mercedes and walked to Daniels's Audi. He had changed jackets, put on a baseball cap and kept his face down. Knowing he would be seen on camera as he approached Daniels's Audi, Yuri acted as if his shoelace was untied by kicking his foot a couple of times. He bent down, out of sight of the security cameras and looked like he was tying his shoe. Instead, he was placing a Geo Tracking device under the front wheel well of Reid's car. Yuri got up and continued toward the elevators. As he got near the elevator, he began checking his pockets and let his shoulders slump suggesting he had forgotten something in the car. Yuri did an about face and headed back to the Mercedes where it was a short wait for Analka's call.

"Okay, agent Daniels is leeving in just a couple of hours ta go ta Ketchikan, Alaska. Want to know why?" Analka said. "To find Shelby Ellison, the inventor of the CP Pak technology whose alias is Kendall Hughes. She has a little shop dare on Creek Street."

"That is a smart move. We could not have found her so easily without your help getting into the FBI files. Can she figure out, as you did, how a person can become animated during a CP Pak transfer?" Yuri asked.

"Yhes, she is brilliant. She is one of my heroz."

"Is he travelling alone Annie?"

"Yhes." Analka didn't know that Robin's libido, in his rush to get home to her soft loving embrace, had delayed the booking of Chris Keller's ticket. In fact, Robin was just completing the booking on his secure phone while driving home to his new sweetheart.

"Annie, contact Fatty Sandwich. Have him book Vadik Kozlov to Ketchikan out of Seattle this afternoon on the same flight as agent Daniels. Then, contact Vadik to let him know where he is going. He will know which explosives he can hide in is luggage," Yuri said. "I don't know if we will need him, but it is better to have an experienced bomber, standing by, ready to do his dirty work just in case we need him."

"Yuri."

"Yes Annie."

"You killed that Chinese man on the CP Pak transport. I never dreamed my discover would be used for that. Why did you have to kill him? Was he trying to kill you?"

"Yes Annie. And now we need to protect ourselves. If you go to jail, there is no one to look out for your mother. We must protect ourselves," Yuri said convincingly.

"I understand Yuri," Analka said.

As soon as he hung up with Analka, Yuri contacted Faddy himself. "Fatty Sandwich (Faddy Zolnerowich), you fat bastard, it is a long time since we have spoken directly," Yuri said cheerfully.

"Hey Yuri, good to hear from you. Do you finally have some field work you can let me in on?"

"Funny you should ask," Yuri responded.

"Do I get to rough up somebody or maybe even kill them?"

"Not so fast, Faddy. You need to show me that you can walk and chew gum at the same time. Here is what I need. Analka is going to contact you soon regarding travel for

Vadik Kozlov. He is following one, maybe two, FBI agents to Ketchikan, Alaska. I want you on the same flight to Ketchikan. I want you to set up a plan to rattle the FBI agent Reid Daniels. Annie will send you a picture. We don't want to harm Daniels. We simply want to give him a little scare."

"Scare him personally, physically?" Faddy asked.

"Not personally or physically. Get into his hotel room. Leave something to let him know you were there. That will show him that we can find him anywhere, anytime," Yuri said. "Analka will give you all of the information you need. This is your first shot in the field; make me proud Fatty!"

Yuri completed his call with Fatty Sandwich and immediately contacted Vadik Kozlov.

"Vadik, you dick, how are you?" Yuri asked.

"I am growing impatient Yuri. Seattle does not have good strip clubs. Too many ugly girls with small tits," Vadik Kozlov laughed.

"Well, your time in Seattle is ending. Analka will be contacting you soon. Fatty Sandwich is booking you onto a flight to Ketchikan, Alaska," Yuri said. "Right now, prepare for your trip, bring what you might need and be looking for further instructions from me."

Yuri loved this part of his work. Directing his staff, like a quarterback on an American football team. He had placed Vadik Kozlov in Seattle to be available for just this type of strategic deployment.

"I must go now Vadik. Your potential target, FBI Agent Reid Daniels, is coming my way."

CHAPTER 9

February 17
Tuesday 11:07am Pacific Standard Time Seattle

As Reid walked to his car, he was deep in thought about what his meeting with Kendall Hughes would be like. *"Would she co-operate with the investigation?"* *"Would she be difficult to work with?"* *"How much of a nerd was she?"* He was directing these questions to Charlie who was walking silently beside him, in his mind.

Suddenly, a black Mercedes was speeding directly toward him. Reid was frozen in place. He could see that the driver was an attractive brunette with large sunglasses. The car was accelerating right at him. The driver remained expressionless.

Reid had only enough time to dive between a white Ford F150 pickup and a light blue Prius. He lunged between the vehicles as the Mercedes sped past and slammed on its brakes. "Still quick like an infielder," Reid thought. He spent too much time thinking that thought and did not get a look at the license plates. His heart was pounding.

Instinctively, Reid had reached for his Glock as he dove out of the way of the speeding car. Not being a practiced maneuver for him he dropped his gun. It had slipped from his hand and slid under the Prius.

"Why couldn't it have slid under the pickup, where there was plenty of room to grab it," Reid was asking Charlie.

Reid was stretching for his gun, when he realized that the Mercedes had stopped. His heart pounded harder. He struggled to make his mind figure out what was going on here. The Mercedes began to back up slowly. He was involved in a murder investigation and now, this woman seemed to be stalking him, but why?

With a great deal of straining, he was able to get his fingertips on his gun. Finally, he had it in his hand. Quickly, Reid got into a crouched position and moved to the front of the pickup; he was shielded from view, as the Mercedes backed past where he had been. Then, just as quickly as the Mercedes had come after him the first time, the brunette driver put the gas pedal to the floor and squealed forward around the line of cars and headed for the exit.

Reid could see that a black card was covering the rear license plate. "What the hell was that about?" Reid said out loud to himself and Charlie. "Maybe the security cameras will give us something."

"That should have him scratching his head," Yuri, who had been hiding below the window line of the Mercedes, said to Petra.

"I am glad he is not the trigger-happy type," said a relieved Petra Zane. "He very easily could have come up shooting when we backed up."

"Yes, now we know that he is a cool and collected adversary," Yuri said.

Yuri's phone rang. It was Analka. "Yes Annie, something new for me?".

"Yhes, my liddle rabbit lover has come and gone," Analka giggled. "I meke a joke.

I was able to hack Robin's verk computer and find that another agent, Chris Keller, will be travelling to Ketchikan today also. The two agents are not seated together, even though they could have been. I research Chris Keller. He is guy. American Indian. Seal Team 6 training."

"It is a forgone conclusion that this agent Keller is there to back up agent Daniels from a distance," Yuri mused. "Okay thanks, I need to call Kozlov and Fatty. Annie, you sound as if you are enjoying your time with Robin Medallon," Yuri said.

"Maybeee," Analka cooed. "Robin is very attentive to my needs, unlike some Russian men and his stamina is amazing."

"Stay focused. We must protect ourselves and we only get paid the big money if we are successful. Focus on the work. I know you need the money to care for your mother," Yuri said as he hung up.

Analka was painfully aware that she needed to provide for her mother and as much as she liked Robin, she would not let anything interfere with that responsibility.

Yuri dialed Vadik Kozlov and explained to him that agent Chris Keller would be accompanying agent Daniels to Ketchikan.

"You may be tasked with distracting an FBI agent, a Seal Team 6 guy, who is silent back up to the lead agent Reid Daniels. I want you to watch the Seal Team guy and occupy him if necessary. We want to see if Daniels can operate on his own. No need to kill Keller. That will draw too much fire power from the FBI and the less people they have working in Ketchikan, the better for us," Yuri said.

"How will I know this guy?" Kozlov asked.

"You will have photos and Fatty Sandwich, himself, will be the bait to draw out the Seal Team man," Yuri replied. "Call me after you have identified the Seal Team man. I believe I will have an explosives job for you at that time," Yuri said. "You may need to take him off the case for a while. Don't kill him, but get him out of the way, so that Daniels is on his own," Yuri repeated his directions.

"Will do boss," Kozlov replied.

Chimes interrupted as Yuri had another call coming in. It was his employer. "Please turn on Microsoft Elucidation voice translation," Yuri's phone directed. Because all his calls with his employer had been through the Microsoft Elucidation voice translation App, Yuri had no idea of the sex, the nationality or age of his employer.

"There is a meeting of The Marco Polo Alliance in Paris, in three days. You don't need to know exactly what that means right now. Park Soo-Hoon, a Trade Diplomat from North Korean is travelling from Viet Nam to Seattle to then transport on a CP Pak to Mexico City. Earn your money," the mono toned computer generated voice commanded. "I'll be back to you when I know the exact Mexico City CP Pak Transport out of Seattle that you and Park Soo-Hoon will be taking."

Yuri knew that there was no need to respond. The call hung up on him immediately. He also knew this was a directive to kill Park Soo-Hoon during that CP Pak Transport from Seattle to Mexico City. He would need Annie's help with travel since Fatty would be occupied with his assignment in Ketchikan.

"I am so lucky to have Analka Hrapla on my team. She is surely the most versatile member of the team," Yuri thought.

CHAPTER 10

Analka Hrapla had grown up in a "working poor" family in Astrakhan, Russia. In the bar where she met Robin, she had pretended to be from Czechoslovakia. She was with another young woman, a model, whom Petra had sent, who, was from Czechoslovakia. Yuri told Analka that he thought Czech women were sexier than Russian women, so she should say she was from Czechoslovakia.

Analka was an attractive, but not drop dead gorgeous, young woman. Certainly, to a computer nerd like Robin Medallon who usually was too nervous to get within 6 feet of a pretty girl, Analka must have been the most gorgeous, sexiest thing he had ever seen. Analka's job was to meet and go home with Robin so she could spy on the activities of the FBI Cyber Crimes team. Planting herself with Robin was an educated gamble by Yuri which paid off when the investigation was quickly assigned to Reid's team. Having sex with Robin was totally Analka's idea. Yuri knew that was not something he could ask of her.

Analka had a strange sense of morality; Stealing was fine. Hacking was fine. Being the technical backup for Yuri was fine. But, if you wanted Analka to sleep with someone or kill someone, that was asking too much. Analka was having sex with Robin because that is what she wanted.

Analka's mother had been a housekeeper for a wealthy family headed by a highly placed executive with Gazprom. Gazprom, a state-run natural gas giant, developed a nearby gas field and the Gazprom executives were the richest people in the area.

At one time the family home, Astakhan, was known for its caviar and fish production, but overfishing had been responsible for killing what should have been a sustainable industry. Analka's father had been a fisherman. By the time Analka was born, he was a drunk and he abandoned the family by the time she turned two.

Analka tested for high intelligence and even though Astrakhan was an exceedingly poor area of Russia, children like Analka were pushed ahead in education. This gave Analka an early introduction to computers and the Internet. At the age of 8 she was sent to a school for *"gifted youth"* called The Thirty School in St. Petersburg. There she was a little girl without her mother, without a father and feeling quite vulnerable. Little girls were not usually pushed in the direction of technology, but Analka was so bright administrators agreed sending her there was the right thing to do. Luckily, she was able to find encouragement and friendship from an older female classmate who saw Analka's talent and took the young girl under her wing. Analka buried herself in the study of the Internet and computer coding, but she deeply missed her mother.

By age 11, when she was not studying, Analka was hacking on the Internet. She developed online scams which were bringing her over $2500 in some months from foolish Americans who were willing to provide banking information to her because they thought they could make some quick money or win a prize.

Analka was the only one making quick money in those hack attacks. She convinced herself that she was not a bad person because she did not take all the victims' money and because they would be wiser from the experience of their loss. Analka was determined to work her way out of poverty.

The geeky little girl was growing up. Her mother was a pretty woman, and Analka was becoming a pretty teenager. Her affable personality made her even more attractive. She knew that her mind and her Internet studies were her ticket to wealth and success.

By her mid-teens, Analka was mining data from retailers, insurance companies and banks, then selling that information to the slimy underbelly of the Russian mob. Those criminals knew how to use the information after they had it, but the mob could not obtain the data as easily as Analka could.

Her bank account, bolstered from her hacking schemes, was too large to remain untouched. Analka started dressing and spending like she was more than a poor girl from Astrakhan. She was also funneling a large amount of U.S. dollars to her mother, who was able to quit her job in Astrakhan and move to a plush apartment in St. Petersburg where they both lived.

Analka's big mistake came when she began to work scams on the executives of Gazprom back in Astrakhan. It was a game to her. It was all about taking money and embarrassing people whom she felt had treated her mother and other poor women so badly for years and years.

Over a period of 18 months, she was pulling in thousands of rubles with creative hacks on the accounts of the executives with Gazprom. Then one day, close to her 18th birthday, it all came crashing down.

Authorities from the State Intelligence Police came swooping in and arrested Analka. Her trial was quick and quiet. The government did not want to publicize that a "gifted youth" had been taking money from overpaid executives of a giant state-run energy company. Her funds were taken by the government, Analka was sentenced to two years in prison and er mother was evicted from the plush St. Petersburg apartment and literally thrown out onto the street.

During Analka's incarceration, her mother was living with a street thug and again cleaning houses of the rich. Analka was heartbroken and bitter.

Analka was granted early release, if she agreed to go

back to The Thirty School and continue her education. While completing two more years of schooling, Analka came to realize that she needed to be smarter about how she made money. She became intensely interested in CP Pak Technology. She was certain she could take the technology further than Shelby Ellison had. This was the perfect time for Analka to be looking for new sources of Internet income. She had to get her mother out of poverty and keep her out.

An anonymous benefactor, who somehow knew about Analka's genius, stepped forward to help fund her research. Soon, Analka was being paid a retainer to be available to crime figures for her hacking brilliance. Her benefactor worked behind the scenes procuring tech talent for the slimy underworld of Russian organized crime. That entity was now Analka's anonymous agent.

When Yuri needed to make money after the Vassily Zaikov killing, Analka's services were made available to him on a piece meal basis. A few years later, when Yuri said he needed to have his own hacker working directly for him on his latest job, Analka was delivered for a fee.

Yuri took Analka under his wing and added her to his team of assassins. Analka was an incredible asset to Yuri as she could make fast money hacking and because her youthful, good looks and winning personality made it easy for her to get close to people. People who could provide Yuri with valuable information.

Analka felt as if she had found a temporary home. Some place she could make money on her own terms and get her mother back out of poverty. Yuri didn't try to have a relationship with his Annie, and he let the other team members know that she was hands off as well. He treated her kindly and with respect. Misguided as it may have been, Yuri was a father figure for Analka, but she never lost her drive to build her own future and to support her mother.

Even though things were going very well again for the young woman, Analka's greatest fear was that she would become trapped in a life of crime. Her moral compass, although somewhat twisted, was still firmly in place. In her mind, Yuri and his team only killed bad guys and that somehow made it okay to work with them.

The sexual nature of this job was something different for Analka. During her teens, she had had awkward sexual encounters with other geeks from The Thirty school, both male and female, but she had not enjoyed it. For Yuri, she had used her charm and flirtation to gather information about or from targets, but until now sex was not a part of her undercover work on Yuri's team.

Robin Medallon was special to her. Most of Analka's previous relationships had been with *"jerks"* and *"assholes"* who wanted to act as if Analka was their private whore. For a time, she put up with these men, because those were the only kind of men she had ever been around. Eventually she dumped them. Because of those experiences, she was surprised at the treatment she received from Robin Medallion. She could see that Robin adored her and placed her on a pedestal.

Why sex this time? She didn't know. It all seemed very normal to her. She went to a bar and met a guy she wanted to get to know better. It seemed like maybe it was what real life was like in America. During their first sexual encounter after she allowed herself to be picked up by him, Robin had been gentle and caring even though she could tell he was quite inexperienced. It was enjoyable for Analka, which surprised her.

Subsequent love making had proven just as satisfying for Analka and with frequency and coaxing Robin became a better and better lover.

Secretly, she hoped this assignment would go on and on, but she had to keep remembering that she was there to gather information from Robin, first and foremost, to help Yuri, stay on track for this *"Job"*. She dreamed that one day she would be away from this life of crime and have a real life with someone like Robin.

CHAPTER 11

February 17
Tuesday 2:00pm Eastern Standard Time Washington, DC

President Charles Parker and his Administration had a full plate of problems that ranged from a lagging economy, growing unemployment, the ever-expanding Social Security crisis and the scandal of sexual harassment charges against his Homeland Security Secretary Coleen Decker. In addition, Charles Parker had come into office two years earlier with a promise of balancing the continuing U.S. Trade deficit with China.

President Parker was in the oval office alone seated behind the Resolute desk with several papers and two laptops laid out before him. Not the photo op scene that Americans are used to seeing.

As leader of one of the largest countries and economies in the world, he knew he always had to be ready for one more problem. Into his otherwise hectic day, Jaime, his personal assistant, Secretary of State Emily Hertz and Defense Secretary Justin Roberts charged into the Oval Office, waving documents. Chief of Staff Blaine Hurwell was close behind.

"Sorry for interrupting sir, but this is something you need to know," said Secretary of State Hertz. "We received, word earlier today, that a Chinese Diplomat was murdered on a CP Pak transport being sent from D.C. to Seattle."

"Did the murder take place in D.C. or Seattle?" President Parker asked.

"Neither! We think it happened during the transport," Secretary Hertz replied.

"How does that even happen?" the President responded.

"We don't know sir, but the Chinese are responding in a manner that we might expect," said Defense Secretary Justin Roberts. "They have placed their South Seas Fleet with their Type 001A Aircraft Carrier Xi Jinping on full alert and they look to be getting under way headed toward Hawaii."

"Jesus, do they ever wait to find out what is going on before reacting?" the President exclaimed. "Jamie, get Director Russell (FBI Director James Russell) on the phone, right now!"

"He's already holding sir. He called right when Secretaries Hertz and Roberts got here," replied the President's personal assistant.

The President punched up his speaker set. "Jim, I hope you are calling me about the CP Pak murder of the Chinese Diplomat," Parker said.

"I am sir, here's what we know. The Diplomat is Xing Tsua Ten. He has worked on agricultural trade with the U.S. for years but is very low level and has never been believed to be a Chinese spy. We have our Internet team in Seattle leading up the investigation, since the murder took place during a CP Pak transport. There are no leads so far, but it's still early. The team at Quantico is helping as well."

"Emily are you in touch with Jeng-Sheng Wei, Chinese Ambassador to the Chinese Consulate in Washington, D.C., about this?" the President asked.

"I have put in a call, and we are meeting in about an hour," Secretary Hertz replied.

"If I may be so bold sir, if the shoe was on the other foot, we would want to be part of the investigation," FBI Director Russell interjected. "Let's offer to let them send some folks to Seattle to help us. My team out there can control that."

"I think that is a great idea," Emily Hertz replied. "If everyone is in agreement, can I have their people contact you, Jim?"

"I agree that is an idea we should pursue as long as we can control them," said the President. "Now, what about our naval response?"

"I have asked Joint Chief McCallum to work up responses for the Chinese move and I should have those within the hour," replied Defense Secretary Roberts.

"Sounds good everyone. Thanks for the fast response. Keep me appraised and let those folks in Seattle know how important this is. We need to find who is behind this and bring them down quickly," the President finished the meeting.

"REID!" It was Regional Commander Sanchez on his ICP. "REID, PICK UP, PICK UP, PICK UP, RIED!" Sanchez was always impatient, as if the person on the other end were taking their time to answer him.

"Yes Carlos, what is it?"

"Do we have anything that I can send to Director Russell and the President?"

Reid personally knew James Russell, Director of the FBI. Russell had been in the position for ten years and had served two Presidents. Reid had met him on several occasions.

"Still at the Airport, we don't have anything yet," Reid said. He made a split-second decision not to say anything about the strange happenings in the parking garage. "Ronni Johnson got back to us that the autopsy at Overlake Hospital in Bellevue did not turn up any cause of death outside of strangulation and there appeared to be little struggle. The passengers we've interviewed didn't see anything suspicious. The victim was a low-level trade diplomat, dealing mostly in agricultural trade. Nothing in his background would lead to this type of murder. The airport security staff has not found anything in the trash, but they are still looking. FBI general office here has not reported in on who the other passengers were in the CP Pak module," Reid reported.

"In other words, you got squat!"

"In just a little over an hour, I am headed to Ketchikan to talk to the primary inventor of the CP Pak technology. Chris Keller will be shadowing me up there," Reid countered.

"Reid, I cannot impress upon you enough that we need to start getting some answers on what happened here. The Chinese Navy is moving a Carrier Group toward Hawaii. Jeng – Sheng Wei, the Chinese Ambassador to the U.S. Consulate in DC, is right at this moment lighting up our State Department and President Parker," Sanchez said. "I don't have to remind you that President Parker came into office promising to even the trade balance with China,"

"You are right, you don't have to remind me," Reid thought.

"Yes," Reid said. "I understand how the President would be very sensitive to this killing of a Chinese Trade Diplomat on a Transport in the U.S."

"This thing is ratcheting up faster than expected. We have a lot at stake here Reid and we are placing our trust in you and your team." Sanchez continued, almost talking over Reid, "Director Russell has offered to allow the Chinese to help with the investigation. Sooo, Hai Chang, the Intelligence and Security officer from Chinese Consulate in Washington, DC, says they are sending Lan Phang, Internet Intelligence Director from the People's Republic of China, out there, to Seattle, to get a first-hand look at the investigation. We need to accommodate that, Reid."

"Oookay," Reid said. His mind was racing. "Do you know when Hai Phang will arrive?"

"It's Hai Chang who is the Intelligence Officer in D.C. and Lan Phang who is coming to help with the investigation."

"Got it," Reid said, but he wasn't sure if he did. "Is Lan Phang a woman or a man?"

"That is a damn good question, Reid. I'm gonna hafta get back to ya on that. Now, be sure and let me know as soon as you find anything."

"It goes without saying,"

Reid hung up and went back to studying the airport

security camera with Janet Ballard, head of airport security. They could see the black Mercedes jumping parking spaces on the 5th floor of the parking garage until it was in the same row as Reid's Audi.

The events on the parking garage security video played out as Reid remembered them. Luckily the camera did not show Reid's clumsiness with his gun. In fact, it did not show Reid at all after he dove out of the way of the black Mercedes.

"It is almost as if the lady just wanted to scare you," Ballard said.

"Seems like it, doesn't it," Reid responded, "Very strange."

Neither Reid nor Janet Ballard thought to look at earlier morning security camera footage from the 5th floor of the parking structure.

CHAPTER 12

February 17
Tuesday 3:00pm Pacific Standard Time Seattle

Reid settled in for his two-hour flight to Ketchikan and opened his portable device to review the dossier from the Marshal Service on Dr. Shelby Ellison or Kendall Hughes as she was known now. He was going over it with Charlie at the same time. Ketchikan did not have CP Pak transport capabilities. He had already contacted Robin, Bert, and Chris to let them know that Lan Phang, or was it Lan Chang, was coming to join the investigation. He was pretty sure it was Lan Phang, which Robin later confirmed after a little research. Robin also found that Lan Phang was a 34-year-old female.

Reid opened the files on Kendall Hughes. The first thing that struck him is that Kendall is a beautiful woman with incredible sky-blue eyes. Not at all the nerd he had expected. Ellison is 45 years old, was born in Kirkland, Washington and attended the University of Washington and MIT. *"Well, you have the University of Washington in common,"* Charlie offered.

In her youth, Ellison, now Hughes, had been quite athletic, playing soccer and golf. In golf, Ellison had placed 2nd in State in the 8th grade before the technology bug bit her. She had never married and had no children. *"Do you think she has regrets about not having children?"* Charlie was asking.

At that very moment, in Ketchikan, Kendall Hughes was having an afternoon meeting with her key employee Kassie Young. The two were looking over what Kendall always called "trinkets and trash" that they needed to purchase for the upcoming tourist season. Even though the item cost was low, and the profit was also low, Kendall always wanted to have the best quality items, even in low priced items, thus pushing the profit on those items lower.

The foreboding feelings from the night before were still forefront on her mind. She kept reminding herself, these feelings did not always mean bad things. The feelings, however, were the feelings. They brought back the death of her parents and the days when she was fighting the government takeover of her work on the CP Pak transports.

At times over her years in Ketchikan, Kendall had allowed herself to believe that she had given up too easily in the early days of the struggle to see how CP Pak would develop. In her mind, she had determined that if she had it to do over again, she would have fought harder; would fight harder today, if she got the chance, but at the same time, she was not going to let the past ruin her current life.

Before she went into hiding, Microsoft, Google, Boeing, Tesla, Lockheed, Airbus, Uber and Lyft all had made lucrative offers of employment; Kendall had turned them all down, she didn't want money.

What she had in Ketchikan was good and, who knew, maybe something else would take her life in a different direction that was even more enjoyable. On her own she had created a full and happy life for herself in Ketchikan. Deep down, however, she knew she was a scientist and the feelings that awakened her last night made her realize that she needed science back in her life.

Kendall had worked hard to immerse herself in her new life in Alaska and to forget about the past, but your past is deep in your skin, deep in your bones and seems to come back when you least expect it. Top of mind for her right now was her mistrust of the government and of men in general.

As Reid read the notes from Bert Hamilton, the thought of it all made him feel a little sick in his stomach. How could the government he worked for do such a thing and how on earth was he going to convince this betrayed woman to help him figure out how the murder had happened aboard a CP Pak transport? *"Just be yourself Reid,"* Charlie said. *"Women love you."* Reid smiled.

It was quite the coping mechanism Reid had worked out with himself. From outward appearances, you would never know that he was having ongoing conversations with Charlie except for an occasional facial expression that didn't seem to fit the current circumstance. To Reid his conversations with Charlie were normal, very natural. Reid Daniels needed help with his mental state. People talk about a *'functioning alcoholic.'* Reid was a *'high functioning delusional'.*

While on his portable device, Reid received a note from Robin regarding accommodations in Ketchikan. Reid would be arriving on one of the last flights of the evening, he would catch a ferry from the airport across Tongass Narrows and go directly to his hotel from there. Robin Medallon's notes said he would send the room information momentarily.

Reid ran through his day in his mind; "Bring your gun!" Head up a seemingly impossible murder investigation, have someone try to scare or maybe kill you in the parking garage, carry the mounting pressure of an international incident on your shoulders and hang every hope going forward on a woman who might be so mad at the U.S. government that she probably won't talk to you.

Charlie might as well have been there with him because that is who Reid was directing all these thoughts to. *"Wish you were here Charlie. I know you would have some great advice to get me through this."*

"I am right here Reid," Charlie said.

In his mind, he could hear Charlie's advice. *"Reid, if you just listen to yourself, you've already broken this down. With all that is on your mind, contacting this woman in Ketchikan, winning her over with your honesty and charm is the most important task before you. The other things will take care of themselves. Oh, and Reid, keep your gun close by."*

Reid said a little prayer for Charlie to watch over him, then he fell asleep listening to some old Garth Brooks hits for the remainder of the flight.

CHAPTER 13

February 17
In route to Ketchikan –Arrival 5:15pm Alaska

Reid had slept for about 45 minutes, when he awoke with a gentle vibration from his portable device. It was a note from Robin regarding Reid's accommodations in Ketchikan.

"Since you will be deplaning at approximately 5:40pm local time, one time zone West of Seattle's Pacific time, you will catch the ferry from the Ketchikan Airport across Tongass Narrows and then go directly to your hotel," the note began.

"Because it is February and the rates fit our budget, I got you booked into the Inn at Creek Street. That way you are close to your meeting in the morning. Now, don't go looking for a place called the Inn along Creek Street. According to the travel brochure online, it is a *collection of small, historic properties stylishly restored with modern amenities and guest services.* The historic, mostly wooden structures, line both sides of the creek. The guest services location for check-in is at 133 Stedman Avenue which joins Creek Street and is right across from the Federal Building. You will be staying in the only room at the Star House. Your Star House room is about one-half block away from The Dog and the Butterfly, the gift shop owned and run by Kendall Hughes. Get this, the Star House used to be the only registered brothel in the territory of Alaska and is on the National Registry. I book you into only the best places. I booked you for two nights in case you need more than one day. Creek Street sounds pretty cool. Online it looks to be about two or three blocks long on both banks of Ketchikan Creek. The creek runs roughly Northwest to Southeast spilling into Thomas Basin, which is an inlet of Tongass Narrows. I sent Chris his hotel information and yours. He is nearby on Stedman. Travel safe!"

As soon as Robin had made the reservations, Analka intercepted the information and contacted Yuri. Yuri immediately sent the information to Fatty Sandwich and Vadik Koslov along with his own message for Fatty. "Fatty, I know you have never done field work for us, and I know how much you want to get involved in this end of the business. This should be an easy way for you to get started. Let me stress this! We only want to scare this target, not harm him! Scare to distract, not harm! Very important! Again, the target is FBI Agent Reid Daniels, the leader of a team that specializes in Internet crimes. You should have received a photo of Daniels and of the trailing agent who is there for Daniels's protection. Work to steer clear of the trailing agent, he is a bad Seal Team dude," Yuri's message read.

Faddy Zolnerowich was an expert forger for Yuri's team. He was born in America to Russian immigrant parents but had deep ties to the Russian mob. Faddy was a geek; over-weight, bad complexion, awkward around women and desperately wanting to fit in with Yuri's crew. He had begged Yuri for a chance to work in the field. Faddy had worked ahead creating false identities and paperwork for Yuri's team in case he ever got the chance for a field assignment. He was thrilled at the opportunity. Faddy Zolnerowich did not mind being called Fatty Sandwich by Yuri, The Thorny Rose. He saw it as a badge of honor to have a nickname from The Thorny Rose.

When he deplaned, Reid was surprised at the size of the Ketchikan airport, full of people and amenities. He was also surprised that more than half of the passengers had cars parked in the parking garages and would take their cars onto the Ferry across the Tongass Narrows to Ketchikan. *"Who knew?"* he thought to Charlie. Shelby Ellison, aka Kendall Hughes, really had found herself a protected hide away.

Reid and by default Charlie, Chris, Faddy and assassin

team bomber Vadik Koslov made their way from the plane onto the old MV Oral Freeman II ferry for the short ride across Tongass Narrows. Chris noticed that only three passengers were carrying small bags. Everyone else had multiple bags, including Vadik Kozlov, and they were using the free Smart Carts. The people with multiple bags appeared to be returning from somewhere warm where they had gotten away from the wet and cold Ketchikan winter. Chris, Reid and the heavy-set gentleman were dressed as if they had learned about this trip at the last minute. Chris became immediately interested in the heavy man.

Without being too obvious, Chris Keller watched the heavy man. Vadik Kozlov watched Chris watching Fatty Sandwich.

Fatty Sandwich made no attempt to watch Reid and Chris. He went immediately to the taxi stand and took a cab looking like a man who knew where he was going. Chris relaxed a little. This guy didn't look like he was a threat to either he or Reid.

The two FBI agents travelled separately to their hotel rooms. Reid checked in and settled into his room at the Star House and started to think about where he might eat and get a beer. Chris checked in, dressed in all black, and went out into the night to see if anyone was following Reid.

Creek Street was as Robin had described. It was not really a street. At roughly 10 to 12 feet wide, Ketchikan Creek flowed moderately fast down a draw bordered by steep banks. Because flat ground is scarce in Ketchikan, buildings on Creek Street were erected on stilts and scaffolds on embankments above both sides of the creek. There were boardwalks on either side, with footbridges connecting the boardwalks at three locations. Between the boardwalks and under the bridges was open air down to the fast-flowing creek.

CHAPTER 14

February 17
Tuesday 6:30pm Alaska Standard Time

Across town, Fatty checked into a room at the Rodeway Inn Edgewater, paying with cash including a damage deposit of $100 cash because he could not say how long he would need the room. The Rodeway Inn Edgewater is a 70's era outside door entry motel on the North Tongass Highway, not far from the Airport Ferry Terminal.

Faddy Zolnerowich had no idea what these two men were planning, only that they were FBI. He ran through his assignment in his mind. Yuri had told him to "scare and distract" one man and be wary of the other.

As soon as he dropped his meager travel bag at his room, Faddy took an Uber to the only Walmart just a short distance away. Fatty's plan was to use a "stink bomb" that he would make from an egg, a little milk, some vinegar, mustard, a soda can and a Ziploc baggy. He planned to detonate this with a very small phone-activated detonator that he carried in his pocket in what looked like a Chap Stick tube. He had gotten the small detonator from the real bomb specialist, assassin team member, Vadik Koslov, years earlier. Koslov would laugh if he found out Faddy was using it with a stink bomb.

After buying his "groceries", Faddy headed back to his room to assemble the bomb. It needed to be mixed, then heated and cooled multiple times, to speed up the chemical reaction of the simple ingredients. When he was done cooking, Faddy walked the short distance to the Creek Street area carrying the bomb in a plastic grocery bag.

Upon arriving at Creek Street, Faddy knew he must establish an escape route, just in case this "Seal Team" guy should catch on to him. He had heard Yuri's experienced field guys talk about the escape routes they had pre-arranged for themselves. Faddy was determined to impress Yuri and the other guys.

Near the point that Ketchikan Creek flows into the Thomas Basin Harbor, there is a marina for local fishermen and sailing enthusiasts, in other words, lots of boats. Over the point where Ketchikan creek empties into the harbor, sits the 100-foot-long Stedman Street Bridge with the boardwalks of Creek Street on both ends of the bridge.

Faddy decided that if he was spotted by the man he has named "Seal Team", his best escape route, if needed, was down the boardwalk of Creek Street to the Stedman Bridge, where he could jump into the water off the Thomas Basin side of the bridge and swim the short distance to the marina, where he could hide on one of the boats. *"A simple plan, really,"* he thought. Faddy has braved cold water before and has heard "the guys" talk about escape routes like this, so, he felt good about his plan.

Now all Faddy had to figure out was how to get his "stink bomb" close enough to his target, agent Daniels, let Daniels know that he is being followed and that these people, Yuri's team, could find him anywhere and take him out any time they wanted. "This should be fun and easy," Faddy mumbles to himself.

Faddy made his way to the south side of Creek Street with his plastic grocery bag in hand. He looked like a guy carrying a sack of food for the evening.

The night was crisp, just above freezing, and the boardwalk looked damp from the dew of the evening and might be a little slippery later. *"Look for little things like this,"* Faddy told himself, *"So you can become an excellent operative on Yuri's team."*

As he walked, he spotted the Star House across the creek,

where Analka had told him "his target" was staying.

While Faddy had shopped for stink bomb supplies and looked for his escape route, Reid had left his room and made his way to the Married Man's Bar and Grille. The Married Man's is a pub that borrowed its name from Married Man Trail, which was a trail one could use, back in the day, to get to and from Creek Street unnoticed. Back when the entire Street offered houses of ill-repute.

As the fat forger walked past the Married Man's Bar and Grille, he recognized Reid sitting at the bar with a half-eaten burger and fries. Reid's chatting with the bartender who's handing him another beer. *"This is too easy, Faddy. You are good at this,"* the fat man reasoned.

Faddy continues walking past the Bar and Grille. He ducks into a dark alcove where he can survey the Creek Street boardwalk. From this spot, he can view the boardwalk, looking both ways for "Seal Team". Seeing nothing, Faddy passes back in front of the Married Man's Bar and Grille, once more. He makes his way past the footbridge that crosses over the creek and passes in front of the Star House where Reid is the only guest.

From the time that Faddy began walking on the Creek Street boardwalk, Chris Keller has been watching. Chris quickly recognizes this fat, somewhat slovenly looking, fellow from the Airport Ferry. Keller does not believe in coincidences. This guy is worth watching.

Faddy turns back to the footbridge. He moves across quickly to the Star House guest entrance where he begins to pick the lock.

Chris Keller closes in fast on Faddy with the stealth of a Navy Seal. As Chris reaches the middle of the footbridge, his footfall hits a loose board making a slight creaking noise.
Faddy doesn't need to look up. He knows who it is. He turns quickly to his right, downhill, toward the Stedman Bridge. He must get to the end of the boardwalk at Stedman. He breaks into a sprint. Though Faddy is giving it all he has; speed is

not the fat man's strong suit. Chris Keller is gaining on him, but still 15 yards behind. As he runs, Faddy reaches into the grocery sack, pulls out the bomb, raises it up over his head and slams it into the boardwalk.

The concoction spreads all over the middle of the boardwalk. Seconds later, Chris hits the slimy, stinky mess, momentarily losing his footing and falling. This allows the slower Faddy Zolnerowich to pull away from him by another 15 yards.

Chris gathers himself. He can't believe the stink of what he has fallen into. He feels no burning in his lungs or his hands, so he concludes it's not toxic. He can deal with it later. Chris closes ground again between himself and Faddy.

Faddy rounds the corner, turning to his right from the boardwalk onto the Stedman Bridge. Angling right, he looks back over his right shoulder to see how close "Seal Team" is behind him. For a fleeting moment, he is pleased that he is going to make it to the water on the other side of the bridge. In the next instant, he runs directly into the path of a Ketchikan Gateway Borough Electric Transit bus. Faddy Zolnerowich is instantly killed!

Vadik Koslov has had a front row seat to this debacle and has a clear view of Chris Keller. He will watch what plays out and deal with Keller later. It appears Koslov's skills as a bomber may be needed here in Ketchikan after all.

CHAPTER 15

February 17
Tuesday 7:39pm Alaska Standard Time Ketchikan

Chris Keller reaches Faddy first. He shouts for the Transit driver to call 911. Chris quickly checks the fat man's pockets and finds only a Rodeway Inn hotel pass key.

"Who the hell is this man and what was he doing? Is anyone else after Reid?" Chris wonders.

When the sirens start to blare, Reid quickly paid his tab and, through force of habit, takes one last gulp of beer with Charlie in his ear saying, *"C'mon. C'mon!"* before going out to see what was happening. He makes his way cautiously down the Creek Street boardwalk toward the gathering crowd, checking to make sure his gun is secure.

Just then, a woman comes running hard at him across the footbridge. Reid pauses and keeps his hand behind him ready to pull his gun. The woman brushes passed him. "Excuse me. Any idea what happened down there? I'm a doctor!"

Reid watches the doctor running down the boardwalk, slipping a little, then recovering. He follows cautiously and soon reaches the stinky, smelly, slippery mess. "What the hell?"

Where Creek Street meets Stedman, Reid sees the downed fat man in the street. Chris is speaking with the local police while paramedics are covering the body. Chris makes brief eye contact with Reid then looks back to the police officers. Chris has shown his FBI badge to local police and contacted Robin.

Bert had previously contacted the Federal Marshal

Service in Ketchikan when she learned Shelby Ellison's alias identity, Kendall Hughes. The Marshal Service was standing by to help if needed. Bert had also contacted the head of Ketchikan Gateway Borough Police to inform them that the FBI would be working a case in their jurisdiction.

"Hi, I'm Sargent Lenny Blankenship, lead Ketchikan officer here right now. I understand you are FBI."

"Chris Keller, FBI Seattle. I suggest that your accident investigators go up the boardwalk here to take a sample of this stinky concoction which I have all over me and gather the debris where the heavy man had thrown it down."

Sargent Blankenship nodded to his officers who heard what Chris had said and they head up the boardwalk with their evidence kits. The officers were quick to agree with that plan because it meant they can get away from the stink on this FBI guy. Little did they know that they were headed for a lot more stink just up the boardwalk.

"With you here, right on top of the scene, this suggests this is more than some guy wandering in front of the bus," Sargent Blankenship states the obvious.

"Give me a chance to take off these stinky clothes, grab a quick shower, get into some clean clothes and I will come down to the station and tell you what I know. Here is a hotel card that I found on him. We need to locate the room for this key and see what can be found there."

"You might have contaminated that evidence," Blankenship replies.

"We have the body, we know he was hit by a bus, and we can get the prints directly from the body," Chris says with a bit of a smile.

"Good point," Blankenship replies sheepishly.

"Look, we will need the prints from the body sent directly to the FBI. We don't know who this guy is, but he was trying to interfere with a current investigation of something that happened in Seattle this morning. Find me that hotel room and that will be a huge help at this point. I am going to get cleaned up," Chris said.

As Chris walks past Reid without eye contact, Reid gets a strong whiff of whatever Chris had fallen in and a few minutes later Reid receives a call from Chris on his Insta-Com phone.

"Reid, I don't know what this guy was up to, but he was trying to get into the outside entrance to your room," Chris half whispered. "When he saw me moving in on him, he took off running. He knew that someone might be watching him, and he ran at the slightest noise. Didn't even look up from trying to pick the lock. Did you smell that stuff I fell in?"

"Yeh. Bad stuff. You might shower before you walk past me again.'

"Shh, blow me dude."

"What are your thoughts on what this guy was up to?" Reid asks.

"Don't know for sure yet. I think we will find this stink bomb to be benign. Seems to me, he just wanted to scare you, let you know that somebody knows where you are, and they want you to know that they know. I am going to go down to the Borough police station and help them jump start the investigation of who he is errr ah was," Chris said. "Did you see him on the Ferry? He was on the plane with us and he was also carrying a small bag, like he found out he was travelling at the last minute. He had to buy the stuff to make that stink stuff unless he has an accomplice here in Ketchikan, but more likely he is working alone here. You were his target. That's for sure."

"Think I should worry about anybody else coming after me tonight?" Reid asks remembering the SeaTac Airport garage incident.

"I'll talk to the Marshal Service and see if they can have someone from their office keep an eye on you tonight. Their office is right down the street from us. I'll explain the sensitive nature of what you are doing and why I don't want to bring in the local Borough police for this."

"Guess I'll sleep with my gun under my pillow."

"Please don't shoot yourself. Talk to you when I know

something," Chris signed off.

CHAPTER 16

February 17
Tuesday 9:15pm Alaska Standard Time

When Reid got back to his room at the Star House, it was 9:15pm Alaska Standard Time, 11:15pm in Seattle. It had been a long day.

He ran back over the day's events in his mind with Charlie. A Chinese diplomat had been murdered in a CP Pak Transport. How was that possible? Someone had tried to scare him in the Sea-Tac Airport parking garage. Someone tried to get to him in Ketchikan. How did these people know who he was and where he was?

Charlie's response, *"Someone wants to distract you from the investigation of the murdered diplomat. Someone in the Cyber Crimes team or the FBI is leaking information and Bert Hamilton is just the person to find out who and how."* Reid smiled and nodded his head up and down in agreement.

Bert Hamilton's ICP buzzed. She answered on the first ring. "Hey Reid, what's up?"

"Hi Bert. Sorry to call so late."

"Not a problem. I was just into my third hour of Get Locked and I am killing it! Get Locked is the latest gamer driven video game."

"Bert, we are dirty. Someone knew my exact whereabouts in Ketchikan and is almost a step ahead of us."

"Do you need me to find them and scrub them out to get us clean again?"

"Yes, sort of. I need you to "get unlocked" and get on this right away. But when you find out who's making us dirty,

I want you to get back to me. We might be able to feed them some bad information for our own purposes."

"Alright Reid, I'm on it Dude! AEEYAA GOT YA MUTHA FUCKA! BOOM! Sorry Reid. I just scored big on some dude from Portland who calls himself Blazer Butthole. Okay, I'm on it for you Reid. Goodbye."

Reid hung up his ICP and laughed out loud as he sat down to start planning his introduction to Kendall Hughes aka Shelby Ellison.

CHAPTER 17

February 18
Wednesday 6:52am Pacific Standard Time Seattle

On Wednesday morning, Yuri was eagerly awaiting news from Fatty Sandwich. When his encryption protected phone rang, he jumped, thinking it was Fatty. The voice on the other end was his client speaking in a voice modified computer monotone.

"Thorny Rose, how are you," the voice asked.

"I am what I am," Yuri replied. "One of my team is harassing the lead FBI Investigator right now. We know their every move."

"Are they any closer to figuring out how we accomplished snuffing the China man?"

"No, we are in the clear! So far, we have been harassing this lead agent to slow him down. We know they will try to find Shelby Ellison, the genius who led the invention of the CP Pak technology. She has been in what they call witness protection. When we have found her, Ellison and the lead agent will have unfortunate accidents."

"I think I told you originally, that a good intelligence officer would have found Ellison before the CP Pak murder. Now you must work on two fronts. Foolish man, you have spent too much time in the West," the voice said using terse words, but delivered in the same modified computer monotone. "You must now climb into another CP Pak transport and take out the second target."

"First, finding Ellison is much easier through the FBI and second, I think it is too soon for another CP Pak kill," Yuri protested. "We need to let the dust settle."

"Don't act like a woman! The time to push forward is now! We have confirmed word that the North Korean, Park Soo-Hoon, is travelling to Mexico City later today. You need to get on that transport and do your JAY-OH-BEE or do I need to find someone else to make this $2 million?" The voice closed, then immediately cut off the call leaving Yuri fuming.

Park Soo-Hoon, the North Korean Diplomat, was ecstatic to be a part of The Marco Polo Alliance and had begged, borrowed, and stolen to get the $50,000 buy-in to join the clandestine group of investors.

Because the investments had had only a little time "to cook", as the lovely Luba Krupin had described it, he needed to continue his real job making trades for Agricultural products to feed the North Korean people. His thoughts drifted momentarily to Luba. He wondered if he might have a chance with her. He felt the wealth he was accumulating through The Alliance could easily erase their age difference. Like most men, he was blind to the fact that a young woman as beautiful as Luba would never fall for a toad like him.

Park was nervous about this trip. He trusted the advice of Shahnaz Latifpour because he knew that Latifpour had a background in intelligence in Iran, but it bothered him that the details of the murder of their friend Xing Tsua Ten had not been made public. The thought of quickly concluding his business in Mexico City and then on to Paris where he would see the lovely Luba Krupin and the others buoyed his spirits while he waited for his transport.

The Thorny Rose was booked on the same transport under the alias Yokov Mikhailov which Fatty Sandwich had created for him before Fatty's trip to Ketchikan. His able computer whiz assistant, Annie, had hacked the CP Pak transport booking computers a second time and had Yuri aka "Yokov" seated directly behind Park Soo-Hoon on the transport.

In addition, Analka edited paperwork previously prepared by Faddy Zolnerowich, which Yuri would need to get out of Mexico.

While the two men were seated in the departure lounge, Yuri received word in a secure text from Vadik Koslov of the death of his friend and team member Faddy Zolnerowich. He was surprised and saddened by the news. Yuri knew that he would need to step up the pressure to slow down agent Daniels's investigation. Because of the work Yuri would complete today, FBI Agent Daniels would be under even more pressure from high levels of the U.S. Government.

It was time to turn up the heat on Agent Daniels. Yuri had little time to think before he called his bomber, Vadik Koslov, on the encryption protected phone. Vadik gave him a brief description of the last few minutes of Faddy's life.

"So they must know by now, that we have access to their moves as they are making them," Yuri said.

"And they will be even more cautious," Vadik added.

"Change of plans, Vadik. We know now from Analka that they are there to see the lead inventor of the CP Pak technology. Her alias is Kendall Hughes. She owns a tourist store named The Dog and the Butterfly on Creek Street near where Fatty met his unfortunate death. We don't know whether they have contacted her yet. After they have met her, I want you to firebomb her store. I prefer that agent Daniels, the Seal Team dude, and Kendall Hughes are all there when you detonate the bomb. Do a sight inspection and get back to me."

"Will do boss."

Yuri then called his most ruthless hit team on his encryption protected phone. Georgy and Luka Pajari were the Russian criminal brothers still on the team after they had helped Yuri kill Property Minister Vassily Zaikov and the other revenge victims. Yuri had them on his team for tasks that take cunning and brawn. They are ex-military, mercenaries and are merciless.

"Georgy what are you and your fagot brother up to today," Yuri teased.

"Thooorny Rooose you must need som top notch unda cova killers to do some important verk for you," Georgy replied.

"I need you now Georgy. Is that going to be a problem?"

"Na na, we are into some tings, but we can be ready quick. Vod you need Yuri?"

"Analka will send you information including travel arrangements. The weather will be cold, dress warm. I need your report twice daily. We'll talk later," Yuri said and hung up.

Yuri quickly thumbed an encrypted text to Annie letting her know about the death of Faddy Zolnerowich and giving her directions to be given to Georgy and Luka Pajari. The brothers were to get to Ketchikan, as quickly as they could, to pick up the trail of Agent Daniels and follow whatever was happening with him.

Yuri wanted as many assets as he could muster now that he knew that the FBI would trace Faddy Zolnerowich back to Russian mob connections.

"Time to move in and shut down this investigation with a dead end and a few dead bodies in Ketchikan," Yuri thought to himself. Revenge was always the best motivator for Yuri and Fatty's death provided the tonic to sooth Yuri's morals.

Analka made the arrangements and sent a message to the Pajari brothers. She warned them about "Seal Team" giving cover for lead agent Daniels. In addition, she informed them that Fatty Sandwich was dead, even though she had no details. They should arm themselves, be careful and await further instructions.

When she had done her work, Analka updated Yuri. Analka informed Yuri that her Robin had had no communication from agent Daniels, but that agent Bert Hamilton had come by Robin's condo to update his computers. Analka let Yuri know that she had checked things out after

Hamilton left and that she still had secret access to any communication between her Robin and lead agent Daniels. In addition, she had strengthened her firewall to keep anyone from reverse hacking and uncovering her operation.

After receiving the message, Yuri was ready to check in for his transport to Mexico City. During the check-in process, both the diplomat and the assassin were questioned at length.

Each took their own metallic stabilization tablets, as is required for CP Pak transports.

Individuals have slightly different levels of Iron and Lead naturally in their bodies. The stabilization tablets bring all passenger's systems into a tighter safe range for these chemicals thus making travel in a CP Pak transport possible. Additionally, Yuri took two more "mineral" tablets which had been supplied to him by Analka. These tablets enabled him to be fully animated during the transfer and mirrored what he had done in the transport with Xing Tsua Ten.

Fifteen minutes later the hatch was closing on the CP Pak pod in Seattle, destination Mexico City.

The same dreamlike, other worldly feeling Yuri had experienced when he killed Xing Tsua Ten was back. His surroundings had become a murky red. He had not seen this in the first killing. The air was not like air and not like water, a combination of the two. His body was warmer than normal. He must commit complete focus to the deed. He cannot let his mind wander to the environment around him.

Yuri felt for the cellulose string in his shirt pocket. He thought for a moment he had lost it. With effort he recovered from the panicked feeling. With focus and skill, Yuri threads the string around the neck of Park Soo-Hoon and pulled hard and tight for the 30 second relative time count. Then, he slid back to his seat and drifted off for transport and arrival.

As the hatch opened, Yuri needed to be awakened by the person sitting next to him. He was groggy and less alert than he had been after his first transport killing. He had a strange metallic taste in his mouth. The flight attendants, ground attendants really, were concerned about his condition, but quickly turned their attention to another passenger who was not waking up normally. Yuri assured them he was okay and made his departure from the pod.

A little shaken and out of sorts, Yuri almost forgot to get rid of the cellulose string. He had to back track and buy a bottle of water in order to dissolve and drink the murder weapon. This delay meant Yuri was caught up in an airport lockdown. The Thorny Rose had a bad feeling about all of this, and that feeling was more than his hangover from the CP Pak transport. It was 1:40pm in Mexico City, 11:40am in Seattle and 9:40am in Ketchikan. Yuri joined a long que to be questioned by security officers.

CHAPTER 18

February 17
Wednesday 9:40am Alaska Standard Time

Agent Reid Daniels and Charlie were at the Inn at Creek Street Café where Reid was enjoying a toasted bagel with cream cheese thinking of how much he and Charlie used to enjoy mornings like this with a hot cup of coffee.

The bagel is perfect; Crispy on the outside with melting cream cheese and a texture that was warm, firm and chewy on the inside. The absolute comfort of it made him forget the messy incident last night. He was smiling in Charlie's direction. Reid shifted his weight slightly and was brought back to reality quickly when he felt his Glock in the back holster.

As he returned from this mini daydream with Charlie, he began preparing to meet Shelby Ellison aka Kendall Hughes at her store, The Dog and The Butterfly, shortly after it opened at 10:00am.

He gave a quick call on his ICP to agent Chris Keller to find out what he now knew about the mystery stink bomber from last night.

"Yo, Chris. Got anything on our guy?"

"Hi Reid, I was just about to call you. We connected prints from the dead man to the hotel room and ran them last night. Seems this was one Faddy Zolnerowich also known by his crime buddies as Fatty Sandwich. He is American, but part of the Russian mob. Usually, a forger, no experience breaking bones, shooting kneecaps, stuff like that," Chris replied. "We can't find that he has ever worked in the field before last night."

"Odd, that a forger, with Russian mob connections, was planting a stink bomb for me. What do you make of that?" Reid asked.

"I've been pondering that. One, it looks like the Russian mob was involved in the transport killing of the Chinese diplomat. We can't confirm that yet, but it sure looks that way. Unlikely the Russian government was involved. Two, they have calculated it only takes a stink bomb to take out the lead FBI agent Reid Daniels," Keller teased.

"Yeh, yeh, yeh. I get no respect. Seriously, let's think about what this tells us and I will bump the information up to Sanchez," Reid said. "They could be waiting for us to lead them to Kendall Hughes because Hughes could help us figure out how they pulled off a murder in the CP Pak transport. That concerns them, because when we figure that out, we get closer to them and closer to the reasons behind the hit."

"And that could mean they don't want us to figure out how they are doing it because they are not done with transport killings," Chris added.

"Maybe their goal at the start of this has been to slow us down, but things are sure to get more serious after last night's accident and after we have contacted Shelby Ellison. My guess is that once we have led them to Ellison/Hughes, they will want to kill her and me, if I am around," Reid said. "How soon can you untangle yourself with the local police and take over the position of covering my ass again?"

"I can be there in a half hour. I've been thinking this through. Let me go into the Dog and the Butterfly store before you Reid. We don't know what her response will be. I'll pass her a note with the safe code Bert received from the Marshal Service and a message for her to meet you at Ketchikan Walmart in the office supplies section. Your approach to her will be to say something like, these supplies are expensive even at Walmart.," Agent Keller said. "There may be someone new following you and if we take your meeting with Ellison/Hughes to the Walmart, they have to follow, and I may be able to spot them."

"I guess, that's alright," Reid said. Charlie was giving her approval. "While I am waiting for you to meet her, I'll contact Sanchez and let him know what we know and what we have surmised. The think tank guys in D.C. can poke holes in our theories and get back to us."

"Look Chris, go gentle. This Ellison lady is our key to moving ahead on this case."

Reid Daniels and Chris Keller didn't know, thanks to Analka Hrapla's skills as a hacker, that Giorgi and Luka Pajari were just now departing for their flight to Ketchikan and would be in position on Creek Street to silence Kendall Hughes and anyone who got in their way, if Vadik Koslov's bombing of The Dog and the Butterfly was not effective.

CHAPTER 19

February 18
Wednesday 12noon Central Standard Time Mexico City

Yuri had been in the que at the Mexico City International Airport waiting to be questioned. He could not leave the airport before he was questioned. He'd been through this dance many times over the past few years. He knew that he was the guy they were looking for, but his calm nature and his forged papers passed him safely through each time previously. Yet, he was bothered by the pulsing headache he had had since waking in the transport from Seattle.

"Mister Yokov Mikhailov what is your business in Mexico City?" the Mexican Officer asked.

"I work for a company that does advance work for Russian firms who want to build manufacturing plants in Mexico. I hope you understand that my work is a little secretive. We look for areas where we can find 15,000 to 30,000 laborers who can be trained to produce internationally utilized products and of course make top wages. We are looking for multiple locations. I am sorry, that is really all I can tell you." Yuri, aka Mikhailov, offered. "It is a very competitive industry."

"Where will you be staying in Mexico City and how long do you plan to stay?" the security officer asked.

"The Stara Hamburgo for ten nights," Yuri confidently answered in near perfect Spanish.

"We'll be able to find you there if we have further questions for you?" the officer said while handing Yuri's papers back.

"Absolutely." Yuri smiled.

"Mister Mikalson, did you notice anything odd on the transport before you left Seattle or upon arriving here in Mexico City?" The officer raised his eyebrows and asked.

"It's Mister Mikhailov and no I did not notice a thing. Did the man become ill in the transport?" Yuri asked.

"Thank you, mister Mikhailov," the guard said, then, he motioned the next person in line to come forward.

Yuri walked at a comfortable pace to the airport dining hub where he bought an enchilada meal and sent a message to Annie for her to get him out of Mexico City as soon as possible.

Analka Hrapla was on top of Robin Medallon, gently brushing her breasts in Robin's face, when Yuri's message came through on her encrypted phone. She was, at that moment, thinking this is the best assignment Yuri had ever given to her. She really liked being with Robin and keeping track of this Daniels guy was a piece of cake. She could get used to this. Her mind wandered to a life away from crime with someone like the man beneath her. Robin was equally delighted with Analka. He was quite certain she was the best thing to ever happen to him.

When they were finished with their mid-morning delight, Analka hacked Yuri onto an airline flight back to Seattle on Alaska Airlines, slow but reliable transportation, departing Mexico City at 2:30pm and arriving in Seattle at 6:00pm PST. His new persona, which had been created months earlier by Faddy Zolnerowich, was Fredrick Hemmel, a German photographer, who specialized in wildlife photos. Faddy had even sent pictures to load onto his phone in case he was asked to show some of his work. Faddy had prepared multiple passports and backgrounds for all of Yuri's crew before the *Job* began.

Yuri's online paperwork, revised by Analka, would show that he had been in Mexico for 6 months. Because he carried just a small amount of luggage, he purportedly had shipped his equipment and other belongings ahead to Seattle via Fed Ex. Yuri, of course, found the passport and identification papers he needed in the many identities which had been prepared for this *Job*. As he prepared himself to be Fredrick Hemmel, the thought struck Yuri that he needed another forger.

CHAPTER 20

February 18
Wednesday 1:45pm Eastern Standard
Time Washington, DC

"Mr. President you have a call from Director Russell," Jamie Lawrence, Administrative Assistant to the President, said.

"Have him hold. I will be with him in five minutes," the President responded.

After he put his meeting with Chief of Staff Blaine Hurwell on hold, the President picked up the phone.

"Hello Jim, tell me you have good news in Seattle."

"I'm sorry Mr. President. We have had another diplomat murdered on a CP Pak transport from Seattle to Mexico City," the FBI Director said solemnly. "This time it is a North Korean. Again, this is a fairly low governmental level person involved in Agricultural trade with the U.S., and again, we have no reason to believe this victim, Park Soo-Hoon, has any involvement in spying. We watch the North Koreans closely."

"This thing is getting out of control. What in the hell are those people in Seattle doing? Do we need to put more agents, different agents on this investigation?"

"We are on it, sir. Our team is tracking down a lead in Alaska," Director Russell answered.

"Okay! But Goddamit Jim, we have to get to the bottom of these murders. This thing is blowing up on us. Is your Quantico team profiling this? Is Tang's (Marcia Tang, CIA Director) team, over at Langley, involved in trying to find an international motive as well? Get it done Jim! I'm counting on you and your team!" The President disconnected the call and punched the line for his assistant.

"JAIME."

"Yes, Mr. President."

"Get Secretaries Hertz and Roberts on the phone immediately!"

After he finished his luxuriously wonderful bagel and coffee and after a conversation with Charlie, Reid wrote a quick follow-up report on the identity of Faddy Zolnerowich and the discussion that he and Chris Keller had had, that morning, about what the Russian American and what his role may have been in this fast-developing case.

Sanchez called him back immediately.

"Carlos, you got my report?"

"Yes, I've kicked it all over to our team in DC, who work on Russian mob activities. We have also sent them the video of the transport concourses in Seattle to see if their computers recognize anyone from the mob. Reid, that is great work, but we must get more. The burners in Washington have been turned on high and the Whitehouse and Quantico want more from us, and fast!" Sanchez pressed.

"Reid, we have had another transport murder or assassination on a CP Pak transport from Seattle to Mexico City. The victim in this one is another low-level trade diplomat. This time, it is Park Soo-Hoon, a North Korean," Sanchez said.

"I am not surprised," Reid said, "I don't know what it means, I'm just not surprised. Chris and I are setting up contact with Ellison/Hughes right now and I think it is of upmost importance to get her under our protection as soon as possible."

"Agree with that Reid. Get that done as soon as possible.

I have another curve to throw your way, and this comes from the Director himself straight from the White House."

"Oh great!"

"We have to expect this when we have diplomats dropping in such unbelievable circumstances," Sanchez said. "We have been instructed to allow that team of Chinese investigators to help us with this."

"We talked about this before Carlos, and I think that's a Shit Show looking for a place to happen. How do you propose we handle this?"

"Your language is more colorful than the Director, but you are both in agreement on this," Sanchez said. "The Director knows that the only reason these high-level security and intelligence officers from the People's Republic of China want in on the case, is so they can learn more about the CP Pak transport process. They could care less about their dead low-level diplomat, but the fact is that Chinese Ambassador Jeng-Sheng Wei has put a lot of heat on the White House to get his people involved in the investigation and the Chinese Xi Jinping fleet is steaming toward the Hawaiian Islands. Before this gets out of control, we must comply."

"Can we slow walk their involvement?" Reid asked.

"I prefer to describe it as thoroughly bringing them up to speed on all aspects of the investigation, before we put them in contact with your team, Reid."

"Hai Chang, Intelligence & Security officer from the Chinese Consulate in Washington, DC and Lan Phang, Internet Intelligence Director from the People's Republic of China, are making their way to Seattle as we speak," Sanchez said.

"I thought only Lan Phang was coming our way," Reid said.

"Well now it's both of them," Sanchez responded.

"Thanks for the heads-up, Carlos. Let me know when you need me to get involved with them. Hope that is all for now, cause I gotta go. Chris Keller is walking into Kendall Hughes' store."

"You are good to go Reid! Let's get Ellison err Hughes on board and get this investigation moving on the fast track!" Sanchez said.

CHAPTER 21

February 18
Wednesday 10:10am Alaska Standard
Time Ketchikan, AK

Chris Keller strode into Kendall Hughes' store wondering what he would find in the genius who invented the CP Pak technology. He stepped up and asked the young clerk behind the counter, "is Kendall Hughes in?"

"Yes, she is in her office in the back. Can I tell her who is here? She doesn't meet with advertising people! That's my job and right now our budget is spent!" the young woman said as curtly as she could.

"Yes, tell her a friend from Colorado, Chris Keller, is here to talk with her for just a moment." That was the introduction safe phrase provided by the US Marshal Service for a government agent contacting Shelby Ellison while she was in witness protection.

No sooner had the young woman disappeared through a curtain in the back, than something, akin to a raging Buffalo, came charging though the curtain.

Kendall knew immediately this was what she had sensed the night before. She needed to cut this problem off at the knees. She did not appreciate the government coming after her for anything.

"They probably fucked something up and need my help fixing it," she thought.

"You government son-of-a-bitch, Chris whatever the fuck your name is, get the hell out of my store and leave me the fuck alone!" Kendall Hughes stormed at Keller causing him to take a step backward.

"This is important ma'am," Agent Keller implored.

"Oh, well you didn't say this was important. Wait right there!"

Hughes walked hard back through the curtain and charged back seconds later with the biggest colt revolver Chris Keller had ever seen. Certainly, the biggest he had ever seen aimed directly at his chest.

"This is what I use to take care of IMPORTANT PROBLEMS needle dick," Hughes half shouted. Her head was cocked slightly sideways and in her right hand, the revolver was fully cocked and ready to fire.

"Unless you want to be sporting a couple of holes made by a 45-caliber antique, you'd best walk your candy assed government outfit back out that door and never come back!"

"Ma'am, you're making a dangerous mistake!"

KABOOM!! Kendall Hughes, AKA Shelby Ellison, fired one round through the rough-cut lumber floor at Keller's feet sending the bullet into the sub-cellar and possibly all the way into Ketchikan Creek below. As fast as she fired, she cocked the old 45 for another round.

Keller instinctively started to grab his Glock from his shoulder holster.

"Make my day motherfucker!" Hughes said, "My Clint Eastwood impersonation isn't very good, but I have another round ready to go here."

Keller thought better and carefully removed his hand.

"Now, like I said before! Get the fuck out of my store, you needle dick Fed!"

Reid heard the gunshot with understandable concern. As he weighed what might have happened and whether he should move toward The Dog and the Butterfly, Chris Keller walked quickly out the door, looking red faced and flustered. "Oh my," Charlie offered.

Kendall was shaken. She was not sure she had done the right thing but there was nothing she hated more than a government man!

"What was that about?" Kassie asked in a shaking voice.

"Old business," Kendall said. Not wanting to elaborate. "If I get any phone calls or messages to our "Info" email address, respond that I am out."

"Do you think it had anything to do with the man getting hit by the bus last night?" Kassie asked.

"I don't know. I am going to work until noon and then take the rest of the day off."

Kendall had just decided to spend the afternoon and the night at a cabin cruiser of a friend which was moored at the marina in Thomas Basin Harbor. She needed time to get her thoughts together on how she wanted to handle this problem which seemed to be growing each minute.

Breaking their earlier protocol, Reid met Chris on the boardwalk. "What the hell happened in there? Where is Shelby, err Kendall Hughes?"

"The Goddamn lunatic bitch nearly shot me!"

"What the hell?" Reid exclaimed.

"Apparently, she has little respect for government employees and doesn't want to talk to us!"

"Did you hand her the note to meet at the Walmart?"

"I think I would have been shot, if I tried."

"Do you think I would have any better luck?"

"Take your chances, if you want Reid, but she is pretty fired up right now. She shot that fucking hand cannon right through the floor at my feet. It's a Goddamn antique Colt 45!"

"Let's let her cool off a little bit. I'll contact Sanchez and see if anyone who has worked with her can help us out," agent Daniels assessed. "We'll give her some time to digest this contact from the Feds and we'll both go in tomorrow morning. I just hope we can break through to her before the bad guys get to her," Reid said after a few moments of thought." *"Any ideas Charlie?"* he thought. Charlie, uncustomarily, was silent.

Reid went back to his room and reached out to Carlos Sanchez to let him know the situation in Ketchikan.

Sanchez immediately contacted Quantico. Within the hour, two Marshals who had worked with Kendall Hughes in the past, were able to send a message to her. Through message encryption, they let her know it might be a matter of life or death if she did not meet with the FBI agents who were in Ketchikan to find her and protect her if necessary.

Kendall Hughes did not confirm that she had received the message. She was maintaining radio silence and did not want to communicate back. *"So much for my feelings being a good thing,"* Kendall thought.

CHAPTER 22

February 18
Wednesday Late Evening Saint Petersburg, Russia

Just as she had done a day earlier, Luba Krupin rushed to Kostya Ivanov's luxury apartment after receiving the news of the death of Park Soo-Hoon.

Ivanov greeted the nearly hysterical Krupin at the door.

"We need to abandon this plan immediately and dissolve The Marco Polo Alliance before this killer comes for us," Luba shouted in obvious distress. "Someone has hacked one of the partners, found out we have piles of money, and they are taking us down one by one!"

"I can't say that I don't have the same feelings Luba, but we cannot jump to conclusions. We need to take time to collect our thoughts and we certainly cannot make the unilateral decision to dissolve the investments, without consulting Shahnaz. He's still in this with us," Kostya Ivanov said, as he pulled Luba into his arms to comfort her. As Ivanov cradled Luba's soft body close to himself, he thought, *my stars this woman is incredible."*

"Luba, my understanding is that the funds that have been set up for Park Soo-Hoon and Xing Tsua Ten will now equally be converted into the funds of Shahnaz Latifpour and me. You of course continue to make your commissions on all funds," Ivanov said coldly.

Luba backed out of Kostya's embrace and emphatically pleaded her concern, "You have no concern for the safety of our lives, or even a caring thought about the loss of our investment partners? What kind of man are you, Kostya? Will you be just as unconcerned after my untimely death? Will you then be dividing my money as well, you greedy," Luba struggled for the word that she would allow herself to say, "turd" she shouted in Russian.

Kostya was taken aback. He did not want to offend Luba. Beautiful, beautiful Luba.

"Luba, Luba, Luba, I apologize. Please accept my apology for seeming not to care. I have always been a very pragmatic man," Kostya pleaded. "I am only looking out for all of us. We must call Shahnaz immediately and get his input. I'm sure there are things we can do to protect ourselves."

Kostya started toward his desk drawer to get his encrypted Microsoft Elucidation Translation phone so he could speak with the Iranian. As he moved past Luba, he reached out to give her one more reassuring hug, but she dodged his advance.

"Luba, I am so sorry for my callous behavior. Please forgive me," Kostya said.

Luba began crying and melted into his arms again as she had done before. In reality, her tears were tears of joy. She would share in the proceeds as well, but showing her greed was not a good look at this time.

Shahnaz Latifpour answered on the first ring. "I have been waiting for your call Kostya." "It seems that we may have a problem," Latifpour said. "Have there been any strange happenings in the lives of you or Ms. Krupin."

"I will put you on speaker phone, she is right here with me," said Kostya.

"My darling Luba, are you there?" Latifpour asked.

"Yes Shahnaz, I am here. What do you think this means? Have we been found out? Do you think Park or Xing could have been bragging about how rich they soon would be?"

"It is possible. I had my concerns about each of them. They had each called me to find out how much money we might receive on our first disbursement," Shahnaz said. "I told them to be patient. I told them that we would be finding out soon enough in our scheduled meeting in Paris on Friday."

"Oh my gosh, I had totally put our meeting out of my mind," Luba said. "Do you think we should still plan to meet?" She was glad he brought it up.

"I believe we should. But first, let's talk about some security concerns. This is, after all, my area of expertise."

"Luba are you certain that no one has hacked your work on the investments," Latifpour asked.

"I checked and double checked, we lost Xing," Luba said. "No one knows anything about The Marco Polo Alliance, except originally, the five of us, and well now, the three of us."

"And Luba, a sensitive question, but one I must ask. Are the accounts set up so that funds can be shifted to the remaining members?" Latifpour asked. "They don't wander off into some other account that can be accessed by some other individual?"

"Yes, a sensitive question that has already been addressed. I guess my greed level is not equal to that of the two of you," Luba asserted. "The accounts, ultimately, shift to the remaining members, but not directly. They go into blind accounts that later will be moved to the members in smaller timed movements. It is all set up into the system that I have designed. In case you are both losing sleep about something happening to me, the controls to access the system will be sent to the remaining members 48 hours after the last time I have accessed The Marco Polo Alliance account."

"I believe you are both insensitive POOPS." Luba had no trouble finding the word she could use this time. "Two of our partners have been murdered and the two of you are only worried about the money. I am now wondering which of you might be behind these murders."

Both men responded, almost simultaneously, to deny that they had anything to do with the deaths of Park and Xing.

Shahnaz responded first, "Luba I am sure there is an explanation for what has happened and while we try to figure that out, we must hire protection for ourselves. I will contact some people I trust to look into these deaths and to assign protection for each one of us."

"Luba we cannot begin to turn on each other. The Artificial Intelligence you have developed, and the hacking of the U.S. stock markets is still a ticket to untold wealth for each of us," Kostya said reassuringly. "We must allow Shahnaz to do what he knows how to do, and we must be brave and not deviate from our course."

"What about our travel to Paris for the meeting? Do you think we are safe to travel by CP Pak transport?" Luba asked.

Shahnaz replied slowly, "Let's follow through with our plans to meet Friday in Paris again at the Spring restaurant. Each of us will make our own travel plans and overnight accommodation. In addition, I suggest, to you, we also make hotel reservations in New York. If someone is after us, that will throw them off."

"That sounds good to me," Kostya said.

"I am still very concerned," Luba said.

"It is agreed. We will meet Friday at 7:00pm at the Spring restaurant and determine where to go from there. We'll decide the timing of the first disbursement of The Marco Polo Alliance account," Shahnaz Latifpour stated. "Everyone in agreement?"

"Yes," the others said in unison.

One half hour after the three remaining members of The Marco Polo Alliance concluded their conversation, Yuri received an encrypted monotone telephone call.

"Well, Thorny Rose, it seems you have been successful again," the monotone voice said. "Are you free and clear?"

After I board my flight back to Seattle, yes, I will be free and clear," Yuri responded.

"Did you have any trouble? Anything we should be concerned about?"

"I am experiencing some symptoms of nausea. It may be

the flu," Yuri said.

"Maybe you are just a pussy motherfucker and can't stand to work hard for a full week," the monotone voice said with a little laugh.

"Yeh, maybe that is it," Yuri responded.

"Well, maybe I can let you take a break from the CP Pak work. Maybe I can give you some old fashion work in Paris, the day after tomorrow," the voice said. "He's a Russian cocksucker, just like you, and he will be at the Spring Restaurant in Paris on Friday at 7:00pm. He will be the only Russian jerkoff at a table of three. I need him dead before midnight on Friday. You can recognize a useless Russian when you see one, can't you?"

"Pretty sure that I can," Yuri replied. And with that, the call ended.

CHAPTER 23

February 18
Wednesday Night

After the first hair raising experience with Kendall Hughes, Chris Keller and Reid had agreed that Chris should watch over Creek Street again on Wednesday night. Not only to look after Reid, but also to keep an eye on The Dog and the Butterfly. They had just uncovered Hughes' hidden identity and that may have been what the people following Reid had been waiting for.

For the stakeout, Chris enlisted the help of Federal Marshal Larry Goddard. Chris also communicated with the Ketchikan Borough police what he and Goddard would be doing just in case the two federal officers needed to call for backup during the night.

Agent Keller set up in the same alcove he had been in the night before when he had watched Faddy Zolnerowich. Goddard set up where he could keep an eye on The Dog and the Butterfly a little further up Creek Street.

It was a cold and damp night on Creek Street. Both men on the stake out were having trouble keeping warm.

The cold and the necessity to remain crystal clear alert reminded Chris Keller of his Navy Seal Training. Mental and physical toughness are the underlying requirements of being a Seal. Chris's mind remained sharp and was fully engaged in the stakeout.

One of the basic problems on stakeouts was evident here on the Creek Street boardwalk. Where to relieve oneself. Walking down to the Federal Building on Stedman every few hours to warm up and use the restroom was out of the question.

Reid had gone about his evening, like the night before, taking in a beer and a burger at the Married Man's Bar & Grille. He also enjoyed an NCAA basketball game between Duke and North Carolina. The game had been played earlier and was being shown now, for Ketchikan evening viewers. Reid was a Duke fan and Charlie loved Carolina for their powder blue uniforms. This was the rivalry that never ended between the two of them.

After the game replay ended locally at 10:00pm. Reid and Charlie made their way back to his room at the Star House. When he was in, he contacted agent Keller to let him know he was safe.

"Chris, are you freezing your balls off out there?"

"Yeh. Are you all nice and cozy and safe?"

"Yes, I am," Reid said feeling a little sorry for Keller.

"Well, tell me Prince Daniels, did you see anything we should know about at the Married Man's Bar and Grille. Any suspicious activity?".

"No one paid any attention to me at all except the bartender. Not even a good-looking woman who was dining alone. Of course, I probably still carry that guilty look of a married man because I can't stop thinking about Charlie." Agent Keller had no idea how true that statement was.

"Jesus Reid! You need to get back into the zone man. It has been long enough. Even Bert Hamilton has volunteered to take one for the team to get you back into action," Chris said in hushed tones from his stakeout position.

"That's not necessary. I am a perfectly happy born-again virgin," Reid replied. Charlie was giving him a palms out at her hips, a shrug of her shoulders, a rise of her eyebrows and a tilt of her head.

"Be that as it may, we'd better sign off. I think Goddard and I need to take turns sneaking down the boardwalk to relieve ourselves. Be safe virgin Reid."

"Thanks, be safe Chris."

Reid knew that he would have trouble sleeping that night. His mind was racing. This woman Kendall Hughes was in danger. Was he doing everything he could to protect her and to find out who was responsible for the CP Pak killings? He felt like there was a countdown clock running in the background.

"Charlie, how do I put Kendall Hughes at ease? You are a woman. What will it take to get her to trust me?" Reid thought.

"Be yourself was the thought which kept running through his mind." It had to be Charlie putting the thought there.

CHAPTER 24

February 18
Wednesday Very Late Night

Agent Keller immediately contacted U.S. Marshal Goddard.

"Larry, I am going to need to find somewhere to piss here in the shadows. I can't do it right here in this alcove. Do you need me to cover for you?"

"Oh hell, I already pissed. I just went in Ketchikan Creek. One time shouldn't hurt anything. Fish do it."

"Okay, I'll do the same. I can go between a couple of buildings just a little down the way here. I can remain in the shadows. Please keep an eye down this way. They have shown interest in going after Daniels twice and I want to have eyes on his door," Chris said.

Keller returned after a minute. Goddard stealthily shifted at his post just beyond The Dog and the Butterfly.

Time passed and the routine needed to be repeated several hours later.

Earlier, Vadik Kozlov, Yuri's assassination team bomber, had made his way up the old Married Man's Trail coming onto Creek Street the historical backway. He had the bomb and supplies in a backpack. Like the Feds, he had also been hiding in the shadows and was ready to step out when he saw movement near Marshal Goddard's position. Being an experienced undercover operator, Kozlov quickly figured out what was happening with the two lawmen.

"Thank God for stupid Amerikans. I just move a little further here and I can meke my way under the support system of the dog store, or whateva it is, and plant my bomb," Kozlov

thought to himself.

From his recon earlier in the day, Kozlov had seen the man, he knew as Seal Team, go into The Dog and the Butterfly and he heard the canon blast of a gunshot with the Seal Team guy coming out shortly after.

Kozlov figured out that the Seal Team guy had been chased out of the store with the gun blast and he guessed that one or both the FBI agents would make another attempted meeting with the woman the next day.

Per Yuri's orders, Kozlov's plan was to plant a bomb under the store to take out the woman and whomever she was standing near the next day. With any luck, he would get the woman, Seal Team and Agent Daniels. He had built a remote-control detonator, which he could trigger from his cell phone.

Kozlov crawled through the support structure under the Dog and the Butterfly. Ketchikan creek flowed beneath him.

"Ezee does it Vadik, that water looks cold. We don't vant to fall into it," Kozlov whispered.

This was not Vadik Kozlov's first night job where he needed to remain hidden. He carried with him a six-foot-by-six-foot black cloth which he used to cover himself and his work while he used his hat flashlight to place the bomb under the building. The charge was designed to send the blast upward, through the floor and into the store where Kendall Hughes and, hopefully, the two FBI men would be standing.

Kozlov had worried that he would not be able place the bomb in the correct spot. As luck would have it, he sighted the hole where Hughes had fired the antique Colt 45 at the feet of Chris Keller. There was a small amount of light coming through the floorboards from the store. "Tanks lady, for showing me where to place the bomb to keel you."

After ten minutes of placing the bomb and setting the radio frequency for the cell phone trigger, Kozlov was ready to climb out from under the building. He planned to sneak back down the Married Man's trail, then return just before the store opened the next morning. "I will spot dem all together and boom, my verk here is done," he whispered to himself.

As he was climbing out from under the building, Vadik spotted the man, who had been watching the store. It was U.S. Marshal Goddard shifting in the shadows of his well-hidden observation position.

"I will just slip down here ta come out a leetle further down the walk und..."

Just then, his foot contacted an immature raccoon which had been hidden there by his mother. When he partially stepped on the animal, it started screaming like an injured kitten. Startled, Kozlov kicked at the young raccoon, but momma raccoon was already coming to attack Vadik's leg. A mature raccoon can be as big as a medium sized dog and have the ferocity of a bobcat. A rule of nature is, don't mess with momma's baby no matter what the species.

The momma raccoon, herself now screaming, sunk her claws then her teeth into the fleshy backside of Vadik Kozlov's calf causing him to let out a low moaning scream of his own.

This was all easily heard by Federal Marshal Goddard. He pulled his gun and moved to investigate.

"Agent Keller, I have something going on up here. Requesting backup!" Goddard thumbed his ICP.

"On my way," Chris Keller answered back. Then in quick succession, he sent an ICP message to Reid. "Reid, Reid, we have something going down out here. Arm yourself and stay put!"

"Got it!" Reid answered.

As agent Keller began moving up the boardwalk, he contacted the local police and requested a squad car to hold at the Stedman Bridge area at the bottom of the Creek Street boardwalk to await further instructions.

Larry Goddard moved cautiously toward the point where he heard the animal and human distressed noises. He held his gun beside his service flashlight. When flipped the light on, he saw Vadik Kozlov half rolling up onto the boardwalk. There was a large amount of blood on the man's pant leg.

"FREEZE! FEDERAL MARSHAL! PUT YOUR HANDS UP!"

Kozlov continued rolling and looking right into the flashlight. On his roll and out of sight behind his back, Kozlov quickly pulled a gun up and fired three shots at the light shining in his eyes. Instantly Marshal Goddard fired at Kozlov, hitting him twice in the upper torso.

One of Kozlov's shots hit Goddard in the right shoulder, causing him to lose control of his gun. Instinctively, Goddard dropped his flashlight and picked up his Glock with his left hand. Able to find and shine the flashlight with his badly weakened right shoulder, Marshal Goddard could see that the man on the ground was bleeding from his bullet wounds, but still moving. He had let go of his gun and was digging into his backpack.

"FREEZE! HANDS UP YOU SON-OF-A-BITCH OR I'LL SHOT AGAIN!" Goddard screamed.

Rapidly losing blood, Kozlov's muddled mind was telling him he had to detonate the bomb now. He was manipulating his cellphone inside his backpack and just as Goddard fired another shot into Kozlov's leg, the bomb detonated under The Dog and the Butterfly sending shrapnel, wood splinters and debris violently upward and to the sides of the blast.

CHAPTER 25

February 19
Wednesday Very Early Morning

FBI Agent Chris Keller was directly in front of The Dog and the Butterfly at the exact moment of the blast. The shockwave blew him violently through the boardwalk's handrail and falling hard onto the steep embankment of Ketchikan Creek. The Navy Seal lay there, deep in the brush, unconscious, with cuts and blast trauma pushing his body to its limits.

The sound of the gun shots heightened Reid's awareness and the explosion shook his room so badly that he thought the building might collapse into Ketchikan Creek. He called Chris Keller on his ICP.

"Chris! What's happening out there? Chris!" he shouted.

Silence.

Panic came over him. Reid holstered his gun, grabbed his coat and headed out into the night. Charlie was not with him.

Where The Dog and the Butterfly had partially straddled Ketchikan Creek, there was a huge gap in the line of buildings. The other side of Creek Street was still intact. The remaining boardwalk and buildings, on the side where the Dog and the Butterfly once stood, were burning bright yellow orange flames which towered into the sky. Reid could feel the heat and hear the sirens in the distance.

Reid called Chris Keller again on the ICP. "CHRIS, LET ME KNOW YOU ARE OKAY!"

Chris slowly came back to consciousness but could not speak or respond. A shard of wood protruded from his neck. He dug deep into his reserves to remain conscious and hang onto life, while feeling for his phone.

Back on the boardwalk, to Reid's left, a woman was suddenly standing by his side. From photos he had seen of a younger woman, he could tell in the firelight glow, that this was Shelby Ellison aka Kendall Hughes.

When she heard the blast, Kendall had cautiously made her way from the boat to the boardwalk. Over several cups of tea and deep thought she decided, she needed to confront this problem head on. "The only way around is through" kept playing in her mind. She was ready to face it.

"The man you are looking for. He is the man who tried to warn me yesterday?" she said without emotion.

Reid stared at her and answered, "yes."

"And who are you?" Kendall asked.

"FBI Agent Reid Daniels."

"Important sounding name."

"I tell everyone that my mother was a serious person. It's a name that's hard to live up to. I am heading up a team investigating a murder and it appeared that the bad guys might be looking to harm Shelby, err Kendall Hughes."

"Looks like you were correct." The woman then put out her hand and said, "I am Shelby Ellison, but better known around here as Kendall Hughes. I prefer Kendall Hughes now."

"Look, I can explain to you why we are looking for you, Kendall," Reid paused, "but. Right now, I must find my team member Chris Keller. Do you have anywhere nearby that you will be safe for the next few hours, then I can explain everything to you?"

"People will be surprised, if I am not here."

"People will be more surprised, if someone shows up and kills you."

"I don't trust the government, but I will listen. Here is my card. Call the cell number when we can talk." With that, Kendall Hughes turned and walked quickly back down the boardwalk toward the Marina. As she passed more fire crew running to the scene, her mind raced and she was struck by the calm nature of the FBI man she had just met. She instantly knew she would need to trust him with her life, and she felt like she could. *"So, this is it,"* she thought.

Reid had to find Chris Keller. He quickly found the fire Captain, who was getting his team lined out to attack the growing blaze.

"Captain...Warner," Reid said reading the badge. "I am Agent Daniels with the FBI. We have two, maybe three individuals up here. One of my agents, a Federal Marshal from here in Ketchikan and a possible bad guy with a Russian mob. I am thinking they are all injured."

Captain Warner eyed Reid's badge and radioed, "Johnson, Miske get over here to help FBI Agent Daniels. We may have three injured people and one is the perp, proceed with caution."

Warner switched channels and double clicked his mic. "Thomas, when you get here with the ambulance, come up quick with stretchers. Also, radio in for another ambulance. We may have to transport three."

As he was getting the appropriate 10-4s, Warner went back to directing the attack on the fire.

"Are you agent Daniels?" one of the two firemen asked. "We're Johnson and Miske. Here, put on this mask and tank."

"Thanks," Reid said.

"Where are the injured people?" one of the firemen asked.

"I'm not sure. We have to find them! One is FBI, one is a U.S. Marshal and the possible other is Russian mob," Reid shouted behind him as he worked his way past the flames from the explosion on the opposite boardwalk. The heat was so intense he felt as if his clothes might catch fire.

As they moved past the worst of the flames from the buildings on the opposite bank, Reid spotted a fireman tending to a man who was quickly identified as U. S. Marshal Larry Goddard. He had what appeared to Reid to be a through and through wound just inside his right shoulder. Goddard was conscious and lucid.

"Guy just up there must have detonated the bomb after I caught him crawling out from under the boardwalk," Goddard explained. "He's the one who shot me."

Miske had run up and across to the opposite boardwalk where Vadik Kozlov lay. "He's dead sir. Two shots to the torso and something going on with his leg, lots of blood," he shouted over the noise.

As Reid looked back down Creek Street wondering where he could find Chris Keller, the entire scene was organized chaos, firemen setting hoses and spraying the main blazes on either side of the gap where The Dog and the Butterfly had stood, and others wetting the fronts of the buildings on the opposite side of Ketchikan Creek to keep them from catching fire.

"I have tried agent Keller multiple times," Goddard shook his head and looked away. "He might have been right in front of the store when it blew."

Medics were arriving to assist Goddard. Reid responded, "You're a good man Goddard, these guys will take care of you," motioning toward the medics with the gurney.

Reid pulled Johnson and Miske together for a quick huddle. "Let's assume he was right in front of the explosion. Seems to me, that would put my man on the bank under us badly injured or dead."

"Up by the dead guy, near the end of the boardwalks, there is room to crawl under buildings and get to the bank of the creek on both sides," Miske said.

"Let's go for it!" Reid shouted as broke into a run to the top end of the boardwalk.

With flashlights shining bright, the three started working their way along the bank headed downstream. It was slow going through and over the thick brush.

After 15 minutes, they had struggled their way along the brushy bank downstream to nearly opposite The Dog and the Butterfly location. The fire team was controlling the blaze up top. From where Reid was, under the structures, the heat was less intense, but he was being showered by water.

"I see him!" Johnson cried out. He charged through the brush like a bull for the last ten feet. "Agent Daniels! I've got a pulse!"

Miske was already on his radio asking for a stretcher to be dropped over the edge for them as well as some morphine. He could tell by what he saw that Keller was in severe pain.

Reid was at his side, "Chris, we are going to get you out of here. Stay with us."

With expert precision, the two firemen had Keller in the stretcher and were carrying him downstream in the shallow water of the shoreline. Their goal was the cross over-bridge, outside of Reid's room entrance to the Star House. There, paramedics began hoisting the stretcher up to the boardwalk level.

Other firemen were there to help Johnson, Miske and Reid up to the boardwalk as well.

Reid looked on as the paramedics got Keller onto a gurney and started I.V.s. As he rolled past, Agent Keller made weak eye contact with Reid, as if to say, "you know what you need to do" and Reid gave a nod back.

As he stood in the wake of the evening attack, Reid reflected that he had only been in Ketchikan for 30 hours and his situation had gone from someone seemingly wanting only to scare him, to people preparing to kill him.

CHAPTER 26

February 19
Wednesday 5:04am Alaska Local Time

Reid retreated to his room at the Star House just steps away. He needed to clean up and he needed to contact Regional Commander Sanchez. It was a little after 6:00am in Seattle.

"Carlos! Are you available," Reid said into his ICP.

"Yes, I'm here. I have been preparing for your call this morning. Glad to hear that you are up and at it early," Sanchez said.

"We have been up most of the night. At about 3:00am, a bomber leveled Kendall Hughes store. Chris Keller was directly in front of the blast and is badly injured," Reid explained.

Reid went on to report on the events of the night. The severe injury of agent Keller, the wounding of U.S. Marshal Goddard and the killing, by Goddard, of what must be a Russian mob bomber.

"I don't think the bomber intended to blow the building last night. We were watching the store and the U.S. Marshal caught him trying to get away after he crawled out from under the buildings. The perp was shot twice in the torso when he resisted. It makes sense that he detonated the bomb out of confusion after he was shot. I think his plan was to take out Kendall Hughes and whomever was with her; Chris, me or all three of us, later in the day," Reid said.

"What about Shelby Ellison, will you contact her this morning?"

"So much to tell Chief, I left that out. She showed up right after the bomb blast. We introduced ourselves. She realizes now her life might be in danger. I asked if she had a safe place to stay, she said yes, and I sent her there. I have a number that I can call," Reid reported. "Oh, and she wants us to refer to her as Kendall Hughes."

"Do you think she will go into hiding, even from you?" Sanchez asked.

"I didn't get that vibe from her," Reid said confidently, but really, he did not know why he had such confidence. It was a good question.

"Reid, I want to get this information to our profiling team in D.C. There is other news as well. I will call you in ninety minutes. Are you in a safe and secure place?"

"I will be. And Carlos, we need to get protection for Chris at the hospital. I really think it is Kendall Hughes they are after now, but we can't be too careful."

Sanchez said, "I'm on it. Ninety minutes," and hung up.

Reid went to his room, finished cleaning up and packed his clothes. When he was done, he pulled Kendall Hughes's card out of his pocket and dialed the number.

"Hello," the voice answered. Reid knew immediately it was her, but he did not say her name.

"My mother was a very serious person. Where can I find you?" Reid asked.

She liked that Reid did not ask her who she was and that he used a clear identifier that only the two of them would know. That meant it could be only him. She didn't trust men, but this one was at least tolerable.

"Come down to the Thomas Bay Marina. I will be waiting for you at Gate C." Then, she hung up.

CHAPTER 27

February 19
Wednesday 5:35am

Reid stopped just outside the Star House entrance to his room and beheld the scene of a beaten fire. There were still flames and coals, but Captain Warner's expert crews had this fire under control.

"Charlie, did I cause this all to happen," he asked. "Did I miss something, could this scene have been prevented?"

"Charlie, it is so much easier to think of you and remember you when I am alone. Forgive me for allowing you to slip to the back of my mind for the past 90 minutes."

Reid could hear Charlie saying, "You've got a job to do Buddy. Get after it. Don't worry about me."

Reid turned and started down the boardwalk of Creek Street.

At the Thomas Basin Marina, he easily found Gate C. It was a typical marina security gate with a 9-foot-high heavy gage wire fence with a wide gate secured on the outside by a keypad lock. As he approached, Kendall Hughes emerged from the shadows.

He had not been able to get a good look at her when she was standing at his side in the firelight. She was a beautiful woman, not appearing, to his eye, to be in her mid-forties. He would have guessed maybe late thirties. Kendall Hughes was fit and trim and her pretty face held a concerned expression. This was not at all the same person Chris Keller must have met in The Dog and the Butterfly yesterday.

"Follow me," she instructed and led Reid ten boats down

the dock to a 34-foot Tolly-Craft cabin cruiser on the left. Reid could tell it was an older boat, but one that appeared well maintained.

They climbed onto the aft of the boat and took three steps down through the hatch into the galley and living quarters. The inside was comforting and warm. A eucalyptus candle gave off a pleasing scent. A candle that was maybe even from her store, Reid thought. Relaxing soft music played. The area was neat and clean and even though small, it felt spacious. The seating areas cushions looked new and clean. The wood accents were polished to a rich shine. The cubbies were neat and not overstuffed. Some had pictures of a handsome graying man with what looked like his grown children and one picture of the man with Kendall Hughes. The relaxing atmosphere reminded Reid of spas that he and Charlie had visited together for couple's massages.

Hughes decided Reid looked like a coffee man, so she offered him a cup. "There are a few sweeteners in the refrigerator, and I made these protein bars while I was waiting for you." Kendall handed Reid a plate with precut squares that had the appearance of fudge.

"This coffee really hits the spot, and these are great! What's in them?" Reid asked.

"Chocolate flavored protein powder, oatmeal, peanut butter and honey," she said, completing the small talk.

Hughes stared straight into Reid's eyes from six feet away, her steel blues piercing deep into him and said, "if my antique Colt had not been lost in the fire, I'd be aiming it at you right now and asking, what in the hell is going on here?"

"Sometimes things work out for the best when guns are not used," Reid raised his eyebrows and said sheepishly.

"I have led a wonderful life here in Ketchikan for 5 years and then you fucking feds show up and the store I have worked so hard to build and a life I have worked so hard to create is blown to smithereens. What the fuck?"

"Can we sit down," Reid asked. "Do you have any more

coffee?"

Hughes poured Reid another large cup of black coffee. Then, she asked, "I have some day-old bagels from the café at the Creek Street Inn, do you want one of those warmed up with some cream cheese?" "*You can get to a man through his stomach,*" Kendall could hear her grandmother saying.

"Are you clairvoyant? Yes, I would love that," Reid responded gratefully.

"I don't know why I trust you more than most feds, but there is something about your manner that disarms me," Kendall said. "Okay, the imaginary gun is not pointed at you but, for the second time, what the hell is going on here?"

Reid started the story with the first killing aboard a CP Pak transport and Hughes did not seem as surprised as everyone else that this could happen. He followed with the garage incident, the trip to find her in Ketchikan, the death of Faddy Zolnerowich, the knowledge that they were being hacked in Seattle then finally, the events of the past few hours.

"So you have come here in hopes that I will help you figure out who these people are," Hughes said with a tone of disbelief in her voice.

"It is not only that, but we guessed, one might say correctly, that they would want to harm you, possibly kill you, to keep you from helping us," Reid said.

"Haven't you created a self-fulfilling prophecy here," Hughes said. "You have led them to me. If you weren't here, they wouldn't be here trying to kill me."

"Maybe you're correct, but isn't it better to have us here now? Isn't there a good chance they would have found you on their own and we would not be here to warn you or protect you?" Reid responded with conviction. "The way I see it, you can help us, help me, find them or you can run to hide and start another life somewhere else. I can't make you help me," Reid continued emphatically.

Kendall Hughes sat quietly staring at Reid for over two minutes, then, she finally spoke.

"There is a professor I had in college who helped me with research when I was developing the CP Pak technology. Winston Eblodskya. Dr. Eblodskya is in his mid-80s and lives in Montana. I have visited him there on two occasions. He lives in Western Montana on Flathead Lake near Glacier Park. Two years ago, when I visited him, he had just returned from a paid Scholar Fellowship position in St. Petersburg, Russia at a school for gifted students. The school name was like a number, the 30, I think.

Dr. Eblodskya knew that the Russians wanted him for his knowledge of the CP Pak transport technology. He was old, but he was not stupid. He could teach gifted students about new uses for the Internet, but not give up U.S. Government secrets. His secrets!

He told me how agents for the Kremlin were always after him, trying to turn him for the Russians to gain knowledge about the CP Pak and how he was able to avoid those attempts. But he also mentioned one student who was always after him about CP Pak technology, a young woman he was quite sure had nothing to do with the government. He spoke of the student as a pretty young woman who was kind of a rebel, bordering on being a young Internet criminal. Her interest in CP Pak was whether there was a time interval at the start or the end of the CP Pak Transport, where a passenger could become animated or have the ability to move around."

"Son of a bitch," Reid said eagerly. "That's exactly the break we're looking for. We have to contact him about this student."

"I knew you would say that" Hughes responded. "Winston Eblodskya has forgone using the Internet since his return from that Fellowship. He is off the grid and can only be contacted by snail mail or in person."

Just then Carlos Sanchez's voice broke through on the secure ICP with the usual urgency, "Reid, Reid are you there, pick up Reid pick up!"

Reid rolled his eyes toward Kendall Hughes and

answered, "Yes Carlos, we are here. Kendall Hughes is here with me."

"Uhh Reid, mind picking up? We should have this conversation alone."

"We are fine Carlos," Reid said with a smile. "The Colt six shooter she used with Chris was lost in the fire. Wonder Woman has lost her powers."

"Reid has convinced me that it is in my best interest to help you, much as I would like to tell you Feds to go fuck yourselves. So, if I am in, I need to know what the FBI knows about what is happening here," Hughes stated tersely.

"Alll rrright," Sanchez said with a little Spanish trill in the word. "Quantico matched the prints from the guy killed by the U.S. Marshal. He was Vadik Kozlov, a bomber with Russian mob ties. Here is what the profile team in D.C. has for us. They believe that the instigator, who is behind the killings, has hired a Russian mob team, to handle the assassinations. Sadly, there is more than one to choose from and we are trying to narrow this down. Our team also believes the instigator wants the killings to be completed quickly, maybe within the next week or less. The team believes that is why attempts have been made to slow you down because these gangs are not inept and are capable of so much more, but now that you have found Shelby Ellison..."

Sanchez was cut off by Ellison saying, "I am Kendall Hughes from now forward."

"Now that you have found, Kendall Hughes, attempts will be made to stop your investigation by killing you and Hughes. I think we need to get you back to Seattle and get you both under protection until we figure out what to do next."

"Thanks Carlos. That is confirmation of what Chris Keller and I had discussed before the bombing last night," Reid said. "Carlos, Kendall and I have just uncovered the first real lead in this case." Reid went on to share the story from Kendall Hughes about Dr. Eblodskya and the mystery student from Russia. He also explained that he and Hughes would need to travel to Montana to question Eblodskya in person, as soon as possible.

"Reid, that is fantastic news! The news that there is a substantial break in the case will go a long way with Director Russell and President Parker. This story of the diplomats being killed on CP Pak transports with American connections is topping international news."

"I am formulating a plan Carlos, but the fewer people who know the whereabouts of Kendall Hughes and me, the better. Can you get us a military flight out of here and back to Seattle as soon as possible?"

"With this news, I am sure that I can. Would you rather go from Ketchikan to wherever in Montana?

"No, just get us to Sea-Tac International," Reid said. "My guess is that there are more Russians here in Ketchikan, right now, ready and willing to kill us."

CHAPTER 28

February 19
Wednesday 5:00am

Before Reid had left the Star House, Yuri was calling Georgy and Luca Pajari the most competent killers on his assassination team.

A hung over Luca answered the phone, "Ja."

"Sorry to wake you two fuck-offs, but I thought that I would have heard from you by now," Yuri shouted. "The television news here is filled with a bombing and fire on Creek Street in Ketchikan in the wee morning hours. Vadik Kozlov was shot to death at the scene. Where were you two limp dicks when that happened?"

"Uhhh," in the background Yuri could hear Georgy. "We were doing research."

"Research this you lazy cocksuckers, you have 24 hours to find and kill agent Reid Daniels and Shelby Ellison aka Kendall Hughes or it will be the last 24 hours you spend alive on this earth! Are we clear?" Yuri shouted into the phone. "Analka will be back to you with their whereabouts. Don't fuck this up! If you don't deliver, I will kill you both when you least expect it." Yuri slammed the phone down.

"I toll you vee should notta gone ta Babe's last night," Luca said.

"Vee'll go again tonigh," Georgy laughed. "They veel have bullets in dare heads before we eat lunch today."

After hanging up with the Pajari brothers, Yuri sent a note to his Annie asking if she could talk. His code encrypted phone rang immediately. "Hello Annie."

"Ehlo Yuri, how kin I help you?"

"Any news for me from your guy there?"

"Eets been quiet here Yuri. Robeen has been digging into the Russian mob, the Thorny Rose team and a few other assassin's teams, but he is getting nowhere. A leetle earlier, he gots information bout FBI agent Chris Keller in da hospital in Keetchikan. Souns like he hurt bad in explosion. Robeen getting people to look afta him," Analka explained.

"Nothing else Annie?"

"That's eet," Analka answered.

"That seems strange Annie, do you think you have been uncovered by the person who came to update Robin's computer?"

"I canna find eet and I am pretty good at this sort of ting."

"I know you are Annie. Well, here is the thing now. There was Vadik's explosion that laid up the Seal Team guy. Vadik was killed in a gun fight afterward. Agent Daniels is not hurt, but we have lost him and the newly found Kendall Hughes. You know. The alias of your hero who invented the CP Pak technology."

"Is she hokay?" Analka asked.

"I think she is. I think she is with agent Daniels and my guess is that he will try to get her back to Seattle as soon as possible. The Pajari brothers are in Ketchikan and will kill Daniels and Hughes as soon as we find them," Yuri said firmly.

Analka winced at the mention of the Pajari brothers.

"When agent Daniels or anyone else from the FBI contacts Robin for travel help, you must get that information to me as soon as possible. We must take Daniels and Hughes out of the game. Do you have that Analka?" Yuri asked tersely.

Analka swallowed hard and said, "Yes Yuri, I have that."

CHAPTER 29

February 19
Wednesday 7:00am Alaska Local Time

Reid finished the call with Carlos Sanchez and Kendall Hughes asked, "What is your plan? Why do you not want the military plane to take us to Montana? We could fly into Missoula or Kalispell and rent a car to go to Eblodskya's house on Flathead Lake."

"Look, I can only imagine that there are assassins here in Ketchikan already looking for us. My plan to get us out of Ketchikan is a simple bait and switch. We have my people book us onto a commercial flight to, say, Portland. We have the plane from Sanchez arrive at the airport to pick us up a little earlier than the commercial flight. We slip the waiting area and get on the government flight to Seattle ahead of the commercial flight to Portland. If we can dodge the killers and get onto the government plane ahead of them, their best chance to keep up with us is to get onto the next commercial flight to Portland," Reid explained.

"Ooohkay," Hughes said with skepticism. *I may have overestimated this guy*, she thought.

"At some point, we are going to need to sleep. If we fly all the way to Montana, I don't imagine much sleep for us on a military plane. If we fly to Seattle, my gas-electric self-driving Audi is at the Sea-Tac airport."

"Uhuh," Hughes occasionally responded. *Where is he going with this?* She was thinking.

"My car is filled and charged so we can go 1000 miles, more than enough to get to Western Montana and we will not have to stop for fuel or a motel where we would leave a credit card trail along the way," Reid said with a pleased look on his face.

"Right now, I wish I had my Colt back, my Wonder Woman powers as you said, because that is the stupidest fucking idea, I think anyone could come up with," Hughes scolded.

"Could you put your arms out and spin around when you use your Wonder Woman powers?" Reid asked, thinking he was being clever.

Reid continued, "Here is some information that you don't have. One of the people on my team has been hacked and compromised by the oldest trick in the book. His name is Robin Medallon. Robin could not catch a pretty girl in a bar with a rope if he snuck up behind her. He is a geek with a capital G. At the same time the killings started, Robin met two Czech girls in a bar, and one went home with him. According to Robin it is non-stop sex with this girl. Whomever is after me has known my every move and now will know our every move." Reid said confident this would end the exchange.

"So why don't you arrest her, genius," Hughes blurted out, but quickly followed, "I'm sorry, but I feel like I know you well enough already to tell you when you are sounding like a moron. It is my life too after all."

"Look, my plan is to feed them misinformation. By the time they figure out where we went, we are secretly on our way to Dr. Eblodskya's on Flathead Lake. Spin around Wonder Woman and give me a better idea."

Kendall Hughes spun around three times and stopped with one arm extended giving Reid the finger.

"While you work on your better idea, I need to call Bert Hamilton on my staff and give her some direction," Reid said.

"Be careful with that because right now, I am not sure you know which way is up," Hughes said hoping to get in the last word.

Reid started to say something but stopped himself. He had lost arguments like this with Charlie and right now it was still a draw. He knew when to quit. Charlie? He had lost track of her again.

Reid called Bert Hamilton on his ICP.

"Hey Bert, you there?"

"Right here Reid!"

"I suppose you have heard what has transpired up here?" Reid asked.

"Yes, Regional Director Sanchez sent a note out this morning. Sounds like Chris had a close call but is pulling through."

"That is good to hear. Wish he was still here to have my back," Reid shared.

"Hey Boss, I have some good news for you on that front. Ya know how all of you old folks say that my generation doesn't take enough initiative?" Kendall Hughes let out a little giggle and Reid rolled his eyes.

"Well, I bit me off a big piece of initiative this morning and I hope I wasn't biting off a big piece of my own butt," Bert paused then continued. "I made a plan with Robin so I could get into his place for a while last evening. I explained to him I needed to check out the devices of his new FF, feature fuck; Told him it was a security mission. We needed to make sure she wasn't pumpin him for pleasure and for knowledge. He was a little hurt, well a lot hurt, but Robin is a professional. We made a plan that I would sneak into his condo precisely at 9:22pm and he would be in the process of starting to bump uglies with the Czech girl. Well, I get in there and it sounded like Robin was getting in there as well and either this girl is a great actress, or our boy Robin has some talent we didn't know about or suspect. I was able to reverse jam the Czech girl's phone and now we will be able to hear whatever from whomever she is talking. Just minutes ago, she was talking to some guy named Yuri and Yuri tells her he had these guys in Ketchikan who are going to kill you and Kendall Hughes as soon as they find you. It sounds like two brothers are after you."

"Great work Bert! Wow, our little girl is growing up! How'd

you leave it with Robin?"

"I told him everything checks out. I thought you should be the one to tell him that his girl is using him."

"Okay, so here is the plan," Reid shoots a quick look across the room to Wonder Woman who throws up her arms with palms up in a "what" gesture. "I am going to contact Robin and request that he books Ms. Hughes and me onto a flight out of Ketchikan to Portland," Reid speaks seriously. "For all that you and Robin know, we are on our way to Portland. Got it?"

"Got it Reid. Be careful out there."

CHAPTER 30

February 19
Wednesday Mid-Morning Ketchikan Local Time

With little additional bickering, Reid and Kendall packed up their belongings and took Kendall's car to the Ketchikan airport parking terminal. In route, they drove directly past two rough looking men standing at the base of the boardwalk where Creek Street meets the Stedman Bridge. The Pajari brothers had no idea their prey had passed by so closely.

After they arrived at the airport without incident, Reid showed his credentials and asked airport security to provide them with a room where they would be safe.

When they were safely behind the scenes, Reid contacted Regional Commander Sanchez on ICP mode.

"Carlos, Reid here."

"Yeh, Reid what took you so long?" Sanchez asked.

"I thought you were going to get back to me about the military flight," Reid said surprised.

"Don't know why you would think that, Reid. Been waiting for your call.

Reid looked at Kendall and she offered a puzzled look back to him.

"Okay, I am here now, what is the story on the plane," Reid asked.

"A Coast Guard plane can pick you up at Ketchikan with a half hour notice. Are you still wanting to go to Sea-Tac International?"

Reid looked at Kendall and she gave a resigned nod.

"Yes, Seattle. I will get back to you in 30 minutes with the time we need them here."

Reid hung up and immediately contacted Robin Medallon.

"Robin, Reid here."

"Yes, Reid. I got the news about the explosion and Chris Keller. Are you okay?" Robin asked.

"Yes, I am good. Robin, it is important to get this done right away. I need you to book Kendall Hughes and me on a flight to Portland, Oregon on the next flight out of Ketchikan today. Use our power to bump people if needed," Reid commanded. "I will stay on the line so you can tell me when that flight leaves here."

"Reid, your flight is at 2:10pm arriving in Portland at 8:35pm Pacific Time. Nearly a 4-hour flight with the time change."

"Got it Robin. Thank you. I need to call Carlos now."

Reid got back to Sanchez to request that the Coast Guard plane be ready to pick them up at 1:55pm at Ketchikan International which would be during the boarding process of the flight to Portland. Reid was hoping his ruse would work and the Russian mob assassins would be on the flight to Portland.

CHAPTER 31

February 19
Wednesday Mid-Morning Ketchikan Local Time

As soon as she could, Analka jumped onto Robin's computer to see what he had been doing for his boss. Analka saw the airline tickets to Portland for Agent Daniels and Kendall Hughes. She knew she needed to contact Yuri and she needed to book the Pajari brothers onto that flight.

Yuri's phone rang three times before he could answer. He was still having physical problems after the CP Pak transport to Mexico City.

"Yes, Annie, what do you have for me?" Yuri asked.

"Yuri, vee have important news. Agent Daniels and Kendall Hughes are headed to Portland, Oregon in a couple hours."

"Interesting," Yuri said. "It would seem that we need to book Georgy and Luka on that same flight just in case they do not get Daniels and Hughes killed in Ketchikan."

Analka cringed at the mention of killing Shelby Ellison. She wondered how much longer she could do this.

"Can you do that for me Annie?"

"Yes Yuri, veel do."

Analka set about immediately booking the Pajari brothers onto the 2:10pm flight out of Ketchikan to Portland secretly hoping that agent Daniels and Hughes would make a getaway.

Yuri phoned Georgy Pajari. "Georgy, are you and your brother sober yet? Do you have a clue where agent Daniels and Kendall Hughes are?" Yuri asked.

"We think dey still out here near explosion," Georgy responded. "We are staked out and vatchin for them."

"It is a wonder you two can find your dicks in the dark!" Yuri shouted. "Your targets are not there! Get your sorry asses out to Ketchikan airport. Daniels and Hughes are booked onto a flight to Portland, Oregon. If they knew that you two worthless cocksuckers were after them, they would feel safe enough to be out having lunch and shopping. Now, move your sorry asses out to the airport and see if you can get eyes on them. Analka is arranging tickets for you on that flight to Portland. It leaves at 2:10pm."

"Do you want vee kill them at the airport?"

"No! Too many people around! Get out there and get eyes on them. Follow them," Yuri instructed then he hung up.

Yuri had a screaming headache. He did not feel well, and he was in a bad mood. He had been pounding down Advil since getting off the Mexico City CP Pak transport after killing Park Soo-Hoon. It had to be something related to the mineral pills he had taken that allowed him to move around during the transport.

Having made his way through security and waiting to board his flight back to Seattle as Fredrick Hemmel Yuri was feeling advancing pain in his head. He began to wonder if he could make it to Paris and the Spring restaurant by Friday to kill the unnamed "fucking Russian" that his employer had ordered as his next hit. Yuri was having a little trouble functioning.

CHAPTER 32

February 19
Wednesday Early Afternoon Ketchikan Local Time

While waiting for their Coast Guard plane to arrive, Reid and Kendall split a toasted cheese sandwich, and each had a bowl of tomato soup brought to them from the cafeteria. Reid filled Kendall in on everything he knew about the case. Obviously, she had a good mind, and she was clearly a problem solver. Because communications with headquarters might be limited in Montana, he wanted her to know everything that he knew because. He may need her insights on problems they might face.

Their agreed plan was to get to Montana, meet with Dr. Eblodskya and, hopefully, be able to determine who the mysterious young woman was who had shown such interest in CP Pak transports. Could that young lady be a part of all of this or was it a dead end? Either way they needed to run it down and time was of the essence. Two dead diplomats were already creating unbearable pressure at the highest levels of the U.S. government and all that pressure was finding its way to Agent Reid Daniels.

Reid was recapping his mind. They had driven through Ketchikan and made it unnoticed across the Tongass Sound to the airport. Soon, they would be free and clear to head to Montana to interview Winston Eblodskya. *"Charlie, if you have any ideas, feel free to share,"* Reid thought. *"Charlie, do you like this lady, Kendall Hughes?"* All Reid got in return was a vision of Charlie smiling back at him giving a slight nod.

Having seen only the bombed out remains of her

store, Kendall wondered about the true capabilities of this "assassination team" as Reid called them. She had worked with Russians before and was not always impressed with anything other than their drinking. Was Reid exaggerating their capabilities because of what seemed to be his inexperience as an FBI murder investigator or was he trying to impress her? Kendall could hear her grandmother saying, "*sadly, in many cases, men are just grown-up little boys. You must develop the skill to sort through the grown-up little boys to find the real men. And Shelby, don't let any man put his boots under your bed until your brand is on his cattle.*" Kendall took that to mean don't give in completely to any man until he is willing to give in completely to you.

A little before 2:00pm a senior airport security officer came to get them.

"Hi I'm Jim Peterson. I am in charge of airport security here. I don't know who you are for certain, and I don't want to know. I have it from the highest levels that I am to get you two safely on a Coast Guard plane that is arriving right now."

"Thanks Jim. Will we be able to get to the tarmac without going through any general areas of the airport?" Reid asked.

"Yes," Peterson responded. "Also, we have brought in additional support. We'll have two extra officers in the waiting area for your phony flight which, by the way, you have already been checked-in for." Puffing his chest, a little, Peterson continued, "The Air Marshal has been alerted that there will be two empty seats on the Portland flight, and he will alert the crew. Nobody should make a fuss about you two being missing at takeoff time for that Portland flight."

"Sounds like you have done a thorough job Peterson."

"Well, we don't have too many issues like this come up and we want to make sure we do it right," Peterson said proudly. "And I know you will like this; we have two Sheriff Deputy coats and fur caps for you guys to put on to walk out to the Coast Guard plane. I will go out with you and it will all look like very official business as usual."

"Damn Jim, you almost make me forget that there might be two Russian thugs trying to kill us," Kendall Hughes interjected.

Missing the irony completely, Peterson said, "just trying to do our best ma'am."

At the same time, Georgy and Luka Pajari were skulking around the airport waiting area trying to make out which passenger was Reid Daniels. They had seen photos sent by Analka days earlier, but they were not seeing that person in the waiting room.

Luka had checked at the front desk and found that his "good friend" Reid Daniels was checked in for the flight. The window behind the check-in desk for the Alaska Air flight to Portland looked out onto the taxi way. An orange and white Coast Guard plane had just landed and come to a stop on the tarmac beyond and to the left of the Boeing 737 parked at the Portland flight boarding ramp.

This piqued Luka's interest and he motioned for Georgy to come over to the window. Three uniformed individuals were seen walking out to the Coast Guard plane which was letting down its ramp.

When they got to the plane, two of the three started quickly up the ramp. The third followed a little behind. At the top of the ramp, the first person, who they could see was a woman handed her coat and hat back out. The second person was now stopped in the doorway of the plane and took off his coat and hat and handed out. In that moment even from 200 yards away, Luka Pajari, who had the abnormally strong eyesight of a sniper, recognized Reid Daniels.

"Vee been fucked Georgy," he said, "they just got on that plane, and I bet they are not goin to Portland."

Georgy was already calling Yuri to get instructions. Georgy quickly explained the dilemma.

"Well, they are leaving Ketchikan and it makes sense that they are headed to Seattle," Yuri said. "Motherfucking shit!

I may have to be on a flight to Paris before they get to Seattle or I could wait for their flight, find them, and snuff them. This weasel of an FBI Internet clerk is causing us way too much trouble. I have lost two valuable team members and now we have lost them." Yuri's headache was pounding.

"Let me think, let me think," Yuri was struggling. "Okay, they have left Ketchikan, that we know for sure. You can leave Ketchikan on your flight to Portland in, what just a few minutes?" Yuri thought out loud. "Get on that flight to Portland, when you get there, I will have further instructions for you."

As soon as he hung up with Georgy, Yuri called Analka.

"Annie, I need to travel to Paris almost immediately," Yuri said. "I am not feeling well, so I believe I want to fly."

"Then, you veel fly. Let me see. I can book you from Seattle to Atlanta, then Atlanta to Paris. Ahhhh looks like you will arrive in Paris Friday early morning hours. Hokee," Analka confirmed. "But you need to be on that first leg to Atlanta in just five hours."

"I guess that works. My flight out of Mexico City is boarding now. Any suggestions on my headache?" Yuri whined.

"Good auld aspirin and lot and lot of water and get some rest," Analka advised.

"Thanks Annie, got to go; Another call's coming in," Yuri closed.

"Yuri here." Then he could hear the click and the command "Please turn on Microsoft Elucidation voice translation. "Thorny Rose, the story of the two diplomats being killed on the CP Pak transports is gaining traction in the media," the mono toned voice said.

"As expected," Yuri said.

"Are you able to quiet down the investigation?" "Has the lead FBI investigator and the Scientist Shelby Ellison been silenced forever? Tell me it is so," the monotone said.

"We have not silenced them, and I have lost another

person from my team in Ketchikan, Yuri said tersely. "And just so you know, the price of doing business with me has just gone up to three million dollars."

"You can't extort me you Russian fuck. I can so easily put someone else on this job," the monotone said. "You need to go fuck yourself."

Yuri could tell that he had hit a nerve, so he pushed on, "You need to make a decision. We are running out of time for me to get to Paris and make the next hit. I can't take the chance of travelling on a CP Pak with cameras and face recognition, so have decided to fly to Paris. This job has cost me two of my best assets and is turning out to be more difficult than anticipated. I believe that the speed of getting this all wrapped up is very important to you. Three million dollars!"

There was a long, long pause. "Are you still going to be in Paris at the Spring Restaurant to kill the Russian fuck on Friday evening?" the monotone asked.

"Yes, if you agree to pay an additional one million dollars.

"Okay," came the monotone response. The line went dead.

CHAPTER 33

Wednesday Evening February 19

Everyone was travelling. Yuri was asleep on his flight to Atlanta. Georgy and Luka were sleeping off their strip club hangover on their way to Portland. Reid and Kendall were exchanging life stories on the Coast Guard plane bound for Seattle.

In Seattle, Hai Chang, the Chinese Security, and Intelligence Officer had discovered a South Korean, he was interested in learning more about who was on the CP Pak transport from Washington, D.C. where Xing Tsua Ten had been killed. He didn't need the Americans.

Carlos Sanchez thought it was the perfect diversion for the Chinese security officer and requested help from Quantico. This could take up some of the time of the Chinese and keep them out of Reid's hair. Lan Phang the Chinese Internet Intelligence Director thought it was a waste of time, but she was outranked.

On the Coast Guard flight to Seattle, Kendall Hughes started telling her life story to Reid, mostly because he was asking.

She was born in Seattle. Her parents were wealthy. Her mother was a surgeon at Swedish Medical Center and her father was an attorney with one of Seattle's largest law firms. Her mother had been treating patients during the Pandemic of 2020 when she contracted and later died from COVID – 19. Her father also became ill and died.

The loss of her parents was devastating, but there was not enough time for all the grief she needed. After her parents' death, Shelby went to live with her mother's parents on a farm near Moscow, Idaho. On that farm in north central Idaho, she learned how to cope with loneliness. She daydreamed about what she might invent to make the world a better place.

Young Shelby Ellison was fascinated by computers and the Internet. At a younger age, she had met Bill and Melinda Gates at a Gates Foundation event for children. Bill had told her small group that anything they could imagine doing with computers and the Internet could be accomplished and Melinda had told her group that if you were a girl, it was your time to excel in computers and the Internet because barriers were coming down for women.

At an early age, Shelby Ellison continued dreaming of sending objects over the Internet as she had done at a much younger age. She was interested by the process of ordering something from Amazon and receiving it the next day. But that took time and people and fuel.

Why couldn't you order something on Amazon and receive it in just a few minutes or the next minute? Why did daddy have to be gone for so long when he travelled to Washington, D.C. for work? Why could a document come from Washington, D.C. in a few seconds, but a person travelling the same distance could take hours and hours?

She started learning about super computers and artificial intelligence. She started learning about 3-D printers. She started learning about MRIs and about the chemical and molecular makeup of living things. As her thirst for science and her ambition to achieve her dream expanded, her social life contracted.

Shelby Ellison had to work hard to be a somewhat normal girl and teenager. She did play some sports and she excelled at golf. But she didn't go to the high school football games like the other kids, she didn't have a boyfriend and she didn't have many girlfriends for that matter.

Shelby poured her heart and soul into her studies and her research. After years of focus and hard work, she was able to achieve her dream of sending living beings and objects in CP Pak transports. But there was no celebration. She was crestfallen and heartbroken to see that the practical everyday benefits of what she had discovered and created were overlooked. More important to everyone in government was how her invention could be used by the military. She was sickened that her invention might be used in war.

She told Reid that she fought it so hard she became ill after she was poisoned and in the final analysis, she needed to run away and hide from it all. It seemed the logical solution at the time and that was how she became Kendall Hughes.

"Wow! What a transition! So, what have you learned as Kendall Hughes?" Reid asked.

"I've learned how to live. I have learned to sail. I have learned how to ski. I have learned about the beauty in nature. I have learned to play softball and improved my golf game, although we have a short season in Ketchikan. I have learned how to slow down to enjoy the moment and I have learned how to love," Kendall said. "I have learned to be open with my feelings about the way it is between men and women."

"That sounds ominous. What do you mean?" Reid said.

"I don't simply see myself as an equal to men, I see myself as being superior to most men with only a few of you as my equal. In other words, I'm not subservient to men," Kendall stated. "I have not yet made up my mind about where you fall in my rating system." She smiled.

"Being a farm girl, I learned to do everything that a man does. I drove all types of farm equipment. I worked beside Grandpa during harvest and helped with maintaining equipment in the winter. I even made my way through college working as a welder at a steel fabricator in Seattle. I'm not simply a pretty science nerd, I am a resourceful and tough girl."

"As evidenced by the gunfight at the Dog and the Butterfly Coral with Chris Keller." Reid smiled.

Even though she smiled back, Kendall worried that she was telling too much about herself, but she kind of had a positive feeling about this FBI guy. She really did know where he was on her scale.

"Any regrets in life?" Reid asked.

"Yes, no children. I've been told that children fill the place in you that you never knew was empty. I guess I will always feel empty in that place."

"What about you Reid, do you have children?"

"Yes. A son, Michael," Reid said. He relayed his life with Charlie and how he missed her. He sounded as if Charlie's death had been very recent, but Kendall could discern through a few things he said that it had been a several years.

"Since we are sharing deep aspects of our lives here Reid, you know how I said children fill a place in you that you never knew was empty? I sense you have been living with a place in you which is now empty? May I tell you what I see in you?" Without waiting Kendall continued. "You are trying to remain fulfilled by a memory of your wife, a wonderful memory it is, but you need to live more in the moment and take in the life that surrounds you now. You need to make room for a new life, new love. You must put the old life and love in its proper place as a memory. That is what I have had to do Reid. Losing my parents then my life dream, all that I had worked for, lived for really, is very similar to you losing Charlie. I can tell you from experience, it will make you a better and happier person to move on with your life," Kendall concluded.

"Oh, I'm fine," Reid replied but he knew that he was not telling the truth.

The two became silent and dozed off for the short remainder of the flight to Seattle.

Reid dreamed of Charlie, but in this dream, Charlie was in danger of being taken away and he awoke unsettled as the Coast Guard craft landed in Seattle.

CHAPTER 34

February 19
Wednesday Late Evening Seattle Local Time

Reid and Kendall departed the Coast Guard aircraft at Seattle-Tacoma International Airport thanking the crew for their delivery and wonderful hospitality. They made their way directly to the Parking Garage and Reid's Audi.

It was a rainy February night and even though it would have been easier to set the Auto Driver mode on the Audi, Reid wanted to drive for a while. Kendall appeared to have fallen asleep immediately.

Reid drove onto Interstate 405 headed up the East shore of Lake Washington toward Bellevue, then he took the turn east onto Interstate 90 to drive across Washington, Idaho and into Western Montana. The dashboard readout said the trip to Dayton, Montana would take 7 hours and 58 minutes with no stops. With a couple of stops that should put them in at Professor Eblodskya's home in the early morning hours.

"*Then what,*" Reid thought. "Would the elderly Dr. Eblodskya even remember the student that Kendall had spoken about? And if he did remember, would he and Kendall be able to find the student to see if she could help them figure out how and why these murders were happening?'

Reid recapped, with Charlie, everything in his mind, trying to find something they must be missing at this point. He also thought about Kendall Hughes and what she had said about moving on in his life. Finally, he thought, they had shaken loose from the Russians who were after them.

The snow coming down in big flakes on Snoqualmie

Pass was starting to windshield hypnotize Reid toward a deep sleep. He decided it was time to turn on the Auto Drive and get that much-needed rest he had spoken about earlier. With any luck, they would stay ahead of the bad guys for good now.

As she was drifting off to sleep, Kendall's "ESP" doubted that she and Reid had rid themselves of the Russians. So far, the Russians had not shown themselves to be too adept. She didn't know what their game was, but she did know that not all Russians were as bumbling as those who had shown themselves. They needed to get to Eblodskya's and get closer to figuring out what this was all about.

Finally, Kendall thought about her life and even though what Reid had gotten her into right now seemed life and death, she welcomed the mental stimulation. This was so much more fun than choosing which trinkets the tourists would be most attracted to this coming season.

CHAPTER 35

February 20
Thursday 2:55am Atlanta Local Time

With a head that was pounding only slightly less than it had been previously, Yuri Rosov was landing in Atlanta for a short layover before he departed for Paris. As he turned on his phone, there was an unexpected message.

The message read: Finder App Tracker Device # 199642 is now mobile.

"Yuri you are one brilliant Russian son-of-a-bitch," Yuri said out loud.

The tracking device he had placed on FBI Agent Daniels's car was giving readings of movement.

Yuri tapped open the App and reverse pinched the map over the red blinking dot to see Reid's car was moving East on Interstate 90 across Western Washington State. "The mouse is on the run, but the cat is close behind," he whispered.

Yuri tapped up a statewide view of Washington and I90, and then he brought up northern Oregon so he could give instructions to Georgy and Luka. He quickly placed an encrypted call to Georgy.

"Ehlo Yuri, hey this Portlan airport is really nice! They gots really nice wine bar and I right here in the main terminal and it's steel open," Georgy said excitedly.

"Isn't that nice for you two," Yuri said tersely. "I hate to interrupt your dinner, but your targets are on the move. You will need to rent a car. I suggest a four-wheel drive with Auto Drive if you can get it. You will want to head east on Interstate 84 to Umatilla, Oregon then turn north to go toward Richland,

Washington, then Ritzville, Washington. I will send a text with all of this, but again repeat after me, Interstate 84, then Richland, then Ritzville."

"84 to Umallila, Reechlan, then Reetzval," Georgy repeated. "84 to Umallila, Reechlan, then Reetzval," Georgy said it again.

"Close enough for now. You need to get going right away! They are probably two to three hours ahead of you," Yuri commanded then he ended the call.

Georgy took another bite of steak and a big gulp of wine.

"He sayd we finish our dinner, then we rent a caw und head east," Georgy said. Then, he ordered another bottle of wine.

Yuri sent a text to Georgy with the instructions and let him know how to sign onto the Finder App Tracker device so they would know where to go next. Something told him not to send a note just yet to Analka. Georgy and Luka would soon be on the hot trail left by the Tracker device, and they would bring an end to the saga of FBI Agent Reid Daniels.

Yuri was feeling better. Much better!

CHAPTER 36

February 20
Thursday 4:35 am Mountain Standard Time

Just outside of Spokane and nearly 5 hours into the trip a soft voice on the console of the Audi let Reid and Kendall know that Spokane was ten minutes away. Reid looked up at the console and punched up Rest Areas. He saw one about one hour away just inside Montana.

From that Rest Area, they would still have nearly 3 hours to travel. The weather had turned colder, and it was snowing heavily. Travel would be slower from here to Dr. Eblodskya's house. Reid set the Audi to stop at that Rest Area and drifted back to sleep.

Light chimes then, a soft female voice announced, "rest area" light chimes "rest area."
Reid reached for the console to turn off the alert that they were at the rest area just over Lookout Pass in Western Montana. The display was showing 2 hours and 20 minutes to Dr. Eblodskya's house on Flathead Lake near Dayton, Montana. Snow was coming down heavy and sideways. The temperature outside was 18 degrees.

He gently nudged Kendall. "We're at a rest stop. Do you need to use the facilities?"

"Boy do I," she said covering her mouth trying to hold back morning breath. "What time is it?" It was pitch black outside except for the heavy snow showing in the headlights.

"It's about 20 till 5:00 in the morning, ahhh, Mountain Time. The console says 2 hours 20 minutes to Dr. Eblodskya's house."

"How cold is it out there?"

"18 degrees. But it's a wet and snowy 18 degrees," Reid said attempting to be funny.

"Oh my God! Where's my bag?" Kendall said. Then she was digging in her bag and pulled out a reddish orange insulated winter coat, that Reid could tell would really make her sky-blue eyes pop in bright daylight, then a pair of black insulated gloves and a warm looking winter hat.

"Wow, you've got the stuff for winter," Reid admired.

"I do live in Alaska," she said as she was climbing out of the car.

"How did that just happen," Reid thought to himself? *"I woke up first. She's already walking into the restrooms and I'm still not ready to get out."* Then he realized how enthralled he was watching her.

It had been a long time since he had started his morning with a woman. He said a little apology to Charlie in his mind even though nothing was going on here that he needed to feel guilty about. He apologized anyway. Charlie said she didn't mind. She liked Kendall too.

Within moments Reid was jumping out of the car and headed to the restrooms. He was not quite as well dressed for the conditions as Kendall.

When they were back in the Audi, he started the car and placed it back into Auto Drive control. He figured that computer would drive better in the snowy conditions than he could, because he really doesn't get much practice driving in heavy snow in Seattle.

Neither one of them seemed to want to talk so they rode along in silence watching the snow and looking at the snow-covered road illuminated by the Audi's headlights. The all-wheel drive car did not seem to be having any problems even though the snow looked to be 8 inches deep on the roadway.

In a short time, they were both back to sleep only to be awakened 45 minutes later by the Audi slowing to a stop. Through the windshield, Reid and Kendall could see a herd of what Reid thought may be up to 40 majestic elk wandering slowly across the road and appearing to be headed down the hill to the Clark Fork riverbank. A few stately bulls walked like kings with their heads high holding magnificent racks of antlers as their crowns.

The rest were cow elk and younger animals. Their bodies were a beautiful mocha tan on their bodies, with darker even auburn brown on their lower bellies and legs sweeping up to a dark cloak wrapped over their front shoulders and neck. Their behinds were a puff of very light tan.

One thing was for sure, not one of them was in a hurry. For five minutes they sauntered across the road. When the path was finally clear, the Audi started and continued the journey.

They were no longer on the freeway and had taken a turn north and were following the Clark Fork River which had been named after William Clark of the Lewis and Clark Expedition; this was a two-lane road.

It is a little unnerving to be driving through 8 inches of snow on the twists and turns of a river road through the mountains of Western Montana. Neither of them felt sleepy now and they still had over an hour to go.

"Are you sure we wouldn't be better off for you to take the controls," Kendall asked.

"We may well have hit the elk, if I were driving," Reid said. "Besides I would think that this is far less dangerous than having your body dissembled and reassembled by a computer while travelling in a CP Pak transport."

"You may have a point there, Daniels," Kendall said with a smile, but it was easy to tell that the bad road conditions were not to her liking.

"You would think that we would see a snowplow sometime," Read said.

"This is a secondary road, so they are probably working on more important roadways first," Kendall said. In a more excited voice, "I wish we were making this trip in the summer and in daylight. It's really beautiful. My other trips to see Dr. Eblodskya were in the summer. We went kayaking on the lake, fishing and even did some hiking on Wild Horse Island. That is a big Island in Flathead Lake which is inhabited by deer, big horn sheep, bears and in fact a few wild horses. It's over 2000 acres and it's just a couple of miles across the water from Eblodskya's house."

"So is Flathead Lake kind of a donut that wraps around this Horse Island?" Reid asked just to be polite.

"No, no Flathead Lake is, I think, 27 miles long and in some places 15 or so miles across. I think Winston said it is 200 square miles of water surface," Kendall said excitedly and then with emphasis "W-i-l-d Horse Island is kind of tucked along the West Shore. I think from the east side of W-i-l-d Horse Island it's probably ten miles or more across the water over to the east shore of the lake."

"Impressive facts," Reid said. "How many gallons of water are there in Flathead Lake?"

"You know, I'm not sure," Kendall said as if she should know the answer. Then she sat back, starred at Reid, and bit the inside of her cheek for a moment and said, "fuck you, Reid Daniels, I'm a scientist, I like to learn and remember things like this."

Reid poked, "How many teaspoons?"

"Fuck you," Kendall said quickly, somewhat amused but not wanting to show it. She turned and looked out the window.

Two hundred miles to the south and west, Georgy and Luka had gone through Umatilla, Richland, and Ritzville to make it to Interstate 90 nearly two thirds of the way across the state of Washington. They had stopped to get a sweet roll, some coffee, and waited to hear from Yuri. At this point, they were about four hours behind the FBI Agent and the Scientist.

CHAPTER 37

February 20
Thursday 4:35am Mountain Standard Time

Over the Pacific Ocean 2900 nautical miles from Hawaii a Chandu J-20A Mighty Dragon II Chinese jet fighter was closing on an American EP4. The EP4 was part of the Airborne Reconnaissance Integrated Electronics Systems or ARIES used to track the naval movements of potential adversaries around the globe.

Captain Gus Martinez was piloting the American plane while tracking the movements of the aircraft carrier group Xi Jinping from China. His radar man had told him that Chinese fighter jets were following their flight while they tracked the PLAN (People's Liberation Army Navy) group out of the South Seas. Captain Martinez had radioed his commanders about the Chinese fighters. He received back the orders to stay the course on the surveillance of the PLAN Group and to avoid confrontation, if possible.

With alarms sounding the Chinese fighter approached. The Chinese pilot was entering into the Intelligence plane's airspace. The fighter jet was above and slightly behind the slower less agile American aircraft. The onboard symmetry radar of the American EP4 showed the Mighty Dragon II fighter flying with the bottom of the Chinese jet just feet above the Americans.

Slowly and carefully the Chinese pilot moved down to bump the EP4. Then, he quickly pulled away. An extremely dangerous maneuver for both planes. Martinez was a burly man who had played football for the University of New Mexico.

Although his craft had taken a little damage, he was able to control the flight. For a second time, The Chinese fighter approached. There was a second bump.

Martinez radioed his Commander to report the incident. He received orders to lower his air speed and drop down 1500 feet. If that did not work, Martinez was ordered to take whatever evasive action he deemed necessary. Martinez carried out the maneuver and leveled off.

The Chinese fighter was back like a mosquito in the night trying to get at you no matter what you do. This bump was the hardest of all. There was more damage. Martinez was using all his strength to control his plane.

As the Mighty Dragon II approached for another bump, Martinez pushed the stick forward to dive, pushing the EP4 to full throttle and executing a roll out dive with the heavier slower plane.

The Chinese pilot was caught off guard and overcompensated for the expected bump that was not there. He was accelerating and chasing the American plane downward. Martinez was diving away from the Mighty Dragon II and began another roll down. As the EP4 started its roll to the left, the turned down left wing of the Chandu J20A collided with the upward tipped right wing of the EP4.

The middle of the main left wing of the Chinese plane struck across the end wing tip of the EP4. The concentrated force at the wing tip was like a karate chop splitting a one-inch board. The result was a warp in the right wing of the American EP4. Catastrophic damage crippled the left wing of the Chinese Mighty Dragon II.

The Mighty Dragon began flying erratically. It was out of control in a downward spiral. The EP4 began shaking violently. Martinez did not know if he could control the plane. With several quick attempts, he was able to find an air speed at which he could control his aircraft. His size and strength helped him to keep the plane in the air. Although his craft had suffered major damage, he knew he could get back to base.

The radar man for the American plane reported that the Chinese aircraft was headed for the drink and the pilot had ejected.

Martinez radioed his commander to report the mid-air collision. This, no doubt, would be reported as a major international incident. A fresh crew and different ARIES would need to be sent to track the Chinese naval group. The urgency to find who murdered the Chinese diplomat increased tenfold.

CHAPTER 38

February 20
Thursday 7:35am Mountain Standard Time

Light chimes then the female voice announced, "destination reached" light chimes "destination reached".

Reid reached out to the console to turn off the alert. The Audi was pulled off to the side of the road at Ptarmigan Lane, just above Flathead Lake. The snow to the side of the road looked to be at least three feet deep. The highway of course had been plowed but Ptarmigan Lane was a different story. Snow there had not been so recently plowed and looked to be about a foot deep.

"You awake? Does this look like the right place," Reid asked?

Kendall looked out the window into the growing morning light and could see Flathead Lake spreading out below with Wild Horse Island and its forested multi-elevation hills becoming the focus of her view. The Island lay just two miles across the water.

What wonderful memories she had of this place. Her trips here were always a respite from the pickup sticks style of her life and work. It was a place to unload all that had piled on top of her. This trip would be different.

"This is it. I could really stand brushing my teeth. What is the temperature outside?" Kendall asked.

"It's 15 degrees," Reid said, then, he slipped the Audi out of Auto-Drive and turned down Ptarmigan Lane. The pitch of the road going down the hill was gentle and mostly tree lined with a couple of straight stretches mixed in with two sharp switch back turns. The road looked to have been plowed the day before. It was still snowing lightly but visibility was good out across the lake. Reid thought how beautiful it was with the Island and the high mountain across the lake to the east.

"This view has got to be stunning in the warmer greener months," Reid observed.

"And not bad now in this early morning light," Kendall responded.

There were a few houses at the top of the hill and houses comfortably spaced out along the lake shore. The lakeshore homes were set back from the lake with what looked like snow-covered lawns leading from the houses down to the lake shore.

"Which of these houses is it?"

"Keep going down the road. It is up ahead through that gate and in amongst those big pine trees."

The Audi pulled to a stop in front of a rustic style modern home with a log base. The house looked like it was in its proper place here, set back in the trees. There are large windows off the front and on the side of the house which offered views of Flathead Lake and the Mission Mountains out to the east shore of the lake. Reid could see now that this was a large, large lake.

"Is that the other side of the lake out there or is that the Wild Horses Island you talked about," Reid asked.

"It is Wild Horse Island," Kendall enunciated. She was feeling vindicated for the ration of crap Reid had given her the night before.

Out the door came Professor Winston Eblodskya holding a pistol in his right hand and looking like a man who must not have any mirrors in his home. He had long tangled and messy white hair and a white beard that looked like small crawly critters could be living inside. He was wearing a black, red and white plaid shirt and a pair of oversized pants with black suspenders. The look on his face of said, "who in the hell are you and what in tarnation are you doing here?"

Reid wondered if this is where Kendall had learned to

shoot first and ask questions later. Reid was going to stay right where he was until the pistol looked safe.

Kendall opened the passenger door which was facing the house and shouted, "Winston, it's me Kendall Hughes or Shelby Ellison, if you prefer!"

"Goldangit Shelby, you scared the beejesus out of me. Nobody comes down here this time of year except old lady Collier from up the road and I just hide out in here when I see her walkin down. Nosey old bitch. What on earth are you doing here and who is that with you?" Eblodskya shouted back.

About that time, an over-weight gray faced golden lab sauntered slowly out the door and gave two raspy barks. "Don't mind my watch dog here. This is Buttercup. Good dog Buttercup. Her way to let me know that somebody is here." Eblodskya patted her head and Buttercup wagged her tail and looked pleased.

"This is my friend Reid Daniels." Kendall said.

"Umph," Eblodskya grunted. "A boyfriend?"

"Well, no. He is a friend. He's here to help me find someone that I think you know. But we don't need to talk about that right now. Can we come in?" Kendall asked.

"Yes, yes. By all means come in. I'll fix ya some breakfast. I just went to the Costco in Kalispell, and I have some fantastic thick slice bacon, some waffle mix and a dozen and a half of eggs. How's that sound?" the Professor said.

The house was warm and cozy with an open fireplace and electric wall heaters. Smooth and rounded river rock created the hearth and the surrounding of the fireplace. Overstuffed leather chairs and a couch were set beside and behind thick knotty pine tables with deer-horn lamps resting on each side table. Reading material covered it all. The ceiling was open to log rafters well above the living room and kitchen; Reid was sure they called this a great room.

Soon after they had arrived, the cabin was filled with the smell of bacon frying on a large built-in griddle that looked like it could have come from a Waffle House.

As she helped Eblodskya fix breakfast, mixing waffle mix and tending the bacon Kendall asked, "So tell me Winston, what have you been up to? Are you still teaching and travelling and tell me why do you stay here all winter and why no communications with the outside world? We were lucky to find you home."

Reid was setting the table and getting cups of hot black coffee for Kendall and himself.

Eblodskya began telling them about what he had done during the past year "or was it two years ago." And, in the manner of an old man telling stories, it went on and on through breakfast and into the breakfast dishes. He loved having people to talk to, or talk at, in his case.

When it appeared, Winston was running out of steam Kendall asked, "I need to call my assistant Kassie in Ketchikan to check in, then do you think I could take a shower?"

"Oh sure, I'll put you and your man right back here in the guest bedroom. It has its own bath. It's really like a second master bedroom."

Reid stood up and started to protest, but Kendall held her hand out in a stop signal at waste level behind her back while Eblodskya led her back to the guest bedroom.

Reid went out to the car and got their duffels then followed them into the back bedroom. As he entered the room, he could see that there was not only a queen-sized bed, but a large couch as well. That must be why Kendall had hushed him when he was going to protest the sleeping arrangements. He remembered that Kendall had stayed with Winston Eblodskya previously.

As he put their bags on the bed and turned to go back to the great room, Reid caught a glimpse of Kendall through the slightly open bathroom door. She was disrobing to get into the shower. Her body was smooth and fit with youthful looking curves. She certainly did not look to Reid's eye like a woman in her mid-forties. He wanted to be polite and look away, but he just couldn't make himself do it. Kendall looked up and saw him watching her, gave him a knowing smile then turned to get into the shower leaving the door open.

The warmth of the shower felt luxurious washing over her, and she was pleased with the look she had seen in Reid's eyes.

Reid turned away quickly, embarrassed, confused. He apologized to Charlie for not looking away when he should have. Charlie gave him only a half disapproving look in return. Reid walked back out to the kitchen where Winston was putting away the last of the breakfast dishes.

CHAPTER 39

February 20
Thursday Morning Western Montana Local Time

Yuri had arrived in Paris and his hotel which was about a mile from the Spring Restaurant. It was 9:00pm at night local time. He had time now to check his Geo Tracker app to see if Reid Daniels's car had finally come to rest. His headache had subsided.

On the flight, he had thought about this *"Job"* and all the *"Jobs"* he had performed for himself and for others. He had lost two long-time associates and for what and for whom he did not know. Yuri didn't know if he was getting soft or just tired. All he knew was that this would be the last *"Job"* and as such he wanted to make sure he was being extra careful.

First, he checked his Geo Tracker app. Agent Daniels's car was stopped in Western Montana on the shores of Flathead Lake near a town named Dayton. He could see that Dayton was about 40 miles from Glacier International Airport where he suspected Georgy and Luka could fly out after ending the Agent Daniels and Kendall Hughes saga.

Georgy and Luka Pajari had been in their rental car in Ritzville, Washington for the past two- and one-half hours waiting for instructions from Yuri. They were bored and had been bickering over who got to shoot FBI Agent Daniels and the woman. Typical sibling bickering.

"Yuri will want me ta do it, because I am a bedda marksman," Georgy said.

"This is crap. Why ve need your marksmanship? I could get close up and shoot them with a peestol or cut their throats,"

Luka argued.

"Maybe when we fine dem, it should be a race ta see who can keel them first and the winner gets sixty per cent of our take on this mission," Georgy fired back.

"Deel," Luka exclaimed, then he spit on his hand to shake on it. Georgy did the same and that seemed to placate the brothers for the time being.

Georgy began searching the Internet to see where they could privately print their composite plastic guns and buy ammunition. He decided it was a city called Spokane which was a little less than an hour away.

Luka was searching where they could find a strip club in Spokane that might be open in the early morning. He knew where there were strip clubs there was usually access to hookers and he decided they needed to make time for that in Spokane as well.

Finally, Georgy's encrypted phone rang. It was Yuri.

"Well, what are the limp dick Pajari brothers up to this morning?" Yuri asked on speaker phone.

"We want to keel somebody before I have to keel my fucking bradder to break the boredom. Will you tell my worthless bradder that you would prefer I keel these peeple up close and personal rather than his sniper type shot?" Luka pleaded.

"Let's talk about that in a minute. Your targets are in a place named Dayton, Montana. It's a very small town on a giant lake. You are about four hours away, but you will need to print your weapons and buy ammunition. I'd say that makes it 5 hours," Yuri said.

"Let's make it six hours. There is no place ta eat here," Luka said which was a lie. There were several places to eat in Ritzville.

"Okay six hours that will put you in the Dayton area just before dusk. I've checked and it should get dark there about 5:45pm. You will be able to scope things out and execute the targets shortly after it gets dark. On Google Earth, they look like they are in a private home. I think we need to assume that there could be some collateral damage as well at this location. We must assume that they may be on the move again before you get to them." Yuri was thinking through all the possibilities.

"What is collateral damage?" Luka asked.

"Other possible witnesses who you will need to silence," Yuri said. "I am sending the directions and coordinates to you right now. I have not slept for hours. I am going to bed and when I get up in about nine hours, I expect you will have good news for me. Do your best and end this! And be careful!" Yuri ordered.

"Veel do," Georgy and Luka said in unison as Yuri disconnected.

Now it was time to take care of something else that had been bothering him on his flight to Paris. Yuri was convinced that Analka Hrapla had been found out. It was time to get her out of there. Georgy and Luka would take care of Agent Daniels and Kendall Hughes in just a few hours. When they were out of the way, it would take the FBI several days if not a week to regroup. There was no need to risk Analka any further.

Analka's encrypted phone rang moments later.

"Wow," Robin Medallon said. "I don't think I have ever heard that phone ring before."

"It is probably my mum. She gets worried about me," Analka said. "Ehlo mummee. How are you? Every ting okay with you?

"Is your FBI man right there with you?" Yuri asked quietly.

"Yes, tings here are just fine. I am liking Seattle a lot. You should come here to visit. Ya?," Analka asked.

"Listen, Annie, I am sending Petra to get you out of there. We are just hours away from taking down Agent Daniels and Kendall Hughes. We will not need you there anymore. I don't want to risk keeping you in place any longer," Yuri explained.

"Mummee you so sneaky! You already here! Maybe I

could bring Robeen with me to see you. He knows Seattle very well. He could be useful in so many ways. What you tink?" Analka asked.

"That is not such a bad idea Annie. After Daniels and Hughes are out of the way, the FBI might look to Robin to pick up the case. Holding him in hiding for a while would give us all the time we need to wrap up this assignment," Yuri said.

In the back of his mind, Yuri knew that Analka was fond of Robin Medallon and if Analka and Petra could get him out of the way for a while, there would be no reason to kill him and upset Analka. He was getting soft Yuri thought to himself.

"Let's plan on that Analka. I will contact Petra and ask her to arrange a location," Yuri said.

"Sooo exciting mummee! We will plan to meet you in the lobby of the Olympic Hotel at seven tonight," Analka gushed as she looked at Robin for approval of the time.

It was set. Robin and Analka would be meeting her mother at 7:00pm that very evening. Robin was excited beyond belief that his new girl wanted to introduce him to her mother. This must be what they mean by cloud nine.

Analka had acted it well, but she was distressed. Ending her secret work here with Robin Medallon distressed her more than anything Yuri had ever asked of her.

CHAPTER 40

February 20
Thursday Early Afternoon Washington, DC Local Time

"Why on earth would the Chinese be so eager to escalate this?" President Parker asked of the assembled group in the Oval Office.

"As can happen, Mr. President, even slight incidents and miscalculations can escalate things out of control if we take the wrong tact on this incident. It could be a Chinese pilot who is trying to show off for his superiors. We can't assume that he was ordered to perform this risky stunt," said Secretary of Defense Justin Roberts.

"We have expressed our sadness and condolences to the Chinese for the midair collision. We are treating it like an accident," said Secretary of State Hertz.

"Our plane and crew will be on the ground within the hour and we will have time to debrief them to see what really happened," the Defense Secretary said.

"Sir, we are still working on the murder investigation, we just aren't there yet. My people are making progress," FBI Director Russell affirmed.

"We have to get this thing solved before we accidentally start World War Three and at the same time, we need to remain vigilant with the Chinese regarding their aggressive behavior. Do we have full alert with our ARIES group? There must be more activity by the Chinese than just this one Carrier task force," the President said.

"Our people think the Xi Jinping Carrier group could be a feint to get us looking there while their real thrust is somewhere else. All of this could be the result of the Chinese using this murder as an excuse to test some of their theories about our defenses and how we respond," said Secretary Roberts.

"It's a dangerous game they are playing if that is what it is," President Parker responded. "If it is chess we are playing, we need to find who murdered their diplomat and put the People's Republic into checkmate."

CHAPTER 41

February 20
Thursday 10:30am Montana Local Time

After helping Winston with the last cleanup of the breakfast dishes, Reid excused himself to go for a short walk where he could check in with Carlos Sanchez.

"Take Buttercup with ya," Winston said. "She can use the exercise and probably needs a little outside time."

"Go fer a walk Buttercup?" Winston encouraged, and with that the old dog dragged herself first into a sitting position, then slowly into a full stand and then waddled herself to the door, tail wagging, where Reid was waiting for her.

"Come on old girl, you can show me around," Reid said. Buttercup crowded her way out the windowed screen door ahead of Reid.

Late morning was inching its way into midday as happens in colder northern states like Montana. The sun was low on the southern horizon and even though it tried in earnest, it was not able to break completely through the high thin layer of clouds and the lower pockets of cold fog blanketing the sky over Flathead Lake. The light snow had stopped. Bushes and trees had large pillows of snow on their branches. Off in the distance there were the sounds of a truck engine and a jet passing overhead at 40,000 feet, probably headed to Seattle, but other than that Reid could hear only the crunch of cold snow under his feet and the occasional shuffling sound of Buttercup at his side.

As he was walking, Reid saw the news report of the

midair accident with the U.S. and Chinese military planes. He knew it had to be connected to the diplomat's murder and therefore his investigation. He felt the pressure. Charlie wasn't with him.

Reid punched up his ICP for Regional Commander Sanchez.

"Carlos, it's Reid."

"Reid, tell me you're making progress. Been hoping you have good news for me."

"Kendall knows the guy well. He is in his late eighties, so she is letting him warm up to us before hitting him with questions about his past student," Reid said. "He met us at the door with a gun, so at least he has put the gun down. I know the pressure is building on this investigation and we will start questioning him within the hour."

"Reid, the pressure has already built on this side, and you need to start questioning him right away," Sanchez said. Reid started to roll his eyes, then Sanchez said, "I am getting calls every half hour from the Director. I had to tell Lan Phang, the Chinese Internet Security officer, where you are. She is demanding to join you in Montana and did seem to have heard about the midair incident out in the Pacific?"

"Yes, I feel the pressure and we are on the questioning very soon. Let Lan Phang know that we are questioning someone, and we believe that will lead our investigation to another location. As soon as I know where we are headed, I will let you know, and she can meet us there."

"Okay, that sounds good Reid. Also, wanted you to know that Bert Hamilton, on your team, said to tell you there has been no outside activity on Agent Medallon's computer. Should I know what that means?" Sanchez asked.

"Not time to go into it now, but good to know."

"Oh! Chris Keller is recovering well! No brain injuries and no internal bleeding problems. Doctors say he has got to be in a lot of pain, but that Navy Seal sonofabitch is up and walking around in the hospital with over 200 stitches on his body most of them on his neck. He wants to get out of there asap."

"That is terrific news!" Reid exclaimed. "Okay Carlos, I have a person here I have to talked to, but as soon as we have anything, I will call you."

"Hi," Reid said as he ended the call.

"Hello, my name is Elaine Collier," Elaine said as she thrust out her hand which had a strong grip. "I see it's your turn to walk Buttercup." Buttercup was deep into getting her ear scratches and pets from Winston's neighbor.

"Very nice to meet you, Elaine. My name is Reid Daniels." Reid could see that contrary to Winston's description, Elaine Collier had a pleasant face, a pleasant demeanor, and a twinkle in her eye.

"How is Winston today? I worry about him. He doesn't take real good care of himself and since we are really the only ones down here in the winter months, I feel like it is my responsibility to watch after him."

"He seems to be doing well, but I can see the reason for your concern. I will let him know that you asked about him."
"That'll probably just make him mad. If you need anything, anything at all, I am just up the road here and I am happy to help," Elaine said as she turned to walk back up the gentle incline of the road toward her house.

"I'll keep that in mind and again very nice to meet you, Elaine.".

"You know what Mr. Daniels? I am thinking of making some chocolate chip cookies this afternoon. Do you think your crew would want some?"

"You bet! I know I would! I mean we would," Reid exclaimed. He had not had chocolate chip cookies since Charlie had passed away. "What a treat that would be!"

Reid watched Elaine turn and walk carefully up the hill. She was not nearly as old as Winston, but definitely a woman starting to show her age. Why is Winston so stubborn about her? She would be a great friend out here in the middle of nowhere.

"Come on Buttercup, you better come back with me," Reid coaxed the old dog to join him headed down the hill.

"Charlie, am I missing anything?" Reid asked.

"You are doing great Reid, but you need to step it up! The problems with China seem serious," was Charlie's response.

When he got back to the house, Kendall was out of the bathroom, dressed and looking fabulous to Reid's eye. She gave him a big smile.

"Winston, one of the reasons I came here, in addition to wanting to see how you are doing, is to ask you a question about a student you mentioned to me the last time I was here," Kendall said.

"Oh, who's that," Winston said as he was placing some more logs onto the open fireplace.

"Well, that's what I am here to ask you," Kendall continued. "When we were talking about the CP Pak technology a couple of summers ago, you began telling me about a Russian student who was very interested in what happened to the human body during the transmission interval, do you remember that?"

"Yesss, yes, I seem to remember that. Let me grab one of my journals back here," Winston said as he walked back into his study. He came back with a small green book which he had opened.

"Yes, here it is. Her name is A. Hrapla, and she was a very bright Russian girl. Maybe Russian and Czechoslovakian parents. I can't remember that part well. Pretty young thing and oh so bright. She was a huge fan of yours. Wanted to know how she could find you. Wanted to, how do the young people say it today, pick your brain," Winston said. "I of course told her that I had lost track of you."

"Curiosity is one thing, but did she do any research about the transmission interval and the effects on the human body," Kendall asked not knowing if their trip had been a waste of time.

"She was amazing! She was able to hack government computers and pull up actual research you had done on the transmission interval," Winston said. She was most interested in the time right before the molecular breakdown.

Kendall shot a look at Reid which told him this was what they were looking for.

"That is top secret stuff Winston. Weren't you worried about being caught for even knowing all of this?" Kendall asked with concern.

"After what the Feds did with your incredible groundbreaking research and invention, I thought it serves them right to have this young lady going through their files with impunity," Winston said smugly.

"Were you, her advisor? Did she share with you, the research she was doing?" Kendall asked.

With that question, Winston opened up with all that he knew about Analka Hrapla and her search for knowledge of the transmission interval during a CP Pak transfer. Over the next several hours, he described how Analka built her own small system and learned to vary the metallic stabilization chemicals to the point that she was able to show that a mouse actually moved around during the start of her transmission of the rodent over the internet.

Reid was totally lost during most of this dissertation, but Kendall Hughes was asking detailed questions, many of which Professor Eblodskya was unable to answer. During all of this, Kendall was intensely taking notes and at times stopping for as long as a half hour to make calculations and then continue with her questions. Several times, Professor Eblodskya had to dig in files in his office and in computer back up files to answer questions.

Finally, Kendall put down her note pad, turned to Reid and said, "Analka Hrapla is the real deal and is the connection to these murders. Now all we have to do is find her."

Reid was taking a breath to answer as a car was coming slowly down the drive. It was Elaine Collier. She left the car running and carefully made her way through the snow with a large plate of cookies. Reid could smell them as soon as he opened the door.

"Here are the cookies that I promised you," Elaine said with a smile.

"Thank you," Reid and Kendall said in unison.

"You must be Elaine. I am Kendall. It is so nice to meet you and for you to bring some cookies. These smell like they just came out of the oven," Kendall said. "Can you come in and sit for a while?"

"No, no. I need to run down the road to the Post Office. Are you going to be here a few days Kendall? Maybe you could come up tomorrow for coffee," Elaine answered.

"What about tomorrow morning? I'll bring your plate back. I remember it is usually lights out around eight o'clock and up early in this part of the country," Kendall said.

"That sounds nice. Winston, do you want me to check your mailbox at the Post Office?" Elaine asked.

"Whatever you like Elaine," Winston said gruffly.

"Okay, you all enjoy those cookies," Elaine closed the door and left.

"Winston, I think it's time that we have a drink," Kendall said. "Where's the liquor cabinet and what do you have?"

CHAPTER 42

February 20
Thursday 4:00pm Montana Local Time

Dusk painted itself across the sky in shades of gray creeping into the Flathead Valley when Georgy and Luka pulled off Highway 93 onto Ptarmigan Lane. They had followed the directions on the GPS file Yuri had sent to them. They were just short of sober again from their short excursion of drinking and whoring in Spokane. They were able to get their weapons printed with fake paperwork from Analka. They had two Glock style pistols and one rifle capable of being accurate up to 40 yards. In addition, Luka bought a hunting knife with an eight-inch blade. He loved the personal touch of a knife to use on his victims.

As they studied the latest live shot from Google Earth, Georgy and Luka were able to determine where Agent Daniels's car should be parked. The brothers decided they would leave their car parked at the top of the road near the highway and trek through the snow about a half mile where they could approach the house undetected from behind. A standard military Op.

As they stepped out of the car, Luka noticed that not 20 yards away, there was a phone box which likely served this section of the lakeshore. Having no way to know Winston Eblodskya's disdain for contact with the outside world, Luka thought it would be a good idea to cut off phone service. Tires crunching on ice alerted him to a vehicle slowing on the highway. It was an older Jeep driven by an older woman. Elaine Collier turned off the highway and drove slowly past the Pajari brothers and then turned down the road.

"Harmless old woman," Georgy said.

Luka took out his hunting knife and pried open the door of the phone box where he could see the connections inside.

"And if she gets in our way, we will keel her too," Luka laughed and cut the main wires. "Collateral damage!"

Darkness was beginning to win the battle over light as if it is being finely sprayed onto the valley floor. Georgy and Luka climbed a fence and took a direction that led them down the hill toward the house where they are certain they would find Agent Daniels and the woman. The snow was about three feet deep, but easy going as they worked their way down through the trees.

The wind was beginning to freshen and was coming across the lake at an angle from the right, blowing out of the southwest. Stars began to twinkle through the high thin clouds that were attempting to block them out.

As they approached the house from behind, Georgy and Luka stayed about thirty yards out and moved around to the right side where they could see through the big front windows which faced the lake. They could see three people inside, an older man and a younger woman who were seated by the open fireplace and a younger man who was standing near them.

Although they were quite certain they were at the correct house, there was still a little nagging doubt in their minds. The only time they had seen Agent Daniels and the woman was from the terminal, looking down on them walking across the tarmac in Ketchikan. The people they saw then were wrapped in heavy coats and hats.

"Whadda ya tink?" Georgy said. "Is that them?"

"I tink so," Luka said very quietly.

"Yuri say to be kerful and make no mistakes, Georgy said keeping his eye on the trio in the house. "Let's break the door down and charge in like door to door combat. Then, we can meke them show identification. When we confirm, we keel them all!"

The two crept in low, quick, and quiet, taking the three steps onto the porch in just two strides. The brothers exploded through the door crashing it inward with the powerful force of combat veterans.

Reid, Kendall, and Winston are completely startled by the force. Reid wanted to grab his gun but thought better of it. The two Russians, stinking of alcohol and body odor from two days on the road, began shouting.

"Are you fucking FBI agent Daniels? ARE YOU? AH YOU?" the older looking and shorter of the two demanded.

Luka approached Reid, found his gun in the back holster, punched him hard in the gut and then hit him across the face with the side of Reid's own Glock.

"How dare you break into my house!" Winston was struggling to his feet from his cushy fireside chair.

Luka knocked him to the ground with the same side of Reid's gun, "sit down you old fucka."

Luka grabbed Kendall's backpack which was hanging on the back of a kitchen chair and began dumping out the contents on the table. When he saw an I. D. case fall out, he picked it up and inspected it.

"Georgy, I'd say we haf the right people," Luka says smugly. "This is Kendall Hughes." He pauses and looks the three over. "Which one we keel first?"

"Good question. First you go up the hill and get the caw. After we snuff them, we need to get outta here quick. When you get back, you get to pick the one you want to keel first. Deal?" Georgy said.

"Okay, I get the caw, because I know you a lazy cocksucker, but you don't keel anyone till I get back," Luka said grudgingly.

After Luka left, Georgy poured himself a large drink and began making lewd comments to Kendall Hughes. Kendall sat down silently, staring straight forward, seeming to ignore him. Without looking, she knew her phone was on a nearby side table. She intentionally mixed metaphors in her mind as she determined that these guys were not the brightest tools in the shed. *"Remain present. Stay sharp,"* she tells herself. *"There might be a chance to get a call out to 911,"* she thinks.

Reid sees an opportunity to ask Georgy some questions. Through his pants pocket, he pushes the send button on his ICP. He hopes Bert Hamilton is getting the conversation.

"You guys are very good. I have no idea how you followed us here, but you finally have us. So, grant the wish of a dying man. Who do you work for? Who sent you after us?" Reid asks.

"Wouldn't you like to know," Georgy said with a smile.

"I would like to know. Are you part of the crew of Demitri Sanoff? We at the FBI think they are the best." Reid throws out a low-level Russian mob name.

"That is bullshit, Demitri Sanoff could not even make the Thorny Rose team, let alone get Luka und me verken for him," Georgy's tongue slips.

"Hey! What's that light in your pocket?" Georgy lunges forward, reaches into Reid's cargo pants pocket and grabs the ICP. The phone is thrown on the floor and stomped into small bits. Georgy saw Kendall's phone on the table and smashes it as well.

"Too bad you couldn't get that message out," Georgy smiled. "We are part of the Yuri Rosov team! We are the best! You are a dead FBI man!"

Luka was pulling their rental car next to Reid's Audi. Georgy glanced outside then back at the trio that he is ready to kill. "Luka's back. Who wants to die first?" Georgy laughed loudly.

Luka stepped out of the car, closed the door and was smashed in the back of his head with the butt of a 12-gage shotgun. He went down hard, nearly unconscious. His hands were quickly and forcefully pulled behind him and he heard and felt a zip tie bind his wrists. Next, he was quickly rolled over and his ankles were bound with a zip tie. Then, his ankles were pulled up and his hands were pulled back and the two are zip tied together.

It all happened in just over 18 seconds and the thought raced through Luka's mind that another "Seal Team" guy has been watching over Agent Daniels. Then Luka caught the faint scent of lavender, the kind that you smell around older women.

Elaine Collier, Ex U.S. Army Special Forces who served two tours of duty in Iraq, got to her feet. Through the broken doorway, she saw and heard Georgy speaking smugly and laughing. She climbed quietly up the steps, across the porch and was standing just to the side of the doorway when Georgy took a half step out the door to ask Luka what was taking so long.

THUD! Georgy took a hard punch from the butt of the shotgun to the side of his face and head. He went down in a heap. Quickly Elaine applies the same zip tie treatment to Georgy that she had performed on Luka.

"Be careful," Reid says as he comes to her side. "There is another one out here."

"Oh, he's tied up too," Elaine said casually. "Are you people okay? I saw these cheesy looking bastards parked up at the top of the hill about an hour ago and I just knew they looked like they were up to no good. Say, that's a nasty looking bump on the side of your face."

"Oh, I'll be fine," Reid said rubbing the side of his face.

"Reid, it's Winston, he is struggling to breath!" Kendall called out.

Reid and Elaine rush inside.

"I think we need to get him to the hospital in Polson, right away," Elaine said after a short examination.

"Can you do that for us, Elaine? We learned information today that we need to act on right away. I'm FBI and we are on a case with international ramifications. You are a damn hero here and you will be recognized later. Do you have a cellphone or a phone in your home that we can use?" Reid was talking fast.

"Which question do you want me to answer first? Yes, I

can take Winston to the hospital. Yes, here's my cellphone, but the main lines are out because these scum bags cut the lines up at the top of the hill," Elaine answered.

"You're a much better woman than Winston led us to believe, Elaine. We owe you our lives. Thank you so much for being here for us," Kendall said. "May I run and get your car for you?"

"Yes. That would be sweet of you dear. Here's the keys. "You'll see the old Jeep parked three houses up at the big turn," Elaine answered.

Reid was contacting Bert Hamilton on Elaine's cellphone. "Bert, it's Reid. We are in Montana."

"Hold on Reid, this looks like an unsecure phone you are calling on. We have no idea who might be listening. Robin's girlfriend may have hacked our phones as well as his computer," Bert said.

"My phone was broken in an attack on us. We are fine, just my phone is damaged. Where can I find a secure phone nearest to Dayton, Montana and get into the NSA system?" Reid asked.

Reid could hear Bert's keyboard clicking rapidly in the background of the call.

"Okay Reid. Your nearest location is Blacktail Mountain out of Lakeside, Montana. It's an old NORAD site where the NSA has equipment. You should be able to drive there in less than hour. You will need the code Grizzlies Kill On Sight 9042 Ask Other People, GKOS9042AOP," Bert said slowly.

"Here, give it to Kendall also, she's the smart one," Reid handed the phone to Kendall Hughes who had just returned.

"Let's get him loaded into your car," Reid said as he aided Elaine in moving Winston Eblodskya out of the shattered front door. "Can you tell me how to get to Blacktail Mountain?"

"Going skiing tonight?" Elaine smiled as she lifted the heavy patient.

"No, there are communications facilities there that I need to use," Reid grunted breathlessly back to her.

"Well, it's a ski area nowadays, but used to be a RADAR station back in the days of the Cold War of the 1950s, 60s and 70s. Easy to find. Go back up to the highway here, turn right onto Highway 93 and follow the highway to Lakeside about 22 miles up the road. You'll see the turn to the ski area off to your left as you drive down a hill to enter Lakeside. Then, just follow the road to the top of the mountain. It's only about ten miles, but it is a winding mountain road, and it takes a while. One of those unique ski areas, where the parking lot, ski shop and restaurant are all at the top of the mountain," Elaine finished as they got the old man loaded into the Jeep. "Help me get Buttercup in the back cargo area here. She'll go nuts if he's not around. I'll just take her with us."

"Here's your phone back, thank you. Please call the Sheriff or whomever you call here to come and get these two characters. They can contact the FBI in Seattle to get instructions on what to do with them. We are leaving immediately to go up to Blacktail Mountain," Reid handed the cellphone to Elaine.

As Elaine drove away Reid and Kendall dragged Georgy across the deck, down the steps and out to the parking area near where Luka lay motionless on the cold ground.

"You two dickheads ought to be easy for the law to find out here," Reid said under his breath.

Kendall got the keys out of the brothers' rental car and tossed them as far as she could out into the snow. After the close brush with death, she was fully engaged. She could see how the murders had been carried out during the CP Pak transports. Having full movement in the nano seconds before the start of the transport was not something she had researched, but she could see how it could be done. Who would want to do that? Now she knew how the men were killed in the CP Pak transports and she was ready to get to the bottom of who was behind the killings.

"Grab your warmest clothes. We're going to the Blacktail Mountain Ski area for some night skiing," Reid said with a little lilt in his voice. After facing death and coming out alive one can feel rather good about life in general.

"Elaine already tried that joke," Kendall said. "Maybe after this is over, we could come back to Montana and ski."

Reid picked up his Glock, checked it over and slipped it back into his behind-the-back waist holster. *"Reid, be sure to bring your gun so the bad guys can hit you up the side your head with it,"* he mimicked Regional Commander Sanchez to Charlie.

"Reid, I feel like I am distracting you. You need to be 100% in the present. Kendall Hughes is a good partner. Trust her. You are doing fine," Charlie said.

CHAPTER 43

February 20
Thursday 6:45pm Montana Local Time

As they approached Reid's Audi, he stopped, went to the passenger side and pulled a flashlight out of the glovebox and began looking under the wheel wells of the car. Near the passenger side rear wheel, he found a little box that looked like it did not belong. He pulled it out from the glue that was holding it in place under the car. A simple Geo tracking device was what allowed these two Russian killers to find Kendall and him so easily.

Reid dropped the device on the icy driveway and Kendall stomped on it with her boot. Reid slid the small high-powered flashlight into his jacket pocket.

No sooner had Reid and Kendall driven out of sight, than Luka Pajari called out to his brother laying just ten feet away, "Georgy, are you awake?" "Georgy, GEORGY, WAKE UP BRAADER, I know that old woman didn't keel us," Luka called louder each time.

"Uuhh, uuhh, what the hell happened Luka?" Georgy responded.

"What happened is them fuckas should have keeled us, because now we gonna catch them and really keel them this time," Luka vowed. "Rock up and down on your belly to get close to me. Come on. Verk at it Georgy. I have a knife in my pocket that can get us free then I know where they are going and how to get there. Blacktail Mountain," Luka said with a new commitment.

Luka and Georgy rocked themselves back and forth on

their bellies working to get closer and closer together. Luka could not believe that they had been bested by an old woman. He was determined to finish the work with the FBI Agent and the woman Kendall Hughes. Then, he would track down the old woman and "keel" her.

Clearly Georgy's head injury was worse than the mild concussion that Elaine Collier had administered to Luka. Georgy's fumbling hands were finally able to extract the hunting knife from Luka's pocket. After more arduous rocking and rolling on his belly, Luka had the knife in his hands. He slowly and methodically worked the knife until he was able to free himself and Georgy.

Luka helped Georgy to his feet and into the house.

"Georgy, you need stay here and wait for me," Luka instructed. Luka then moved a couch in front of the fireplace and helped Georgy to lie down. Luka stoked the fire with more wood and hung a blanket over the doorway to protect his brother from the cold.

"Here's your gun. Take care of yourself and I'll be back soon," Luka said as he walked out the door.

As he opened the door to the car and checked for keys, Luka shook his head in disbelief, "Stupid people. They leave our guns and the second set of keys in the glove box. They shudda keeled us. Stupid people. I keel them all now," Luka vowed.

While Luka was turning the car around in the driveway, Georgy, who had gained more clarity, was up and coming down the steps, "Luka, Luka wait. I go with you. We always better as a team."

Luka ran around the car to help his brother with tears forming in his eyes, "get in bradder. Good to see you getting better."

The two sped up the driveway in heated pursuit of their prey causing the car to fishtail and throw an occasional patch of gravel as the tires broke through the snow packed road.

Reid and Kendall reached the Blacktail Mountain turn off in Lakeside and started the drive up the mountain. There were cars coming down the hill. Skiers, who had stayed up at the lodge for a little alcohol to soothe their aching muscles while they told stories and laughed about the day's skiing adventures.

Reid remembered the days that he and Charlie had spent skiing and the times they had stayed after for a beer or two and maybe to split a chicken sandwich and some fries. Occasionally, Charlie insisted they have a salad.

"Are you a skier Kendall?" Reid asked.

"Yes, more cross country than downhill though," she answered. "Got started really late in life and I think downhill is something you need to learn when you are young."

"Charlie and I did mostly downhill and some snowboarding living in the Northwest," Reid said.

"Reid, we almost died back there. If not for that wonderful neighbor of Winston's, we'd be dead right now. I'm having a little trouble wrapping my head around that."

"Near death experiences have the effect of making a person appreciate life. We've all heard it before. Make each day count," Reid offered.

"I guess, but these fuckers are trying to kill us. Likely there will be more," Kendall said.

"With luck, the local sheriff will apprehend those two and it will be harder for The Thorny Rose to get more killers after us, now that I found his Geo tracking device on the car. In addition, we have shut down the spy who was following us through my contacts with my team member Robin Medallon. I have to say though, Kendall, every time I think we are in the clear, more of them keep coming. I am so sorry you had to be dragged into this," Reid reached his hand across the console to squeeze Kendall's hand. She squeezed back. Reid continued, "We have to stay alive and figure out who killed those diplomats and if any more people are in danger."

"This all seemed like a welcome adventure with a good-looking younger man until that stinking Russian was pointing a gun in my face," Kendall said. "It is more than that now. Now, it's personal. These guys are starting to piss me off." Kendall could feel the rage she had for men in general now building, focused on these Russian assassins.

"Good looking younger man," Reid thought. He liked Kendall's spunk. He had not been around many people as intelligent as Kendall, but her ability to be a normal person and show that spunkiness was an attractive characteristic, he thought. Charlie was right. Reid could trust Kendall in tough situations.

They drove into the parking lot of the Blacktail Ski area just as the last cars were heading out. The lot was not quite as level as most ski area parking lots. This lot, because it was on the top of the mountain, sloped up and away from them as they drove to the main building. The lot was about 100 yards wide and a quarter of a mile long.

A bearded man, driving an older model Ford F-150 pickup toward the exit road, waved them down as they approached to pass him by, "Can I help you? Everything is closed now. We don't have any night skiing."

Reid, who rarely did so, pulled his FBI badge to show the man. "I need to find the communications tower where the old NORAD Radar site used to be."

"Sounds serious. I can walk you up there. It's not far," the man said.

"Would we be able to find it without you?" Reid asked.

"Probably, but it will be easier for you officer, or do I call you agent, if I just show you where it is. My name is Bill Barrows. I am the manager of the bar and restaurant up here."

Bill parked his truck and Reid followed suit. The three walked up a snowbank on the uphill edge of the parking lot just to the right of the ski lodge. About 30 yards up, they passed the drop off of a chair lift. They could see and hear snow cat grooming machines working in tandem headed down the hill. At a point that Reid and Kendall might have missed the turn without him, Bill cut out into the ungroomed snow onto what looked like it might be a jeep trail in the summer. They slogged up the hillside through the hip high snow toward a small summit.

The communications building was well fenced and larger than Reid thought it would be. There were three radio towers of varying height, with the tallest being maybe 100 feet high, Reid estimated. There was also a domed building. The towers each had communications dishes and antennas suspended on them.

"This area up here at Blacktail Mountain is where the old radar dome used to be deployed. From here they could cover hundreds of miles on all points of the compass to scan for enemy or I guess Russian aircraft trying to come into our air space flying at low elevation. The original dome was big enough to cover, maybe three tennis courts and had this big sweeping dish that covered most of the space inside. That big antenna continuously swept around in big circles reading the sky. I came up here with my Boy Scout troop when I was a little guy. Guess the Air Force or Army or whoever had these things spread all over the mountains in the west. They overlapped each other in scan area. This smaller doom came along as electronics got smarter and smaller. Now, I think everything is done via satellite, but there are still people who come up here to check on things every month just in case the satellites lose communications. Anyway, here you are. I'll leave you to your business," Bill concluded his tour and not soon enough for Kendall Hughes.

Reid stepped up to input the code at the gate. Let's see, "Grizzlies Kill On..."

"That's GKOS9042AOP," Kendall impatiently broke it down for him.

The code worked at the gate and worked at the door of the larger of the two buildings. "Thank you, Bert Hamilton," Reid said almost under his breath.

There were three phones, not your normal looking sets, but phones, nonetheless. Reid picked up the first phone and had to punch in the code one more time to get a dial tone. With a dial tone he called the number of his main Seattle FBI Field Office and from there was able to call Carlos Sanchez directly on his ICP, all of it on secure lines.

"Carlos are you there?"

"Reid, you son-of-a-gun, I was worried you were dead. Where have you been? What's happening? I cannot stress enough how important solving this case is to our government. This thing just keeps getting more complicated as time goes by," Sanchez answered.

"Carlos, we found the connection to how a murder can take place during a CP Pak transport. Take this down. The name is A. Hrapla, more on her in a minute and, we know who is running the Russian gang that has been harassing us and is now bent on killing Kendall Hughes and me. Yuri Rosov, The Thorny Rose, is the gang leader. He is a hired gun. We still don't know who or why someone has hired his team for these murders and hired them to harass or shut down our investigation." Reid said.

"I will get these names to our team at Quantico. I don't recognize them, but that don't mean nothing, if you know what I mean. I also need to call pass your information up the chain of command," Sanchez responded. "What's your next move Reid? Do you have any information on where we can find these characters?"

"We've got nothing for sure Carlos. We were held at gun point just an hour ago, our phones were destroyed. I am calling you from a mountain top in Western Montana. As soon as I hang up from you, I am going to call my super sleuth Bert Hamilton to see what she can find out about Yuri Rosov and to have her coordinate with the general office in Seattle, through you, for the arrest of the young woman who has been hacking our team through Agent Robin Medallon's computer. Analka is her first name."

Kendall interrupted Reid, "listen to yourself. The girl with Robin is named Analka, a brilliant hacker it seems. The student of Winston's was a brilliant young woman named A.

Hrapla. I think it is one and the same person. Analka Hrapla is the key to the CP Pak transport murders."

"Reid, I think I heard all of that and I am on it. Do you need backup in Montana? I've alerted our guys in Missoula, Great Falls and Billings if you need them," Sanchez said.

"Right now, we are good. We don't plan on being in Montana for more than a few hours at this point. I'll call Bert and then we'll head out. Talk to you when I know more Carlos," Reid closed.

Reid hung up, had to input the code one more time and then he called Bert Hamilton in Talk-Back mode.

"Bert, it's Reid, you available?"

"Reid. Finally. I was worried you were dead. Commander Sanchez said you might be and that it would be a shame because this is so important to Director Russell and President Parker," Bert Hamilton blurted out with the sound of a busy restaurant in the background.

"We are not dead," Reid responded. "Sounds like you are in a restaurant, can you take down these names?"

"Give me a second, okay go ahead, I'm recording you right now. Totally secure," Bert said.

"We need to find the high-tech whiz named Analka Hrapla and a Russian gang leader Yuri Rosov aka the Thorny Rose," Reid instructed. "Does the girl's name ring a bell for you?"

"Reid, that girl who has been banging and hacking Robin, I'm pretty sure that he said her name is Analka. I don't know if that is a common name in Russia or Czechoslovakia, but quite sure that is hers," Bert said excitedly.

"Kendall and I believe she is the same person and that would be a huge break for us. It would be great to get two birds with one stone," Reid said.

"That bird stuff is a great cliché. Haven't heard that for a while. Love working with old people. I will get the paperwork handled and see if Chris feels well enough to pick her up," Bert said.

"Chris Keller is out of the hospital and back in Seattle?" Reid was amazed.

"Yeh, that Indian stud got out of the hospital, took a flight down from Ketchikan and arrived this evening. Don't expect me to show that kind of dedication if I get blown up on the job."

"Point well taken Bert. That is wonderful news. Say hi to him for me. We are going to finish up here and head back to Seattle tonight. As I said earlier, my secure phone is down, so the only way I will be able to contact you is on an unsecured phone. Keep that in mind. Find out what you can about our Analka and Thorny Rose being friends and have Chris pick up Robin's Analka," Reid instructed.

"Also, law enforcement in Polson, Montana is apprehending two Russian thugs who came out here to kill Kendall Hughes and me. Please contact Polson and let them know that these guys are extremely dangerous. They will need to hold them until U.S. Marshals can pick them up. Please get all of that in the works," Reid continued.

"Oh, Reid, just so you know, I am at dinner with Lan Phang, our Chinese counterpart. How much of this should I tell her?"

"Check with Commander Sanchez on that..." At that moment a gun shot rang out from the direction of the parking lot. Reid paused. A few seconds later a second shot was heard. "Gotta go Bert!"

Bill Barrows had left Reid and Kendall at the communications towers and realized he had forgotten his list of supplies that he needed to purchase in Kalispell the next morning. He trudged back up to his office to grab the list. Lucky thing running into those FBI guys, he thought.

As he came back out of the lodge, Barrows saw a man kneeling by Reid's Audi. He approached to see what was going on. As he drew near, he saw that the man was running a large hunting knife into the right rear tire. Before Barrows could say anything or turn away to run, the man with the knife pulled what looked like a toy pistol out of his pocket, aimed at Barrows and shot him in the chest. Barrows fell to the ground clutching his chest. Luka Pajari stepped over the struggling man and shot him in the head.

CHAPTER 44

February 20
Thursday 8:04 pm Montana Local Time

Reid and Kendall had to use the code to back out of the communications building and the fenced area. Rather than go down the trail they had come up, they worked their way around the fence to the other side of the summit and down a steep embankment in waist high snow. Adrenalin was pumping and they were able to make it through the deep snow for 200 yards downhill then hit the main road just short of the ski area parking lot.

They were moving through the shadows on the edges of the parking lot where they could see Bill Barrows on the ground and a dark pool around his head. They also recognized Georgy's and Luka's car.

"Damn, those bastards must have gotten themselves free before the law got to them," Reid gritted his teeth and clutched his gun from his back holster.

"Is that them on the far side of the parking lot?" Kendall asked.

"As soon as they go around the building, let's make a run for my car," Reid said.

In an instant they were in a sprint to Reid's car. When they got there, they hid on the driver's side out of view of where they last saw the Russians. The punctured tires were clearly visible.

"Fuckers," Kendall hissed.

"Stay here, maybe Bill's keys are in his pockets," Reid said. He stayed low around the corner and was back moments later.

"They must have pulled the keys," Reid said. "I don't know if that old truck is the best getaway vehicle anyway."

"We will discuss later how we did not grab all of their keys, but right now I have an idea Reid. What if we ski out of here back toward Winston's house? While you were making your calls up there, I was looking at a topographical map on the wall. Here look at my hand. We are at the top of four ridges."

Kendall held out her right hand with the back of her hand up. She made a fist, straightened her fingers out to the middle knuckle which she kept bent, then she parted her fingers with the ends still in the bent position.

"The ridges look like my half open fist and my four fingers. Right over there is the ridge for my middle finger. We can start down that ridge on cross country skis, cross over to the right when that ridge tails off, then one more time to the right at the next ridge and that takes us down to within a walking distance of Winston's house," Kendall explained.

"I'll just get the skis off the rack on the car, and we can start right out," Reid said sarcastically.

"Don't be a ninny. We can find gear right over there." Kendall pointed at the Ski Shop.

Georgy and Luka had made their way around the building travelling uphill past the ski lift to where the trail took off to the right toward the dome and the communications building.

They moved a little more slowly as they approached the building.

Meanwhile, Reid and Kendall were breaking into the ski shop.

"It's got to be cross country," Kendall said. "You okay with that."

They quickly fitted themselves out, grabbed a backpack to hold their regular winter shoes and moved out the front door. The ski shop crew had a box of Cliff Bars which Kendall grabbed and put in the backpack. She then ran over to the vending machine and bought four bottles of water.

"Good God woman, hurry up. This is not going to be a picnic. They have to be coming by now."

"You burn a lot of energy cross country skiing. Okay let's go." Kendall pushed past Reid and out the door.

Far across the parking lot a shot rang out but came nowhere close to them. Georgy and Luka had followed their tracks around the fence and down to the road on the backside of the summit and were running and swearing from more than an eighth of a mile away.

With skis in hand, sprinting as best they could in cross country boots, Kendall led Reid straight across the 100-yard width of the parking lot and scrambled up and over a snowbank.

"Mount up cowboy! Get your skis on," she shouted as she scrambled down the other side of the snowbank.

In little time at all, with powder snow up past their knees, they began stepping and gliding down the mild descent of the top of the middle ridge. By the time the huffing and puffing Pajari brothers had reached the top of the embankment, Reid and Kendall were well out of range of the 3D rifle. The two Russians sat on top of the mound of snow catching their breath.

"What we do now?" Luka gasped.

"They headed down to the old man's house, I tink," Georgy tried to think things through. "But we cannot let them go. You need to follow them Luka."

"I cannot ski," Luka protested.

"Yes, but this is a ski place. They got to haf two-man snow sleds. Follow me." Georgy was gaining his clarity.

The moon was nearly full, the cloud cover had thinned, and visibility was clear. Snow encrusted treetops looked like an army of ghostly figures standing on the mountain. Reid and Kendall were making good time letting gravity do the hard work, but that didn't last forever. They came to a steeper embankment and had to step turn across the hillside to go down. It was a good half mile down the hill to the second ridge.

Kendall led the way. As she skied, she shouted back to Reid who was struggling a little.

"Remember, keep your weight out over your downhill ski, that will help you to keep turning back into the mountain. We're going to stop here in a little and rest a bit."

This was now hard work. Their thighs burned with exhaustion. Their muscles were not used to this kind of work. When skiing outside groomed boundaries like they were, they had to avoid tree wells. Tree wells are caused by snow around a tree trunk and under the branches not being packed as tightly as the snow out away from the tree. If skiers get to close, they can fall in next to the tree like falling into a well, usually face first, head down with skis on top. Loose powdered snow falls in around them and they can suffocate easily by being trapped upside down in a pile of snow.

Kendall stopped about a quarter of the way down the embankment to the next ridge. Reid turned into a stop beside her.

"It's time to catch our breath, grab a drink of water and share a cliff bar," Kendall breathed heavily as she reached into the backpack Reid was carrying.

Georgy and Luka had located the equipment shed. Sure enough, there were two snowmobiles parked there. The first one they tried started right up.

Georgy shouted, "Okay Luka, you follow their tracks and I'll drive down to the old man's house and wait for you. When you catch them, you keel them!"

Luka gave a determined nod, gunned the throttle of the snow machine, and raced across the lot jumping up and over the snowbank on the opposite side.

Georgy could hear the whine of the snow machine getting further and further away as he walked back to the car. "You may have short time to live FBI man," he said under his breath.

"You okay," Reid and Kendall questioned each other in unison. They laughed a little at that.

"People bent on killing us and here we are laughing," Kendall said with a smile as she looked directly into Reid's eyes.

They each had a long drink of water, assured one another they were good to go, then they turned down the mountain again. As they began their descent, the sound of the snow machine could be heard off in the distance. With the strenuous effort needed to stay upright and moving down the steep incline, Reid and Kendall did not hear it.

Kendall again let Reid know she was going to stop. They were each gasping for air and at the same time gazing at the incredible nighttime winter beauty of the moon shadows that surrounded them. As they came to a complete stop, they could hear the faint sound of the whining snow machine.

"Do you think that's our guys?" Kendall asked.

"I'm sure of it. Maybe we miscalculated."

"Maybe they miscalculated," Kendall said. "That snow cat will need to back track to make it down this steep stretch here. That might just give us time to lose them."

The skiers cut their rest short and pushed on down the hill, finally making it to the flatter descent of the next ridge. The sound of the snow machine was getting louder and louder. They could hear it back tracking trying to traverse the steep embankment which they had just come down. It sounded as if it would be just a few minutes before it caught up to them.

As they approached an open edge of the ridge where the wind was blowing the snow around in circles, Kendall pulled to a stop.

"I think we can pull off through this windy area and head down into the trees. The wind looks like it can cover our tracks and going through those trees will be tough sledding for the snow machine," she said.

"It's worth a try," Reid answered.

It was at least 100-yards to the trees. The strong wind continued at that point on the ridge. The blowing snow was burying their tracks, but it also made the skiing extremely difficult. Just as they were able to slide out of sight into the trees, the snow machine went speeding past at the top of the ridge. Soon the whine of the engine was growing faint again.

"We've lost him for now. This is a big mountain. Maybe we have lost him for good," Reid said.

Kendall handed Reid the water and a half a Cliff Bar.

For the next half hour, they worked their way through the densely treed hillside coming out on top of the final ridge. It had been a while since they had heard the snow machine.

Suddenly, it was back and growing louder. This time, it was coming uphill from in front of them. They could not go back up hill to get away.

"We can't outrun it. We need to set a trap. I have an idea," Kendall said.

"A trap?" Reid questioned.

"Yeh, let's get to those trees and I will tell you what I am thinking," Kendall said as she pushed off.

Luka was unhappy with himself. It had been easy with his head light following the pair of ski tracks down the ridge lines. But now, he had lost them. He felt that circling back lower on the hill would allow him to pick up their trail again, but so far nothing.

With the sound of the snow machine getting closer and closer, Kendall, then Reid, came to a stop. When death chases you and is drawing near, you have hidden reserves. Neither of them was as tired or as exhausted as before.

Kendall turned to Reid with urgency in her voice and in her eyes.

"Here's my plan. We are going to make it look like I have fallen into a tree well. Hurry!" Kendall said while taking off her skis, boots and pants with the snow machine growing louder.

"Help me stuff snow in my pant legs. We want the skis upside down and the bottom tips of my poles sticking out of the snow. You'll be digging trying to get me out," Kendall said.

The snow machine was meandering, looking for their trail, drawing closer, but still out of sight.

"Why don't we have me fall into the tree well?" Reid

asked.

"Don't be crazy. These are sexist Russian assholes we are dealing with here. Of course, they will buy the ruse of the weak little woman falling into the tree well," Kendall said snidely. "At your signal, I will pop up out of the snow and shoot the fuckers with your gun."

"Wait a second," Reid said.

"We don't have time to argue, we've used your crazy ass plans before. Now, it's time to use my very well thought out plan. All you need to worry about is the execution and what the signal is, hurry!" Kendall demanded.

The snow machine was closing in from a few hundred yards away. Reid was arranging her skis along with her poles to make it look like a tree well accident. Kendall went to the adjoining tree and began carefully working her way under the snow.

"Hand me your gun," she held out her hand. "I know what I am doing Reid, I have shot more than an antique Colt 45. Do I have 14 rounds?" she asked as she slid one into the chamber and worked her way under the powder.

"Yes, and my signal is Russian asshole," Reid said. "Got that?"

He heard a muffled "yes".

"Jesus, she is going to freeze to death. If she can't take him down, I will have to rush him," Reid was thinking. Reid turned toward the fake scene with his back to the sound of the snow machine that was closing fast now.

When Luka saw Reid, he was still 50 yards out and could not quite see what was going on. He slowed the snow machine and drew closer. There he could see that one of the two had fallen into a tree well. He had heard of this, but never seen it. He killed the motor.

"What we got goin on here?" he said smugly. As he walked closer, he had his 3D gun in one hand and his knife in the other.

"She's going to suffocate, if we don't get her out of here!"

Reid said as he was digging frantically.

"That means I only have to keel you," Luka continued walking closer.

When he was right on top of Reid, Reid turned and shouted, "you Russian Asshole, help me get her out!"

Nothing!

Reid's mind panicked. *"Was she still conscious?"*

"How bout I keel you first?" Luka was raising the gun.

"YOU FUCKING RUSSIAN ASSHOLE," Reid shouted at the top of his lungs.

Like an ancient snow creature, Kendall Hughes began rising out of the snow. It was as if she was in slow motion or at least that is how Reid saw it. Kendall began unloading the Glock into Luka Pajari. The shots split the night air with small flames coming out the barrel.

Luka was caught totally off guard and was not able to return fire or take a shot at Reid. Kendall fired until Luka dropped to the ground.

The phrase from Carlos Sanchez echoed through Reid's mind again, *"and Reid bring your gun, so a woman can rise up out of the snow to kill the bad guy and protect you."*

With Luka Pajari gurgling blood, Kendall walked over to him, aimed the gun at his head and said, "this is for Bill Barrows." With that she pulled the trigger again. Kendall then dropped the gun where it steamed in the snow. A tear ran down her cheek.

CHAPTER 45

February 20
Thursday 6:54pm Seattle Local Time

Robin Medallon and Analka Hrapla walked arm in arm into the lobby of the Olympic Hotel in downtown Seattle. They were there, ostensibly, to meet Analka's mother.

The Olympic Hotel held the old-world charm of its 1900s era construction. At one time, the building was the site of the University of Washington. The hotel had been upgraded over the years and the ornate lobby had the appearance of a classic large lobby hotel like those found in Europe. The ceiling was two and a half stories high with four giant chandeliers placed across the vast expanse. The floor was marble with huge inlaid rugs, multiple seating areas capable of holding 6 to 8 people each on comfortable love seats and cushy armchairs arrayed around French coffee tables. The walls and columns were covered with a rich honey maple wood. The kind of place that made Robin Hamilton feel like he was somebody.

Analka parked Robin in one of the seating areas and asked him to relax there while she went to call her mother's room.

Robin was excited to meet Analka's mummee. He had never known anyone who stayed at the Olympic Hotel, and he had never been asked to meet a girl's mother. This was heady stuff for a computer geek.

"Mummee wants us to come up to her room. She has a

suite of rooms," Analka cooed in Robin's ear when she came back. She grabbed his hand, "Come on."

As they got into the elevator, Analka said, "mummee is in room four oh four on the fourth floor. Isn't that romantic?" She pulled herself to him and gave him a deep kiss that lasted from the lobby to the fourth floor. Robin's head was swimming.

Analka wanted to make this as easy as possible for Robin. She did not want him hurt and certainly did not want him killed.

They walked to Suite 404 and started to knock, but Analka saw the door was held open by the safety lock extended. She gently pushed the door open, turned to Robin and whispered, "she must still be getting ready." Analka walked in and motioned for Robin to follow.

As he was taking in the grandeur of the white and blue décor of the spacious luxury suite, a hand quickly came from behind and forcefully held a wet cloth tight over Robin's nose and mouth. He could feel Analka had grabbed his wrists and was holding them from pulling the cloth away. In a split second, Robin was unconscious and slumped to the floor.

Petra Lane and Analka stripped Robin down to his boxers, put his clothes in a laundry bag and placed it in the hallway by their door. They tied him spread eagle to the posts of the bed. Yuri had trained Petra that when holding hostages, always take their clothes away from them. This makes it more difficult for them to escape.

In normal circumstances, Robin would have found his position of being tied up by two pretty young women to be quite exciting. However, for the next hour or so he would not feel a thing and hereafter his life would experience a dramatic shift from his previous reality.

Bert Hamilton and Lan Phang, Internet Security expert of the People's Republic of China, were digging to find information on Yuri Rosov, the Thorny Rose. They were working from the FBI Internet Crime Division offices in downtown Seattle. They were taking a forward view of where Yuri was right now, while a cyber forensics team at Quantico was looking backward to see where Yuri had been.

Bert had ordered pizza and salad from Pagliacci Pizza, and they were enjoying it at the snack bar in the kitchen. Lan Phang loved it. Bert thought that they were hitting it off well. Lan's English was very good, exceptional really, Bert thought. She had challenged Bert to a game of ping pong if they took a break in the middle of the night.

Quantico was able to track Yuri back to his days as a student at the Wharton's School of Business at the University of Pennsylvania.

"Why is it that all of these people are always educated in the United States," Robin asked rhetorically.

"Because the United States is the best place in the world to learn to be a criminal," Lan Phang responded naturally without thinking.

"Lan," Bert said, "what would you think of narrowing our search to photos of Yuri Rosov, then start connecting into public cameras in all the places where we know murders have taken place? Bert would have the team at Quantico expand from there into areas of deaths of diplomats over the past three months, six months, a year."

"I like that, Bert. By seeing where he has been, we can build a timeline coming forward. If we do it well enough, we can fast forward on him and catch up to where he is right now," Lan said enthusiastically.

"I think we can save time Lan, if we use each other's systems and share breakthroughs as we make them," Bert offered.

From her coat pocket hanging over a chair across the room, Lan's encrypted communications device chirped. "I think that is a great idea, Bert," Lan replied as she went to answer her phone.

Lan answered her encrypted phone in crisp Mandarin, "Hello Lan here."

"Hello Lan, this is Jen-Sheng Wei and Hai Chang," Chinese Ambassador to the U.S. Consulate in Washington, DC and Intelligence and Security officer from China's Consulate in Washington, DC who had returned to DC from Seattle. "Are the Americans making any progress on this murder investigation? We must report to Xi Jing Ping."

"It looks like the murder is by a Russian assassination team, seems there is no government involvement from old man Putin, but we do not know yet the why of the murder," Lan Phang reported. "The Americans are very co-operative. I am working side by side with them." Lan Phang hoped her role sounded even bigger than it was. This was important to a young security officer, especially a woman.

"That is very good progress, Lan," Hai Chang said. "Not sure why we have not heard this from the Americans yet. Stay in the middle of things and report in often. Goodbye."

"I will. Goodbye."

"My bosses," Lan said. "They were happy to hear that we are making progress."

"Let's see if we can make some more. I am ready for an all-nighter," Bert said as she popped open a Red Bull.

"An all-nighter?" Lan questioned.

"That's when we work through the night."

"We just call that a normal day of work in the People's Republic," Lan said with a big smile at the joke she made.

The two young women laughed and dug back into their searches.

2700 miles to the east, President Parker was receiving a briefing from his Secretary of State Emily Hertz. The other cabinet members were in attendance.

"It would seem to me that with all of the technology that the American people pay for, we would be able to find this

Thorny Rose guy in a snap," Parker said snapping his fingers for emphasis.

"We have known who he is for over an hour and still we have no clue where he is or why he is doing this. With the Chinese playing the serious stakes war games, it is not tolerable that we, ALL OF YOU, have not pinned him down. Any change in the Xi Jing Ping carrier group?"

"The group is still steaming toward Hawaii. We also have some probing by Chinese subs in the Philippines and Australia. Those parries have been blocked and we are tracking them with our subs," Secretary Hertz said.

"We have 12 ARIES planes in the air around the clock tracking the Chinese and Russian Navies. The North Korean's have used this unrest as an opportunity to launch a newer version ICBM over Japan and the Russians have subs probing defenses along the western and eastern coast of South America. It is a damn mess out there, sir," reported Secretary Roberts while CIA Director Tang pulled up charts on the table vision.

"They are all looking for some sign of weakness in order to further their own positions," Tang said. "Our intel shows that none of them, including the Chinese have any real plan to get into a skirmish with us, but they are ready just in case we or one of the others makes a mistake. It's all quite volatile. Any missed steps now and we could have a hot war on our hands."

"What's our FBI team on the ground doing," Parker demanded.

"They are moving as fast as they can sir," Director Russell responded. "We're running down facial recognition in Seattle and Quantico. The Chinese are helping us in Seattle with their own AI computers in China. This Thorny Rose has a very advanced hit team, and they must be using incredible makeup and disguises to beat the cameras."

"Emily, have we informed the Chinese consulate what we know about this Thorny Rose team," Parker asked his Secretary of State.

"Not yet sir, we have waited for your order on that," responded Emily Hertz.

"Dammit, we need to be better than that. Their people have likely already reported in. It will look like we are trying to hide something," Parker said. "From now on, when we know, they know. Is that clear?"

"Anything else? Anything we should be doing that we are not? I want to be briefed again at 5:00am," Parker demanded as he stormed out of the room.

CHAPTER 46

February 20
Thursday 9:30pm Montana Local Time

Reid held Kendall in his arms as she shook uncontrollably for the next several minutes. Clearly the life and death pressure of the past four hours all came bubbling to the surface after she had killed Luka Pajari.

As she began to calm, she pulled her head back and gazed into Reid's eyes while still in his comforting embrace. In the bright moonlight he could see moisture along her eyelids top and bottom. She looked tender and vulnerable.

"We'd better get a move on," he said gently. "We don't know where that other nut job Russian is right now. Let's get you back into your pants again and put on our own shoes. We can ride this thing down the hill."

Not forty yards away, first one howl, then more timber wolves broke the silence of the forest. Reid pulled the flashlight from his jacket pocket and shined it in the direction of the howl which had started again a little to their left now. Six sets of eyes were in a semicircle behind them.

Reid picked up his pistol from the ground and popped in his reserve clip. Slowly he moved toward the snow machine pulling Kendall with him.

"Not sure why we did not think of this, in the first place," Kendall said. "But I am very happy our man pulled it around for us."

"Have you ever driven one of these," Reid asked.

"Of course," Kendall said as she climbed into the front position on the sled and turned the key. The snow mobile roared to life, Reid climbed onto the back, and they pulled away from the scene of Luca's death, slowly at first, then Kendall advanced the throttle. As they sped out of sight, the wolves moved in to inspect the blood they could smell. It was not likely that there would be much left of Luca Pajari by morning light, maybe his hands and the bottoms of his feet, Reid thought. He'd read that once in a book written by David McCullum.

Kendall got her bearings and started moving along the right side of the bench they had been travelling on and toward the next bench to the right which would take them back to Professor Eblodskya's cabin.

With Kendall driving, Reid knew that they were only half done with the Russians. He had no plan. But he knew that they were going to have to deal with the other Russian before the dim light of the northern sun shed warmth on tomorrow. He remembered the conversation he had had with Chris Keller and their determination that whoever it was that was after them was working to slow down the investigation and at this point, they were accomplishing that goal. He wondered what was happening in Seattle, in D.C. and he thought about Charlie. He hoped that Charlie was able to forgive him for the feelings he had for Kendall Hughes which were stirring ever stronger.

Though focused on driving the snow machine, Kendall was pleased with what she had done, and she was mentally preparing herself to face the other Russian. She guided the snow machine along the right side of the bench. She was looking for a point where they could safely turn down the hill toward the last bench to the south. That would take them back to Edblodskya's cabin.

Suddenly, the shorter trees were beginning to move around them. She quickly recognized that they were sledding up to the edge of an elk herd. This was an incredible sight. At least 200 elk, to Kendall's estimate, were grazing on this moonlit night on the tops of grasses that had been cleared of the recent powdery snow by the Southwest winds. The wind had been gaining strength all evening. This herd would explain the wolves earlier, she thought. Wolves' main source of food is sustained by following elk herds.

"How do they keep warm out here in this frigid weather," Reid half shouted to be heard over the rattatatat of the snow mobile engine running at slow speed around the elk.

"Promise you will not make fun of my knowledge," Kendall responded.

"Pinky swear," Reid said. "As soon as we can get our gloves off.

"Okay, they have two sets of fur. Fuzzier, wool-like fur close to their skin and a longer hairier fur on the outside of that," Kendall explained. "And, they have big bodies as you can see. That also helps them stay warm out here."

Even in the moon light the majestic coloring of the elk is shown through. Kendall picked a path to the right edge of the herd and moved slowly past the animals. When she was sure that they were clear, she throttled up and continued down the ridge.

In a half hour, they pulled to a stop at the break over the last bluffs and where they had pulled clear of the trees. They could see Flathead Lake shimmering in the moon light before them. It was now easy for Reid to see Wild Horse Island tucked along the west shore on the right of this picturesque view. In the panorama there was a large expanse of water stretching off the eastern edge of Wild Horse Island on the left. The east shore of the lake lay up against the base of the Mission Mountains some 17 miles way. They stopped for a moment to take in the moonlit breath-taking beauty of it.

Puffs of grainy already fallen snow was pelting them painfully in the face as the wind was beginning to gust from about two o'clock out of the southwest across the lake and then gaining speed as it climbed the hill to them. Kendall started the snow machine up again taking long zig zags across and down the hill until they were just above the main highway near where they had turned off to go down the road to the Professor's house that morning. It was ten minutes past midnight.

"Okay, what do we do from here?" Kendall asked as she shut down the snow machine.

"Let's hope that Elaine has returned, or the sheriff is waiting here so we can call for an extraction," Reid breathed. "That's my hope but my gut tells me that the other Russian is down there waiting for his brother to come down the hill with the good news that we are dead. When he finds out that we are alive, he will know that we got the best of his bradder," Reid mimicked the Russian, "and he is going to want to "keel" us."

The wind had picked up dramatically. In the moonlight, they could begin to see whitecaps coming across the lake toward the shore below them. Temperatures were dropping.

"This wind should dampen the sound of the snow machine," Kendall said. "That could give us time to idle down to Elaine's house at the big switchback corner. From there we can see if she is back home or has any other transportation. I think we should be able to see if the Russian's car is back down at Eblodskya's place as well. Whadaya think?"

"I like the idea of moving down there as far as we can on the snow mobile. I also think instead of being the hunted, we become the hunters," Reid said with intensity.

"Let's go. Elaine may have more weapons at her house as well," Kendall said as she started the machine.

With the light off and running only at an idle, they began working their way slowly down the access road toward Elaine Collier's house. They pulled through the sharp corner at Elaine's house alongside a large juniper shrub and shut down the machine. They were hidden behind the shrub out of view from the Professor's house.

They listened for a moment. The wind was loud blowing through the evergreen trees. Faintly, they heard a voice coming from down the road, "Luka, Luka, is that you?" "Luka, Luka," Georgy called out. This time a little closer.

Reid pulled his gun and crouched by the snow machine

expecting Georgy to burst around the corner of the shrub at any moment.

Kendall grabbed Reid's sleeve and jerked him in her direction. They both slid out of sight down a landscape embankment toward the lake side of Elaine's house. But, not before Georgy was able to catch a glimpse of the two of them. He fired two shots.

"YAH FAWKING KEELERS!," Georgy screamed. "WHAT HAVE YAH DONE TO MY BRAADER?" Georgy was carrying a bolt action deer rifle. He carefully came down the embankment after them. He was on a rampage, but also moving with some caution.

Reid and Kendall quickly broke the glass of a sliding glass window on the daylight basement of Elaine's house. As he passed through the broken glass behind Kendall, Reid reached back to fire two shots at Georgy to slow him down. It worked and gave them a little time to scramble out of the basement to the kitchen upstairs. They needed to use Reid's flashlight intermittently to show them the way.

Georgy was still coming after them and firing a second weapon which sounded like a .22 pistol. Reid fired two more shots to slow Georgy down. During the exchanges as Reid held Georgy in the stair well, Kendall quickly explored the garage. Elaine did not have another vehicle. She also found that Georgy had taken every weapon from a gun safe he had broken into.

"I'm down to my last six in the clip," Reid whispered. "The rest of my ammo is in my car at the top of the hill. We can't sustain a gun battle with this guy. We are dead ducks out in the open and he shows no signs of stopping."

"How are you in a Kayak?" Kendall asked.

"What are you thinking?" Reid asked.

"I know the next-door neighbors have two kayaks under their deck. They have let me use them before," Kendall said. "Hold him off. I am going back into the garage. I think I saw sleeping bags in there."

Georgy reached around the corner of the stairwell and fired into the kitchen. Reid was holding the line. He got off a shot that he knew hit the Russian on the forearm because he heard him grunt in agony. Georgy took a moment to assess his wound. He determined it was only a flesh wound, but it gave Reid and Kendall the time they needed.

They exited the house through the man door of the garage and closed it quietly behind themselves.

"Five left," Reid said. "We probably have only a minute and he'll be on top of us."

The wind was blowing hard, and it was growing even colder. They carefully ran to the house next door on the frozen road leaving no tracks. The kayaks were under a large deck off to the side of the neighbor's house. Reid and Kendall were able to walk under the eaves of the house. They were leaving minimal tracks which the blowing ground snow quickly covered.

When Georgy realized that he was alone in the house, he cautiously exited through the garage man door. Weary of an ambush, he was moving slowly checking all around himself. Visions of his brother were haunting him. He could see Luka as a small boy, a teenager and a young man. How could Luka have allowed these two to get the best of him? These thoughts made him even more cautious. That caution allowed Reid and Kendall the time they needed to prepare to escape on the lake using the kayaks.

Kendall whispered, "Take off this cover like this. You should have one of these in your kayak. It's called a skirt," she whispered. "You put it over your head and pull it down to your waist. You then fasten it to the kayak when we get in the water. It keeps the water from getting into the kayak."

Reid did as Kendall had shown him. "What are you thinking with these?"

"I am thinking we can go with the wind up the shoreline about a half mile and lose this nut job," Kendall said quietly. "He can't move as fast on land as we can move in the water.

Just a few hundred yards up the shore with the wind, we come to a cove. The water will be protected there, and we can move faster. I got the sleeping bags so maybe we can stay in one of the buildings along the shore up there. Let's drag these down to the water."

They started the150 feet downhill to the water's edge. The waves were breaking hard on the shore with the strong wind coming at an angle from their right. The left side of a concrete abutment, built to create a swimming area in the summer, gave just enough protection for them to get into their kayaks. They fastened their skirts while bobbing on the protected water.

"Follow me." Kendall set out into the three-foot waves and turned to go with them. A shot rang out and Reid heard it whistle past extremely close to his shoulder! A wind muffled THAWK! Then another! And another!
Georgy was running downhill toward them in the deep snow stopping every few steps to shoot at them with the 3 D pistol which was notoriously inaccurate from this distance. He was hoping for a lucky shot.

Kendall was correct. They were quickly out of Georgy's range in the kayaks. Just as quickly, aided by the wind, they were well away pulling into the half-moon shaped cove. The cove had about a half mile of protected water which came nearly two hundred yards out into the lake.

"How are you doing?" Kendall slowed to allow Reid to pull alongside her.

"Good, so far. What do you think are the chances that one of these places has a phone that works?" Reid asked.

"I'm hoping these homes are on a different circuit than the one that was cut by the Russians. Let's paddle to the far end of this protected area and we will get out and try to find one," Kendall responded. "We can hide the kay..." Two gunshots rang out in close proximity!

Georgy was coming on strong in a canoe and was closing the distance quickly. He would be on top of them in less than ten seconds.

Kendall wheeled her kayak to the right to head straight back into the direction of the waves in the unprotected water. "We have to run for Wild Horse Island," she shouted. "He can't come out there in the canoe. He will eventually get swamped and capsize. PADDLE REID! PADDLE!"

Reid's turn into the wind and the waves put him almost right next to the fast closing Georgy. Georgy was now trying to put down his canoe paddle and get his gun in his hand. He could shoot Reid from very close range. Rather than try to get away, Reid took two more strong quick strokes on the left side. This brought him even closer to Georgy in the canoe. In the next stroke action, he swept his paddle out of the water and punched the end of it into Georgy's neck catching him totally off guard.

The move knocked Georgy off balance. It was just the time needed for Reid's kayak to race directly past the canoe and head out into rough water behind Kendall. Georgy could handle neither the canoe paddle nor the gun and had to use both hands to balance himself in the canoe. By the time he was balanced, Reid was out of range. He fired a shot in anger anyway. It missed wide.

Kendall and Reid were fighting for their lives. Not with Georgy. With the freezing winter winds on Flathead Lake. It was two miles across the lake to the protected waters of Wild Horse Island. The Island was off to their left, but if they tried to head straight toward it, the wind would blow them right past the Island. They'd be swept into the open water and eventually blown to the east shore ten miles away. They had to head directly into the wind while working their way to the left toward the Island. It was two steps forward, one step to the side.

Without changing direction, Kendall slowed to let Reid catch her so she could shout some coaching on how best to paddle. "Use your waist more than your arms. Turn at the waist rather than just pulling with your arms. Your torso is stronger than your arms. Pull with your torso. Set a pace of paddling that best suits you. Just keep following me. I will make sure I don't lose you. Use those muscles in your core that you have worked so hard to keep in shape," she smiled.

"That smile would keep anybody going," Reid said.

"Oh my God, that fool is trying to bring the canoe out here," Kendall said in wonderment.

Reid turned to look. Georgy was a football field behind them and struggling mightily. Water was breaking over the front of the canoe and filling it around Georgy's feet and ankles. Georgy was paddling as hard as he could to no avail.

Reid and Kendall had on winter ski coats, gloves, and kayak skirts. Georgy was clothed only in a jacket and in the rage of avenging his dead brother. The elements were the greatest protection that Reid and Kendall had. It was the elements that would complete the job on Georgy Pajari. Small drops of ice were forming in the cold wind and blowing off the kayak paddles. Soon sheets of ice might be forming on Kendall and Reid and most certainly on Georgy.

"Nothing to do now Reid, but paddle using your torso and make it to Wild Horse Island," Reid thought.

CHAPTER 47

February 20
Thursday 11:35pm Montana Local Time

Kendall and Reid arrived at the Northshore of Wild Horse Island exhausted from paddling across the wind. Ice was starting to form and soon would cover them like dipped ice cream cones. After they dragged their kayaks up onto the snowy bank, they were shivering uncontrollably.

"You ma-ma-might na-na-not la-la- like this ba-but, it is wha-what we ha-have ta-ta do and ssa-survive ri-right na-now," Kendall said in a shivered voice. She was digging with her kayak paddle to clear the snow under a yellow pine tree where the branches hung low to the ground and created some protection from the icy wind.

Reid started helping with his paddle. They pushed snow to the sides and the back building up a little berm around the area and then dug down to pine needles. Kendall moved back to her Kayak as fast as she could, which was not fast at all, a stumble really, and grabbed the sleeping bags. She then pulled off her gloves so she could handle the zippers. Working as quickly as her cold hands would allow, she stuffed one bag into the other. Then to Reid's amazement, she started stripping off her cold wet clothes. She got down to her Cuddle Duds on the bottom and nothing on the top and climbed into the bag.

"Ga-Ge-Get that dumb sta-struck la-la-look off ya-ya-yer fa-face Ga-Reid, ga-get ya-ya-your clothes off and ga-get ya-yer ass in here so wa-we ca-ca-can ga-get wa-warm," Kendall demanded during shivers.

Reid complied, stripping down to his boxer briefs.

At first there was not a lot of warmth coming from either one of them, just their warm breath on each other's faces. They were cuddled face to face, their arms holding the other, their legs slightly inter-twined.

"This is kind of weird, huh," Kendall asked, her voice now steadying. "I took a survival course. It is what you do when you live in Alaska. This is what they say to do when faced with what we just went through. I never dreamed I would have to do this when we discussed it in the class. We, of course, never practiced it in the classroom." She was talking nervously, talking too much.

"Shsh," Reid quieted her. "It is okay, you needn't be embarrassed or worried. You did the right thing for us. It is the second time you have saved my life tonight."

After a time, the warmth was beginning to flow back into their bodies and with it came the realization that they were body to body, skin to skin with a person to whom they were attracted. Reid noticed it first. Men have an involuntary response to being wrapped so tightly to a half-naked female body. As Reid had seen before when she had stepped into the shower at Eblodskya's, Kendall's body was fit and amply curved. She felt incredible with her nude torso and the length of her body lying against him. Reid was beginning to warm up.

Kendall was feeling the same thing build inside of her. She liked this guy almost from the start. Reid's disarming manner had been winning her over since she had first met him and now she could feel his arousal pushing against her.

Without hesitation, she grabbed the sides of his face and pulled him in for a deep and passionate kiss. It was the kind of kiss that young lovers have, starting slow when they are not sure where their passion is taking them. Soon all of their energy was feeding into this powerful spine tingling kiss.

They kissed deeper and deeper for several minutes until the dam gave way and they were scrambling to get each other out of the boxers and Cuddle Duds.

The love making was hot and intense as all of the

emotions of the night dissolved. The sex was a runaway train with the waves pounding and the wind howling around them. They feverishly consumed one another. They finished mutually satisfied and exhausted and remained in each other's arms.

Reid fell asleep immediately. Kendall remained awake a little longer thinking how strange life is. Eventually, she drifted off as well. They awoke hours later and made love again. It was Reid's first time with another woman since the loss of his Charlie. After the second session was over, he didn't know how to feel. The normal guilt he had been feeling was barely there. He drifted off to sleep again.

Reid found himself at his condo home on Mercer Island with Charlie. He was just finishing a call and she was reading on the loveseat next to the picture window that had a view through the trees down to Lake Washington. The sunlight was washing over her casting a glow and she looked more beautiful than ever.

"That was the Segmillers, they have a tee time at 4:35 and the couple they were going to play with, have cancelled at the last minute. Do you want to join them?" Reid asked. "They are inviting us to dinner at their club afterward."

"You should go," Charlie said.

"They are inviting us," Reid responded. "I wouldn't feel right going on without you."

"Reid, you should go. You should never feel bad about enjoying your life without me," Charlie said softly.

"I just can't do it," Reid said. "My happiness without you seems to me to be unfair, unfaithful to you."

"You should never feel that way. I know how much you love me. That will never be a question," Charlie said in a soothing voice. "The best thing you can do for me Reid is to live your life and be happy. That is what I want most for you."

The crackle of a fire gently brought him out of his dream. Reid lay in the sleeping bag watching Kendall spreading their clothes around the fire to dry and reflecting on his dream.

For the first time he could remember, he had no guilt and no questioning for Charlie.

It seemed to him for that brief moment, this entire adventure was designed to help him come to peace with the loss of his beloved Charlie, then, in the next moment he remembered how much was at stake in solving this case. He had to move on.

CHAPTER 48

February 21
Friday 12:30am Montana Local Time

Bert Hamilton and Lan Phang had been working for nearly eight hours straight. They were making headway on tracking past movements of Yuri Rosov. By using a new processing algorithm software from Quantico and new Recogni'tione software from China, Bert and Lan were able to break through the facial enhancement disguises Yuri employed. They were finding The Thorny Rose in the crowded concourse at Sea-Tac International in the minutes after the murder of Xing Tsua Ten. Bert saw that he had stopped for a bottle of water, but she couldn't make out what he was doing with it.

Using a video enhancement and analysis software of her own from her security sources, Lan Phang was working on taking the grainy video of the surveillance camera to begin to bring into focus what was happening with the water bottle. It was taking some time for Lan's software to process, so they stopped to take a break.

"So, are you a government cop like I am Lan?" Bert asked quizzically.

"I am not allowed to go into that Bert," Lan answered apologetically.

"You and I may be getting closer to who actually killed Xing Tsua Ten, but we are no closer to the why," Bert said. "Do you have any idea of the why, that you can share with me?"

"I can share that we have no idea of the why. The death of this man is a total mystery to us. He is a relatively unimportant low-level diplomat, from all that we can find."

"We learn in our training that in crimes like this, you either follow the passion or you follow the money," Bert said.

"We also follow that logic in cases like this," Lan said.

"After the murder of Park Soo-Hoon, it seems we can rule out passion. There would have to be some kind of lover's quadrangle for passion to be the case," Bert said.

"That would be very strange. I think you are correct that this is about money," Lan laughed.

"Occam's Razor helps us rule out passion versus money at the root of this." Bert said.

"I agree totally," Lan replied.

Bert, who was never at a loss to treat people like people commented, "I understand your involvement in the investigation, what I don't understand is the saber rattling of your government on this issue."

Lan Phang stared back at Bert Hamilton for some time. A very pregnant pause before she spoke.

"Like the classic Kabuki Theater of the Japanese culture, all things are not always as they seem."

"Understood," Bert said, "but why take it so far? It seems a very dangerous provocation to come from the loss of a relatively low-level person from your government."

"Never underestimate the actions or the resolve of the leaders of the People's Republic of China," Lan said solemnly.

Lan's computer dinged to show that it was done processing the video from Sea-Tac airport from two days ago. Lan figured it was perfect timing to end the conversation, but it left Bert wanting for more about what China was up to in the Pacific. She had been instructed to dig for information by FBI Regional Commander Sanchez and she was employing a little Kabuki Theater of her own.

With stop action and slow motion on the enhanced video analysis, the women were able to see Yuri Rosov take what looked like a heavy string, maybe nylon, out of his pocket and drop it into the bottle of water. After a few shakes of the water bottle, over the next two minutes as he walked down the concourse toward the exit, he drank the whole thing and discarded the bottle.

"I think we just saw him drink the murder weapon," Lan Phang said in amazement.

"Amazing," Bert said. "I don't know about you, but I need to call this in."

Both ladies rushed to their phones and took up positions in opposite ends of the FBI office.

Bert reported everything to a sleepy sounding Carlos Sanchez including the comments made regarding the Kabuki Theater of the Chinese government regarding their military actions.

"Thanks to your live feed of information from your computer, we have 24 people at Quantico working along with you to find Yuri Rosov," Sanchez instructed. "We have even processed the video to see what you are seeing with the string. Our experts think it is a celluloid string, like heavy fiber that dissolves in ordinary water. We have our people at the airport going back through the garbage to find that bottle. You must continue to make the Chinese investigator think it is just the two of you making all these findings. You are doing great!"

"Thanks. Will do boss," Bert closed and hung up.

Lan Phan seemed normal when she ended her call. After their calls to report in, the two Internet investigators began pulling up concourse video from the Mexico City airport in the minutes after the realization of the murder of Park Soo-Hoon on the CP Pak transport's arrival there.

Even though it was nearly 5:30am in Washington D.C., phones were buzzing with the news that the FBI had extremely high confidence that they had identified the actual killer of Xing Tsua Ten and that they were focusing on that individual to gain access to his whereabouts. They still did not know why the diplomat was killed.

After his Whitehouse staff disseminated the updated information on the investigation, President Parker ordered a phone meeting minutes later with cabinet members Hurwell, Hertz, Russell, Roberts and Tang.

"Emily, the first order of business when we get done here is to call Ambassador Jeng-Sheng Wei and tell him what he surely already knows about this report. Also make sure we convey the information to Ambassador Yoon Byung-Chul (North Korea) and we hope to have word on that investigation soon as well.

"Jim, are we devoting all resources possible to this investigation?" the President asked.

"Yes, our whiz kid in Seattle, the Chinese whiz kid out there and Quantico are following up on the Mexico City murder of the North Korean to see if Yuri Rosov was the culprit in that one. We are also fanning out the search to look for this Thorny Rose, as Interpol calls him, to see if he has travelled on any real time flights or CP Pak transports since the Mexico City murder."

James Russell continued, "Sir, we have a team of 24 Internet agents at Quantico working behind Bert Hamilton's computer. We figure that the less the Chinese see about how we are truly conducting the investigation, the better."

"Justin, what do you make of the comments about the Chinese and their intentions with the Xi Ching Ping aircraft carrier task force and other provocations? Have you finalized recommendations from the Pentagon if the Chinese continue?" President Parker asked of his Defense Secretary.

"Yes, Mr. President, the Joint Chiefs believe we need to meet force with force in all areas. If the Chinese are using this as a chance to probe us in all areas, we need to show them that we take all their actions very seriously. We have the carrier group George H.W. Bush steaming to intercept the Chinese west of the Hawaiian Islands. We have intercepts moving in all areas and we await your approval of DEFCON 2," responded the Secretary of Defense.

"I'll take the steps to approve that. I know we all have a lot of other things on our plates, but we must give this highest priority. Marcia (Tang CIA), if this moves overseas, we will have NSA and CIA involved, so thank you for sitting in on these briefings. Thank you everyone," the President closed.

◆ ◆ ◆

Yuri had awakened in Paris at the Hotel Mercure Paris Centre Tour Eiffel, well rested and feeling like his old self. He had tried to contact Georgy and Luka to get the good news on Daniels and the woman but had been unable to reach them.

He applied his facial enhancements, donned a baseball cap, pulled it low over his eyes, put on sunglasses and went out to walk in Paris. He stopped at the Boulangerie Suffren 55 for beignets and a press coffee. He was looking and acting like a tourist.

After his breakfast, he walked near the Eiffel Tower and then to L' Auberge du Champ de Mars to check out the neighborhood and the Spring Restaurant.

Upon seeing the restaurant, he determined that plan A would be to take down the "Russian cocksucker" in the men's room during the dinner meeting. He had brought along a coldcock device, the type sometimes used by thugs and police. It was custom made for him with a finely stitched leather strap handle and a 2 lb. ball stitched into the end. It was made to knockout a person with one blow to the head and not care how much brain damage might be included.

While at the restaurant, he made a reservation for 6:45pm that evening. He wanted to be there a little early, but not too early.

His encrypted phone rang. He hoped that it was Georgy to tell him that the deed was complete. Instead, he got the brief static delay of the voice converter.

"How is the Russian camel fucker today?" the monotone voice asked. Are you in place to handle tonight's work?"

"Yes," Yuri replied succinctly.

"You are over feeling ill as you were feeling a few days ago are you? I would call you a pussy motherfucker, but my mother taught me to have greater respect for women."

"No, I'm good," Yuri was working not to show his distaste for his employer. *"His employer might be the next person that I kill, when this is all over,"* Yuri thought.

"The Russian you will kill has a 7:00p.m. dinner reservation with two other people, a man and a woman," the voice said. "Whatever you do, they must not be harmed or endangered. Do you understand? I am paying you a lot of money and so far, all you and your team have done is fuck things up. Have you eliminated the lead FBI agent and the woman inventor?"

It was all Yuri could do not to answer yes to the question, but it nagged at him that he had not heard from Georgy.

"That is in the works, but not quite completed," Yuri responded.

"Your limp dick Russian associates don't seem to be able to complete the job. I can't help but think that I should have hired another team for this *"Job"*. One last thing. The dinner group will be seated against an inside wall by the brick feature. When you complete this task tonight, there will be one more waiting for you. Happy hunting." The monotone voice converter ended the call.

Yuri was seething. He had never been treated so badly by an employer and he did not like the feeling. There was arrogance in this person that was growing intolerable. What was even more intolerable was the wait to hear from the Pajari brothers. Yuri had a sinking feeling in his stomach.

CHAPTER 49

February 21
Friday 4:00am Seattle Local Time

Tied to the bed in his underwear, Robin Medallon was brooding about his predicament. It had all seemed to be too good to be true. It was all coming together in his mind. Usually, women like Analka Hrapla were not attracted to him. Bert Hamilton must have known that Analka was playing him and was hacking his computer for information on the investigation. He was feeling like a fool.

Robin's biggest fear was that he may have caused the death of Reid Daniels and Kendall Hughes or someone else on the team. What a fool he thought himself to be.

As he lay there in the dark considering his next choices, he was trying to remember if there was anything in his condo that would give a clue as to where he was now. He knew they would not keep him for much longer and that he might surely be eliminated when Analka's boss showed up.

"Why am I alive now?" he thought. "Think Robin! Think!" Then it hit him. Analka did not want him dead, or she believed he could give them more information. Either way, this was a plus for Robin and might just keep him alive long enough to be found.

Robin had no way of knowing where the murder investigation was at this point. Obviously, Bert and Reid knew Robin was being hacked. That was why communication from Reid stopped late on Wednesday the 19th. This was now Friday the 21st by Robin's best estimate.

The door to the living area of the Suite opened a crack. A woman came into the room. Robin could tell by the perfume scent that it was Analka.

"Coming in to make sure that I am still tied up," Robin asked.

"Yes," came the quiet response.

"Analka, what have you gotten yourself mixed up in? Whatever it is, we have been onto your hacking for a couple of days now, so we have not given you any good information," Robin's lie was the truth.

"Analka, I care for you, and I think you care for me," Robin gambled.

Analka sat at the side of the bed and reached out to touch Robin's face tears running down her face.

Robin kept talking. "Look, we don't have a clue of what is going on here with these CP Pak murders. It seems like you guys are throwing us curve balls every step of the way. The last communication that I got was that my boss was leading your guys on a wild goose chase..."

"Curve balls? Wild goose chase?" Analka asked.

"We're running in circles to keep you busy, because we don't know what else to do," Robin clarified. "That way it looks to our bosses in Washington, DC like we are doing something, but believe me, we are nowhere on this. My point is, leave me here. Get away while you can."

Analka knew she could not leave. First, she had to protect Robin. She would not be a part of his murder. Second, she had a job to do to take care of her mother. She pulled back her hand quickly and turned to walk out of the room, but she stopped short and turned to stare into his eyes.

"Robin, I do care for you." She continued out and closed the door.

Bert Hamilton and Lan Phang were in the process of giving the team in Quantico more "tells" they had noticed on Yuri Rosov. These then could be researched against airport security cameras all over the U.S., Europe and Asia. The way a face looks when the person is trying to be pleasant at security, the way the face relaxes when no one is looking, the eye movements in a crowd and in conversation, or the way a person walked. It was a painstaking task with AI computers making it only slightly easier.

In the back of her mind, Bert did not like the fact that Robin had not checked in with her for almost 12 hours now and that was not like him. She knew that his new room-mate lover had been hacking his computer, but she had never felt Robin was in danger until now.

The team at Quantico was also digging into and finding information about Robin's Analka Hrapla. Was she the young woman that Professor Eblodskya had identified only as A. Hrapla, the person so interested in the CP Pak transfer process? They had to be the same person.

"OH MY GOD," Bert exclaimed! "How could I have not connected these dots before this?"

Her outburst startled Lan Phang who was querying her own AI computer to show Yuri's characteristics in a middle-aged woman and run those images against the world's airport security cameras.

"What on earth Bert? Have you found something?"

"Maybe, I'll let you know in a short time when, I am sure."

When she had gone to Robin's apartment to see if Robin's computer was being hacked, she also installed a stealth camera feature that would take a photo of the person hacking Robin's computer. She needed to recover that photo now and see if that could help the people at Quantico.

Within seconds of sending the photo to Quantico, Bert got a positive response that Robin's Analka and the A. Hrapla of

Professor Eblodskya were indeed the same person. Find Analka maybe find Yuri. Find Robin maybe find Analka.

Bert grabbed her ICP. "Chris, I need you to wake up! This is Bert. Are you there?"

A sleepy voiced Chris Keller responded, "Yes, (pause) Bert, (pause) what is it?"

Against doctor's orders, Chris Keller had checked himself out of the Ketchikan Regional Medical Center and flown to Seattle on a late-night flight.

"I have been up all-night Chris, so at any point this does not make sense, just stop me."

"Just speak in plain English and don't use any of your young hip words and I should be able to keep up."

"Okay, here's the drop down. Robin has been having a few hot rolls in bed with honey. Honey has been hacking his computer allowing the bad dudes to be one step ahead of us on this investigation. In Montana, Reid and Kendall Hughes uncovered a genius hacker who may have made the CP Pak transfer murders possible. Her name is Analka Hrapla. Robin's honey is the one and the same Analka Hrapla. I think she is still in Seattle. Robin is missing, let's hope not dead. Finding Analka Hrapla solves a lot of things for us, and you win Fort Night. There did I keep it in your generation?"

"You did," Chris laughed. "I am on my way to Robin's condo as soon as I shower, dress a couple of wounds and take a couple of Advil. I'll check in after I get there. Oh, are Reid and Kendall Hughes okay in Montana?"

"I'll check on them right now. That'll keep me from thinking about you in the shower," Bert joked.

"That's just wrong on so many levels. Let me know when you hear from Reid," Chris said.

"Will do," Bert chuckled.

First, she tried Reid's ICP, then she remembered that he told her it was smashed out of existence last night. Then, she tried the cellphone number she had for Kendall Hughes. Nothing. Then, she remembered that he had called her on someone else's cell phone the night before when he was headed to Blacktail Mountain Ski Area. Elaine Collier's phone had run out of power as she had spent the night at the hospital with Winston Eblodskya, so Bert got no answer on that phone as well.

This is not good, she thought.

Next, she called the Lake County Sheriff's office. The call was answered immediately.

"Lake County Sheriff's dispatch."

"Hello, this is Roberta Hamilton with the Northwest Cyber Crimes Division of the FBI in Seattle," Bert introduced herself.

"You folks are sure making our lives interesting in the last 12 hours. This is Sheriff Deputy Colleen DeMers. We have dead bodies, people in the hospital, home break-ins and your agent's car at a ski area with four slashed tires sittin beside one of the dead bodies. Do you know where your agent is? We have questions? You Feds come rollin into town and start shootin things up and never even tell us what you are up to," Deputy DeMers said. "Ever stop to think that we might be able to help Roberta?"

Thinking fast on her feet Bert asked, "do you have a helicopter?"

"We have squad cars, 4-wheel drives, ATVs and snow mobiles, but we don't have helicopters," DeMers replied.

"When you do need a helicopter, where do you get it?" Bert asked.

"We have a contract with the Tribe for search and rescue and fires and such." Deputy DeMers answered.

"How do I talk to the Tribe," Bert asked.

"406-AIR-CSKT," Colleen said.

"Thanks," Bert said. She immediately called the number. Dead bodies that are not Kendall Hughes or Reid? Sounds like Reid has been in some gun battles Bert thought.

After several rings, "hello, this is the Confederated Salish and Kootenai Tribes air services Marcia speakin. Sorry, I was just puttin on the first pot a coffee for the day. We don't get calls this early normally, but we're here and ready for em every day. How cun I help ya?

Bert explained who she was and why she was calling. She wanted a chopper up as soon as possible flying over Dayton and the Blacktail Ski Area and everything in between looking for any sign of human activity in places you would not expect to see it. She gave the FBI office billing info, which Marcia asked to receive. Bert was impressed by that.

"It's still a little dark here, but by the time Billy Walks Horse gets here, he'll be able to take off," Marcia informed. "Just so ya know, we don't have a chopper, we have a Fourfly. You know. Four blades. All electric. More stability. More lift. Wherever your people are, Billy cun get em in the Fourfly.

"Hey, you're in the Seattle office of the FBI, right?" Marcia asked. "Do you happen to know a big, good looking native guy named Chris Keller?"

"Yes, I do, I work with him," Bert said. "How do you know Chris?"

"He was featured in Native Heroes magazine a few months back and then he spoke out here at the College in December about missing indigenous women," Marcia said. "He don't know it, but I have a huge crush on him, so say hi for me," Marcia giggled.

"Will do," Bert promised with a smile.

"We'll get Billy in the air real soon and let you know what he finds."

CHAPTER 50

February 21
Friday 8:10am Montana Local Time

The fire Kendall had built next to their little camp site on Wild Horse Island was putting out plenty of warmth now and the wet clothing was starting to dry out. They would smell like a campfire, but their clothes would be dry soon.

"Here, let me try to clean up the side of your face a little," Kendal said.

"About last night," Reid said.

"Reid, that was real. Real good, I might add. As crazy as it seems in the situation we are in, we are attracted to each other and for me this morning, that is all that matters," Kendall said as she stacked small broken tree branches on the fire.

"So, you are not going to report me to my bosses," Reid said with a half wistful smile.

"If you hadn't been ready for a second time, I might have had to report you," Kendall turned to face Reid and give him her winning smile across the fire light.

"What do we do next?" Kendall asked. "Do you suppose anyone will come to check out this fire?"

"Fire or no fire, I am sure my staff in Seattle has been working the phones this morning to get people out looking for us." Reid said. "They know where we have been in the past twelve hours and people will be looking for us. I just hope they have found the whereabouts of one Yuri Rosov, the Thorny Rose."

The morning light was beginning to creep over the Mission Mountains with a faint touch of blue backlight lining the tops of the mountains in the east. The strong winds of the night before had ushered in the start of a beautiful clear day. It was a very cold morning, probably under 20 degrees, but neither Reid nor Kendall seemed to notice. They were glad to be alive and happy to be together.

Out of the growing light came the quiet whirr and flashing red lights of Billy Walks Horse and his Fourfly. The Fourfly consisted of four blades incased in donut shaped protective rings. It looked like a much larger version of a small personal drone except the blades rotated to horizontal for hovering, landing, and takeoff and to vertical when in flight. The body containing the cockpit and the passenger compartment was sleek and bullet shaped. The Fourfly could achieve speeds of 225 miles per hour. It was a lovely sight.

Billy set down in a clearing just a few hundred yards from the fire. The Fourfly was azure blue with white stripes waxed and polished to a beautiful shine. It looked very much like a larger version of the four-blade drone that Reid had received one Christmas when he was eleven. By noon, Reid had flown his toy into the side of his neighbor's house, and it never flew again. He tried to put that mishap out of his mind as he looked at the beautiful machine in front of him.

Minutes after putting out the fire and securing the kayaks, Reid, Kendall, and Billy were airborne and headed toward civilization, or at least that was the way that it felt to both Reid and Kendall. They held hands as they took off.

Shortly after landing at the Fourfly's home base in Pablo, Montana, Reid was patched through a secure FAA channel to Bert Hamilton. Reid learned from Bert that Yuri Rozov had been tracked to an air flight that had taken him to Paris just last evening. That was the good news. The bad news was that the airport cameras quickly lost the Thorny Rose in Orly Airport upon arrival.

As Bert was catching up with Reid, Chris Keller checked in. He was at Robin's Condo. Bert conferenced the calls.

"Chris, how are you doing? Are you sure you are alright

to come back to work so quickly?" Reid asked with concern.

"I had a concussion and needed some stiches. They needed the bed for sick people, and you needed me here. As long as I don't walk past another explosion, I'll get along okay." Chris said. "The doctor was a little upset that I checked myself out."

"Happy to hear you are on the mend so quickly," Reid approved.

"I was elated to learn it was an explosion that got me and not you," Chris joked. "I had pain from a shard of wood in my neck and I was worried you had shot me. The knowledge that it was just an explosion lifted my spirits and is helping me recuperate," Chris responded. "Have you used your gun on the bad guys yet?"

"Sort of, it's a story best told over a burger and a beer," Reid said, protecting the secrets of his gun. "Bert just told me that Robin is missing. Any sign of him at his condo?"

"I am calling in to get approval to pick his lock, because no one is answering his door," Chris said.

"You are good to go. Everyone who uses their home as an office, signs a waiver so you are good to go in," Reid advised. "I'd like to stay on the phone while you go in. I want to hear what you see there."

"Okay, I've got my earpiece in, (short pause) I'm in and there does not seem to be anyone here. Checking all the rooms." Chris paused as he cleared each room. "Everything is clear here. No sign of a struggle," Chris said. "To my eye, Robin left here and expected to be back."

"Thanks Chris. Keep checking and let Bert or me know what you find. Bert, can you get a protected ICP in my hands as quickly as possible? I need to call Sanchez and we'll need to talk strategy."

"I already have an agent coming to you out of Missoula. He or she, Agent Fitzgerald, should be there within the half hour," Bert said with a little pep in her voice.

"I'm gonna have to start calling you "Radar" for that

guy on the old M*A*S*H television program," Reid chirped. "You read my mind before I can say it."

"How about NOT calling me "Radar" gramps! Like it's hard to stay ahead of your sorry middle-aged ass. How about you call me Bert and give me a raise," Bert fired back.

The sleep deprivation may have been setting in for Agent Hamilton or it was Bert's weird sense of humor. Reid couldn't tell which.

"Okay, after I speak with Sanchez and we've formulated the next move, I will be back at you Radar," Reid went with a sense of humor.

"Bite me old Man," Bert replied with a smile in her voice.

Agent Clair Fitzgerald arrived with the phone just minutes after Reid got off the secure FAA channel with Bert. Reid asked Fitzgerald if she could hang around to give them a ride to Missoula.

"Carlos, pick up, it's Reid."

"Good God Reid, where have you been? I've been worried sick, and I have not had anything to report to Washington for hours. You can't go this long without reporting in Reid. This thing is way too important. You should know that," Regional Commander Sanchez admonished.

"We have been a little busy, Commander," Reid started. "We have managed not to get killed by two Russian assassins and we managed to take them out in the process. Just came out of the deep woods in Montana and I've learned that we have traced Yuri Rosov to Paris. We lost him there at Orly Airport."

"How long have you had this information? I'll have our boys at Quantico contact French DGSI (Directorate-General for Internal Security French equivalent of the FBI) and DGSE (Directorate-General for External Security French equivalent of the CIA) to see what help they can provide," Sanchez said.

"I think Bert Hamilton and what's that Chinese Intelligence person's name, Lan Phang, may already have the French involved, because we have been studying airport security from all over the world for the past 12 hours," Reid said.

"Well, we will just kick it up a notch to a higher level," Sanchez defended. "So, what do you think is happening in Paris?"

"My guess is that he is there for another assassination. We should warn every nation we have diplomatic relationships with to warn their assets to take extra precautions and maintain a high level of security," Reid advised.

"I will communicate this with Director Russell immediately. How soon can you get after this guy in Paris?"

"It is a long way from Pablo, Montana to Paris, France. Can you send a plane to get us back to Seattle? We can CP Pak transport to Paris from there." Reid said. "I'm told that Missoula is the nearest airport large enough to handle one of our jets," Reid said.

"Will do, Reid. I'll get the aircraft information to our Missoula office. Let me know when you find out more information on Yuri Rosov," Sanchez said. "I'm told the U.S. and Chinese are making military moves and counter moves. The FBI is the best bet to keep this thing under control and a lot is riding on you. You are doing a great job Reid. As always, let me know what I can do for you."

Reid took a deep breath as he came out of the private room at the CSKT Helipad Office and looked at Kendall Hughes and Clair Fitzgerald. "Looks like we are headed to Missoula to meet an FBI plane, but first," he turned to Billy Walks Horse, "what are the chances that you can fly us up to Blacktail Ski Area to gather our belongings from my car?"

"Not only can I do that, but I can give you a hop to the Missoula airport to catch your plane also," Billy Walks Horse replied. He was more than happy to get some extra billing from the FBI. Every profit center needs revenue.

FBI Director Russell was eager to share the news with President Parker that they had tracked the assassin to Paris. The President was a little less eager to hear that they needed to warn diplomats of all levels who might be in Paris to be on guard and to use the highest levels of precaution until further notice from the U.S. State Department. Secretary of State Hertz immediately put her team to work communicating the warning for Paris.

Lan Phang had also communicated with her superiors and assured them that Yuri Rosov was a prime suspect and that he had been tracked to Paris. She trusted Bert Hamilton and thought in the back of her mind that women would do a much better job of ruling the world than men had done for centuries.

After Lan's report, the Xi Jinping Carrier group did not slow down, but they did change course to cruise 200 nautical miles South of the Hawaiian Islands. The U.S. Navy had the H. W. Bush carrier group protecting the Hawaiian Islands. Two other carrier groups and three fast attack groups had moved into closer range to military bases China had developed over the past 20 years on man-made Islands in the South China Sea. Both China and the United States were flexing their military muscle as a result of these inexplicable assassinations.

President Parker and his team knew that provocations and tensions from small events can take on a life of their own and grow to the point that they are hard to contain. They were doing everything in their power, including their own communications with the Chinese, to keep the Genie in the bottle.

CHAPTER 51

February 21
Friday 8:55am Montana Local Time

Chris Keller was concluding his search of Robin Medallon's condo. He had not found anything that would indicate where Robin had gone. He was concluding that Robin had been lured away from his apartment and possibly kidnapped by Analka Hrapla and her people and that Robin could be in grave danger or worse.

With those thoughts running through his mind, Chris stepped out of Robin's Condo and encountered what looked like one of Robin's neighbors.

Chris reacted quickly and stepped forward to introduce himself. One, to make sure it was a neighbor and two, to see what this guy knew.

"Hi, I'm Chris Keller. I work with Robin, and I'm surprised to see that he is not home."

The man was taken aback by this abrupt approach and responded slowly. "I'm Justin Grace, Robin's neighbor. Soo, are you with the FBI also?"

"I am," Chris responded showing his badge, "and I am a little worried about Robin. He hasn't checked in with us since late yesterday. Did you talk with Robin in the last 24 hours?"

"I did," Grace said. "We talked a little when we were taking our garbage out yesterday afternoon. I asked him how things were going with his girlfriend. I don't want to sound like a perve, but a lot of the guys who live here in the Condo complex are very interested in the comings and goings of his girlfriend, because I don't know if you have met her, but she is a hot."

"That's what I hear," Chris said, keeping his ears tuned to anything that might help him find Robin.

"What did he have to say?"

"He said he was meeting her mom for dinner last night and he asked me if I knew how expensive the meals were at the lobby restaurant at the Olympic Hotel. I told him that I didn't have a clue, but did her mom need a date. I figured her mom had to be pretty hot also and maybe even under 50 which is kind of my limit if you know what I mean."

"What did Robin say to that?"

"He laughed and said he would let me know, thanked me and said see ya later."

"Thanks Justin. If you see Robin let him know that I stopped by. Have yourself a good day."

"You too, nice to meet you," Justin said as he walked away without a clue how much he had just helped.

Chris immediately placed a call to Bert to let her know that he was headed to the Olympic Hotel. Twenty minutes later he was at the front desk showing his badge and asking to speak to the manager.

At the same time on the fourth floor, Analka was receiving a call from Yuri in Paris.

"Annie, my dear how are you doing?" Yuri asked.

"All is gud here Yuri. How can I help you? Is your verk done in Paris?"

"Not just yet, but soon. I will need to take one of the conventional flights out of Paris tonight. One of the ones that you booked earlier for me," Yuri said. "I want to take the one out of Charles de Gaulle, what is my alias for that flight to New York?"

"Let me look. You are Francis Jamieson. That's F-R-A-N-C-I-S J-A-M-I-S-O-N and you have been in Paris on business for an art company Plum Brothers. You are headed home to New York," Analka dutifully reported. She had set up three different flights two days ago from three different airports in Paris.

"Your flight is at 10:45pm on British Airways."

"Excellent, make sure I have my boarding pass and other documents I will need on my phone on my encrypted phone," Yuri instructed. "Please put Petra on the phone."

"Petra, about Analka's FBI friend. I have been thinking about this. I see no use in him any further and at this point, he is likely a liability. You need to kill him in the same way that you did the Polish businessman in Minsk."

In Minsk, Petra had killed the Polish businessman using autoerotic asphyxiophilia, cutting off his air supply during sex until he was strangled to death. It looked like a man who had paid for kinky sex and his perversion had killed him. He would not have been the first.

"Kill the FBI guy and then you and Analka head for the Canadian border in your car. She will not be on board to kill him at first, but she will see the wisdom in it later. You will need to distract her, get her out of the room and get it done quickly. The sooner you can kill him and leave for Canada, the better. I cannot wait to see you again Petra. Maybe when this is over, we can spend some time in a warmer climate, soaking up the sun during day and making love at night."

"Yuri, that sounds nice. Tings are goings fine here. You take care and we will see you in couple of days and we will see about what you say," Petra said.

"Thank you, Petra. I know I can count on you. Goodbye."

"That was a long conversation," Analka said.

"Yes. Yuri making sweet talks to me about what he do to me when he get back," Petra smiled.

"That's just like a man. Thinking sex when there is verk to be done," Analka said. They both laughed.

"Hey, you dressed. How bout going down to get lattes for us?" Petra asked.

"I think I can do that." Analka grabbed her room key and her oversized purse which contained her laptop computer and headed out the door.

The hotel manager and at least two of the desk clerks

on duty remembered the woman that Agent Keller was describing. She had been with a man that met the description of Robin Medallon. The front desk had given her information about a specific room. As one of the clerks looked up to Chris to give him the room number, instead of giving him that number, her eyes got big and she said, "the woman we are talking about is crossing the lobby behind you right now."

Chris turned slowly to see a pretty, young woman crossing the lobby turning more heads than just his. She was walking toward an espresso kiosk. "What's the room number," Chris asked. "I need a key."

"I don't know if we can give you a key," the desk manager protested.

"I have reason to believe there is a crime going on in that room, so you can give me the key, or I will break the door down," Chris said firmly staring the manager in the eye.

"It's room 404. Here's the key," the clerk said above her boss's protests.

"Call the Seattle police and tell them an FBI agent, Chris Keller, needs immediate backup and ask them to call the Federal Marshals." With that Chris hurried across the lobby to the bank of elevators.

An elevator door was closing, and he couldn't make it. Chris had to wait for the next one. It seemed like an eternity to him. Finally, he reached the fourth floor. He stopped at room 404 to listen. There was minor noise coming from the suite.

Agent Keller opened the door quietly and quickly got his gun in his right hand and his badge in the left. The noise was coming from the bedroom.

Chris entered the room to see Petra Lane performing sex by riding on top of a spread eagle and tied down Robin Medallon, who was gasping for air. Petra was tightening a leash around Robin's neck.

"FBI! FREEZE," Chris shouted as he quickly moved toward the couple.

Petra yanked the leash as tight as she could while rolling

off Robin over the right side of the bed away from Chris. She came up with a gun in her hand pointed directly at the Navy Seal.

Chris had never taken his eyes off Petra and shot her point blank in the center of her forehead. That was the only part of her showing over the side of the bed. He then released the stranglehold on Robin's neck.

Robin gasped for air. Chris took photos of the scene with his ICP, then, began freeing Robin from his restraints.

"(cough) How on earth did you find me here?" Robin wheezed. "Oh my God, you arrived just in the nick of time!"

"Dumb luck," was Chris's answer. "Here are your clothes. Looks like they got cleaned. Get dressed out here and leave the room just as it is. I need to go back to the lobby to get your friend, if she is still there. Will you be okay here?"

"Yes, yes go," Robin waved his hand at the door.

Robin was buckling his belt on his jeans when he heard a key in the door. It was Analka. She closed the door slowly behind herself.

"What's going on here," she said cautiously as Robin took a step toward her. She could see the severe red marks on his neck and began to put two and two together.

"Did Petra do that?" She was pointing at the red marks on Robin's neck.

"It's over Analka, a partner of mine from the FBI was here. Is here. Down in the lobby looking for you now." Robin was wrapping his hands around her wrists. "Petra is dead, and you are under arrest." He recited her rights to her, then said, "Analka, your best chance not to spend the rest of your life in Federal prison, is going to be to tell us everything you know."

Analka struggled a little, but Robin was able to maintain control of her. He was able to tie her hands behind her with one of the ropes from which he had just been released.

"Analka, I really thought we had something," Robin said. "I think I love you."

"We do have something," Analka responded. "I love you

too," she said as she gazed up into his eyes.

CHAPTER 52

February 21
Friday 9:40am Montana Local Time – 5:40pm Paris

The Thorny Rose, his persona while he was working, put on his best slacks, shirt and jacket and walked out of the Hotel Mercure Paris Centre Tour Eiffel. He looked nice, he thought. Not bad at all for a man who was out to take a life. It was a crisp and cloudy evening with a possibility of rain later. He had a few things he needed to do before he got to the Spring Restaurant at 6:45pm.

Yuri walked toward the river Seine and stepped into one of the high end hotels visited by the wealthy and elite. He was looking for a hooker to join him at dinner at the Spring Restaurant. He approached a lovely curvaceous brunette at the bar and asked her if she was available for dinner, while handing her $500 American.

"What room she asked?" in perfect English.

"The Spring Restaurant at 6:45pm," Yuri responded. "Ask for Mr. Jamieson."

"I will be there," she said demurely with a slight but sexy turn of her head.

Yuri was off now looking for a drug store. The doorman gave him directions to one a few blocks away.

Even though Yuri felt he had totally recovered from the ill feeling he had after the second CP Pak transport killing, he was pushing his pace since he knew he was short on time and this made his heart race more than usual. He felt like his heart was skipping beats and sweat was trickly down his temples. *"Be calm Yuri"*, he told himself.

Upon arriving at the drugstore, Yuri asked the pharmacist for an over-the-counter diuretic, one that would work within an hour. He also picked up an umbrella. With the bottle of pills and umbrella in hand, Yuri walked to the nearest public waste can where he took two pills out of the bottle and tossed the rest in the waste. The two pills were placed in his pocket as he began his walk to the Spring Restaurant.

The Thorny Rose arrived at the restaurant at 6:40pm on the dot and made sure he was seated along the wall where he would have a view of the entire dining area. His heart rate and sweats had calmed down. He ordered a glass of water and began going over the plan in his mind.

Yuri would ask the hooker to make a deal with one of the waiters to get the diuretic pills into the water glass of the target. He did not care what deal was made, but he figured it would be a blow job for getting the pills into the drink. Not many waiters would pass that up.

The diuretic would do its job and the target would need to use the men's room. Yuri would follow, disable the target by bashing his head into the wall and then drown him in the water of a toilet bowl. This was a tactic he had learned and perfected by watching American mafia movies.

At 6:45pm the hooker arrived and was seated at Yuri's table.

"My name is Suzette, by the way. If all I have to do is eat a meal here, this is the easiest money I have made all month. What's your real plan here Mr. Jamieson?"

"Let's order drinks and just sit quietly for a few minutes," Yuri responded.

After a few minutes, a table nearby began to fill up. First came a well-dressed man who was obviously Middle Eastern. Just a bit later, a man arrived who was not quite so well-dressed and reminded Yuri of many of the men he had seen all his life. The man looked Russian. Finally, a gorgeous young woman, who looked totally out of place with the other two, arrived and sat down.

The Middle Easterner took an Apple Elucidation box out of his satchel and handed out ear buds. Obviously, they didn't all speak the same language. *"Interesting,"* Yuri thought, but they all seemed happy to see one another with hugs and cheek kisses all around. On second observation, the men seemed to be more eager for the hugs and kisses than the young woman.

After what looked like small talk, they began what seemed like serious discussions. Yuri was able to hear for certain that the rumpled man was indeed a Russian, but the woman was speaking Russian also. *"Also, interesting,"* Yuri thought.

The Thorny Rose shared with Suzette what he needed her to do with the pills, but they were thrown a curve when the person taking the drink orders at the two tables was a woman.

"Don't worry," Suzette said as she followed the waitress back into the kitchen. After several minutes, she returned to the table and said, "It is done. Now what?"

A young blonde man came out from the kitchen shortly after and delivered water to both tables.

Yuri was impressed with Suzette's work. "Now you order the finest meal you see on the menu, make eyes at me while you eat and then bid me au revoir."

At the table nearby, Shahnaz Latifpour was emphatically making the case that he had no involvement in the deaths of their comrades in The Marco Polo Alliance.

"In fact, my actions to protect you are probably the reasons you have not been attacked like the dead men," Latifpour boasted.

Anyone who has spent any time dealing with Iranians, knows that they easily become boastful when they try to protect their lies.

"Save your breath. This will all be over soon enough. I think Luba has some things she wants to say," Kostya Ivanov said. "And you should know Shahnaz, both Luba and I have bodyguards on duty in the restaurant, should you be thinking of trying anything this evening."

Drinks had arrived and all were drinking them down quickly as might be expected with the tension at the table.

"Kostya my friend, you misjudge me completely. I have no...," Shahnaz was saying softly when he was abruptly interrupted.

"Please save it Shahnaz, Luba wants to speak," Kostya said firmly.

With her voice shaking, Luba started to speak. "I would never have entered this work arrangement had I known the level of greed that this arrangement would bring forth. I had a simple plan which I have executed. It was to make all of you several millions of dollars, but that was not enough for you," Luba said looking directly at Shahnaz Latifpour. "Now all I want is to get out of this horrific Marco Polo Alliance."

That cold and angry stare made Shahnaz think that maybe Luba was not the woman of his dreams.

With her voice still shaking, Luba continued, "I have made arrangements to go to New York on the Monday, this Monday the 24th, to disband the Marco Polo fund. If you want your BLOOD MONEY," she said loudly, "YOU WILL BE THERE." Tears began to wash down her cheeks. She was so angry; the tears came with no effort at all.

"This might be a good time for a break," Kostya said. "If you will excuse me."

Kostya pushed himself away from the table and headed toward the men's room. The diuretics were working.

The Thorny Rose followed shortly thereafter as did a third man. Yuri saw the third man out of the corner of his eye. This would not be as easy as the first two hits on this "Job".

The third man clearly gave up that he was a bodyguard when he entered the men's room and stood by the door until Kostya Ivanov was done and had exited. Yuri could not pull off his American mob style murder here.

He went back to his table where Suzette was about halfway done eating her Buckwheat Galettes with Salmon,

Capers with Dill. "Sorry darling, but I have had a call and we need to leave," Yuri said in near perfect French.

Without saying a word, Suzette put down her knife and fork and placed her napkin on her plate. As she brushed past him, she half whispered, "Will there be other services tonight Mr. Jamieson?"

"Yes, other services and more pay," Yuri said and gently took her hand. "Walk with me."

Yuri and Suzette walked hand in hand out of the Restaurant and down the avenue until they came to a bench where they sat down. They were still in sight of the front doors to the Spring Restaurant. After a short time, the two Russians and the Middle Easterner walked out of the restaurant and parted company walking in different directions. The bodyguards of the Russian man and woman followed them.

The Thorny Rose and Suzette, still holding hands, followed the Russian man and his bodyguard.

The street was lined with trees. Without the leaves of summer, the intermittent streetlights provided ample light for those who were out for a stroll. Rain was beginning to sprinkle down as was forecast.

"Do you see the gendarme up ahead? Here is another $500. I need you to cause a problem with that man who has been following the other man and have him detained by police. Can you do that Suzette?"

"Without a doubt Mr. Jamieson. Then where do I meet you darling?"

"You don't. You are off my clock. Here's another $500 since you have been so efficient. Maybe I will see you again when I am in Paris."

Suzette raced ahead and caught the bodyguard right next to the gendarme and began shouting and pointing and raising holy hell by Yuri's judgement. *The prostitutes in Paris are the best in the world,*" Yuri thought to himself.

It was time for the Thorny Rose to go to work. Kostya Ivanov was clearly rattled. First, he stopped to watch what was happening behind him with his bodyguard. He stared and thought he had seen that woman. Yes, one of the beautiful women from the restaurant. Quickly he panicked. He whirled to hurry back to his hotel. He now knew he was in danger.

He took one last look over his shoulder and was hit hard in the side of the face and the back of his head by a rock or a brick. It was the custom-made ball and leather strap. He was losing consciousness. He was being pulled into a darkened doorway. Then he felt a wire around his neck and he could not get air. He was too far gone from the blows to the head to put up a real fight.

Kostya Ivanov died in the shadows of the doorway to a millinery shop. The Thorny Rose quickly arranged Kostya's body so that he appeared to have had too much to drink and had passed out. He in fact had pissed himself during the attack.

Yuri moved slowly down the street, with his umbrella over his head to protect him from the sprinkling rain and from the security cameras above. His plan was to go back to the Hotel Mercure, spend some time listening to the singer in the hotel lounge, make a point of stopping at the front desk to leave a wakeup call and then to go to bed. He had no intention of answering that wakeup call. He would go to his room, gather his bag, apply his disguise and head to the Charles de Gaulle airport for a 10:45pm flight to New York where he would hide out until payday on Monday. He wanted to be in New York to personally oversee the movement of his "Job" payment from the New York bank to his accounts in the Grand Cayman Islands.

CHAPTER 53

February 21
Friday 1:30pm Local Time Seattle 9:30pm Paris

When Reid and Kendall walked into the FBI Northwest Cyber Crime offices, Robin, Chris and Bert were all hard at work. Kendall was impressed by the offices which looked more like a high-tech operation than an FBI office.

Reid introduced Kendall Hughes to each of them. "Sorry that I called you a needle dick fed," Kendall said to Chris.

"No need to apologize for that ma'am, it was the gunshot that scared me." Chris answered.

"Sorry," Kendall wrinkled her nose sheepishly.

"Believe me she could have hit you if she had wanted," Reid added.

When he came to Bert, Reid thanked her for the great job she had been doing. He also used the opportunity to give her some good-natured ribbing. "Kendall, I want you to understand that Bert doesn't always look like a fuzzy dog toy that has been mouthed and chewed at for months. It's just that she has been up all night for maybe two nights in a row. This young lady works hard."

Bert's tired eyes perked up. She was genuinely thrilled to meet Kendall Hughes and took no offense at Reid's ribbing. As tired as she was, Bert did not miss noticing that Reid was acting just a little differently around Kendall.

"Other than those bruises on the side of your face, you look pretty rested boss. Did you get a good night's sleep?"

It was a joyous home coming even though Reid had been gone only two days, underscoring the danger which had brushed so closely near Reid, Kendall, and Chris.

Lan Phang was asleep on a cot in a back office. Bert swore that she herself had gotten two hours sleep earlier, hoping that would put everyone at ease regarding her sleep deprivation.

"What do we know people," Reid asked rather seriously.

They all started talking at once.

"Okay, okay. How 'bout we go around the room? Bert you are first."

"We tracked Yuri Rosov to the Orly Airport in Paris, but we lost track of him there. There was a killing of a low-level Russian diplomat along the Seine near the Eiffel Tower just hours ago tonight, you know what I mean. It's 9:30pm there now. French authorities are questioning people there tomorrow. Those being questioned are a Russian woman who was seen at dinner with the victim earlier and an Iranian man who was also at dinner with the victim. Also, a couple of restaurant employees are being questioned."

"French police are also looking for a prostitute who may have aided the killer. Rene' Bernal of the DGSI (General Directorate Internal Security) in Paris is willing to hold off on additional interrogation until you get to Paris, provided you can be there by tomorrow morning. I told them you would be there. The French have an all-out manhunt currently underway in Paris for Yuri Rosov. They believe Rosov may have gone underground or left by train for Germany. They are sounding like they are not certain he was involved in the killing of this Russian tonight, aaa today. But the M.O. is the same and it follows because he is another low-level diplomat."

"Chris. What do you have?" Reid asked.

"We have Analka Hrapla under lock and key at the Federal Building awaiting charges. We have her laptop computer and Robin is working to hack it. Robin was kidnapped by Analka and a woman we now know as Petra Lane. Lane is dead. I shot her when she leveled her gun on me. Internal investigation and Seattle PD says the shooting was justified."

"Are you available to accompany me to Paris, Chris?" Reid asked.

"Sorry boss, no. Due to the internal force on my organs from the blast up in Ketchikan, medical does not want me to travel for another 48. The doctor I mentioned to you earlier is quite upset that I flew back here last night. She says we are pushing it in terms of the internal damage I may be doing to myself. Can't fly. Can't Transport."

"Robin, what do you have for me?"

"Chris saved my life Reid. I know that there will be an investigation into how I allowed myself to be duped so badly, but I am here 110% until that time. I am on the verge of breaking into Analka's computer."

"We will get to your investigation later Robin. How close did you get with this Analka Hrapla? Do you think you and Kendall could pump her for information?"

"Do you think you could pump her one more time for us Robin?" Bert asked without looking up from her keypad.

"All kidding aside," Kendall interjected, "if Robin does continue to have a close relationship with her, I may be able to probe her (Bert snickered) for information on how she discovered individual animation during a CP Pak Transport."

"Analka and I mutually feel as close to being in love as you can be in this circumstance. I think she would meet with Ms. Hughes and me," Robin said.

"How soon can you get me on a Transport to Paris and are you certain that Yuri Rozov is not here in Seattle waiting to kill me when I jump on a Transport?" Reid asked no one in particular.

"Already have you booked to Paris before you walked in. You'll depart Seattle at 3:00pm via CP Pak transport and arrive a little after 11:00pm Paris time," Bert confirmed, "and, Lan Phang and I are certain that he has not used public transportation to leave Paris. Chinese Intelligence has allowed the French to use their latest version of Recogni'tione software to watch all forms of travel. You are safe until you get to Paris,"

Bert added with raised eyebrows realizing how that sounded.

"That gives me little more than an hour and a half to get out to Sea-Tac. Chris, can you take me? I need to swing by my condo to grab some clean clothes," Reid said.

"Can do boss," Chris Keller said, rising out of his chair.

"Kendall, are you good interrogating," Reid emphasized interrogating while giving a glance toward Bert who raised her eyebrows again in acknowledgement, "Analka Hrapla without me?"

"Absolutely! The question is, are you okay being alone with Yuri Rosov in Paris?"

"I have my gun. I know how to take care of myself."

"You be careful. We'll get someone from the Embassy to meet you at the airport. Don't get cocky," came the almost simultaneous responses from Kendall, Bert and Chris.

"Alright! You all know what to do," then Reid and Chris were out the door.

As Chris drove to Mercer Island to shower and pick up some clean clothes, Reid used his new ICP to call Regional Commander Sanchez.

"Carlos, it's Reid Daniels, pick up."

"Reid, you're back. When can we meet?"

"That's why I am calling. As I am sure you know, there has been another murder in Paris, a low-level Russian Diplomat. Bert Hamilton and Lan Phang tracked Yuri Rosov to Paris on surveillance video less than two days ago. The DGSI in Paris are holding off questioning of the last people to see the Russian victim alive. If I can get there by tomorrow morning, they'll wait for me. I am headed to Sea-Tac right now to take a CP Pak transport to Paris," Reid said.

"Who's going with you Reid, for backup?"

"I have the French DGSI people and someone from the Embassy is meeting me at the Airport. CIA, I assume."

"I'll report all of this to Director Russell. Do you have the name of the person from the Embassy in Paris?"

"No."

"I'll check with Director Russell to touch bases with CIA Director Tang to make sure you get strong back up. Do you still have your gun with you?"

"Yes, I do."

"Reid, be careful over there!"

CHAPTER 54

February 21
Friday 9:30pm Local Time Paris

Yuri had had a drink in the hotel lounge and listened to the jazz vocals of a pretty, young French woman whose name he did not catch because his mind was on getting out of Paris. He had gone to his room to pack and then to head to the airport. His packing was interrupted by the ringing of his phone. *"Oh finally, Georgy is reporting in,"* he thought.

There was a pause and an electronic click. Yuri knew the monotone voice was next. "Great work Thorny Rose. I am surprised that you didn't fumble things like your staff and pleased you can think on your feet." Yuri detested this voice. He was certain now that when this was completed, he would kill this person.

"Which one are you? The slick Middle Easterner or the beautiful girl?" Yuri never jumped to conclusions.

"Ha, ha, ha, ha," the monotone voice was haunting. You Russians really are simple mother fuckers. Ha, ha, ha, ha. You can become the great detective after you have finished your *"Job"* for me fuck stick. For now, call me the Cobra, if you like. Pay close attention halfwit. There is a CP Pak transport to New York clicking out of Paris at 3:30pm on the 24th. I will book your seat. You will kill the person sitting directly in front of you. Get this right my limp dicked Russian friend and the $2.5 million will be in your account by 5:00pm on the 24th and we will have pulled off the international crime of the decade. What name do I book your seat under?"

"Francis Jamieson. F-R-A-N-C-I-S J-A-M-I-E-S-O-N and it is now $3 million!"

"You cocksucker!" the monotone said. "You surprise me goat fucker. You bargain like a rug merchant. That impresses me. I'll pay you $3 million. (pause) Here is some interesting news for you. The Gendarmes have tracked me down and I am to be interrogated tomorrow morning by DGSI and lead FBI Agent investigator, Reid Daniels following your trail of murders. You know, the man who has killed your entire team? The man you were to delay or to kill. Your team fails their assignment and now I must face this person and answer questions about my relationship with Kostya Ivanov," the monotone voice said. (pause) Maybe I tell them who you are and where they can find you at 3:30pm on the 24th. Then, I pocket your $3 million. Orrr, maybe you figure out how to finish the "Job" I am paying you for, so I will not face Reid Daniels for questioning. You decide."

"Now tell me Thorny Rose, if that seat in front of you has a child, or a crippled old man or a beautiful young woman, will that concern you?"

"I will kill the person in that seat. The guilt of killing that person resides with you," Yuri said.

"Goodbye Thorny Rose. This will be the last time we will speak," the phone clicked off.

Yuri's blood was boiling. Not only did he want to kill the person with that monotone voice, but he also wanted to kill the FBI man whom he was now sure had killed Georgy and Luka Pajari. This man had to die for what he had done to Yuri's team.

Yuri quickly booked two more nights at the Mercure Hotel. He had made the decision that he was going after Special FBI Agent Reid Daniels, who he had just found out was coming to Paris. He would not contact anyone else on his team and he would not answer his phone again. He was too close to the end, and he did not need them.

Yuri pulled up a CP Pak transport schedule. If Reid Daniels was to be at an interrogation tomorrow, he had to be in the transport arriving in one hour and ten minutes at the Orly International Airport terminal.

Yuri had planned before to kill at this air terminal and that plan was refreshing in his mind right now. Tonight, he would tie up loose ends and tomorrow, he would dawn a disguise he had never used, buy sunglasses and a hat and Yuri Rosov would be again a tourist in Paris.

CHAPTER 55

February 21
Friday 2:05pm Seattle Local Time

Immediately following his conversation with Reid, Regional Commander Sanchez called to update FBI Director Russell. Russell called President Parker who hastily went to the Situation Room with his Chief of Staff for a conference call with Sec. State Hertz, Sec. Defense Roberts, CIA Director Tang and Director Russell.

"We are getting great news, ladies and gentlemen, our Cyber Tech team in Seattle has tracked the Diplomat Killer (the term being used by the press) to Paris. Sadly, there has been another killing there of a low-level diplomat from Russia. Emily, please reach out to give our condolences and give them just enough information to keep them happy for now. Consult with your people on how much to share," the President stated.

"Yes, Mr. President."

"Jim, please update us on the manhunt," President Parker said.

"Yes sir," FBI Director Russell started. "Our Special Agent in charge of the Cyber Tech team in Seattle, Reid Daniels, has been doing an outstanding job. There have been at least four assassins sent after him personally and not only has he foiled every attempt, but he has taken down all four of them. This is a Russian mob assassination team we are dealing with, and they have years of experience all over the globe and the head of our computer team in Seattle is taking them down."

"This Daniels guy sounds like a stone-cold lawman," interjected Secretary of State Emily Hertz. "Has he been in the field before?"

"No." Director Russell continued, "right now he is headed to Paris to go after the leader of the team, one Yuri Rosov or The Thorny Rose as he is known. We expect to have The Thorny Rose dead or alive within the next 48 hours."

Comments of American bravado were dancing across the phone lines among the group on the call.

"Thanks Jim," the President said.

"If I might interrupt Mr. President," Secretary of Defense Roberts spoke up.

"Yes, Justin what are you hearing on that Chinese carrier task force?"

"More good news Mr. President. We saw them swing wide of Hawaii and now we are getting reports that they are turning south and appear to be headed toward South America. They may be headed for Cape Horn. The Navy Admirals tell me that the Chinese did this three years ago. A Chinese Carrier force sailed hell bent for election toward Hawaii, then turned south to Cape Horn. After rounding the cape, they headed north to a point about 200 miles off the coast of Argentina and Brazil to Fortaleza, Brazil which is the eastern most point of the South American continent. It was a speed run. They wanted to know how quickly they could be in position with a Carrier group just off our Southern flank.

This current run could be provocation resulting from the killing of their diplomat or it could have been planned for months and just serendipitously aligned with the loss of their diplomat. Whichever it is, our Navy minds think they will get to just east of Fortaleza, Brazil and then head for the Cape of Good Hope around the tip of Africa and back toward home waters. Our estimates are that the Xi Jinping Carrier group will not reach the waters east of Fortaleza, Brazil for another three and a half days," Defense Secretary Roberts explained. "When the Chinese come around Cape Horn, we will deploy the USS H.W. Bush Carrier Group and the Bush Carrier Strike Force to travel south along the east coast and into the Caribbean. We will match force with force."

"Your timetable makes it Monday around noon our time. Goddamn, that's cutting it awfully close for our computer wonder cop from Seattle to catch this Thorny Rose and put an end to this," the President exclaimed. "But this Daniels sounds like the man for the job."

Shortly after the Situation Room call ended, CIA Agent Harlon Sturm received a call at his Paris apartment. It was CIA Director Marcia Tang.

"Harlon, this is Director Tang. Your ICP should verify my identity."

"Yes, Director, how can I help you?" Agent Sturm was a no-nonsense guy and that is exactly why he was receiving this call.

"No doubt you have heard about the murders of the several low-level diplomats from various countries which have taken place in the last four days?" Tang asked.

"Yes."

"At 11:09pm this evening a Special Agent, Reid Daniels with the FBI, is arriving at Orly Airport on a CP Pak Transport from Seattle. I need you to be there to meet Special Agent Daniels and be his back-up and assistant for as long as he needs you here in Paris. Are we clear?"

"Yes, Director Tang."

"The man suspected of murdering the diplomats is a Russian Assassin named Yuri Rozov. Have you heard of him?" Tang asked.

"Yes. The Thorny Rose has come across in some of our investigations," Sturm replied.

"Rosov's team has been trying to kill Special Agent Daniels for a couple of days now. It is my understanding that Daniels has put down four of Rosov's top team members and Rosov may come after him personally here in Paris," Tang explained.

"Daniels sounds like a pretty tough dude. I am happy to assist him," Agent Sturm said with conviction.

"Keep me apprised of your activities at least on a thrice daily basis," Director Tang ordered as she hung up the call.

CHAPTER 56

February 21
Friday 10:15pm Local Time Paris

Yuri Rozov's pulse had quickened as soon as he had learned that FBI Special Agent Reid Daniels was coming to Paris.

"Sometimes you are good and sometimes you are just lucky," Yuri thought aloud to himself. "I am both," he said as he smiled into the mirror at his hotel. "Now I get to work."

Yuri was always motivated more by revenge than by money and revenge was what he had in mind for Special Agent Reid Daniels

Yuri arrived at Orly International Airport 45 minutes before Reid's CP Pak Transport was scheduled to arrive. Yuri was dressed as an old Parisian; He wore gray slacks, light gray shoes, a light blue shirt, a dark blue sport coat and a jaunty plaid fedora pulled low on his forehead.

Though it was after 10:00pm at night, the terminal was busy. He had practiced all of this in his head multiple times for a previous assignment which had been canceled. Yuri was pushing an unreturned rental luggage cart he had found in the parking lot.

He first had to locate two Security Gendarmes working together near a security check point. They were easy to find, and they were young and just about Yuri's size, exactly what he was looking for. The new guys always get the night shift, he thought to himself.

Yuri saw his next necessary targets nearby and approached. When he was in range, he rammed his luggage cart into the Achilles heel of an older woman. She jumped forward and fell to the floor immediately screaming. Yuri had made sure he had hit the back of her ankle with enough force to pop the tender Achilles tendon. She was screaming and writhing in pain. Yuri began shouting his apologies in broken French sounding a little like an American.

There is nothing that the French despise more than a rude American causing trouble and the people travelling with the injured woman began yelling back at Yuri about "Why was he so careless". "You may have crippled her." "Don't you watch where you are going?" "She is an old woman."

Yuri began responding defensively. The scene was growing louder and louder thanks to Yuri's continued provocations.

One of the two young Security Gendarmes came running to the scene to calm things down and to give aid to the woman. As soon as he arrived Yuri shouted in broken French, like an American, that the "Stupid woman stepped in front of my cart." The others reacted and were ready to physically attack Yuri.

The young officer knew he had to get this American away from the accident. He turned to Yuri and shouted for him to move away, even pointing in the direction of his partner over near the security checkpoint. Yuri turned and ran in his best "old man" run through the gathering crowd to where the other security officer was standing. The second Gendarme was calling in the accident and asking for medical help and extra security for the gate. He was close enough to see everything but had been unable to make out what was being said.

Yuri ran up sounding flustered and completely out of breath. "He needs an AED device," Yuri huffed and puffed in near perfect French. "She's going into cardiac arrest." The Gendarme looked at the scene where the woman was down just as the officer attending to the woman looked up through the crowd with a look of questioning and exasperation that easily could be interpreted as *"What are you waiting for, bring the device".*

The Security Gendarme next to Yuri turned quickly and broke into a hard run toward the AED Device hanging on the wall next to a secured door marked Airport Personnel Only. Yuri was right behind him running like a big cat in pursuit of prey rather than the old man he had appeared to be just moments earlier. The two got to the device a split second apart. The young Gendarme reached for the box holding the device and felt a sharp prick go an eighth inch into the left side of his ribs as a powerful hand pulled him left toward the security keypad by the door.

"Don't do anything crazy. Place your hands in front of you like a choir boy," a harsh voice demanded.

With slightly more pressure on the blade, Yuri reached around and grabbed the officer's security card and held it to the keypad. The lock buzzed open, and Yuri pushed them through. With the door closing behind them, Yuri grabbed the guard's gun which he had unsnapped a split second earlier. Now, the gun was pressed into the back of the young Security Guard.

Yuri pushed him into a janitorial closet about thirty feet down the hall closing the door behind them just as another person was coming through the security door from the terminal. Yuri was ready to shoot the Gendarme and this other person if anyone started to open the janitorial closet door. Lucky for them all, no one did.

"Now it is time to quickly take your clothes off, everything, even your briefs." Yuri ordered.

The young security guard complied and stripped until he was totally nude. Yuri looked around at the supplies and grabbed a roll of duct tape.

"Wrap this around your ankles. Six times! Hurry or I'll have to shoot you. Now, put a strip over your mouth." Yuri grabbed the tape.

"Now put your hands behind your back." Yuri taped the guard's hands. He checked the tape on the mouth, then quickly dropped the young Gendarme to the ground and bound his feet and hands together behind his back. He pulled the Gendarmes underwear over the man's head and with all of the strength he could muster, Yuri lifted the young man headfirst into a 75-gallon rolling garbage can and slammed down the lid.

Two minutes later Yuri had dumped his clothes into the garbage can and was exiting the closet wearing the officer's uniform. He looked at his watch and realized he had used 30 minutes of his time before the CP Pak transport from Seattle was to arrive. He had just over 15 minutes left. There would also be a few minutes to spare while people got out of the transport.

He had plenty of time to get to the correct terminal and wait for Special Agent Reid Daniels. The only person he wanted to kill more right now was the monotone voice, but as he got to the Seattle transport arrival terminal, he encountered a problem. A well-dressed good-looking man with square shoulders was holding a sign which read R E I D D A N I E L S. Clearly CIA.

CHAPTER 57

February 21
Friday 11:09pm Local Time Paris

Reid was seated in the CP Pak transport pod with 143 other people. He was paying close attention to people seated around him. Bert Hamilton had booked him in the last row, so there were no passengers behind him.

People in the front were seated and he began to relax. The doors would be secured in a few minutes. Reid had spent the night before making love in a sleeping bag in Montana with a woman that he now had very strong feelings toward. His emotions were no longer conflicted about the loss of his wife two years earlier. Charlie had come to him in a dream and released him.

Reid decided it would be a good time to listen to the soft perfect harmony of the Judds, the mother daughter duo who had worked their way onto the country music scene in the early 1980s. Reid whispered *"Grandpa"* – (*tell me bout the good old days*) into the music App of his ICP and drifted into the soft harmony of the Judds. The song ended as the doors were being opened in Paris.

The first thing that Reid saw as he exited the transport Pod was a man neatly dressed in dark tan raincoat.

The man was holding a sign which read R E I D D A N I E L S. Reid did not make eye contact as he walked with the crowd in the man's direction. This was likely his CIA escort.

Also in his sight was a Security Gendarme with light gray shoes that did not seem to match his uniform. Both men were looking intently in Reid's direction. Reid continued walking with the crowd.

The ear buds were still in his ears, so he heard Bert immediately on the ICP.

"Reid, our apps have a positive hit on Yuri Rosov at Orly Airport. He's dressed as a Security Guard. Let me know you are getting this."

"Yes, mother we just landed. I'll be there soon," Reid said in perfect French as he walked past the two men while staring straight ahead and keeping up with the crowd.

A horn of low tones began repeating on the terminal sound system then, a voice was telling people to stop where they were and get to the ground.

Reid stopped and kneeled, reacting with the group he was with. There were three uniformed security officers running down the concourse toward the Seattle passengers opposite the two individuals who had Reid's attention. Reid turned back to look at the two men. The man dressed as a Security Guard had drawn his gun first and fired two shots at the man with the sign who was able to draw his gun and return one shot before he slumped to the floor.

Reid left his bag on the ground, jumped up and began running toward the two men pulling his own gun as he ran. He stopped, knelt on one knee and steadied with his left hand holding his Glock with his right. He was waiting to shoot for the split second when the man in the gray shoes stopped to swipe the security keypad.

THAWK! A baton came down hard across his right hand dislodging the Glock. Two Security Gendarmes knocked him to the ground. The smaller of the two, a woman, put her knee in Reid's chest and quickly sprayed mace, point blank, into Reid's face. The concoction overwhelmed him and he passed out.

The third Security Gendarme continued running to the downed CIA Agent, sliding to his knees next to him. The Thorny Rose slipped relatively unnoticed back through the Security door.

Luba Krupin was preparing for bed with her bodyguard

on duty just outside her door when her Microsoft Elucidation translation phone rang. She saw who it was and went directly to the door of her room to peer through to make sure her bodyguard was still outside.

It had been a difficult evening. First, she had had to attend The Marco Polo Alliance dinner where the person behind the killings was in attendance.

Second, she had a call from Inspector Rene' Bernal of the French DGSI informing her that Kostya Ivanov had been killed and she was to appear for questioning at 1:00pm the next afternoon. After Bernal had soothed her tears over the phone, he informed Luba that she would be picked up if she did not appear as requested.

"Agent Bernal, I think I know who was responsible for this," Luba had said tearfully.

"We'll talk about it tomorrow, Ms. Krupin," Bernal responded. Bernal was quite sure he knew who committed the murder, he just did not know why, so Krupin's comment piqued his interest.

"Shahnaz, I have nothing to say to you," Luba said as she answered the call from the Iranian.

"Luba, clearly you have not heard. Our friend Kostya Ivanov was murdered this evening shortly after we all departed our dinner at The Spring.

"YOU EVIL, EVIL MAN! LEAVE ME ALONE! I WILL TELL THEM THAT YOU HAVE DONE THIS! THAT YOU HAVE KILLED THEM ALL! I WILL TELL THEM!"

"Luba, do you have a guard outside your door? Do you have other security protecting you as well? LUBA, WE MIGHT BE IN DANGER!" Shahnaz shouted back.

"MIGHT BE IN DANGER," Luba shouted sarcastically! "YOU EVIL, EVIL BA-BA-BASTARD! YOU CAN HAVE THE MONEY, BUT YOU WILL NOT GET AWAY WITH THIS. YOU WILL NOT!" With that Luba slammed down the phone.

"Miss Krupin are you alright?" The bodyguard was knocking at the door.

"Yes Michel, but you and Jean Claude must be extra vigilant all night. There is a man trying to kill me. You must stop him!"

CHAPTER 58

February 21
Friday 3:00pm Local Time Seattle

Arrangements had been made for Robin and Kendall to interview Analka. They rode together in Robin's car. They exchanged pleasantries. Robin was guarded, but Kendall was skillfully breaking down the barriers.

Kendall was looking for clues to verify that the affection Robin displayed for Analka was reciprocated by Analka. Kendall was not as interested in hearing about the science of the "animation interval" in the CP Pak transport, she understood the science. She was looking for clues that might help the FBI catch Yuri Rosov. Every minute he was on the loose was an opportunity for him to harm or kill Reid. The irony of her wholeheartedly helping the government was not lost on her, but her feelings for Reid overpowered her hate of the government.

In the interrogation room, Kendall leaned in close to Robin and spoke so he could barely hear her.

"Robin you must have very powerful feelings toward Analka and if what you tell me is true, she feels the same about you. Even though you know that neither of us has the authority to offer anything, you have to know that her co-operation will help the government to go easier on her. You know the law better than I do, but right now she must be an accessary to multiple murders and that could mean life in prison or even possibly death for her. With a lighter sentence, there could still be time for the two of you to have a life."

"I know all of that and I have been thinking about it,"

Robin replied.

Kendall leaned in again. "I am going to give you 15 minutes alone with her before I come in. You have got to get her to co-operate with us to stop the assassin and get to the bottom of what this is about."

Analka was led into the room and Kendall excused herself with no introductions.

"Oh Robin." Analka tried to reach out to him, but Robin held back.

"We can't Analka. Not in this circumstance."

Playing a hunch, Kendall found the Federal Marshal who had shown them into the private interrogation room and asked to be connected with Eileen Wisdom at Marshals headquarters in Arlington, Virginia.

After a few minutes to set up the call, the officer led Kendall into another room and handed her the phone.

"Eileen its Shelby Ellison. Better known as Kendall Hughes now. How are you sister?"

"I am well, ah ah, should I call you Kendall? It has been a long time since I helped you disappear. I understand that you and FBI guy Reid Daniels have had quite an exciting past few days. It's all the talk in the halls around here." Marshal Wisdom replied.

"Yeh. It is not exactly anything I would have signed up for, but your guy Reid is one hell of an agent and without him looking out for me, I am quite certain that I would not be alive to be talking to you right now," Kendall said. "Have you been keeping up with this investigation?"

"I haven't been working directly on the team that is supporting Bert Hamilton, but tell me what you need," Wisdom said.

"The team here in Seattle captured an individual who was a plant in their midst and who is part of the assassination team. This person was intercepting key information during the investigation, allowing the assassination team to know Reid Daniels's every move. A young woman named Analka

Hrapla seduced one of the men on the team here in Seattle. Let me say he's no dummy, but being an introvert, he was fairly susceptible on the relationship side. Reid and I have established that she has a genius level IQ. She studied with one of my mentors, Professor, Winston Eblodskya. She studied all my work and took it further than even I was able to do. Analka Hrapla discovered how a human could become animated inside the CP Pak transport process thus making it possible to murder two diplomats in transit."

"Oookayy," Eileen Wisdom followed.

"Stay with me Eileen. I'll get to the point," Kendall half laughed.

"Hard to believe, but this assassin helper, Analka, and the FBI geek, Robin, have fallen in love. I believe Robin can turn her to give, what do you call it, states evidence and to help us. To do that, somebody is going to need to show her how that is in her best interest. That is why I called you, to advise me. As you know, time is of the essence on this case." Kendall continued.

"So, you really think our guy, Robin is it, can flip her quickly?" Agent Wisdom asked.
"Yes, I do. Even though I am a scientist, and most people don't give us credit for being touchy feely, I can see it in their eyes," Kendall said.

"Hold on while I get a couple of other people on the phone with us," Eileen put her phone on hold.

In the interrogation room, Robin and Analka had spent the past several minutes simply staring at each other. The hurt in their eyes was palpable.

Robin was the first to speak. "How could you be so devious and full of deceit to have done this to me? What kind of person are you?"

"Oh Robin, Ahm so sorry. I have reasons you don't understand," Analka sobbed.

"Sorry doesn't even start to cut it. You've broken my heart. You've ruined my career. I trusted you. I fell in love with you," Robin said angrily fighting back his tears. "How could you do this to me? How could you do this to anyone?"

"Robin pleez, I have made a terrible meestake. My mother was in trouble. I had discovered some ting big, really big. Yuri Rosov a very nice man. He hires me to computer hack. He wants to use my discovery. He tells me that men will die but they are bad men, and the world will be a better place without them. Yuri needed me to get in tight with you so I can tell him where the FBI is so he can do tings to slow FBI down till he keels all the bad men," Analka explained.

"Yuri tells me he'll pay me a lot of money so I can help my mother," Analka pauses. "I never thought I would fall in love with you. I never knew Petra would try to keel you. I was going to let you go when she was not looking. Please forgive me Robin. I love you so much!"

Again, the star-crossed lovers stared deeply at one another across the table.

Eileen Wisdom was back on the phone with Kendall. "Kendall, I have a legal team with me. Without going into formalities, they are Karen, Marcus, and Eric. They have 70 plus years of prosecutorial experience among them. They know the situation and they have some questions for you."

"Kendall, this is Mawcus." He had a New England accent. That accent always made Kendall think of the Kennedys. "Do you think your love-struck guy can get us some real useful infahmation?"

"I'm confident of it," Kendall said.

"What kind of infahmation and how will that help us," Marcus asked.

"There are other of your agents who know more about this than I do, but from what I know, she was a main contact for Yuri Rosov, the head of the assassination team. She may be able to lead us directly to him," Kendall responded. "In addition, she developed the process for human animation, human movement, during a CP Pak transport. That is how the first two murders happened and from a scientific standpoint that is huge."

"And you know this science, how," Karen asked.

"Trust me, Kendall knows the science on this," Eileen offered firmly.

In a heavy Oklahoma drawl Eric joined in. "This is Eric. Ah'm the leader of this gang. Let's get this little gal to the point that she wants to make a deal, then the three of us can put that together. When we get to that point, I want you ridin silently long side, on the phone, so we can make sure we are gettin the deal we want. Let's get 'er all roped and tied and catch this Yuri sons a bitch. Put an end to this thing."

Kendall promised to get back to Eileen as soon as there was any sign from Analka that she was willing to make a deal.

With that deal now in play Kendall headed directly to the observation booth of the interrogation room to see what was transpiring with Robin and Analka.

"Robin what can I ever do for you to forgive me for what I have done? (pause) I love you Robin; I want for you to love me again."

"You could start by showing me that you care more about me; more than that murdering assassin Yuri Rosov. Maybe, if you help enough, I can save my job and maybe you can save spending the rest of your life in prison," Robin said. "Annie, this is an international incident and
it needs to end quickly before something worse happens. You could start by telling the FBI everything you know about how and why these murders are happening."

"Robin, I will tell ever ting I know, if it means getting back your love," Analka said still sobbing.

From the observation room Kendall, said quietly to herself, "that's my sign to go back in."

Kendall entered the interrogation room and sat down next to Robin.

"Is this the FBI person I should talk with?" Analka asked.

"Analka, I am Shelby Ellison. I learned from Winston Eblodskya that you are a fan of my work," Kendall said.

Analka was dumbstruck and her face displayed the guilt of child who had just been caught with her hand in the cookie jar. "I am so sorry for what I have done with your discovery. You must hate me."

"You have things to be ashamed of in all of this for certain and you have things for which you can be proud," Kendall said. "Robin and I want to help you, each for our own reasons. Robin loves you very much and I want to help save your wonderful mind so you can use it for good for the rest of your life instead of wasting it in prison."

A surge of pride bolted through Analka's mind and body. Someone she respected was respecting her. Here she was with the man she loved and the person she had admired most in all of her life and they both cared about her. Analka knew it was time to do as Robin had said and begin to help the FBI unravel the mystery of these murders and put a stop to them.

CHAPTER 59

February 22
Saturday 6:30am Local Time Paris

Out of the darkness, Reid could hear his name being called softly.

"Reid. Reid Daniels (pause) I thought he was coming to," a man was speaking softly in French.

"Oh, he will wake up soon. His eyes have been kept still for the past six hours while we have had him in an induced coma," the pleasant female voice said also in French.

"What coma? What are you doing to me?" Reid was fighting the premise but speaking French himself.

"Reid, I am Rene' Bernal with DGSI and with me is Dr. Eloise Marchand."

Dr. Marchand began to explain, "Mr. Daniels you are at the American Hospital of Paris. Do you remember what happened to you?"

"I was trying to apprehend a gunman at the Orly airport. I am FBI," Reid said calmly although being in total darkness did not make him feel at all that way.

"You were pepper sprayed in the eyes at very close range by one of our Airport Security personnel. The spray was so close and at such pressure, you almost lost your eyesight," Dr. Marchand explained. "We were able to get you here very quickly and began a chemical wash of your eyes. We put you into a coma, so that you would not fight the process. We also treated those small abrasions on the side of your face. You have been out for over 6 hours. It is Saturday morning a little before 7:00am."

"Am I going to be able to see again? It is completely dark for me right now." Reid could hear the noises of a hospital; there was a whirring machine very near him, a heart monitor playing softly behind him, a gear noise every several seconds, several voices in the hall and the squeak of wheels rolling by an open doorway.

"We think we have saved your eyesight, but we will not know for a couple of days. We have your eyes wrapped up pretty good right now. You will need the bandages on at least another 36 hours and you can have only limited activity," Dr. Marchand explained.

"I have already cleared it with Dr. Marchand for you to come with me for the questioning of the people who were at dinner with the latest Diplomat Murder victim. I will take you to our offices later this morning and bring you back to the hospital when we are done. That is, if you want to do that," DGSI Agent Rene' Bernal said.

"Yes, yes, of course," Reid replied with enthusiasm.

"We will be escorted by two other officers of the DGSI, and I have two people posted here at the hospital to guard you around the clock," Agent Rene' Bernal explained.

"Did you capture Yuri Rosov? I am quite certain that was him that I was about to shoot. And oh, was the man he was shooting at from our CIA and how is he?" Reid asked.

"Bad news all around, I am afraid. We did not capture Yuri Rosov and the CIA agent is in pretty bad shape, but still hanging on," DGSI Agent Bernal replied.

"Our questioning of Luba Krupin and Shahnaz Latifpour is scheduled to start at 12:30 this afternoon and could run several hours. We also have two people to question from the staff of the Spring Restaurant. We'll start with them at 10:30am. Dr. Marchand believes you are up to it, do you agree?" Agent Bernal asked.

"I think so. Right now, I am a little bit hungry, but other than not being able to see, I feel fine," Reid answered. "I have a question for Dr. Marchand. You said American Hospital. Is there some kind of segregation of Americans in Paris?"

Dr. Marchand laughed, "No, we treat you Yanks at our other hospitals as well, but American Hospital is very close to Orly Airport and we happen to have an outstanding Optical Surgery team, so it made sense to bring you here. I am sure you will find your stay to be above satisfactory. We take great pride in keeping our American patients happy and that is not always easy to do."

"Thanks Doctor, I completely understand," Reid replied. He said it with some resignation knowing how Americans can be.

"I will send in one of our nurses who will get you taken care of in terms of food and will help you get ready for your work with Agent Bernal," Dr. Marchand said.

"And I will be back in about two hours to pick you up for the interviews. I will brief you in on the people we are seeing on the ride over," Agent Bernal said.

"That all sounds fine. Who do I talk to about food?" Reid did not want to sound impatient, but he was starving. He couldn't remember when he had eaten last. He wondered how Kendall and the team in Seattle were doing. He would check with them a little later due to the time difference between Seattle and Paris.

In Seattle, the FBI had placed Analka in contact with a defense attorney. Marcia Sherman was a very qualified international defense attorney and agreed to work for Public Defender wages if Analka Hrapla could not pay for her services. The key was to make sure that Analka had top drawer legal counsel before the government would make a deal with her.

The arrangements took place all afternoon and most of the evening. As time was the most precious commodity in this situation, the DC legal team leader made it clear to Marcia Sherman that unless a deal could be secured quickly, there would be no deal at all. National Security was at risk. Councilor Sherman was nonplused by this argument but agreed to begin the negotiations at 7:00am the next morning.

Reid got this news when he called in to Bert Hamilton. When Bert picked up the secure ICP immediately, Reid wondered if this girl ever slept at all.

Apparently, the CIA had not informed the FBI that Reid was in the American Hospital in Paris nor that he had lost his eyesight, at least temporarily, having been pepper sprayed at point blank range, and that Yuri Rosov was likely attempting to assassinate him at Orly Airport the night before.

"Sufferin Baldheaded Hannah Reid is there anyone there to protect you? You know that as soon as I tell Chris Keller about this, he is going to be on a CP Pak transport immediately to have your back. You lay low boss until he gets there," Bert Hamilton instructed.

"Well, I can't do that Bert because I must question some people. Please call Carlos Sanchez and fill him in. Get his permission for Chris to come over the water or through the wires and please let Kendall and Robin know as well," Reid said.

"Do you have your gun, Reid?" Bert asked.

"I have no idea where my gun is and I am not sure I could use it if I had it. I can't see a thing. What do they say, It's as dark as ah, ah ...." Reid was saying.

"As dark as a well digger's asshole, that's what they say. GOOD GOD REID, YOU ARE GOING TO GET YOURSELF KILLED. BE CAREFUL! Ohhh Reid, I don't feel good about this at all," Bert said.

Bert called Chris Keller and began booking him to Paris on a CP Pak Transport out of SeaTac, and then she called Regional FBI Director Carlos Sanchez to get his permission to do that. Chris was due to depart at 2:45am Seattle, so he should be at Reid's side by noon in Paris.

Commander Sanchez was shocked to hear the news about Reid and gave immediate permission for Chris Keller's already scheduled trip to Paris. After his call with Bert, Sanchez reported to FBI Director James Russell and the legend of Special

Agent Reid Daniels grew even larger.

"Apparently, he had a gun battle with the diplomat assassin, Yuri Rosov, at Orly Airport and was still working from the American Hospital in Paris. He'll send more information when he has it, but clearly they are hot on the trail of the assassin," Sanchez explained to Director Russell.

"Is Special Agent Daniels available to accept a call?" Director Russell asked.

"Yes. I am sure that he is," Sanchez responded.

Ten minutes later Reid's ICP rang from his bed table in the American Hospital.

"Special Agent Daniels this is Jim Russell and I have someone here I want you to meet."

"Yes, Director Russell," Reid responded.

"Reid this is the President of the United States Charles Parker," Russell said.

"Hello Reid. Sounds like you are doing some great work out there," the President said.

"Thank you, sir," was all Reid could muster.

"Look Agent Daniels, we are between a rock and a hard place with a Chinese carrier fleet. We have known for over a year now that the Chinese have been looking for a reason to test our military forces and the death of this low-level trade diplomat looks like just the excuse they may have been looking for. Their fleet is being very provocative. Reid, honest assessment, how close are you to wrapping this up?" the President continued.

"I can't say with 100% certainty sir, but I believe we can make an arrest within the next 72 hours," Reid replied.

"That may not be fast enough son. How can we speed that up? We could be in a hot skirmish or even full out war with the Chinese before that. Are you getting all the help you need? Do we need more assets in France?" the President emphasized.

"Here's the situation, Mr. President. We know the ringleader, a man named Yuri Rozov is in Paris. We are using

AI driven FR (facial recognition) so we don't think he can get out easily. I am involved in the interrogation of people who we believe relate to him within the hour. We may apprehend him sooner, but I don't want to mislead you sir," Reid stated.

"Godspeed agent. We will do what we can to dissuade the Chinese from taking action against us. Go get your man and put an end to this," President Parker demanded.

"Yes sir," Reid said.

Reid could feel the pressure closing in on him. He reached out to Charlie, but she was distant as if she was across the room and inaccessible to him.

As promised, Rene' Bernal was back at 9:30am to collect Reid for the interviews at the DGSI Paris Headquarters, which he said was a twenty-minute ride away. As they walked out of his room Reid noticed things he had never noticed before. People talking, some to each other, some clearly on the phone, computer key clicks, the whirring and soft beeping of equipment in the background, the soft padding of shoes probably worn by nurses, the heavier harder sound of the shoes of the officers of the DGSI, the antiseptic cleaning smell and the smell of things that weren't quite right. The bell of the elevator door opening startled him. It seemed so loud.

The noise on the street seemed like being on an airport tarmac with jet engines all around, but then Reid realized it was really just normal. His senses were shifting to compensate for the loss of sight.

In the car, DGSI Agent Bernal began bringing Reid up to speed on who they would be questioning. First, they would meet with Lizette Bergen a waitress from the Spring Restaurant and then Pater Skons a kitchen worker at the Springs. Lizette was French and Pater was from Norway. The preliminary investigators had learned some interesting things from these two.

Next, they would meet with the two people who had been dining with the Russian Diplomat murder victim, in the minutes before he was killed. They were Luba Krupin and

Shahnaz Latifpour.

"In what order will we speak with them?" Reid asked.

"I think it is best to talk to Lizette first then Pater," Agent Bernal said.

"Will I be able to record these on my ICP or do your laws prohibit that?" Reid asked.

"Yes, record them on your phone. We will be able to provide a transcript of them as well," Bernal answered.

Lizette Bergan was led into the interrogation room. Questioning started with general inquiries about her and about her employment at the Springs Restaurant. Then, Agent Bernal got to the crux of what they wanted to know from her.

"Lizette you are aware that two nights ago a person, whom you served, was murdered shortly after he left the restaurant."

"Oui," she answered timidly.

"Was there anything strange about that evening?" Reid asked.

"Oui." Lizette stared intently ahead as if she was waiting for something else.

"Will you tell us about it?" Reid asked.

"Oui." She paused, folded her hands in her lap, opened her eyes a little wider, exhaled and seemed very pleased with her answers and how things were going. Then, a little embarrassed, she said, "oh, you mean tell you now?"

Bernal nodded.

Reid noticed the fragrance of hair product and a nice perfume. They were light and neither was overwhelming.

Lizette began in a measured voice, "on that night a gorgeous woman came back into the kitchen like she was looking for something. She spotted my co-worker Pater who was putting together a tray of waters and she walked directly to him like she knew him. Pater serves water and picks up empty plates and such. He was startled by the beautiful woman and what she said to him must have embarrassed him at first. He turned red and he got a nervous smile on his embarrassed face. I was watching all of this from the corner of my eye, not really looking directly at them. She beckoned him to follow her, and they moved to the back of the kitchen in a hallway where we bring in the food shipments, fish, poultry, vegetables, wine everything comes in through that back door, but at night when we are open, it is just a dark hallway."

"Did you know what they did back there?" Agent Bernal questioned.

"Oui." Again, Lizette was pleased that she could answer the question yes.

There was an uncomfortable pause.

"Please continue," Bernal coaxed.

"So sorry. Um, I moved to where I could look around the corner to see what was going on and she was giving his wiener a good sucking. Her, all dressed to the nines and kneeling down in her beautiful dress, working on his cock. I moved away quickly. Apparently, Pater was quick as well, because they came out right behind my moving away," Lizette Bergen explained.

"Did you ask Pater what that was all about?" Reid questioned.

"Oui." Again, silence from Lizette after she answered the initial question. Again, the look on her face showed she seemed pleased with herself.

"Aannd?" Reid continued.

"So sorry. He told me to mind my own business." Lizette said abruptly.

"Please tell us if there was anything else strange about that evening," Bernal said.

"Oui, there was," Lizette answered.

"And that would be?" Reid came in quickly to keep things moving along.

"There was a loud discussion at the table where the murdered man was dining and everyone there, all three of them, got up quickly and left without even finishing their meals. And do you know what else?" Lizette said.

"What else?" Agent Bernal mocked excitement about her

answer.

"The woman who was doing the business in the hallway with Pater and the gentleman who was with her, also got up and left their meals unfinished. The Spring Restaurant is a fine restaurant and people dine there leisurely and all people finish their excellent tasting food, but these two tables were in a hurry to get out of there. Why do you suppose that was?" Lizette questioned.

The interview with Lizette Bergen took a little more than an hour. Reid was not sure what they had accomplished.

DGSI Agent Rene' Bernal led Pater Skons into the interrogation room.

As with Lizette, they began with general questions for Pater. He was from Stavanger, Norway and had grown tired of watching hundreds of thousands of tourists pass through to see the Petroleum Museum and the rock outcropping of Preikestolen. Not that these were not interesting things to see, but he "wanted to be the one getting out and away and seeing new places."

Pater had been in Paris for about ten months and "was loving" it.

"So, Pater, you are aware that one of your customers just two nights ago was murdered shortly after dining at The Spring Restaurant, where you work?" Agent Bernal asked.

"Ja, that was terrible," Pater responded.

"Did anything strange happen at the restaurant that evening?" Bernal asked.

"Mmmm, not really," Pater looked earnestly at the two men.

Reid could smell a little body odor and a heavy layer of cheap cologne trying to cover it up. Reid could also hear that Pater was breathing a little heavily.

"You sure there is nothing you want to share with us?" Reid asked. "We don't think you were involved in the murder we are simply trying to put together the pieces of what happened in the hour or so before it happened."

"Nothing out of the ordinary," Pater answered quickly.

"Pater, we have word from some of your coworkers that a beautiful woman came back into the kitchen and gave you a blow job. If that is ordinary, I might have to get a job in a restaurant kitchen. Is it ordinary as you say?" Agent Bernal questioned.

"Who ever said that is lying to you and you should be interested in why they are lying about me," Pater protested.

BAM!!! Agent Bernal slammed his hand down on the table and stood leaning into Pater from across the table. The move startled Reid.

"YOU NEED TO STOP IT RIGHT NOW! WE DON'T HAVE TIME FOR YOUR GAME! IF YOU DON'T START TELLING THE TRUTH, YOU'LL BE BACK TOURING THE PETROLIUM MUSEUM IN STAVANGER BEFORE THE SUN GOES DOWN TOMORROW NIGHT!" In a lower voice Rene' Bernal continued, "if we boot you out, you will never return to Paris. Never return to France." "GIVE US THE TRUTH!" For effect, Bernal slammed his hand down again.

Reid was not as startled at this one. He was waiting for Agent Bernal to blow his stack. He was sure that the degree of body odor coming from Pater had ticked up a couple of notches. In a calm voice he said, "Pater, just tell us what happened. You are making us think you are trying to hide something, and we have no reason to believe that you were involved in this murder, but you have to stop trying to hide something from us."

Pater started in a shaky voice, "Ssshh Shh she said he wouldn't notice it. She said it would not hurt him. Just put the two tablets in the man's water before it was served and if I did that, she would suck my cock right then and there."

"What color were the tablets?" Reid asked.

"They were small and white, and they dissolved quickly in the water," Pater answered. "Did I kill him?"

"No. You did not kill him. Did you notice anything else Pater?" Reid asked.

"After my uhh encounter with the woman, I kept looking over to her table and watching the man as well. When the man who got the pills got up to go to the rest room, two men followed him. A man, who was sitting at the bar and the man who was with the woman," Pater replied.

"Did you notice anything strange there?" Agent Bernal asked.

"They all came out together almost. The man at the bar seemed to be watching over the man who got the pills, because when that whole table got up to leave, he moved to the doorway to get with them."

"What about the man with the woman?" Reid asked.

"He and the woman got up and left immediately before the other table," Pater answered.

"Do you remember what those two men looked like?" Reid asked. "The one with the woman and the one who seemed to be watching over."

"The man at the bar looked like a thug. He had close set eyes and seemed to stare right through you. The man with the woman looked like a well-dressed, good-looking, dark-haired businessman. He was fit, maybe forty years old. He seemed to not pay too much attention to anything but the woman whom I have guessed was a prostitute?" Pater said. "But when the man who got the pills got up from the table, the man and the woman were already outside. No one from either table finished their meals. It was such a waste of delicious food."

"The person Pater described could easily have been the same person he was trying to shoot at the airport. Yuri Rosov," Reid thought.

"Do you think if you saw the man and the woman again you could identify them?" Reid asked.

"I'm not sure," Pater responded. "I'm not very good at that kind of thing."

Agent Bernal got up and walked to the door. "I think we are done for now, but we may have more questions for you later. We would appreciate if you don't speak to your co-workers about any of this." With that Pater departed the interrogation room.

"If I were a betting man, I would say that the man who left the restaurant with the ahh, Pater's beautiful woman was the man who committed the murder," Agent Bernal hypothesized.

"I believe you are correct, and I believe that this man is Yuri Rosov, The Thorny Rose. the man we are looking for in connection with the other diplomat murders," Reid agreed.

"Let's break for lunch and then we can see what connection the murdered man has with Luba Krupin and Shanaz Latifpour," Bernal said.

"Good idea, because believe it or not, I am hungry again," Reid said enthusiastically.

CHAPTER 60

February 22
Saturday 2:00pm Local Time Paris

DGSI Agent Rene' Bernal was struck with how pretty Luba Krupin was, sexy really.

The fragrances that Reid could discern from Ms. Krupin were lovely and a welcome change from Pater Skons. He could identify an alluring blend of lavender, orange, and almost cinnamon, and other spices in the background. He wanted to find out what that was so he could get some for Kendall and for a moment he could imagine himself burying his face into Kendall's neck and bosom with that scent surrounding them.

"Ms. Krupin what was your relationship to Kostya Ivanov," Agent Bernal began abruptly shocking Reid out of his daydream.

"He was my mentor and for a time he was my boss." Luba said fighting back the tears.

"What was the purpose of the dinner? Was it social? Was it business?" Agent Bernal asked.

Luba Krupin looked down and drew a deep breath. "It was meant to be social, but it was really business," she started. "We had an investment group. Kostya, Park Soo-Hoon, Xing Tsua Ten and Shahnaz Latifpour."

Reid's heart skipped a beat. *"Sweet mother of Jesus! We are finally getting somewhere,"* he thought to himself.

"I managed the money in the New York Stock Exchange. All these men knew each other from their work in diplomatic circles. They all worked on trades and agreements related to American agriculture for their own countries. Like most diplomats, they did not make a lot of money. I was Kostya Ivanov's assistant. He knew that I had a gift for trading in stocks and it was really Kostya who put the group together. The investment group known as The Marco Polo Alliance was supposed to be a way for them to save some money for retirement. The group started nine months ago, and the dinner was going to be a report on how the Investments were doing."

Knowing that you always follow the money Reid asked, "How were the investments doing?"

"They are doing a little better than average. We are making about a 15% return against a market that is averaging 7% this year," Luba said with some pride. The return was of course much higher than that due to the Intercepted Trading, but there was no reason for Luba to reveal that now. After all, she thought, maybe they will find that I am guilty of a Securities crime, but that is not likely. She would save that information for now.

"Who would have a reason to kill your partners in The Marco Polo Alliance, who is it?" Bernal asked slowly. "Last night, you told me you know who it is."

Luba, who had been looking down at her hands, as she told the story, looked up briefly and burst into tears.

"The only pa-person I can think of is tha-that son of a mother, Shahnaz Latifpour," she forced out through the tears.

Luba sobbed uncontrollably. Reid could hear her sobs and sniffling and he asked Agent Bernal to get her a tissue. This girl was clearly distraught. *"Was she correct about Latifpour?"*

"Why do you say this?" Reid asked.

"WELL, IT WASN'T ME! WH-WHO ELSE IS THERE?" Luba shouted!

Reid could feel spittle hit his hands from across the table.

"Shahnaz has been so calm after the murders. He-he sseems to know about them before they happen. He is the one who called Kostya and me right after each of them to let us know about the murders," Ms. Krupin explained.

"Well, there must be more than that," Agent Bernal probed.

"Yes, there is. We set up The Marco Polo Alliance so if something happened to one of the members before the disbursement of the funds, the remaining members would split the funds. Now Shahnaz Latifpour is the only one left," Luba explained.

"*Wow,*" Reid thought. "*She may have just handed us the case wrapped and tied in a neat little package. Maybe a little too neat, but not if we can connect the dots between Yuri Rosov and Shahnaz Latifpour.*"

"After the death of Kostya Ivanov, what happens with the investment club now?" Reid asked.

"We had already made plans, before Kostya's death, to travel as a group to New York on Monday morning to disburse the funds from the investment," Luba answered. "I want it to be over. We have all booked passage on the same CP Pak transport."

"Do you think that is wise?" Agent Bernal asked. Luba Krupin would not know that the authorities from France and the U.S.A were hot in pursuit of the killer Yuri Rosov. Ms. Krupin would not know that they had not apprehended him or may not have thought clearly that he had killed twice on CP Pak transports already.

Still crying softly Luba said, "I just want it to be over and to get on with my life."

"Ms. Krupin did you see anything that caught your attention at the Spring Restaurant last night?" Reid asked.

"Like what do you mean?" Luba responded.

"Anything that just seemed a little strange," Reid replied.

"No, I am sorry, nothing caught my attention," Luba said confidently.

There was a brief pause as Rene' Bernal whispered something to Reid and Reid responded, "no."

"Well, we thank you Ms. Krupin. We really cannot

keep you from taking the CP Pak transport to New York on Monday, but we do ask you the courtesy of keeping the French government informed of how we can contact you for further conversations should that become necessary," DGSI Agent Bernal said.

Agent Bernal escorted Luba Krupin back to the lobby area of the DGSI headquarters.

"Well, that was interesting," he said in a rather booming voice, startling Reid, as he came back into the interrogation room. Bernal's dramatic entrance with long strides and arms opened wide would have looked to Reid like a Broadway performer, if only he could have seen it.

Reid responded, "Yes, it was. An investment group, where the last man standing gets all of the money. Money is the motive more times than not in crimes like this. Someone with knowledge of this group or someone from the group has hired Yuri Rosov and his team to eliminate the other partners. It is not clear to me if Luba Krupin had a stake in this money if all of the Alliance partners were to be killed by The Thorny Rose."

"Do you really think that sweet young thing could be responsible for this?" Agent Bernal said as his phone beeped letting him know that Shahnaz Latifpour was in the lobby.

"Let's see what our friend Shahnaz Latifpour has to say," Bernal said as he walked out the door to retrieve Shahnaz Latifpour.

"Gentlemen, I am very pleased to meet the men who are going to bring an end to this unfortunate business of murdered diplomats," Latifpour stated solemnly.

Reid noted that Shahnaz Latifpour smelled of expensive cologne, expensive wool, a starched shirt and newly polished shoes. It is amazing what your nose picks up when you no longer have eyesight to fill in the blanks.

"What can you tell us about your dinner last night? The last meal enjoyed by Kostya Ivanov before he was murdered," Agent Bernal started the questioning.

"I was accompanied by my bodyguard back to my room at the Luxor Hotel just a few blocks away from the Spring Restaurant in the opposite direction from the murder. A hotel room I might add, where I remained until this morning with my guard outside my door the entire time. I heard about the murder on the television," Latifpour said.

"Good to know. What was the purpose of the dinner?" Reid inquired.

"We are friends. Were friends in the case of Kostya and the others," Latifpour replied.

"How do you know one another?" Reid continued.

"We make trades with America for agricultural products. You could say we run in the same circles in American lingo," Shahnaz smiled big at Reid and Rene'.

"Kostya Ivanov was not the first Diplomat murdered in the past several days. Are you aware there are others?" Rene' Bernal asked.

"Uh yes, the others were also people that I knew from diplomatic circles," Latifpour said.

"These murders must have made you concerned for your own life. After all, you had a bodyguard with you last night," Reid stated.

"Yes, of course. I retained a bodyguard after the murder of Xing Tsua Ten. You can never be too careful. I even offered to arrange for protection for the others in our little group. I worked in security, and I know of these things," the Iranian explained.

"What things are those?" Reid jumped in.

"That people sometimes get involved with things that are over their heads, above their level to handle, when they are allowed to travel all over the world. Without investigation on my part, it is hard to tell what those other diplomats were involved with. You see, things are not always as they seem," Latifpour dodged.

"How do they seem to you Mr. Latifpour?" Reid bore in.

Latifpour gazed upward with a look of arrogance and

knowing and said, "These men got involved in something that has gotten them killed. The temptation of money or sex or drugs is too great for some men. I stay on the good side of Allah and do not give in to these temptations of weaker men."

"You mentioned your little group. What little group is that?" Rene' Bernal questioned.

"We were all a part of a little investment club. Xing, Park Soo-Hoon, Kostya and I had all put in a little money for Luba Krupin to manage for us. Have you met the delicious Luba yet?" All of the sudden Latifpour was chatty. "I was hoping to see her here and maybe get a dinner date with her before we leave for New York on Monday Morning."

"Was Luba Krupin making a lot of money for all of you?" Reid asked.

"Who knows? My family already has money. We have distant connections to the Royals in Iran and we are in good favor with the ruling powers. Hence, my job on the diplomatic corp. My involvement in the investment group is singularly focused to get closer to Luba Krupin. Have you seen her yet? She is stupendous! I don't wish to sound like a pig, my mother taught me to hold women in high regard, but I want to conquer that woman in a Biblical sense as you Christians say," Latifpour said.

"Who else might have known about your club? Did you have a name for it?" Rene' Bernal asked.

"The Marco Polo Alliance; that is what Luba named it. I do not know who might also have known about us, but obviously, there is someone," Latifpour answered.

"Continue that thought," Bernal said.

"From the beginning of all of this with the murder of Xing Tsua Ten, I suspected an outsider. Not one of the others had the brains or connections to do something like this. A murder on a CP Pak transport? Are you kidding me? These others needed directions to cross the street," Latifpour said arrogantly.

"What about Luba? Could she have done this?" Reid

asked.

"Possibly. In our line of work, you never rule anything out. But the Luba Krupin I know could not kill a spider and could not have comprehended a plot that would kill three men," Latifpour said confidently. "And additionally, she does not stand to get any of the money from the investments. No, you need to look at who knew about this from the outside of our little group. That is where you will find the master mind of these murders," Shanaz leaned in to give his advice. "There is someone who wanted one of these people dead and has gone to elaborate means to accomplish that goal and has killed others to hide their real motive."

"Will you be travelling to New York with Luba for the disbursement of the funds from The Marco Polo Alliance?" Agent Bernal asked.

"I would not miss the opportunity to spend time with Luba Krupin," Latifpour said somewhat cautiously realizing these policemen knew more about the Alliance than they had let on.

"And you are not worried about travelling on a CP Pak transport? You may be travelling with a murderer," Reid asked. "What if that person is still looking to kill members of your investment group?"

"I have never been the target of these murders," Latifpour said boldly. "And, I will have my bodyguard with me. Besides, whomever the mastermind is and what their real reasons may be, I get all the money no matter the small size of the purse," he said dismissively. "I, of course, will keep you informed of my whereabouts as I travel. I suspect you gentlemen will be working on this for quite some time and may need to speak with me again."

"You are correct Mr. Latifpour. We'll get you some paperwork showing how to keep us up to date on your whereabouts. I will show you out," Agent Bernal gestured to the door.

After they left the room, Reid was almost overwhelmed

with exhaustion. Keeping his brain totally concentrating on the words, sounds and smells in the room, plus the general lack of sleep over the past 36 hours had taken a toll on him. But he must remain alert long enough to debrief Agent Bernal.

"So, what do you think?" Agent Bernal burst back into the room.

"Pretty amazing that the two people who likely would have a reason to be behind these murders spent a lot of time trying to send us in the direction of the other. Offering thoughts on the responsible party is a bit of a hot potato. Are you familiar with that term Rene'?" Reid asked.

"Yes, I am. Which of those deflections from self has the most logic behind it, Reid? Seems to me, that Luba Krupin's assertion that Shahnaz Latifpour is behind this carries the most weight. In addition, to me, he is more than capable of masterminding this and she does not seem capable," Rene' Bernal pondered.

"I have been thinking about that myself. And while I was thinking, three questions came to me. One, does Shahnaz Latifpour really have the money he says he has, thus negating money as a motive for him? Two, does Luba Krupin have a bigger stake in the invested funds than Latifpour believes? If she out lives everyone else, does she get the money? And three, is something Shahnaz Latifpour said. I have it cued up here." Reid pushed play on his phone recorder and Latifpour's voice boomed forth, "Luba Krupin could not kill a spider and could not have comprehended a plot that would kill three men,"

Reid hit the stop button and said, "Shahnaz said three men. If Luba Krupin is the mastermind, she would plan to kill four men. Only Shahnaz Latifpour would be interested in killing just three men to get the money."

"Yes, and he also said that he was not worried about traveling with Yuri Rosov, because he was never a target of the killer," Agent Bernal pointed out. "Latifpour just seems a little too arrogant and confident to me."

"I am beginning to see that myself," Reid said nodding

his head. "Instead of relying solely on our gut instinct, lets dig into the money." "Let's investigate how much wealth the Latifpour family has, and I will have my team in Seattle get warrants to look into the investment account and see if the sweet and fine smelling Ms. Krupin has any skin in the game."

"I could not agree with you more Reid," Agent Bernal said. "I will have our people investigate the wealth controlled by the Latifpour family."

"Let's stay in touch on both of those items. Now, I am exhausted, can your people deliver me back to the American Hospital of Paris? I am expected there for another treatment for my eyes," Reid said.

"Yes, yes." Then Agent Bernal's phone beeped again. With a questioning look he said to Reid, "I'm being called to the lobby again. I'll be right back."

A few minutes later, Agent Bernal burst back into the room. "Look who I found down in the lobby."

"I can't look with my eyes, but I recognize that cologne and the cat-like footsteps. Chris Keller I am beyond happy to have you at my side!" Reid exclaimed.

After a joyous reunion that belied the fact that they had been apart only 12 hours, FBI Agents Chris Keller and Reid Daniels left almost immediately for the American Hospital of Paris. They had a lot to catch up on; the aftermath of the bombing in Ketchikan, the survival in Montana and the incident at the Orly International Airport.

As they arrived at the hospital, Reid asked the DGSI driver and Chris Keller to get out of the car. He needed to call Regional Commander Sanchez.

He was glad to have a secure ICP in his hand. He punched in the code for Sanchez.

"Carlos. Reid Daniels here. Are you free to talk?

"Yes, Reid. Absolutely. Gimme a second," Sanchez said as he motioned the people he was meeting with out of his office. "Tell me it is good news. Have we captured the killer?"

"Not just yet Carlos, but we have what we think is the

motive and we have two very strong suspects, one of whom is most likely the person who hired The Thorny Rose and his team," Reid informed. "We have every reason to believe that we still have Yuri Rosov pinned down in Paris."

"Reid, I can't impress on you enough what a service you are performing for our country. Is there any good news from Paris that I can send up the chain of command?" Regional Commander Carlos Sanchez pleaded.

"I called because we need a Warrant to get into a banking account controlled by one of the primary suspects and this banking account involves all three victims in this case. I can't impress upon you how much we need this warrant and how fast we need this warrant, so my people can track down this account," Reid allowed the stress to show through. "Carlos, we are all feeling the pressure. We are working as fast and as smart as we can," Reid said.

Carlos Sanchez was taken aback. "As soon as you can get the details to us, we will present the Warrant request to a Judge. Get back to work Reid. You and your team are doing a fantastic job."

"Thanks," Reid said.

CHAPTER 61

February 22
Saturday 8:00am Time Local Time Seattle

Robin and Kendall arrived at the Federal Building in Seattle at 8:00am sharp to continue their conversations with Analka Hrapla. To their surprise, Analka had already been meeting for an hour with an attorney sent to her by "her boss". Kendall was furious with the U.S. Marshal Service because they had not reached out to the Seattle FBI Cyber Crimes offices to let them know of this new development. Kendall contacted Eileen Wisdom at Quantico immediately to get some help with this situation.

Inside the private room where they were meeting, Analka and her new attorney, Maria Fedorova, were wrapping up their discussions.

"As we have discussed Analka, it is not all a bad thing to try to get a lighter sentence by helping the FBI, as long as you do not give them too much information. You have the chemical technology card to play that can be especially useful to them," Maria Fedorova said. "So, we will extract as much as possible from the FBI for that tasty morsel of information."

"I understand," Analka said while staring seriously at her attorney.

"What is going to happen now is that your Robeen, as you call him, and Kendall Hughes are going to come in here and we are going to tell them that you want to meet with them alone without me. As we discussed, they will likely want to get their FBI lawyers on the phone, and you will give up your rights to have me present for those discussions. You need to build their trust so you can get from Robeen what is happening in Paris. Our boss needs to know completely what is happening in Paris and you will only get that information if Robeen trusts you." Maria Fedorova explained.

Analka nodded in agreement.

Eric White, the legal team leader from Oklahoma, and Eileen Wisdom called back to Kendall and Robin almost immediately.

"Let's not git our undies all in a wad just yet, pardon the expression. We knew we hadda git'er legal reperzentation before we made a deal with her anyway. We did that but now this surprise attorney has come on the scene, so let's find out what this surprise attorney has to say, and then we'll deal with that," White said. "Git on in there and git us on the phone and we'll git this rodeo underway."

After all parties were in the room and on the line, the FBI side was surprised to hear that Analka wanted to speak with them alone without her attorney present.

"Well, that is highly uncommon," White said with his heavy drawl. "We got that racordor going so there is a record of this?"

"Yes, I can vouch for the fact that the recorder is running and at my client's request, I will leave the room now," Maria Fedorova said. "Analka, I will be just outside, so if you want me back at any time, all you have to do is request that I come back into the room. Just say, I need my attorney present."

Over the next four hours Analka, in her sometimes-broken English, explained how she met Yuri's team because of her work toward unlocking the secrets of the CP Pak transport. She left out the part about her benefactor agent and her work as a hacker for hire for Yuri Rosov. She spoke of her studies with Professor Winston Eblodskya at the 30 School for gifted students in St. Petersburg.

Eric White suggested a break for lunch and as Analka brushed close to Robin she whispered, "my lawyer does not represent me," then she hurried out the door with her jailers from the U.S. Marshal service.

Analka knew she was dancing on a thin wire. Trying to aid the FBI on one side while trying to protect her relationship with Robin and on the other side giving no information that would harm the *"Job"* thus protecting her mother. She had no idea who sent Maria Fedorova to her. She assumed it was Yuri. She knew she was between the rocks and a hard place as the Americans say.

Kendall and Robin headed back to the FBI's Northwest Cyber Crimes offices. On the way, Robin shared what Analka had told him about Maria Fedorova.

They arrived at the office to find Bert Hamilton and Lan Phang typing feverishly on their keyboards. The Banking Warrant had been granted and Bert was digging for the mysterious financial account managed by Luba Krupin. Lan Phang was digging for general information about Luba Krupin.

Kendall placed a call to Reid to make sure he was okay. It had been hours since they had talked.

"Reid are you there?" she spoke over Robin's ICP.

"Yes, I am here, and I am available to talk Mi Amore," Reid responded joyously.

"Oh Reid, my dear, I have been so worried about you!" Kendall gushed.

In the other room, Bert Hamilton raised her eyebrows, but did not look up from her computer work. She allowed a small smile. No one else in the office seemed to notice Kendall and Reid's conversation.

"Tell me right now what is happening with your eyes," Kendall demanded.

"Eloise hmm, Dr. Marchand, the Ophthalmologist here says I am doing really well, and she believes I will be out of the heavy bandages in two days," Reid shared.

"Oh, you're on a first name basis with your doctor already," Kendall said somewhat disapprovingly. "How old is your French doctor?"

"She sounds like thirties, and she smells really good," Reid said, realizing full well how this was sounding.

"Well, I am looking at a picture of her on the Internet right now, which of course she was not, and she is closer to 60 and quite a bit overweight," Kendall responded.

Reid laughed. "Okay, I get it. I will keep that picture of her in my mind from now on. Right next to the perky thirty-year-old that I already have there."

"What's happening on the case Reid? Did Chris Keller get over there with you in the past few hours?" Kendall asked. "I don't understand how he is standing."

"Yes, he's here. I don't understand that either. Let's get Robin and Bert on the line right now and I will brief everyone," Reid said.

When they were all assembled Reid started again, "I have been going over recordings of the interviews with Chris, who is here with me. We are focusing on the answers of the two people who had met for dinner with the Russian diplomat in the hour before he was killed. Agent Rene' Bernal of the French DGSI and I interviewed those people and two people from the service staff at the restaurant."

Kendall bit the inside of her lip at the mention of Rene' Bernal and thought to herself, "*could I really be this prone to jealousy after less than a week of knowing this man. Is Rene' another good looking thirty-year-old woman? Snap out of it Kendall. Let it go. You are more intelligent than this. Concentrate on the problem.*"

Reid had continued, "Turns out all the murdered diplomats and these two people were in an investment group. One of the two people at the dinner is Luba Krupin who managed the investments and the other is an Iranian diplomat named Shahnaz Latifpour who is now the only surviving member of the investment group,"

"A little Stock Club where you can end up dead?" Bert said.

"How old is Ms. Krupin?" Kendall asked.

"Lan Phang says she is early thirties," Bert offered. "I'm working with a FISA Warrant to find this Investment Account, which is managed by Krupin, so we can see how much money is there. Lan is digging to find out everything we can about Krupin."

"The French team is doing the same type of research with this Latifpour fellow," Reid said.

"Of the two, she seems the least likely to have hatched this plot," Reid suggested.

"Just because she comes across as young and vulnerable to a middle aged temporarily blind FBI agent, that is no reason to dismiss her as the possible leader of this entire affair," Kendall interjected.

"I second that," Bert said making eye contact with Kendall.

"Did I mention that I have not seen her, but she sure smelled good?" Reid asked which got a round of laughter out of everyone.

Reid got serious again. "Seriously, can you confirm that Rosov is still here in Paris?"

"Yes," Bert said, "Lan Phang and I, with the help of the French DGSI, are 99% certain that he is still there."

Lan Phang who was now standing in the doorway was nodding her agreement.

Reid laid out his plan, "Our two suspects will be on a CP Pak transport from Paris to New York on Monday morning and my thought is that Yuri will be on that same transport and if you all agree, Chris Keller and I will be on that transport as well."

"It sounds dangerous Reid, unnlesss, unless we can get Analka to provide us with the magic she has discovered which will allow you and Chris to be animated during the Transport," Kendall said looking directly at Robin.

"If we can't give you that protection, then you and Chris should not be on that CP Pak transport," Bert said emphatically.

The alarm from Bert Hamilton's and Lan Phang's computers went off simultaneously startling everyone on the call.

"Boss, stay on the line, while we check this out," Agent Hamilton shouted over her shoulder.

Hamilton and Phang were quickly going through pages on their screens as the alarm continued. Hamilton's phone rang. It was her contact at the DGSI in Paris.

"Are you seeing what we are seeing," the French DGSI agent asked. "Yuri Rosov is at the American Hospital of Paris. We have Gendarmes on the way. Can you alert your people?"

"YES! AND YES," Bert shouted. "REID, YURI IS AT THE HOSPITAL RIGHT NOW! CHRIS KELLER SHOULD DEPLOY AND REID, YOU SHOULD SHELTER IN PLACE! SOME FRENCH POLICE ARE THERE AND OTHERS ARE ON THE WAY!

Yuri had entered through an employee entrance at the side of the hospital. Always the professional, he had studied the schematics of the hospital to learn the back stairways to use and to plan his escape route. A stairway camera caught just seconds of Yuri Rosov before he had disabled it. The AI computers identified The Thorny Rose in those few seconds.

Yuri made his way to the basement laundry where he overpowered a young man working there. He taped the attendant's mouth, zip tied him, lifted the bound man into a laundry cart and covered him under a pile of dirty sheets. Yuri found clean scrubs to pull over his own clothes and prepared one of the dryers for his getaway in case he needed it. He started a drying cycle, opened the door, then closed it again to make sure the dryer would resume its cycle automatically once the door was closed a second time. It did.

Just outside of the laundry Yuri took the stairs to the third floor. He peered carefully down the length of that floor of offices and saw no police security. He walked to the far stairway at the other end of the building. He would use this far stairway to approach the fourth floor and Reid's room. When he reached Reid's floor while still in the stairway, he pulled the silencer from his gun and fired it three times. He stuffed the gun and silencer back into his pocket and burst out of the stairway. Police were already running down the hall toward him with guns drawn.

In his hospital scrubs, running as fast as he could toward the police, Yuri shouted in perfect French as he passed them, "There is a man on the stairway, who shot at me from above."

The officers ran past him, through the door, then started up the stairway.

Yuri quickly reassembled his silenced gun and oriented himself to find Reid's room. He walked slowly down the hall with a clipboard in his free hand. He was looking for there to be more security outside the door to Reid's room. He was surprised to see that there was none.

The door to Reid's room was closed and the lights were off. Yuri walked past the room and could not see much inside the room other than a body lying in the bed. There was not the usual heart monitor or IV bottle that one might see in a hospital. That made sense to Yuri since Agent Daniels's eye condition did not require that kind of care.

Yuri quickly stepped back past the room. He wondered for a moment to himself, *"is this the right thing to do?"* In all the *"Jobs"* he had completed for others, he had been entirely dispassionate about his targets. They were people that Yuri's contracted bosses needed dead.

Yuri slowly opened the door to Reid's room. He saw movement to his right and fired his silenced gun quickly. PUH PUH. The body in the shadows slumped and fell to the ground. The fact that Yuri was wearing the blue green scrubs had put fatal doubt into the mind of Reid's protector and cost him his life. Yuri saw movement in the bed. He flipped the light switch just inside the door to see Reid appearing to look in his direction, but the eyes were covered.

"FBI Agent Reid Daniels, I presume. Let me introduce myself. I am Yuri Rozov. Some call me The Thorny Rose," Yuri said quietly as he peered out the door to make sure no one was coming. Reid's heart was pounding. Yuri stepped over to the fallen body and PUH he put a bullet into the back of the head of the fallen man.

Reid was losing control. His breathing was erratic. His heart felt like it would pound out of his chest. He was disoriented by the darkness, the all-encompassing darkness. He had been given a sedative just minutes earlier to help him sleep. He was screaming in his mind for Charlie to help him. Nothing.

Reid tuned in through the terror to hear Yuri talking again. "Mister FBI man, usually I only keel people who need to die and normally I would not go out of my way to keel someone like you." Reid's mind was racing and sweat began oozing out of every pore. Reid was certain he had just seconds to live. "I must keel you not because someone else needs you dead. I must keel you for me."

Fear was consuming Reid! Pitch black fear! Suffocating fear. Reid had thought once shortly after losing Charlie that he wanted to die too. But now that was the furthest thing from his mind. He wanted to live for Michael. He wanted to live for Kendall. He wanted to live!

Suddenly Charlie was at Reid's side.

"The thing is I must keel you because I need you dead. You have keeled too many of my friends and associates. This is personal to me now agent Daniels." Yuri said in a cool and calm voice.

Charlie shouted, *"Reid! Chris Keller put your gun in bed with you. It is on your left side."*

Reid's foggy mind was coming back. He did have his gun. He was reaching for it as Yuri continued and at that point, the nano seconds of time were expanding for Reid. Everything slowed down. Yuri's speech slowed down.

Slowly raising his gun in Reid's direction, Yuri was saying, "Iiittt isss almooooost funnnnyyy, donnnn't youuuu thiiiink? I haaad theee chaaance tooo keeeel youuu innn theee parrrkkkiiing gaaragggge aaat Seeea-Taaac. I haad theee chaaance tooo keeeel youuu aat Orrlyy Airrporrrt. FFFBBBIII Aaaggeenntt Daaaniiiels, yooouur tiimmee ooon earrrth hhaaas..."

Reid knew that he might die. Still, he could hear Charlie shouting at him to "GO DOWN FIGHTING." Yuri was caught in mid-sentence. BLAM BLAM BLAM BLAM. Reid was firing under the covers in the direction of Yuri's voice. Yuri had to duck and dodge sideways. At the same time shouts and running footsteps were coming from down the hall to the left. Yuri quickly peered out, ducked back into the room, and bent his arm around the doorway and fired two silenced shots at the three officers coming his way. PUH PUH Those advancing ducked into doorways for safety. Yuri looked back in Reid's direction to see the bed was now empty. He fired two quick shots at the bed PUH PUH, then Yuri turned back out the door to his right firing down the hall behind himself as he broke into a run toward the exit at the end of the hall.

Just as Yuri cleared the outside of Reid's room, Reid fired three shots holding his hand just over the top of the bed at a level which he felt might hit the assassin through the wall. BLAM BLAM BLAM

Before Yuri made two steps toward the exit door, bullets were breaking through the shatterproof window of Reid's hospital room. They were coming from Reid inside the room. The 9mm bullets were slightly deflected by the safety meshed glass. Bullets didn't strike him, but he was struck by hundreds of pieces of shattered glass. The tiny pieces of glass hit his right side doing primary damage to the right side of his face. The scrubs over his clothes protected his body, but his face and his right hand were exposed to the glass shrapnel.

When Yuri had been spotted by the Hospital's cameras, the AI / FR applications being monitored by Bert Hamilton and Lan Phang had sounded the alarm to Reid. Chris Keller immediately placed Reid's gun under the covers near his free left hand and had gone to meet with gendarmes who were hunting for Yuri. Keller had given instructions to the unfortunate police officer who had stayed in the room with Reid.

Now with Yuri racing through the EXIT door at the end of the hall, Chris was back bounding into Reid's room to find his friend on the floor beside the bed. Chris helped a sweat soaked and shaking Reid Daniels back into the bathroom of his hospital room.

"Good job dude," Chris was panting and reloading Reid's gun. "You fired your gun and didn't hit yourself or me. You're safe now. A gendarme will be here to protect you."

Agent Keller placed one of the three French policemen on guard duty with Reid, then Chris broke into a sprint toward the EXIT door which Yuri had gone through. He shouted over his shoulder to the other French officers, "follow me."

The three ran to the stairway door with guns drawn. Chris looked through the window, opened the door slowly from the side. Seeing that it appeared safe, he motioned for one of the French officers to take the stairs up and for the other officer to follow him.

The two of them started down the stairs quickly, but quietly. They heard a door close five floors below them and quickened their pace. On their way down the stairs, they passed a fallen gendarme who had been killed by The Thorny Rose.

The delay of Chris Keller's pursuit allowed Yuri to make it to the laundry room. He knew that he would need to use the getaway tactic he had prepared. Yuri quickly got out of the scrubs and mixed them near the top of the laundry cart where he had placed the bound laundry attendant. He then ran to the dryer he had prepared. He set the timer for four minutes, let it start, then he opened the door and climbed inside.

Yuri knew the dryer would start again as soon as he closed the door. He hastily wrapped himself inside of sheets in the dryer and braced himself with his hands and feet against the inside of the dryer drum. He had seen American college students do this on a YouTube video. He reached out, grabbed the bottom of the door and quickly pulled it toward himself. He got his hand tucked inside just in time for the dryer door to close. With the luck that Yuri always seemed to have in these situations, the dryer door closed, the dryer started and Chris Keller along with the French police officer, slowly opened the swinging doors to the laundry room.

Keller quickly assessed the situation. The laundry room looked to him to be 60 feet long and 40 feet wide, painted an off-white color. It was an open structure ceiling with bright overhead lighting and a waxed concrete floor. There were a half dozen oversized, industrial, stainless-steel washers with big tip-out doors. There were maybe 18 larger than consumer size white dryers. About half of the dryers were running, but no washers were running.

Keller did not speak French, but the female officer with him did speak English at a level that allowed them to communicate. Keller wanted to make sure that all the exits out of the Hospital were covered by gendarmes. The officer keyed her radio to verify that the exits were covered.

Keller asked the French officer to stay out of sight in the laundry room and call for support to help search the room. Keller said he would check a couple of side closets and the door at the end of the big room. He assured the officer he would be right back. The officer, with her gun drawn keyed her radio to ask for backup support in the laundry room and then she moved out of sight behind one of the large washers, just as the FBI Agent had requested.

Since their arrival in the laundry room, some dryers had shut down, but a few dryers were still running. One particularly important dryer finished its cycle and stopped. Inside, Yuri Rozov in his dizzied state peeked out the window of the dryer to see Chris Keller and the French gendarme talking. Then she moved out of view behind one of the large washers and Keller headed toward the far end of the laundry room.

Yuri counted to thirty, giving himself time to regain his

equilibrium. At thirty he gently pushed open the dryer door a crack. He could see the big ex- Navy Seal FBI agent walking from a closet in the middle of the room to the door at the far end. The agent peered through the door, opened it and walked through.

Yuri sensed this was his moment. The running dryers were making just enough noise in the big room. He knew if he could not see the French policewoman, she could not see him.

Yuri rolled out of the dryer, stuffed the towels back in and gently closed the door. He pulled his silenced gun and headed for the entrance where he quietly passed through the swinging doors.

He took the steps two at a time and was two floors up when he heard an elevator door opening and several voices headed toward the laundry room entrance.

The doors to the floor where he had stopped read EMERGENCY ROOM RECEIVING written in red in French. There was a small window in the door where he could see the emergency room at the far end of the hallway. He tucked his gun away and started walking down the hallway. About halfway down the hall, he encountered a nurse who, when she saw him, came running to his side.

"Do you speak French or English? Were you in the auto crash?" she asked as she grabbed his arm to support him.

Yuri nodded his head and muttered "French" and leaned heavily into her support. The nurse led him up the hall and pulled back white curtains to find a place for him to sit. She came back to him shortly with what looked like a young female emergency doctor or physician's assistant.

"He speaks French. I found him wandering in the hall," the helpful nurse said.

As she worked on Yuri, the doctor gave a running explanation of why Yuri may have been in the hall, "It looks like he has shattered glass in his face from the auto accident. He looks better than the other car crash victim they brought in. He was probably set off to the side during the first triage and nobody came back to care for him. Is that what happened?"

Yuri nodded and grunted.

The doctor gave him a quick exam while the nurse helped him take off his jacket. "You must have a gold bar in your jacket," she said.

"Multiple cell phones," Yuri muttered rather sheepishly in French.

The doctor was able to determine that Yuri did not have any broken bones and that he was not suffering from a concussion. "You, my man, are very lucky. Other than that glass in your face, you are the miracle passenger in this crash. Margot here will get the glass out of your face and treat the wounds. After she is done with that, she will have someone come in to take down your medical information. Sound good?"

Without waiting for a response from Yuri, she turned to Margot and said, "let me know if you run into trouble on any of that glass and I will be right back in to help you with stitches if necessary." And then she was gone.

Yuri could not believe his luck. He was wondering how he was going to get his wounds treated. Margot worked quickly and soon had tincture and little bandages all over the right side of his face. When she left to get someone from administration to take down his medical information, Yuri simply got up, grabbed his jacket, and limped, for effect, through the emergency room passing two gendarmes on the way. He then strolled out into the night. Some people are just born lucky. Even when they obviously knew he was in the hospital they could not catch him. The only thing that had gone wrong was that clearly cameras had identified him and just as clearly Reid Daniels was not dead in his bed.

It took three minutes for the AI computers to identify him limping out of the hospital with bandages on his face and that was all the time that The Thorny Rose needed to disappear into the night.

CHAPTER 62

February 22
Saturday 1:30pm Local Time Washington, DC

President Charles Parker got the ad hoc weekend crisis meeting underway.

"Ladies and gentlemen thank you for coming in on such short notice," President Parker addressed the cabinet members assembled in the oval office.

"Jim what do we hear from our super cyber cop Reid Daniels," the President asked.

"Reid has been in Paris for just over 24 hours and he and his team are growing closer to making arrests not only of the assassin, but also the master mind of this odd plot to kill diplomats. It seems that all these victims were a part of an investment club intentionally designed to allocate all of the funds to the last living member," explained FBI Director Russell.

"It seems strange that something so relatively benign has caused such a stir in the world," observed Secretary of Defense Roberts. "The China threat seems to have dissipated only to be replaced by false outrage from the old teddy bear, Vladimir Putin."

"Yes, Vladdy while expressing outrage to us and the world has his hands full explaining to China and North Korea how Russians seem to be heavily mixed up in all of this," said NSA Chief. "We are now, and we'll continue to let him drift in the wind."

"Our Press Secretary is doing an outstanding job of releasing just enough information to show that we are moving very quickly on this case, but not getting out ahead of the investigation itself," the President remarked. "Please let Kristin know of my appreciation."

The Chief of Staff nodded her head.

CIA Director Tang interjected, "Have you heard the latest on our man Reid Daniels?"

By now they were all taking ownership of Reid's escapades. "Seems Reid was blinded by a pepper spray mishap at the airport when he arrived last night, and I would like to hear more about that. Anyway, Daniels is at the American Hospital of Paris..."

"I was treated for the flu there a year ago. Great medical people there," Secretary of State Hertz interrupted.

"...where he is being treated for temporary blindness. According to my sources THE ASSISSAN tried to make a hit on blind Reid and totally sightless Reid got shots off that wounded the assassin while suffering no injuries himself. We need to clone this guy."

"Well, let's not get out over our skis too far," President Parker reeled in the enthusiasm.

"We need this wrapped up in 48 hours. If I remember correctly, that is about the time the Xi Jinping Carrier Group will either lay off the coast of Brazil, which will put us on the alert again, or they will turn and head for Cape of Good Hope on the way back to their own waters," Parker said to no one in particular.

"There are some details we can't get into at this time, because a few things need to fall into place, but the good Lord willing, Reid will have it wrapped up in 48 hours," FBI Director James Russell responded.

"Give him all the help he needs and say a few prayers to get this thing off our plates. We'll plan to reconvene in approximately 48 hours, unless another unforeseen event comes out of left field," the President said.

At the Northwest Region FBI Cyber Crime offices in Seattle, Kendall Hughes was just off the phone with Reid where she was making sure he was okay after The Thorny Rose's attempt on his life. She pulled Robin aside from his computer search of Luba Krupin.

"We have to get Analka to share the secret of how a person can actually move in a CP Pak transport," Kendall said.

"Can't I just finish up on Luba Krupin? I'm really close," Robin asked.

"NO! We have to solve this puzzle first, then you will have time for Ms. Krupin," Kendall said firmly.

Within minutes Hughes and Agent Medallon had taken an Uber through the rainy streets of Seattle to the Federal Building. On the ride over Kendall and Robin had discussed giving Robin a chance to find out what Analka meant that her attorney did not work for her.

Analka and her mystery attorney, Maria, were in an interrogation room waiting for them. Kendall asked Maria if she could have a word with her.

When they were alone Robin took Analka's hand and began with the question why Maria did not work for her. Analka's grip was warm and affectionate.

"She's verkin for the boss not for me," Analka answered.

"You mean Yuri Rozov?" Robin asked.

"She wants to find out what ia going on with Yuri."

"What do you mean what is going on with Yuri?" Robin said completely puzzled.

"She wants to find out if FBI knows where Yuri is," Analka asked blinking her eyes heavily for effect, but Robin could tell it was not the usual way she looked at him. It was a desperate look. "Robeen they will keel me if you do not help me." Tears were welling in her eyes.

Robin realized that Analka did not know a thing about what was happening in Paris. Yuri had shown himself in Paris too many times for there to be any doubt about where he was. She wanted information on what the FBI, more importantly, what Reid was planning to do in Paris.

"I don't know anything Analka. Why would they tell me

what's going on?" Robin asked.

He let go of Analka's hand and got up to see if Kendall and Maria were ready to come back into the room.

Analka grabbed at Robin as he got up. Somehow in her orange federal prisoner garb and without that let's have sex right now affectionate look in her eye, Analka, though still beautiful, did not have the same attraction for Robin as before. He'd be damned if he allowed her to get any more information out of him.

Analka could see all of this in his eyes and his demeanor. She had to do something to regain Robin's affection.

When all four were back in the room, a call was placed to Eric White and Eileen Wisdom at the FBI headquarters in Quantico where the two had been waiting for the call.

"Gud mornan everbody," Eric White started pouring it on thick with the good ole country lawya routine. "Miss Hahrapla you are facing multiple counts of wire fraud, theft of U.S. govment property and at least three counts of accomplice to murda and Ah am sure we can find a few more charges to throw in there. You are just about to spend the rest of yah life in prison. What is it that you have that would make any sense for us to make a deal with you?

All of the sudden Analka Hrapla was firm and resolute. "I have what you need to stop Yuri Rosov from killing again," she said.

Kendall glanced at Robin.

Eric White did not miss a beat. "Well now, mebe you do have somethin that would mek sense to us, why don't you tell us why you should not spend the rest of yah life in prison,"

Analka looked down and took a deep breath, "I was fascinated by the CP Pak transport process. I wanted to study everyting about it. I did and, in the process, I determine, even though no accident had ever taken place, an accident was possible. All lives on the transport would be lost." She looked at Kendall, "it can happen in the spin-up process and can be detected inside of the transport."

"After discovering this, I was determined I would find a way to detect and avert such an accident. I discovered, developed, and tested a "mineral pill" that would slightly and briefly change the composition of the body minerals which allows for animal...human movement in a CP Pak transport. In other words, it allows awareness and movement in those few nano seconds before molecular breakdown and reconstruction in transport. A way for at least one person on board to be able to be aware and to avert an accident. It had nothing to do with committing murders," Analka explained.

"I had done hacking for hire jobs for Yuri previously, to make money to support my mother. Yuri paid me a sizeable sum of money as a retainer to work for him scamming people for money. I was poor and desperately needed the money to take care of my mother. I did not know if what my research had found would even be considered my invention, so I took the money and kept the success of my research to myself," Analka explained.

"A year went by, then Yuri contacted me and said he needed to try some of the "mineral pills" that he knew I had and, oh by the way, was I interested in being a spy. I don't know how Yuri found out about my mineral pills, but he convinced me that it was necessary for him to use it to protect himself and the team," Analka continued.

"Yuri made it all sound very exciting. I went to Berlin to meet with Yuri and his team. I should have known it was wrong. Georgy and Luca Pajari were bad men," Analka put her head down moving her head back and forth and tearing up, "I should have known."

"Do ya need a minute," Eric White asked sensing Analka was having a difficult moment.
Robin reached his hand across the table to comfort her.

"No, I will be fine," Analka paused. "It seemed that crime was destined to be my life no matter what I invented."

Kendall Hughes and the others could see the pain deep within this vulnerable young woman.

"Yuri tried one of my pills and made a trial run in a CP Pak transport. He said the pill worked brilliantly," Analka continued.

"Yuri was honest about the fact that he wanted to use the pills to kill a bad person who was trying to kill him. He said sometimes when your back is against the wall bad guys had to die, but he never told me that he and his team were assassins for hire. He never, never told me and I guess I didn't want to know," Analka pleaded with tears running down her face as she squeezed Robin's hand.

"Yuri, Petra Zane, and I spent an entire month planning how I would stalk Robin and become close to him so that I could get information from him to feed to Yuri. I hacked the Cyber Unit's computers and hacking the ticketing computers of the airlines and the CP Pak transports. I am very good at hacking," she said with humility. "Hacking is a way of life in Russian and the old Soviet Bloc countries."

"Even though I have a high IQ, I don't read people well," Analka glanced down seemingly in shame. "I thought we were finding a way to get money from these diplomats or their countries. By the time I came to realize that Yuri and his team were assassins for hire, not just cyber criminals, they had already killed two diplomats and were planning to kill Reid Daniels and you," Analka said looking at Kendall with tears again trickling down her face. "I am so sorry Shelby."

Kendall got up, walked around the table, and gave Analka a motherly hug.

"What do I do when I know that telling Robeen the truth would get both of us keeled by Yuri and his assassins?" Analka asked. "What would you do?"

"When Yuri wants Petra to keel Robeen, I convince Yuri that we should kidnap Robeen and continue to try to get information out of him. I was buying time to spare Robeen's life, and I guess it worked."

"I am now out of contact with Yuri so I can't tell you where he is, but I can supply you with mineral pills. You may need to use them to stop him from killing again," Analka said. "I am not a strong negotiator because I don't read people well, but Maria will watch out for my interest, I guess. I have told you all that I know and what I can do for you," Analka ended.

"I got one more question, Ms. Hrapla," Eric White asked. "Do you know who hired Yuri Rosov and his team of assassins?

"I do not know," Analka said. "That is a question for Yuri."

"Well, give us some time to talk it over and we will get with yer attorney on what a judge will let us do for you in return for yer confession and yer pills. I must say you have been very helpful, and I want to thank you for yer candor." Eric White said.

After Analka and Maria Fedorova had walked out of the room, Eric White asked, "Do we have any reason to believe that she is not tellin the truth?"

"We don't know what we don't know, but her story as it relates to me seems to be the truth," Robin said. "She would not have had time to be doing a lot more than a quick report on where Reid was headed or hacking for airline or transport tickets."

"I need time to talk with Analka about her research and the mineral pills. I need a few questions answered before you finalize a deal," Kendall said.

"I can't imagine how she could have been involved in the plot other than as a hired hand so to speak," Eileen Wisdom said. "Look at me, I am picking up your Oklahoma talk. I don't think I have ever said "hired hand" before in my life," causing a round of laughter.

Eric White summed it all up. "Well, I'll get this assigned to a reasonable Federal judge, hopefully the Honorable Elizabeth Johnson, and we will see if we can getter reduced to Reckless Endangerment, Hacking Govment Computers and Wire Fraud for the airline tickets. If we get all of that wrapped into one sentence, Ms. Hrapla might get as little as Seven Years with time off for good behavior. She may only hafta serve three years. Plenty of time left for a brilliant young woman ta make somethin otta her life without crime."

CHAPTER 63

February 22
Saturday 11:30pm Local Time Paris

Reid had spent an unsettled evening going over the past few hours. Charlie was there with him part of that time, but she kept stepping away. She encouraged Reid to think about Kendall Hughes. Charlie's last thoughts of the evening for Reid were profound.

"Darling, you started on this adventure to find a killer and yet, you have found so much more," Charlie said. It made Reid think long and hard about his life; the time he was wasting, the life he had come so close to losing just hours ago.

Reid spent a restless night at the American Hospital of Paris. Extra guards were deployed in the hospital and Chris Keller was seated in the shadowy corner of the room alert to everything happening around them. Reid's eyes had had a treatment and even though Dr. Marchand had bandaged them up again, during the exam he could tell his sight was returning.

As he drifted off to sleep, Reid dreamed that he was having coffee at a sidewalk table on a street in Paris with a man he did not recognize. The day was sunny and warm for February. The trees with new spring buds. The air smelled fresh and clean. The couples drifted by walking amidst the beauty. He thought he saw Kendall Hughes on the arm of another man. Across from him, a man was pulling a gun with a silencer out from under the table. An alarm started to sound, but the man paid no attention and was leveling the gun at Reid. The alarm was growing louder. Reid woke up with a start covered in sweat and realized that his phone was ringing.

Kendall was calling at 6:16am on Sunday morning Paris time. "Ehlo ahnd gouda morning Mr. Daniels," she said in her best French accent imitation, which was awful.

"Kendall, it is so good to hear your voice," Reid said enthusiastically. "You would not believe what I was just dreaming."

"I can imagine with all of those beautiful and good smelling women all around you," she replied.

"Nothing quite as exotic as that," Reid said. "It is so good to hear your voice. Everything that happened yesterday would be hard enough, but when you add being blindfolded and sightless, that really made it difficult. I sure could have used having you around."

"Lucky for you, I will be there soon," Kendall said.

"Is that a good idea? I mean that would be great, but I'm not sure that is a good idea," Reid said.

"Well, let me tell you what is happening here," Kendall said. "Robin and I have been interrogating Analka Hrapla with the help of Federal Prosecutors in D.C. She has given us a lot of information and she has turned over the mineral pills that she developed while advancing my research. The D.C folks say that depending on how things go in closing this case, she may have reduced her time in jail from a life sentence to just several years. She seems to me to be credible and earnest in her confessions and the help she is providing will surely help you put an end to this."

"That all sounds great, but I don't see how that requires you to come to Paris and be placed back in danger with Yuri Rosov."

"We have tested the composition of the Analka's pills and though they can put the body a little out of balance of key minerals, if taken in small doses, they are relatively harmless to the human body. That is why I am coming to Paris via CP Pak transport. I'll take one of Analka's pills and gain experience in transport awareness and animation. I'll be able to report to you what the effects are and I will be able to put mineral pills into your hands that you and Chris Keller can use if necessary. It will place you on a level playing field with Yuri Rosov," Kendall explained.

"You'll be in danger by experimenting on yourself and jumping back into front lines of this investigation," Reid protested.

"Reid, I am the scientist that invented CP Pak transport. I have a better understanding than anyone other than Analka of what these pills do to the human body in the transport process. Regional Commander Sanchez and FBI Director Russell have both asked me to do this. It is out of your hands Pal. I am taking a pill and coming to Paris in 9 hours," Kendall said firmly.

CHAPTER 64

February 23
Sunday 7:30am Local Time Paris

Yuri awakened early and was preparing a shopping list for Suzette whom he had contacted at the Hotel Garmond. He had previously told the beautiful prostitute that he may need her services again, but he had not known at the time how quickly that would be. Suzette had come to his room on Saturday evening and had stayed the night sharing Yuri's bed. She was a sweet distraction for the troubles he had on his mind.

Yuri needed help buying and applying the items he would use for his disguise on the CP Pak transport on Monday. This would be his most elaborate disguise ever. He had determined that it should be because this was his last *"Job"*. Even though he felt luck was always on his side, Yuri had the nagging feeling that his luck could easily be running out.

Yuri had lost his entire team. He was on his own and the failed hit on Reid Daniels at the American Hospital of Paris had shown him that the AI computers could track his face, his eyes and his body movements to anywhere. His time was over as an assassin, because travel and simply walking around a large city was becoming too dangerous for him.

He would perform this last hit, collect his money and go into long term hiding. The $3 million for completing this job, plus what he had already saved, would be more than enough to disappear and never be seen or heard from again.

Yuri made plans for Monday's travel based on what he knew and what he could make educated guesses about.

The FBI knew there were two people remaining from the dinner party at The Spring restaurant with whom his most recent target had dined, the beautiful young woman and the arrogant Middle Eastern man. He knew that his current target would be one of those two people and that person would be seated directly in front of him on the CP Pak Transport. Although it was not a key element to this last hit, he assumed that the other party from that dinner would be on the transport as well. That person was most likely to be the "mono toned voice" who had masterminded this entire scheme. Yuri hoped "monotone" would be nearby on the Transport as well.

The FBI man would know that one, maybe both, of the people from that The Spring dinner would be on the Transport, which meant that the FBI man would be there. If the FBI man was there, his big Seal Team partner would be on the Transport as well.

Yuri also knew that there would be several CGSI and Airport Security officers at the terminal when they departed Paris. The same number or more of FBI and Airport Security officers would be at the terminal when they arrived in New York. He needed a way to neutralize Mr. Seal Team, the CGSI and Airport Security in Paris and to distract the FBI and Airport Security in New York. *"Extremely difficult, but not impossible,"* he thought to himself.

Alternately, he could just write off this last assassination in this seemingly never ending *"Job"* if things looked too difficult. He could leave the scene and begin his life of hiding. Yuri's ethics would not allow him to do that. He had given his word that he would carry out this assassination and complete this *"Job."* If he didn't, his team would have all died in vain. The irony of that righteous thought process was lost on Yuri. If things were going terribly wrong, Yuri would simply not take the CP Pak transport to New York.

If that were the case, even though it pained him, the killing of FBI Agent Reid Daniels and the killing of the "monotoned voice" would need to wait for another time.

Those killings would be delayed but not forgotten.

The plan for getting on the CP Pak transport out of Paris required Suzette to find 10 to 30 people who could create a distraction. There was no illegal activity required, but they would all need to be at the airport just before departure of the CP Pak transport destined for New York.

As Yuri described the plan to Suzette, she smiled. "I have a nephew who is 12 years old and sings in a Boys Choir. They travel by bus as a group wherever they go. We could offer them money as a fund raiser. Will that do? I could tell them that we are helping a donor celebrate his birthday. I will call my sister. You promise that they are not doing anything illegal?"

"That is brilliant Suzette and no, there is nothing illegal about what we will ask them to do," Yuri said as he thought of how useful a resourceful a person like Suzette could be if he were rebuilding his team. *"It is hard to walk away when you are successful at what you do,"* Yuri thought.

As they went over the list, Yuri and Suzette determined that calling ahead to have a wheelchair available at the door of the Paris airport and on arrival in New York was easier than Suzette purchasing a wheelchair.

Even though the list was a bit long and quite diverse, Suzette was certain she could find it all on Sunday afternoon. In the meantime, on Sunday morning, she suggested that they begin watching the new Netflix series Lillyfield based on the British DCI, Violeta Lillyfield, who brought down the infamous Transit Station Killer.

Assassins and prostitutes rarely get the feeling of normalcy like binge watching a Netflix series. It was a rare treat for each of them.

CHAPTER 65

February 23
Sunday 9:30am Local Time Paris

The images were a little blurred, but Reid thought it was because the light was so bright rather than the damage to the surface of his eyes. Dr. Marchand had just removed the bandages covering his eyes and she was examining those surfaces.

Each second brought more clarity to his vision, but the light was intense to the point of giving everything a halo. Dr. Marchand looked like an angel to Reid, which one might expect. But so did Chris Keller and you would never mistake him for an angel, Reid thought.

Quietly, there was another beautiful angel in the background. Kendall had just walked into the room. She was beaming and haloed.

"Kendall, baby! Come here and give me a hug," Reid exclaimed. "I am so excited to see you and I mean that in every way possible."

"Reid, your sight is coming back," she answered with a questioning look to Dr. Marchand as she was giving Reid a big hug in his hospital bed. "It's long past time to see you as well." It had only been two days.

"Mr. Daniels's sight is coming back to normal, but he will need to keep his eyes covered for the next few days," Dr. Marchand said. "I am guessing that things are looking a little haloed to you Reid."

"Yes, you all look like angels to me and I gotta say it is a little slice of heaven to know that I am getting my sight back,"

Reid answered.

"I am going to lay this towel across your eyes, and I'll send over Pamela from Optical to fit you with some smoked dark glasses that you can wear to protect your eyes from the light," Dr. Marchand said. "I'll turn off these lights too. I needed them for the exam, but they can be off again now. I'll sign your discharge papers and have your clothes brought around. We had them cleaned to get the Pepper-Spray out. You are also free to take a shower. It has been a pleasure working with your Reid."

"So, tell us about your experience with the pill and the CP Pak transport," Chris Keller said getting right down to business. "What was it like? Are there more? Will we be able to use them?"

Kendall was holding Reid's hand. "It was like moving in thick water, but not water. Floating but still barely touching bottom. I moved around a little bit. Time was not a real dimension as we know it. Time stretched out. Movement was difficult."

"Could he have committed the murders the way we thought," Reid asked.

"Absolutely."

"Could we stop him from doing it again?" Chris asked.

"Yes, we could," Kendall said.

"So, what's the plan boss," Chris asked.

"I have a plan, but let's wait until Rene' Bernal is here from the DGSI. He may have additional information for us," Reid said.

"Rene' is a man?" Kendall asked.

"Yes. Were you thinking Rene' was another beautiful woman?" Reid asked.

"Why would I care?" Kendall said smugly.

"What do we know about Luba Krupin and the bank account?" Reid said as he removed the towel from his face and headed for the bathroom.

"Robin says that Luba Krupin is buried deep on the

Internet," Chris answered. "Maybe not quite the innocent that you think she is. And Bert and Lan Phang are having trouble breaking into the account and how it is set up," Chris said. "Seems that Bank of America was hacked to put further third-party encryption on this account. They are making progress with the help of American and Chinese AI computers. Even with that, we know nothing more about Krupin or the account, at this time."

"Alright, well, you guys chill while I get cleaned up. Maybe you can go get some breakfast for yourselves," Reid paused. "And bring some back for me.

"Maybe I could stay and help you," Kendall offered with a smile. "I could wash some places you can't see?"

"Get a room," Chris replied. "Something other than a hospital room, though that might be kind of turn on. Weird, but a little sexy."

"I have a room for us at the Hotel des Grand Hommes. I think it is the same place you are staying Chris. Bert Hamilton arranged it for us. I assured her that Reid and I needed only one. Maybe you are right next door to us," Kendall said with a smile.

"I may need to move my room," Chris said.

"I'll go it alone in the shower," Reid said. "You guys go see what they have in the cafeteria."

Reid showered and the entire time he concentrated on how they would bring down The Thorny Rose. The Rose was becoming too confident and would make a mistake. Hell, it was a mistake for The Rose to even show up on the CP Pak Transport that Luba Krupin and Shahnaz Latifpour would be taking to New York tomorrow. A big mistake, but Reid was sure that Yuri Rosov would take that chance. After all, Reid was sure Yuri had grown to believe he was "smarter" than everyone else. The attempted hit at the hospital proved that. That CP Pak transport was where it would all go down tomorrow afternoon.

In his thoughts, he thanked Charlie again for her help

the night before. Charlie nodded from across the room.

Rene' Bernal arrived at 11:00am with two Lieutenants from Orly International Airport, Security personnel who would lead the security forces at the airport. The French hoped they would take down Yuri Rosov as soon as he was identified at the airport. They had incredible confidence in their camera systems and the AI computers to which they were connected.

"Here's my plan and I am open to suggestions at any point here, so don't be shy with ideas," Reid started.

"We know that both Luba Krupin and Shanaz Latifpour will be on the CP Pak transport at 3:30pm tomorrow. They want to get their money as soon as possible. I believe Yuri Rosov will be on that transport as well. That means we have three chances to catch him, at Orly Airport, on the transport and at Kennedy Airport. With any luck, we will catch him shortly after he steps foot into the airport in Paris. Then, all we have to do is figure out who he is working for."

The Frenchmen nodded in agreement.

Reid continued. "We need to control the seating on the Transport. We know or strongly suspect that Yuri has been seated behind his targets."

"There wouldn't be time for him to move from anywhere else to have accomplished those previous murders," Kendall interjected.

"We want to look at the current seating chart to see where Krupin and Latifpour will be seated, so we can put Chris and one of your agents right beside each of them. I will sit a row behind and off to the side with Kendall right next to me. I believe it is valuable to make it appear that I can't see and that Kendall needs to guide me. If it gets to that point, the more comfortable he feels the more certain I am that he will attempt the hit and we will get him," Reid said.

"I want us all to be carrying handcuffs and everyone, with the exception of Kendall, will be carrying a weapon. Not that she doesn't know how to use one, we simply have to keep this all legal both in France and in the U.S. We don't want any legal technical mistakes that might ultimately allow Yuri Rosov or his contractor to walk away from a court," Reid finished.

Chris Keller questioned having Reid and Kendall a row back of Krupin and Latifpour. He suggested that he and the Security officer be seated a row back and that Reid and Kendall be seated in the same row and next to Krupin and Latifpour. Chris felt their training and skills would be better deployed in that manner. Everyone else agreed.

It was decided that they would meet in the waiting area at 3:00pm on Monday, but they would remain apart from one another. Everyone would be on the lookout for The Thorny Rose. Yuri would likely recognize Reid and possibly Chris but would not know the Security officers.

Once the plan was agreed upon by all, there was nothing to do but wait for tomorrow. As Tom Petty said, '*The Waiting is the Hardest Part*'.

After the French departed, Reid, Chris and Kendall left the American Hospital of Paris and headed to their hotel.

With time to kill. Kendall suggested that they binge watch the new Netflix series Lillyfield based on the British DCI, Violeta Lillyfield, who brought down the infamous Transit Station Killer.

Reid had time in the afternoon to think about what Charlie had said, "You started out to find a killer, but you have found so much more." He was certain Charlie meant Kendall was what he found and how she was moving into that space that was empty inside him.

Kendall had time to think through where she wanted her life to go. She needed something more than the Dog and the Butterfly. She needed science. She needed to use her mind. These past five days had been the most exciting of the past five years. She also had found a man she respected. A man she was sure she loved.

CHAPTER 66

February 24
Monday 3:00pm Local Time Paris

Reid was feeling confident that his eyesight was returning to 90 percent, yet he kept his eyes with the dark glasses and held tight to Kendall who was leading him about. His other senses remained heightened.

Around the waiting area, Chris Keller, Rene' Bernal and the Airport Security Officers each had staked out pre-determined positions to wait. Kendall handed Reid his *mineral pill* and a bottle of water. Chris and the Airport Security officer followed suit with their pills.

Reid was thinking about the hard work that went into Victoria Lillyfield catching the Transit Station Killer. It was not lost on him that she searched for the Killer for two years. He had been on the trail of Yuri Rosov for just over one week. He wondered if anyone would ever make a Netflix series about capturing The Thorny Rose.

DGSI Agent Bernal phoned Reid from across the room. "I just got the report back regarding Shanaz Latifpour and his family wealth. Latifpour's family does have an extreme amount of wealth. He was telling the truth about that. The only problem is that he has been shunned by his family. His personal wealth is less than $100,000. Money could clearly be a motive for him to commit the murders."

At 3:12pm and 3:14pm respectively Shahnaz Latifpour and Luba Krupin arrived in the waiting area. Ms. Krupin was accompanied by her bodyguard.

At 3:16pm a beautiful young woman arrived pushing a

much older woman in a wheelchair. The old woman's wrinkled hands were festooned with jewelry. Her azure blue and gold paisley skirt, light golden blouse and deep Hawaii blue jacket gave the impression that she was a fashion conscious woman even in her advanced years. Her aged face had more makeup than older women wear, but she was not too overdone. Her head remained motionless. Her eyes stared straight ahead, and she did not move at all. The makeup, the outfit and the aloof demeanor worked for her. Kendall thought this was a woman she would like to know. "I bet she has some stories to tell," she whispered to Reid.

Reid could make out the older woman in the wheelchair and the attendant helping her. "One of them has on a delicious smelling perfume. Can you smell it?" Reid asked.

"Faintly," Kendall answered.

Reid's attention was on a man, about 6 feet tall and fit. Dressed in a dark blue suit with a bright sky-blue tie, he held a camel hair overcoat across his arm and a fedora pulled low over his eyes. He looked to be about fifty, had a graying nicely trimmed beard and was making eye contact with no one. No other person in the waiting area had the team's attention like this man.

Just then, each of their phones was lighting up. Reid answered his.

"Reid, he's there!" Bert's voice was excited and breathy. "Yuri Rosov is at Orly Airport! He is out in the ticketing area! No, he's on the concourse coming toward you. No, he's on another concourse walking away from where you are. No, he's back coming at you. This is very confusing. There seem to be multiple Yuri's all over the airport!"

Reid looked around and the others on the team seemed to be getting the same message.

In fact, there were multiple Yuri's all over the airport or rather multiple images of Yuri all over the airport. Suzette had passed out life sized 14-inch by 18-inch pictures of Yuri's face and the choir boys began holding them up over their own faces at exactly 3:19pm. The boys were spread all over the ticketing area and outside security.

She had passed out a few more pictures to actual passengers going through security and gave them the instructions to hold their pictures up to their faces at 3:19pm which many did. She had told everyone that it was a birthday surprise and that they should begin singing Happy Birthday at exactly 3:30pm. She described it as a kind of "flash mob" event and the people who accepted the pictures were excited to take part.

The AI computers were getting positive hits on Yuri all over the airport and were continuously attempting to self-correct for the real Yuri Rosov.

Reid and the team had no idea what was really happening.

The call came to board the transport. The 144 people in the waiting area were shuffling through the loading door.

Things were happening fast. Reid hastily made the decision to deploy Chris Keller and the Security Officers to guard the door entering the transport pod. They would not make the trip to New York. Reid was convinced that Yuri would attempt to board at the last second. He was trying to watch the man in the blue suit with the fedora.

Kendall and Reid began moving to their seats. Shahnaz Latifpour was right behind them.

"Agent Daniels, good to see you. It's Shahnaz Latifpour. How are your eyes?"

Reid turned slightly, but not directly to Latifpour. "Still can see only shadows," he said as he intentionally bumped into the door jam.

"Sorry to hear that," Shahnaz said as he moved to his seat.

A few people back, Luba Krupin was boarding with her bodyguard at her side looking timid and a little scared. She seemed appalled that she was seated side by side with Shahnaz Latifpour and asked her bodyguard to change seats with her.

Shahnaz protested and tried to get Luba to remain in her seat right next to him. He protested a bit too much Kendall thought, "why would he care so much?" "It was only a 90 second transport."

Behind all of them, the beautiful woman and a flight attendant were helping the old woman into the Pod. When she was seated, she was right next to Reid and directly behind the bodyguard. Kendall was to Reid's left.

The attendants called the flight one more time and closed the doors. Within a half-minute the passengers were going into the brief transport sleep. All passengers, that is, except Reid Daniels, Kendall Hughes and Yuri Rosov.

Yuri could not believe his luck. He was seated right next to FBI Agent Daniels. He had seen that Ms. Krupin had changed seats. She was his target on this transport, but he could not allow Agent Daniels to get away when he was now so close.

As soon as he could move as the transport process began, Yuri was standing and turning to his left side. He would strangle Reid first and then the beautiful young woman. Based on his own deductions, this meant that the slick looking Middle Easterner was the "mono-toned voice". Yuri would save this man to kill for another day.

He had to hurry as best he could. His previous experience was serving him well, he was quickly getting the cellulose string wrapped around the Daniels's neck, but the many bracelets he wore in his old woman disguise were getting in the way.

In that instant when he pulled back the bracelets, the FBI Agent and the woman next to him began to move and to fight him. Yuri was shocked. He was not the only person on the transport who was animated.

Yuri fought back the woman and for a moment it appeared that he was going to strangle Reid to death. Then, as if out of nowhere, handcuffs were going around his wrist. In the same instant, a gun was being pushed up under his chin. Kendall Hughes had pulled Reid's gun out of his holster and was holding it ready to fire under the chin of Yuri Rosov. Yuri released his grip on the cellulose string.

Just as quickly, from his right, Suzette was pushing a moist cloth into the face of Kendall Hughes. Yuri, in preparing for a situation like this, had given Suzette a mineral pill.

The cloth was drenched with chloroform which temporarily incapacitated Kendall. She slumped back into her seat. They were all losing consciousness. The molecular breakdown had begun. In the next few moments, the lights came up and the CP Pak transport had arrived in New York. FBI agents, including Regional Commander Sanchez with guns drawn were at the door of the Pod and were not allowing anyone to depart.

Old woman Yuri had gathered her satchel and was making her way quickly to the door with Suzette helping him.

"These people are having extreme difficulty," Suzette said in broken English pointing at Kendall and Reid. "They need help now!"

"I must get to the ladies' water closet! I have not worn my Depend undergarment! You must let me out. I am about to pee myself! Please!" the old woman Yuri pleaded in broken French.

Carlos Sanchez acquiesced to the request sending a female Airport Security officer to accompany old woman Yuri and Suzette to the Women's Restroom just down the concourse.

"Come right back here after you have relieved yourself," Carlos said. "We need to speak with you before you leave the airport."

Carlos and the other Airport Security were boarding to aid Reid and Kendall while departing passengers were being detained.

Kendall's violent coughing was subsiding. She was looked about for the old woman.

"Where did she go? The old woman who was sitting here! Where did she go?" Kendall was sputtering. "The old woman is Yuri Rozov!"

Carlos Sanchez turned and ran to the door taking one of the Airport Security officers with him. He turned toward the Women's Restroom and broke into a sprint. He did not notice that he was passing Suzette walking the other direction toward Baggage Claim and the exits. She had worn a reversible raincoat and had turned it from beige to blue and she was wearing a Yankees hat and blue Chuck Taylor Converse high tops.

Yuri was further down the terminal heading the opposite way dressed as a maintenance man pushing a mop and a bucket. He had carried the maintenance clothes complete with an official looking identification lanyard in his satchel. Yuri's heart was pounding.

Sanchez and the other officer burst into the Restroom. There was no old woman. There was no good-looking attendant. Only the Airport Security officer remained, unconscious, on the floor in one of the stalls and draped in the old woman's clothes.

Sanchez was frantic. He reported to Airport Security that he believed they had allowed Yuri Rosov to escape from the Transport Pod. "Shut down the Terminal!"

Yuri had ducked into the Men's Restroom and was mopping the floor. There were no cameras to recognize him. He would simply mop for a while. It gave him time to think. He knew the authorities would be closing the terminal. He had to remember the way out. So far, his trademark luck had prevailed. He was orienting to exactly where the Pod had been delivered in the terminal.

It was becoming clearer now. He had studied diagrams of CP Pak Terminal at Kennedy Airport. There was security access to the tarmac about 50 yards down the concourse toward Baggage Claim. He needed to pass the Pod which he had just come from. It was his best chance to escape. He had to do it. He was feeling good about his luck again. Someone would let him through that door. He simply needed to get there before being identified on the cameras.

Yuri was wearing a matching gun metal colored shirt and pants with black shoes, dark framed glasses and a dark painter's style hat. Not a great disguise, but he was working to hold his face pulled to one side and he was chewing gum. And then, there was always Suzette.

Sanchez headed back to the Pod. Kendall and Reid were now outside standing in the concourse. Both were shaken.

"Everything is locked down. No sign of him yet on the Camera's. He is somewhere hiding," Sanchez said.

"Where did he go first?" Reid asked.

"The Women's Restroom down the concourse, right down there," Sanchez pointed.

BEEP BEEP! BEEP BEEP! ICPs were going off. It was Bert Hamilton.

"We have hits on Yuri near the exit," Bert said.

"I'm on my way. Warn security that he may be armed," Carlos Sanchez broke into a sprint. "You stay here and watch the concourse," he shouted over his shoulder.

Suzette had been hiding two pictures of Yuri under her sweater. They were a little wrinkled, but she handed them to two young men entering the airport and gave them the same story as she had given the choir boys. Only this time it was, "hold them up in two minutes. You'll see others doing the same thing."

Yuri was pushing his mop and bucket passed Reid and Kendall as Sanchez ran off.

"You are one lucky bastard, Yuri Rosov," Yuri said to himself. "Thank you, Suzette." Yuri continued walking and chewing out the side of his mouth.

"Do you smell that, Kendall?" Reid said. "Yuri just walked by. That's him. I can smell the old lady's perfume."

Kendall Hughes still had Reid's gun and she jumped into action. Quickly she was ten feet behind the maintenance man. "FREEZE YURI!" she shouted.

Yuri continued walking. Reid was now walking beside

Kendall seeing Yuri as a shadow.

"FBI! STOP OR WE SHOOT THORNY ROSE!" Reid shouted.

BLAM! BLAM! BLAM! Kendall fired three shots just behind Yuri's feet shocking Yuri and Reid.

Yuri stopped. His luck had just run out!

"On your knees, hands behind your head," Reid commanded.

Yuri complied and Reid cuffed him.

Yuri was read his rights, placed under arrest and taken to a private room. Shahnaz Latifpour and Luba Krupin were detained for questioning in separate rooms at the airport. Suzette got away, for now.

"That was some job you did with Reid's gun back there Ms. Hughes," Carlos Sanchez said. "Things could have gotten messy, if you hadn't acted quickly."

Kendall said a quiet, 'thank you." 'That sonofabitch is lucky I didn't put one into each of his legs." He had tried to kill her Reid.

Reid and Carlos Sanchez went to the airport security offices to begin to interrogate Yuri Rosov, The Thorny Rose. Reid set up his ICP to capture the interrogation and send the signal to Bert Hamilton to be recorded.

After reading Yuri his rights Reid said through his smoked glasses, "Nice to finally meet you Thorny Rose."

"I easily could have killed you in the parking garage," Yuri said calmly.

"Why didn't you?" Reid asked.

"My contractor wanted you distracted, not killed. Distracted for long enough to do whatever he needed to do," Yuri said.

"Why do you say he?" Reid asked.

"I'd like to see my lawyer before we talk any further," Yuri requested.

"A lawyer has contacted us that she is on the way," Carlos said. "Maria Fedorova should be here any minute. It's like she knew you would be captured."

Yuri did not respond.

"Okay, your attorney is on her way, but in the meantime, I'd like to commend you on placing Analka Hrapla inside my organization. That was smart. How did you find Analka Hrapla to be on your team?" Reid asked.

"Where is that lawyer," Yuri said. "No more answers until my lawyer is here."

"Here's the thing Yuri," Reid said. "We have detained the middle eastern gentleman and the pretty young girl, because we think one of them is your contractor. You had to see them both at the Spring Restaurant the night that Kostya Ivanov met his demise. We believe you were there with that beautiful woman who accompanied you in your travel today. By the way, that was a great disguise, and the distraction was first rate."

"To continue, these two people are about to split several million dollars and unless we have a reason to arrest either one of them, your contractor could disappear into the world and you go to Federal prison for life or possibly execution in Mexico," Reid said.

"Sorry, I don't have anything to say until my lawyer gets here," Yuri said.

"We'll be back," Reid said.

After they were in the hallway, Reid said, "let's talk to Shahnaz Latifpour first."

Reid and Carlos Sanchez entered separated security room with Shahnaz Latifpour and began recording on Reid's phone.

"Shahnaz, we have some questions for you," Reid said.

"Why were you so insistent that Luba Krupin sit next to you on the transport?" Reid asked.

"Who does not want to sit next to a beautiful girl any chance you get?" Shahnaz answered more seriously. "I still hold out dreams that Luba and I will be together one day. She needs a strong man to protect her."

"One thing bothers me," Carlos Sanchez said. "All facts

have come down to either you or Luba Krupin being the mastermind of these murders and the person who contracted Yuri Rosov. It seems to me that the only reason you don't believe that it could be Luba, is because it is you who is the mastermind."

"Do I need an attorney?" Shahnaz asked, "because from where I sit, you are blowing this case. You have captured the assassin, but you don't have a clue about who contracted him because it is not me and I tell you, it is not Luba."

"You can wait for an attorney if you like, but you are not under arrest yet," Reid said as he got up to leave the room.

Reid and Carlos entered the room with Luba Krupin. Again, Reid set his phone for recording.

"Nice to finally see you Ms. Krupin," Reid said.

"You can call me Luba," she said in a very charming and unassuming manner.

"Why did you not want to sit next to Shanaz Latifpour?" Reid asked.

"Because he is a creep and I believe he is behind this entire series of murders," Luba answered. "And he is not as wealthy as he says he is. His family has shunned him. He needs the money," Luba said confidently.

Reid paused, then asked, "How long have you known Analka Hrapla?"

Luba Krupin stopped short. The confidence had disappeared from her face.

"I think you met her at The Thirty School where you were both students. You were a little older, but, if one brilliant young woman ends up at The Thirty School, why not two?" Reid asked.

"I am guessing that you are in line to collect all the money from the investment account when there is no one left. In the best case, you frame Shahnaz Latifpour for being the mastermind and you get it all or in the worst case, you share the money with him. My guess is that this is a much bigger account than you let on when we talked in Paris," Reid continued.

Luba Krupin grew stone silent. The charm had disappeared.

Kendall Hughes knocked on the door and was welcomed into the room. She pulled Reid and Carlos Sanchez aside.

"Do you have news on Ms. Krupin here?" Reid said.

"Yes," Kendall responded.

"Well, I am sure there is nothing that Ms. Krupin does not know already, so share it with all of us," Reid said staring directly at Luba Krupin.

"Luba Krupin befriended Analka Hrapla when they were at The Thirty School. Bert and Lan Phang have found money transfers from Luba through a blind account when she bailed out Analka when she needed help. Luba then became Analka's agent renting her out for hacking and other sophisticated Internet crimes all the while remaining anonymous to Analka. Also, Bert and Lan have found the account which is called The Marco Polo Investment Account. It is extremely large. The account is now valued at over $300 million and was amassed through an illegal hack of SEC computers," Kendall said.

"I need to have my attorney present. Maria Fedorova is her name," Luba Krupin said staring at the table.

CHAPTER 67

Ten Days Later At
Il Terrazzo Carmine in Downtown Seattle

"Carlos, you didn't have to do this for us, but I want to impress upon you how important this is to us," Reid said to a few chuckles from the group.

"Your team solved this difficult case in just over seven days," Carlos Sanchez said. "And Ms. Phang, we wanted you to be here as well because you were a big part of solving this."

"I had to stay and finish the ping pong tournament with Bert," Lan Phang said.

"The President insisted that we give you all a little party. He couldn't do it himself because it would set the wrong precedent. He can't hold a dinner for every FBI team that solves a case," FBI Director James Russell said.

"A little something you did not know is that the Chinese Carrier Group Xi Jing Ping, which had us so worried, turned toward home shortly after the arrest of Yuri Rosov," Director Russell said. "The President is very pleased."

"Here's to the President Parker," Bert Hamilton toasted with her glass of expensive Paradiso cognac.

"Here. Here," Director Russell continued holding up his glass. "I want you to know that U.S. Chinese cyber relations have never been better, and we want to thank you for that Ms. Hamilton and Ms. Phang."

"I want to put in a big Thank You to Kendall Hughes who kick started our investigation and ended it," Reid said as he held up his glass and gave her a hug to his side.

"Let's not forget that Kendall saved your life in so many

ways boss," Chris said holding up his glass with a big smile. That brought a round of laughter from the entire team, even Robin Medallon.

Robin was on probation with the FBI but was able to retain his job for which he was extremely grateful.

"How did you know to hit Luba Krupin with the connection to Analka Hrapla," Carlos Sanchez asked.

"Two of the three most intelligent women associated with this case were from the same part of the world and went to the same school. No coincidence. They had to know each other. When I asked Yuri how he found out about Analka he got a strange look on his face. Like he was realizing something for the first time," Reid said. "The most likely person to have sent Analka to Yuri originally, in my opinion, was Luba Krupin."

"What will happen with the $300 million dollars in The Marco Polo Alliance account?" Robin asked. "Will it go to Shahnaz Latifpour?"

"Right now, it is being held by the government. The SEC is working with us to figure out exactly how Luba did it, but it is looking more and more like ill-gotten gains, so it will most likely go to the U.S. Treasury," Director Russell said.

"Reid, I know this is last minute, but do you think I can take a week off. A young friend of my family in Idaho is missing and they fear she has been abducted," Chris Keller asked solemnly.

"Absolutely, Chris," Reid said. "And let us know if we can help personally or professionally."

Regional Director Sanchez and Director James Russell both nodded.

"Reid, simply curious. Are you carrying your weapon full time again now after the experiences you most recently encountered?" Carlos Sanchez asked.

"I only carry my gun when I think Kendall might need it," Reid said softly.

EPILOGUE

Life has gone back to normal for Reid and Kendall or maybe it should be called the "new normal" for them. They are spending 20 nights a month with each other.

Kendall is quite pleased that the late-night premonition she had before this all started turned out to be one of the most positive things to ever happen in her life. Meeting Reid and taking down Yuri Rosov was extremely fulfilling for her. She rebuilt the Dog and the Butterfly and had turned most of authority for running the store over to her assistant Kassie.

Reid is the happiest he has been since Charlie was alive. He is again fulfilled by love. The fond memories of Charlie are always there, but now Reid is living again. As strange as it might be, he longed to be back out on the trail with Kendall evading death and solving another murder.

Reid, Bert, Robin, and Chris are busy again tracking Cyber Crimes. Robin is spending 6 months on probation and has had his pay grade dropped down for his involvement with Analka.

Analka Hrapla turned "states evidence" about her dealings with Yuri Rosov and her anonymous benefactor agent Luba Krupin. Analka is serving an 8-year sentence and working part-time for the Cyber Crimes Seattle Office from prison. Analka will get out of prison early with less than 2 years served.

Robin visits Analka at least three times per week and they talk of their life together after she gets out and the family they will raise together.

Because of the international implications, Luba Krupin's

trial has proceeded quickly. She is being charged with three counts of murder in the first degree, wire fraud and felony grand larceny and could receive sentencing of 200 years in Federal Prison.

Yuri Rosov's case did not move as quickly. In addition to the charges in the U.S., Yuri has been sought for extradition to other countries for previous crimes he has committed.

Yuri's attorneys are making headway in the public relations trial in the U.S. They claim that he is not the real Yuri Rosov. They claim an alias which had been prepared by Faddy Zolnerowich is this man's "real" identity and that he is not Yuri Rosov.

Further, they claim this innocent man was illegally apprehended in U.S. The claim is that Agent Daniels, through his girlfriend Hughes, was attempting to kill this man and pass him off as Yuri Rosov. They claim it was a cover up by Daniels and the FBI to solve the case.

The man, who is being placed on trial as Yuri Rosov answered to the commands in the airport because he feared for his life. His attorney's claim this man is only alive today because Kendall Hughes, being a woman, was unable to handle or aim a gun properly. Agent Daniels, they claim, had gone rogue and was attempting to have this person killed by Kendall Hughes. It is being claimed that the FBI and Agent Daniels had botched this case and Daniels needed to close it quickly and this man they have in jail is a scapegoat and not the real Yuri Rosov.

Always believing in his own luck, Yuri is convinced he will beat the charges or escape one day soon. When he does, he is planning to kill the "monotone voice" woman who had fooled him into believing it was the Middle Easterner.

And then, he will take great pleasure in ending the life of Special FBI Agent Reid Daniels and his protector Kendall Hughes.

ACKNOWLEDGEMENT

Without Seattle celebrity and close friend Pat Cashman I may have never completed this work. I asked Pat to read through my first draft. He painfully waded through the muck of my typos, misspellings, and misplaced punctuation in order to tell me whether the story made sense from beginning to end. Pat helped me to get the storyline streamlined and on the right track. Thank you dear friend for being so patient with me.

Thank you also to my beta readers, my wife and biggest fan Ann Mary, my daughter-in-law Kjersten Oylear, high school classmate Cindy Beebe and my sister Sharon Ripley for their input on the storyline.

After I cleaned up the story, my sister-in-law Sara Peck tackled the momentous task of cleaning up those typos, misspelled words, and the punctuation. Amazingly, she still speaks to me. Thank you for the great work Sara!
Finally, thank you to Amazon/Kindle for creating a way for a writer like me to have my work published.

Made in United States
Troutdale, OR
08/06/2024

21792531R00196